I AM TRUTHSEEKER

The sword spoke to Dain. Great power flooded within it. Long ago, many battles had it fought. Images of blood and death mingled with war cries in tongues that he had never heard before. He shuddered and opened his eyes as the draped sword was pointed straight at his heart, and then turned sideways and laid at his feet. Gold wire was wrapped around the two-handed hilt and a row of fiery emeralds studded the straight edge of the guard. Glittering and gleaming, Truthseeker lay on the floor in humility, but even the cloth could not mask its greatness.

Ace Books by Deborah Chester

THE SWORD
REIGN OF SHADOWS
SHADOW WAR

Lucasfilm's Alien Chronicles™

THE GOLDEN ONE
THE CRIMSON CLAW

The Sword, the Ring, and the Chalice

BOOK 1

THE SWORD

DEBORAH CHESTER

ACE BOOKS, NEW YORK

THE SWORD

An Ace Book / published by arrangement with
the author

PRINTING HISTORY
Ace mass-market edition / February 2000

For information address: The Berkley Publishing Group,
a division of Penguin Putnam Inc.
375 Hudson Street, New York, New York 10014.

The Penguin Putnam Inc. World Wide Web site address is
http://www.penguinputnam.com

Check out the ACE Science Fiction & Fantasy newsletter
and much more on the Internet at Club PPI!

ISBN: 0-441-00702-3

ACE®
Ace Books are published
by The Berkley Publishing Group,
a division of Penguin Putnam Inc.,
375 Hudson Street, New York, New York 10014.
ACE and the "A" design are trademarks
belonging to Penguin Putnam Inc.

PRINTED IN THE UNITED STATES OF AMERICA

10 9 8 7 6 5 4 3 2 1

The Sword

PART ONE

1

THE DOGS WARNED Tobeszijian that something was wrong.

It was only midday, but the sky hung low, as dark as weathered steel. Snowflakes like tiny chips of ice dropped steadily, turning the shoulders of his burgundy wool cloak white and gathering in its folds where it lay across the powerful rump of his stallion. The king was large, his human blood having given him the same vigorous frame as his father, with broad shoulders, long arms bulked with muscle, and a neck like a pillar. When geared for battle, encased in full plate armor and a crowned helmet fitted with the full spread of gold danselk antlers, he was massive, truly an awe-inspiring sight. But today the king was hunting, and he wore only chain mail and a breastplate embossed with the lightning bolts and hammer that symbolized the connection between Netheran kings and their gods. A bow was strung across his strong chest; a quiver of arrows was tied to his back at his belt. His sword, Mirengard—spellcast and eldin-forged, which no man's hand save his own could touch—hung at his side, its two-handed grip twisted with goldwire and studded with a great emerald set in a gold gryphon's claw. His riding gauntlets, crafted of the finest, most supple leather upon his hands and flaring wide to his elbows, were embroidered with gold thread, again displaying his royal crest of lightning bolt and hammer. Hunting spears of pure white ash clattered in his saddle quiver, and his spurs jingled with the clear, ringing sound of pure silver.

The king's dogs, tall slender beasts with white curly hair feathering thickly on their long legs, ran ahead. Cresting a rise, they lifted their slim muzzles and barked excitedly. The king and his lord protector rode right behind them. They parted to dodge a stand of snow-laden fir trees, and plunged down the slope toward a thicket of briars and choked undergrowth. Tobeszijian's gaze swept the snow ahead of him, noting the scuffed tracks—not fresh—and the nibbled tips of branches. Deer had come this way, all right, but not as recently as Count Mradvior had led him to believe.

Clamped between his strong thighs, his black stallion stretched its muscular neck and fought the bit, trying to outrun the dogs, who were bounding gracefully over the snowdrifts, baying now with a sharp, shrill unfamiliar note. Tobeszijian reined back, forcing the excited stallion to slow.

Half of the hunting party came into sight behind him, shouting encouragement to the dogs; the rest galloped in from his left.

Ahead of him, the dogs reached the thicket, snapping and growling, then one of them yelped sharply and sprang back. Blood stained her white coat.

"That's no hind!" Kuliestka shouted.

Tobeszijian felt a surge of excitement. Since rising at dawn, he'd been eager to course the deer that Mradvior and Surov had claimed was out here. He'd dressed swiftly, eaten light, and kept his horse at a ground-eating canter right behind the dogs. "Nay," he said. "I'll wager my spurs it's a stag that's gouged the bitch like that."

Another dog yelped and dodged, the snarling and snapping taking a vicious quality unusual when they cornered a deer. Tobeszijian frowned, but could see nothing in the thicket except a violent shaking of the branches and brambles.

"Thod take the creature!" Prince Kuliestka said. "Will it stand here or will it run?"

An arrow skimmed Tobeszijian's left arm just above the elbow, ripping his cloak and sliding harmlessly off his chain mail. It nicked the shoulder of his horse, which reared, screaming.

Fighting to keep control of his animal and furious at whoever had shot so carelessly, Tobeszijian tried to look to see who was shooting, but his glance took in only a confused blur of snow and trees, rapid movement as the hunting party galloped closer, and a series of rapid jolts as his horse bucked. From the thicket, something suddenly exploded forth, racing away black and swift, with the dogs in rapid pursuit.

Tobeszijian spurred his stallion, who galloped after them. Blood was still streaming from the horse's shoulder, splattering back across Tobeszijian's gauntlets and thigh. He put his anger aside, knowing he would deal with the matter later, and bent low over the stallion's whipping mane, urging him on faster.

In minutes, he grew certain they chased no stag. The creature was larger, fully as big as a danselk, but too swift. Now and then Tobeszijian caught glimpses of it, too fleeting to tell what it was, except that it was black, the color of no stag that he knew, nay, and no danselk either.

They were rapidly leaving the gentle rolling country behind for steeper hills and sharp little ravines where half-frozen streams plunged. The forest grew much denser here, in some places impassable. It was hopeless trying to keep the rest of the hunting party in sight. Tobeszijian focused on his quarry. He was curious about it now and fevered from the thrill of the chase it was giving him. By Thod, he thought joyously, this was good hunting.

He stayed low in the saddle, his stallion flashing through trees and under low-hanging branches far too fast and wildly for safety. The dogs streaked ahead of him, almost but not quite able to catch their quarry. He realized he had left Kuliestka behind, and wondered how that could be. His lord protector's horse must have stumbled or blown its wind from the furious pace. The sounds of the others crashing and shouting behind him grew fainter, heading in a different direction. The other dogs must have scented another deer. Tobeszijian cared not. His own dogs were running easily, their pink tongues lolling. His horse was strong and not yet tired. If necessary Tobeszijian could keep up this chase for another hour, surely long enough for the quarry to tire and begin to slow.

He lost sight of it and reined up sharply, listening to his breath panting in his throat. The dogs were running in silence now, and for an instant he heard nothing except the snorts of his horse as it champed the bit. His saddle creaked beneath him, and he stood up in the stirrups, shielding his eyes from the sting of snowflakes as he peered ahead.

He had stopped halfway down a steep hill. A ridge rose sharply before him, blanketed almost entirely with snow-dusted trees. If the dogs lost their quarry in this tight country, he would not find it again.

Even as the thought crossed his mind, the creature bounded into sight in a small clearing halfway up the rise before him. It paused there, holding its head high, puffing white from its nostrils. It was a stag, brown with a white throat and belly, antlers spreading a full twelve points.

The dogs came into sight at the bottom of the hill, yelping and casting for the creature's trail along the bank of a narrow, ice-scrimmed stream. Calm, even noble, the stag gazed across the valley at Tobeszijian. He reached for his horn to call the dog ; back onto the trail, but confusion suddenly swirled in his mind and he never blew it.

Was this another deer? He'd been chasing something black, not brown. He'd seen no flash of white from its flag and hindquarters. Had the dogs confused two trails?

From far away to his left came the low blat of the huntsman's horn, startling Tobeszijian. He hadn't realized he'd gone so far east. Or maybe he'd lost his direction entirely in this rougn country. It was easy enough to do with the sun hidden behind such dark snow clouds.

The dogs suddenly found the trail and leaped the stream. They went streaking up the hill, glimpsed here and there through the dark green of the firs and spruces. The stag remained motionless, except for flicking one ear in the dogs' direction. It seemed unworried by their approach.

Tobeszijian told himself to spur his horse forward and catch up. This was a fine stag indeed. What did it matter if the dogs had lost whatever he'd been after?

He felt a shiver brush the back of his shoulders beneath his clothing, like icy fingernails scraping there. An unexplainable but powerful reluctance to go farther seized him.

That hillside, he felt certain, held his death.

Tobeszijian had never been able to part the veils of seeing and gaze into the second world, or even the third, despite his being half eldin. It was said his father's human blood ran too strong in his veins, blinding him from having the sight. He'd never cared much if he lacked the eldin gifts, until now when he found himself wishing violently for the ability to see what had become of his mysterious quarry.

A second shiver touched him, and he felt a dark, malevolent presence, unseen and unsensed even by his horse, which was tugging at the bridle and pawing with a forefoot.

Danger lurked behind Tobeszijian as well. Remembering the close call with that arrow, he leaned forward and touched the wound on his stallion's neck. It had stopped bleeding. The cut was shallow and would cause no harm to the animal, but had the angle been different, had the arrow gone into his armpit instead of glancing off his elbow . . .

A chill swept through Tobeszijian, and his nostrils flared in a mixture of anger and alarm. There had been too many near misses and almost accidents already during this hunting expedition, enough to make any sane man cautious.

But he could not sit here all day if he was to bring down this stag. His horse pawed again, rested now, and the stag's ears pricked toward the dogs, which were nearly upon it. Again the stag glanced at Tobeszijian, as if to say, *Why don't you come?*

He let his horse trot forward down the rest of the slope, then canter across the stream, kicking up water and ice around him. He could still see the stag, standing motionless amidst the trees. Tobeszijian believed it was waiting for him, tempting him. By now, the dogs had reached it, and were yelping in excitement, but their barks suddenly changed to that shrill, frenzied noise they'd made earlier.

It was the sound of fear, Tobeszijian realized. He saw the stag whirl around. It charged forward with its antlers, then sprang aside and went bounding through a stand of thick pines. As it did, the air around it seemed to shimmer. The pines themselves rippled, and Tobeszijian glimpsed something black and sleek instead of the flash of white he should have seen off the animal's hindquarters. A smell rolled down the hill to his nostrils, a thick decayed smell of carrion left to ripen.

Shapeshifter.

Fear burst in his chest, and he reined so hard he made his horse rear up. Tobeszijian's head nearly cracked against an overhead tree limb, but he paid no attention. He was hauling back on the reins, yanking cruelly at his horse's mouth before finally succeeding in pulling the animal around. Feeling breathless and choked, he spurred it hard, and the horse plunged back across the stream. For an instant he could still hear the excited barking of his dogs, those brave handsome creatures coursing tirelessly after their prey. Regret flashed through him, and he reached for his horn to call them off.

But then his hand dropped from the horn hanging on the front of his saddle. The dogs had the creature's scent well in their nostrils and they were close enough now to course it by sight. They would not turn back no matter how much he called.

Tobeszijian fled in the opposite direction with his heart pounding too fast and his breath tangled in his lungs. There was little enough in this world that he feared, but no one but a mad fool took on a shapeshifter alone in a deserted wood.

After a few minutes he realized he was bent low in the saddle, shaking all over, mindlessly urging his laboring horse yet faster. Coming to his senses, he reined up, making his horse stumble. He nearly pitched forward out of the saddle, and had to grab the pommel hard to hang on.

Together, horse and rider paused there in a small hollow next to a fallen log overgrown with ivy now burnished red and gold by the autumn frosts. Tobeszijian willed his pounding heart to slow down, willed his mind to start thinking.

He was drenched and shivering with clammy, miserable sweat beneath his clothing and mail. Wiping his face with an unsteady hand, he realized he was alone out here. The members of his hunting party were well to the west of his current position. He could hear them, but they were too far away. His lord protector was either among them, or separately searching for him, or dead of an arrow in his back.

Frowning, Tobeszijian pushed that last thought away. The afternoon was well advanced by now. The gloomy skies were much darker than before. Nightfall would come early tonight.

Nightfall with a shapeshifter in the forest.

A keeback burst from a nearby tree with a loud flurry of its wings, making him start violently, and flew away, calling *kee-kee-kee.*

Tobeszijian believed the shapeshifter had been leading him into a certain trap. How far would he have chased it, galloping to his death like a mindless fool, before it turned and attacked him? Or led him to an ambush of soultakers?

He shivered again, drawing his cloak tighter around him.

His horse stood with its head low and sides heaving, blowing hard through its nostrils. Steam rose into the air off its shoulders.

The arrow, he understood now, had been intended to spring him into the chase. Everyone knew how much Tobeszijian loved hunting, how obsessed he could become, especially when he escaped court and Grov and fled into the snowy wilderness up north to the World's Rim. There, mountains stood as a barrier to the ice-coated Sea of Vvord, and bottomless fjords held water so clear and still it seemed to be made of glass.

Every autumn Tobeszijian allowed himself this one excursion for pleasure, taking himself far from the cares and intrigues of politics, the day-to-day management of his kingdom. Summers were for war against Gant and sometimes Klad. Winters were for remaining denned up by the fire, clothed in wool and heavy furs against the bitter cold, plotting strategies while the harsh weather raged outside. Spring was for taking his lady wife out into the forests, officially to hunt with her dainty falcon, but in reality to let her visit her people in privacy away from the disapproving stares of his subjects and the churchmen. But autumn was for hunting; autumn he saved for himself.

Gladly he abandoned the mundane duties of his office for two months of glorious play, hunting and camping in the wilds with his most stalwart knights and whatever courtiers were in favor. It was a way of clearing his mind and restoring himself. He had gone forth every year since taking the throne, telling himself that his enemies could not wreak too much havoc in his absence.

His fear had left him now. Reaching out, Tobeszijian scooped a handful of snow off a pine branch and rubbed his face with it. The snow was dry and powdery, burning his skin with its cold. He ate some of it and tossed the rest away. He felt hollow and a little embarrassed by his extreme reaction. Still, he knew himself to be no coward. It was not foolish, but prudent indeed, to flee one of the Nonkind.

Frowning, he put the other incidents of this trip together, piecing them into place the way Princess Thiatereika might solve one of her puzzles.

The first incident had been with the white beyar.

He always started his hunting trips by traveling far to the north in search of the fabled white beyars of Omarya Fjord.

Sighting a white beyar was considered a very good omen. To capture one was rare indeed, and he had set his heart on someday having white beyar fur draped across his winter throne. Every year, he always came home without it.

But this time, he had actually sighted one—a huge male with intelligent black eyes. The animal's throat was banded in dark gray, and he stood on an ice floe bobbing on the surface of the fjord, staring right back at Tobeszijian as though in recognition.

Holding his bow undrawn, Tobeszijian had found himself transfixed, unable to breathe. A voice tugged at his mind, and he could almost hear the words *who/who/who/who.*

"Look at him," Prince Kuliestka said, breathing the words in Tobeszijian's ear. "Magnificent devil! He's not afraid of us."

"He's waiting," Tobeszijian said in sudden understanding. "Waiting for his rider."

Kuliestka's hand tightened on Tobeszijian's shoulder. "Shoot him now. It's a clear shot, perfect."

But Tobeszijian did not move, did not draw. The beyar was still staring right at him, as though he knew everything they thought and said. A cold shiver ran down Tobeszijian's spine. He glanced around, at the steep snowy slopes of the hillside that ran straight down into the water. Tall pines, spruce, and firs grew in heavy thickets, snow bending their branches almost to the ground. The eld rider could be anywhere, close by or a league away. Tobeszijian had not sensed his presence, but then he had been killing game all day. The smell of blood hung thick in his nostrils, and the proximity of his human companions was smothering his senses.

A short distance away, angled up the bank from Tobeszijian and kneeling behind a fallen log, Count Mradvior nocked his bow and aimed it right at the king, who was in the line of fire between him and the beyar. The count rose as though to shoot over the head of the king, and Tobeszijian sensed rather than saw him. Anger flooded his mind. He stood up, turning in one fluid motion, and hurled his bow like a spinning scythe at Mradvior.

The heavy bow hit the count, knocking him over and spoiling his aim. His hastily released arrow flashed in a short, high arc, coming down harmlessly into the water.

"He is not your game!" Tobeszijian said angrily.

Mradvior stood up, floundering in the deep, powdery snow, and swore long and loud. His voice echoed up the hillside, bouncing between sky and water. Keebacks flew from the treetops, making their plaintive *kee-kee-kee* sound.

Mradvior glared at Tobeszijian. "I was trying to pin him for your majesty. I was trying to help your majesty get the perfect shot."

Tobeszijian was not appeased. He needed no help in shooting his game, but that was hardly the point. Mradvior was always trying to step in where he was not needed, helping where no help was wanted, offering assistance that was in the way, hastening to perform tasks of service such as plucking a freshly filled wine cup from the serving boy's hand and bringing it to Tobeszijian himself. New to court and far too ambitious, Mradvior seemed to think he had to work hard to win favor, when that was the surest way to lose it. Tobeszijian had regretted bringing him on this hunting trip from the first day. And now he was certain he had made a mistake.

"Surely our noble companions have informed you by now that I need no help in making my shots," Tobeszijian said furiously. "I am not enfeebled. My eyesight is not gone."

"No, your majesty," Mradvior said, beginning to turn red as everyone stared at him. "Forgive me, your majesty. I was only trying to help."

"Couldn't you see the beyar is an eld-mount?" Tobeszijian said in disgust.

Mradvior looked puzzled. "I—I—"

"They are never to be killed." Disgusted, Tobeszijian turned away from him. Of course, the ice floe was now empty.

Prince Kuliestka, holding his helmet in his lap so that the fading sunlight spangled red highlights in his golden hair, still crouched on the bank, staring intently at the fjord. It was getting late now in the day, and mist was forming over the water, obscuring the ice floe and curling in among the trees on the bank.

"He dove off the moment you moved," Kuliestka said without turning his head. His keen eyes, wrinkled with squint lines at the corners, swept the mist and water again before glancing up at his king. "Fast, for such a big one. No splash of water. I knew he'd go and I kept my eyes on him every second, but he was gone from sight in a blink."

"The legends say they can swim underwater for many minutes," Tobeszijian said, feeling disappointment encompass him now. He'd wanted to watch the beyar, to communicate with him. If he'd had time to share his thoughts, perhaps the beyar's rider would have returned and made greeting. It was rare to communicate with the eldin this far north. Tobeszijian sighed. "He is long gone by now."

Now, that memory faded as a scream from the throat of nothing human rose into the twilight air and echoed over the hills. Shivering under his cloak, Tobeszijian patted his tired horse, scraping off the lather foaming on his neck. At the time, he had been caught up in the wonder of having seen a white beyar that close, that clearly. He had realized he could never shoot one of the magnificent animals, for they were not meant to be trophies on display in the palace. That day, the hunting party had ridden on and pursued other creatures. But now, chilled and worried, Tobeszijian considered the incident in a new light and asked himself if Count Mradvior had been aiming at the beyar or at himself.

And what of the night a drunken Count Surov had stumbled into the fire while Tobeszijian was standing close to it with his back turned, talking to some of the younger members of the party? Surov had tipped over a huge cauldron of boiling stew. Only the quick intervention of Prince Kuliestka had saved the king from being seriously burned. Young Fluryk had been splashed in the face, and he would be scarred for life.

In the morning, a humbled Surov had apologized on his knees before the king, who had pardoned him kindly. Surov had promised not to let himself get drunk again, and he had kept that promise. Only now, thinking about the matter with a mind full of suspicion, did Tobeszijian realize Surov had not been drunk a single evening prior to the incident. Nor was Surov ever one to lose control of himself. He was a dour, somber man, more a companion to the king's half-brother than to Tobeszijian himself. But he had asked to come on this year's hunting trip, and proved himself to be a competent hunter, although he seemed to take little enjoyment from the sport.

Then there had been the boar, which had exploded from a thicket without warning, squealing and attacking savagely. The horses had panicked, bucking and rearing away. Leaning over to grab one of his hunting spears, Tobeszijian had been rammed from the side by another man's horse and nearly knocked from the saddle right into the path of the charging boar. Prince Kuliestka had spurred his own frightened mount between Tobeszijian and the boar, managing to stab the creature in the neck. By then Tobeszijian had dropped out of the saddle, which was slipping dangerously around his horse's belly. With his horse running backward away from him, he managed to draw a spear from the saddle quiver and turned to stab the boar in one eye just as it reached him. The boar squealed horribly and fell over at his feet with a final kick of death.

Tobeszijian wondered who had knocked him off his horse. Was it an unavoidable jostling in the confusion of out-of-control horses, or yet another attempt on his life? Tobeszijian realized he could explain away each incident, dismiss them all if he chose. Had there only been one or two, he would have. But there had been too many. And after today, when he'd come so close to falling into a terrible trap, he no longer wanted to dismiss any suspicion.

The scream came again, a long, wailing shriek that made the hair on the back of his neck stand up inside his mail coif. He felt a fresh surge of fear, but controlled it this time. He knew the shapeshifter now realized it had lost him. Would it come back for him?

His mouth felt dry, and he swallowed, resisting the temptation to gallop blindly away. He had to use his wits now and not fall into another trap.

Who among his thirty or so hunting companions could he trust? He realized that Prince Kuliestka was the only one he could be absolutely sure of. And his lord protector was missing.

Mouthing an oath, Tobeszijian steeled himself and took his time about finding his bearings. He had lost his dogs and his party, but he himself was not lost.

He kicked his horse forward, heading back toward camp at a cautious trot. He had to conserve his horse's strength now. If he broke the animal's wind he would be alone and on foot when darkness fell. That would surely be the end of him.

He rode for a grim hour, keeping his wits and senses sharp. The snow had stopped falling, but the air was heavy with damp and bitterly cold. It was growing steadily darker, making the forest close in around him. With the hills and ravines and thickets any man could easily have become lost. But Tobeszijian's eldin blood gave him a sense of direction superior to any human's. He followed his instincts and knew himself close now to camp.

That's when he heard the sound of hoofbeats and the jingling harnesses of several riders. In the gloom and snowy mist, he could barely see more than a few feet ahead of him.

He stopped his horse and backed the reluctant stallion beneath a fir whose branches were bent low under their burden of snow. Dismounting, he held the animal's nostrils to keep it from whinnying at the other horses. They rode past at a weary walk, close enough for him to recognize Nuryveviza, Varstok, Surov, and Mradvior.

"We'll be at camp in a few minutes," Varstok was saying. His voice was gruff, hoarse with cold, and unmistakable. A huge beyar of a man, he wore a black fur cloak lined with white wool and layers of sheepskin padding beneath his plate armor for warmth. He looked like a mountain being carried by a horse. "What do we tell them? What do we say?"

"What we know," Mradvior said, sounding short-tempered. "The king chased a stag from sight. We lost him. We have called and searched, but he is not yet found."

"Kuliestka will make us search all night," Surov grumbled.

"The lord protector is missing too," Mradvior said.

Someone laughed, and Tobeszijian's fingers tightened too hard on his horse's nose. It flung up its head, almost pulling free of his hold, and one of the riders glanced back.

"Did you hear something?"

Mradvior clapped him on the shoulder. "Don't jump at shadows, my friend. Let us find fire and wine to warm us."

They vanished into the gloom, and Tobeszijian stood there in snow up to his knees, shivering and cursing beneath his breath.

He knew now he could not return to camp. Not alone, with no one to witness what had happened except a handful of frightened servants. They could be killed or bullied. Mradvior and his friends had said enough to confirm Tobeszijian's suspicions. His five-year reign had been a difficult one from the start. Following in the footsteps of his father, Runtha, had not been easy, and he'd made mistakes at first.

The worst one had been to believe his half-brother, Muncel, would ever accept him as king.

He'd tried to make peace with Muncel, had awarded him a rich holding in southern Nether near the Mandrian border, but Muncel was not appeased. Every day he listened to the steady drip of poison that was his mother's voice, whispering in his ear. He listened to the churchmen who were opposed to Tobeszijian because of his eldin blood. When Tobeszijian took an eldin wife as queen, following in the tradition of his father, the church had raised violent objections. Tobeszijian ignored them, and had made himself more enemies as a result. There were plenty who said that Muncel, fully human, should be king—never mind that Muncel was a vain, petty, small-minded, conniving cheat who could barely wield a sword and did not understand the concept of honor.

Tobeszijian had the sudden, overwhelming urge to be home in front of a fire, supplied with a brimming wine cup, his boots off, watching his small children trying to climb inside the boots and toppling over with peals of laughter.

It was his children who had surely goaded his enemies into such desperate measures. First had come Thiatereika, so delicate and beautiful, like her mother. She was four now, straight-backed and clear-eyed, her eldin blood stamped strongly on her features even without her distinctive blue eyes and pointed ears. Two winters past had come Faldain, named for an eldin king, in defiance of Tobeszijian's critics. Little Faldain with his black hair and chubby cheeks and eyes a pale gray. Eldin eyes that frightened his nurses, who murmured he would put a spell on them. Faldain could point at a supplicant cringing before the throne and yell, "Liar!" and be proven correct in his accusation. Faldain, gone missing, only to be found sleeping in the midst of the king's pack of tall, slender dogs, his chubby arms cradled around the neck of Shaiya, the pack leader who would let no one but the king touch her without biting. Faldain, who this summer had stood up in his cradle and loosed a shriek of temper that blew out all the candles in the room. And who a few minutes later had laughed, igniting them all again.

Prince Faldain, heir to the throne of Nether, was three-quarters eldin. Unlike his father Tobeszijian, who looked human and rarely exhibited any gifts of eld, the child was clearly nonhuman. His face might be sweet and chubby, but already the pronounced cheekbones and pointed chin were showing. His eerie gray eyes were tilted at the corners and saw into the minds of men and animals alike. The people feared him, and rumors said that Muncel had vowed the boy would never supplant him as king.

Tobeszijian had kept his concerns to himself. Five years of uneasy rule had taught him to conceal his reasons and motives whenever possible, to give away little, to confide never. He had decided to take the boy with him in public as much as possible once Faldain grew a bit older, for he wanted the people to see the boy and grow used to him. Already he had started negotiations with the people of eld, asking for a tutor who could train the boy in private to govern his special gifts.

But the rumors kept spreading that Faldain was of the evil, that the eldin were hardly better than the Nonkind of Gant. Religious factions in Grov, Lolta, Trebek, and other towns of Nether wanted complete separation between humans and eldin, saying they didn't belong together and never had.

That was false, of course. Tobeszijian knew the ancient histories, of how the folk of eld had lived in Nether first, all the way back to the time of the War of the Kingdoms, and how, following that fearsome time when the gods had battled and slain each other, humans had crept from the Sea of Vvord and ventured into the land. They had been welcomed by the people of eld. An alliance had been formed, now very old, with bonds still true, that said eldin and humans could live together in peace. Over the centuries, more separation had gradually come, but it was not until the reformation of the Church of the Circle, ushered in by zealots and evangelists from other lands such as Mandria, that prejudice and distrust had been born.

They were thriving now, driven by greed and the ambitions of men.

If they have grown so bold that they would take my life, what have they done to my family? Tobeszijian asked himself.

He mounted quickly and left his hiding place, ducking beneath the low branches, which unloaded snow down the back of his cloak. The horse turned toward camp, its ears pricked forward now, but Tobeszijian swung around, spurring the animal when it fought him, and headed to the road and home.

His enemies would not catch him unawares again.

2

TOBESZIJIAN'S HORSE STUMBLED over something in the near darkness. Although it snorted and shied away, the animal was too tired to bolt. Tobeszijian brought him swiftly under control and turned around to squint through the gloom at whatever lay on the ground.

He could see only a motionless man-sized shadow. His nostrils caught the scent of fresh blood.

His heart seemed to stop. *No,* he thought. *No.*

The horse would go no closer. Dismounting, Tobeszijian tied the reins to a branch and drew his dagger. Cautiously he approached the prone corpse, keeping himself alert in case this was another trap.

The snow was well trampled here. His shoulder brushed a broken pine bough, dangling, and he could just make out dark patches on the snow. Bending, he scooped up a patch and sniffed it. Blood on the snow.

There had been a fight here.

His senses told him that the dead man was Prince Kuliestka. Grief pierced Tobeszijian, but he slammed a door on all his emotions and knelt beside his friend.

Kuliestka had not gone easily. His sword was still clutched in his hand. Three arrows protruded from his back.

Touching the fletchings, Tobeszijian scowled. "Cowards," he muttered aloud.

Gently, although it did not matter now, he gripped Kuliestka's shoulders and rolled him over on his side. The heavy smell of blood rose up, and Tobeszijian could see it pooled black beneath his friend's body. There was another smell, something foul and decayed. Tobeszijian's nostrils flared, and he slid around on his knees to stare into the surrounding gloom.

Breathing hard through his mouth, Tobeszijian stripped off his gloves and touched Kuliestka's face. His friend's skin was cold and hard. The heavy ring on Tobeszijian's forefinger glowed suddenly in warning, and he snatched his hand back from Kuliestka's flesh.

Curling his fingers into a fist, he tried to breathe through his mouth, wanting none of the rank smell to enter his lungs.

The light coming from the ring grew brighter. He lifted his hand, feeling himself sweating lightly now beneath his clothes. The pale, clear light shone down upon Kuliestka's corpse, showing the bloody mess where his eyes had been torn out and the huge rents that had been sliced through his chain mail as if it were parchment. The bulge of his intestines showed, and his left hand was missing. Swallowing hard, Tobeszijian averted his gaze. A large paw print showed clearly in the snow nearby, and Tobeszijian lowered his hand unsteadily, not wanting to see any more.

A hurlhound had killed Kuliestka.

Grief submerged Tobeszijian momentarily, but at the same time his thoughts were swirling in a tangle of new suspicions. A hurlhound had attacked Kuliestka, and a shapeshifter had nearly led Tobeszijian to his doom. Mercy of Thod, what had unleashed the Nonkind here in the depths of Nether, where none of them should be? On the shared border between Gant and Nether, yes, there was always trouble, but these creatures should not have been able to come so far without detection.

Unless someone was opening Nether to them, opening forbidden doorways between the first and second worlds, and tampering with the spellcraft that protected the boundaries.

"No," he whispered in horror, and drew back from Kuliestka's corpse.

Was Muncel the one? Tobeszijian did not want to believe that his half-brother would turn to such allies in an effort to gain the throne. But to tell himself that Muncel did not harbor excessive hatred and ambition was to be naive. Of late, it seemed that Muncel was a seething mass of rage and resentment. Tobeszijian had been warned to watch his half-brother and stand guard against treachery.

Until now, Tobeszijian had discounted such warnings, certain that someday with patience he could find a way to make peace with his half-brother.

Now, with Kuliestka lying dead before him and the echo of Mradvior's ugly laugh still in his mind, Tobeszijian finally believed the rumors and suspicions. Evil men consorting with evil Nonkind had infiltrated his court and his circle of friends. Today, they had meant to see him die.

Yet Mradvior was no controller of demons; Tobeszijian's senses would have warned him of that. One of the Believers had to be nearby, had perhaps joined the hunting party today in disguise.

Tobeszijian's thoughts spun rapidly. His emotions were too chaotic for him to think clearly.

But he knew he could not tarry here. It was almost fully dark, and these woods were not safe. He had to get home, and he had to hurry.

He pulled on his gloves, concealing the strong light that still shone from his ring. Thinking of it, he paused a moment in temptation.

The Ring of Solder had been passed down from father to son in a long line of kings. It, along with the Chalice of Eternal Life, had been awarded to mankind by the gods at the Dawning. Forged by the gods, and imbued with their power, the Ring and the Chalice together held the spiritual center of Nether and served as its twin guardians against the darkness. The Ring of Solder alone had the power to transport its wearer from the first world into the second or third. It crossed boundaries of distance and time in the space between heartbeats. He could use it now, and be home just that fast.

Tobeszijian drew a deep breath and reached out his mind, calling, *Nereisse/Nereisse/Nereisse/Nereisse.*

It was too far. He could not hear her—but something had heard him.

He felt a sudden connection, a sudden, sucking darkness that focused on him. Gasping, Tobeszijian closed his mind and stumbled back from his friend's corpse. The evil was close by, too close, perhaps even next to him.

Swallowing hard, Tobeszijian watched Kuliestka's corpse intently to see if it moved. He would know then if a soultaker had consumed what the hurlhound had left.

Behind him, his horse whinnied nervously, and Tobeszijian jumped. His heart was thudding in his chest. He was a warrior, trained in battle, seasoned by war. He had fought the Nonkind before, but never without his magicked armor, his darsteed, and a spell of blessing humming through his sword.

Go, a voice said in his mind.

Tobeszijian whirled around, his sword Mirengard drawn and in his fist without thought. He stared at the forest surrounding him in the darkness. He listened with all his senses, but no further warning came. All he heard was the creaking of the trees in the cold wind and the faint rushing gurgle of a nearby stream.

Running water. He hesitated, then sprang to Kuliestka's corpse. Swiftly he wrested the sword free of Kuliestka's frozen fingers, determined to return it to the prince's family. He pulled the arrows from his friend's back and rolled Kuliestka up inside his yellow cloak. Taking one end of the garment, he dragged the corpse through the trees and undergrowth, gritting his teeth and hearing every tiny sound as though magnified a thousand times. The air of menace and evil grew increasingly thick about him, pouring through the silent trees of the forest. A terrible stench rose from poor Kuliestka's body, warning him of what was coming, of what was trying to seize the flesh and bone of his friend's corpse.

Tobeszijian knew he was playing with fire. At any moment the prince might stir, might reach out for him from the folds of this bloody cloak, might turn his sightless face to Tobeszijian's and speak dreadful spell words that would freeze Tobeszijian in his tracks, render him unable to move while the hurlhound came back to tear him to pieces and the soultaker claimed his spirit for eternal damnation.

The Ring of Solder was now pure fire encircling his finger inside his glove. He gritted his teeth and pulled faster, staggering and stumbling backward through the snow. He knew he owed his dear friend this final chance of release. Kuliestka's soul might be gone into the darkness, or perhaps a piece of it remained tethered still to this mangled body. Either way, Tobeszijian intended to spare the prince's body from becoming a plaything for the Nonkind, to be possessed and used for evil.

Tobeszijian realized he was weeping and saying aloud passages of Writ. He stumbled over a fallen log and fell backward, falling into a snowdrift and tumbling down the bank almost into the stream. The shock of his arm falling into the icy water brought him back to himself. He jerked his arm out of the water, slinging droplets everywhere, and flexed his hand swiftly. He was tempted to strip off the wet glove, for he knew it would soon freeze hard and immobilize his hand, but from the corner of his eye he saw Kuliestka's wrapped body move.

His mouth went dry. Tobeszijian slung his hand, flinging

droplets of water across the corpse. It flinched, and Tobeszijian took an involuntary step back.

He wanted to run, but he knew there was yet a moment of time. Not giving himself the chance to think, he finished dragging the corpse the rest of the way down the bank. He could feel it struggling feebly in his grip, the legs moving sluggishly.

Part of him wanted to call this a miracle and say Kuliestka was still alive. The rest of him knew better.

"Thod protect me with all thy strength," he prayed, and heaved the body into the stream.

It splashed water across his boots, and the corpse bobbed a moment. A thin, ghastly shriek ripped through his mind, and Tobeszijian clapped his hands to his ears, turning away and stumbling to his knees.

"Forgive me," he said through gritted teeth while the shrill keening went on and on inside his head. "Forgive me, my old friend, for bringing you to this."

Finally the horrible sound faded from his mind. Gasping, his face wet with tears, Tobeszijian straightened in time to see Kuliestka's body bobbing away downstream. By morning it would be encased in ice, floating far from here. As long as it stayed in running water, the Nonkind could not possess it, could not use it. All winter, Kuliestka would lie in his coffin of ice, and perhaps, if the gods smiled fortune on him, by spring he would be deep in the Sea of Vvord, his bones safe for all eternity.

Shivering, Tobeszijian lifted his hand in farewell, then scrambled up the bank and went hurrying back through the woods to his horse. As he climbed into the saddle, he could still feel the warmth of the Ring inside his glove, drying it from the inside out. Again, he felt the urgency of too little time.

He could use the Ring and be home in seconds.

But fear or prudence stayed him from such a desperate course. He had never used the Ring. He knew a wearer could use it only thrice in a lifetime. His father before him had never used it. Tobeszijian hesitated, and told himself he was not desperate yet. Worried, yes, but he could reach Grov in a matter of hours, riding cross-country rather than by road. If no one came after him, if none of the Nonkind took his trail, he could make it before dawn.

He clenched his fist, feeling torn, then made his decision.

The Ring was to be used for the protection of the Chalice. It had not been given lightly into his keeping, and it was not to be used for personal reasons.

Grimly, Tobeszijian swung his horse's head around and spurred it hard. He had a throne to save, and a friend to avenge. By Thod's hammer and the vengeance of Olas and Vlyk, he would do both.

Shortly before dawn, he reined up his weary horse on a hilltop overlooking the valley where Grov spread itself along the banks of the Velga River. He felt saddle-galled and frozen to the bone. Ice crystals had frozen themselves to his eyebrows and eyelashes. All night, he had wished himself capable of growing a beard to warm his face from the merciless cold, but his eldin blood prevented that. Swathed in his cloak, he had ridden with few pauses, using his eldin sense of direction as he never had before.

Here and there, he had come across ancient markers carved in the trunks of long-dead trees. It was the old eldin road to Grov, long since forgotten and abandoned, save by those with the blood of eld. It had brought him here faster than he'd dared to hope.

At the last crossroads, he'd hesitated, debating whether to ride to Prince Spirin's hold and call for all his liege holders to raise their armies in his support. Riding back to Grov alone might simply put him inside another trap.

But what would he tell Prince Spirin? That he'd nearly been killed? That the Nonkind were hunting in the forest? That Prince Kuliestka had been murdered? That he feared his half-brother was behind a plot to depose him?

He had no proof, nothing tangible except his lord protector's sword, and that said only that Prince Kuliestka was dead. Tobeszijian knew a king had to be strong. He could not show up wild, bedraggled, and alone and command the respect of a harsh warrior like Spirin. No, his only hope was to do the unexpected, and get to Grov quickly.

Now, the city spread before him, quiet and sleeping still in the gray pearly light before daybreak. On one side of the Velga sprawled the city, with its wooden houses, gilded church spires, and multistoried trade halls. The round expanse of the fur market stood at the city's center. Barges colored vividly in reds, blues, greens, and purples were moored along the river docks, bobbing empty or resting low and heavy in the water. The Velga had not yet frozen, but in the depths of winter it would grow still, and solid, and silent. Then the merchants would travel on it by horse-drawn sleigh, dragging logs and furs to market.

On the opposite side of the Velga stood the palace within its vast walls, high and grim on the sheer rock bluff overlooking the river. The mighty fortress had held for three centuries, proud and unfallen. He squinted through the mist and gloom at the walls, hearing the faint stamp and call of the sentries patrolling the top in their chain mail and long, fur-lined tunics striped in the burgundy and gold colors of their king. With thick, curved mustaches and tall hats of black beyar fur, the palace guards were fierce fighters and intensely loyal to their king.

Or were they?

On the horizon the sky grew steadily lighter. He could see the tallest tower, where the royal banners should have been waving, but weren't.

He squinted, his eyes burning from sleeplessness and fatigue. Where was the queen's banner? Where was the blue-green flag of Nether with its field of white stripes, the crimson banner with the gold circle signifying the church's sovereignty of the spirit, the fluttering ribbons of various colors denoting the knights who were in residence at court?

Nothing flew from the poles, not even a tatter of ribbon. He saw no curls of smoke rising above the rooftops. He listened, knowing the bells should start ringing soon, but all lay quiet, as though an enchantment had brushed away the very life from the place.

His heart froze inside him. For a moment he could not breathe. Were they gone? Were they dead?

He could not believe it. Did not want to believe such infamy could happen in his kingdom, in his own palace.

But he was here in the woods, frozen to the marrow, and skulking about like a refugee instead of the king. He had no baggage, no servants, no guards, no attendants, no courtiers, no crown, and only the torn and dirty clothes on his back. His lord protector was dead. He had ridden away from here more than six weeks ago, in blithe high spirits, shoving aside his lady wife's concerns and fears, telling himself that Muncel's arrival in Grov shortly before his departure signified nothing, ignoring the dark looks and the dour sermon of Cardinal Pernal's mass, which was supposed to have been a blessing of the hunt.

"Give the hunters strength, great Thod," the cardinal had intoned while the incense smoke rose and curled on either side of him. "Let them strike hard and take life swiftly, that all may be made new."

Considered now, after the brutal events of yesterday, those words took on new significance.

Tobeszijian sighed and rubbed the ice from his face. Brooding about betrayals and intrigues served him no good now. If Nereisse was not here, if she'd fled or been taken prisoner, then his coming here alone was a mistake. He needed an army at his back.

Nereisse! he called with his mind, seeking her.

A tiny, nameless feeling came to him, so faint and weak he almost did not perceive it.

His head lifted. He tried to still his rage and worry in order to listen.

At last he heard her calling back, *Come/come/come/come.*

She was in trouble. She was hurt. She was afraid.

He could sense all of it in that faint plea for help. His rage and grief exploded inside his chest. Without further hesitation, he spurred his horse forward, galloping down the long, treeless slope of what served the town as common pastureland. Sheep, clotted together in dirty wool, sprang up with bleats of alarm as he thundered past, his horse's hooves throwing up clods of dirt and ice. A shepherd lad, muffled to the eyes in rags and dirty sheepskin, stumbled out of his hut and stared openmouthed as Tobeszijian swept past.

There was no way inside the fortress save one, not even for the king. Tobeszijian reined up at the massive gates of wood as thick as the walls themselves. They were reinforced with straps of iron. The hinges were as long as his forearms, their pins as thick as his wrists. It took five men and a winch to pull the gates open every morning. Trumpet fanfare always marked the ritual, timed just as the sun broke above the horizon.

He was early, and the guards had not yet assembled. The gates, scarred and splintered, some of their green and black paint peeling, stood shut, dwarfing him where he circled his restless horse.

It was not seemly for a king to have to sit at his own gates, shouting for someone's attention. Tobeszijian had always come home with heralds riding ahead of him to give notice. The gates were always wide open, with guards assembled on either side at attention and horns being blown in the crisp fanfare of greeting and announcement while he and his riders trotted inside.

Had all been normal, he would have ridden home with his hunting party in a few days, his friends windburned and invigorated, their laughter and chatter loud. In their wake would have come the pack animals, laden with game: huge danselk carcasses dragging massive antlers, rows of white ermine tied up by their hind feet, snow-hares with long ears dangling, an enormous black beyar as tall as a grown man with shaggy fur and a set of long claws that could tear the intestines from a horse's belly in one swipe, boar frozen stiff, their tusks protruding long and yellow from the sides of their mouths, and silky-furred lyng cats with their white bellies and coats of distinctive gray and black swirls much prized for hats and muffs by ladies of the court.

Instead, nothing was normal. Nothing was as it should be. He sat shivering in his saddle, locked out and unnoticed. Frustration filled him, but he curbed it as he did his horse. No doubt the stallion wanted his stall and a ration of grain as much as the king wanted his bed and a trencher of steaming breakfast. If the sentries recognized him not, or chose not to, he would never get inside.

He had never felt so helpless, but he wasn't going to reveal his worry. After a few minutes, when no one looked over the battlements and saw him, he unstrapped his hunting horn and blew it.

Heads appeared atop the crenellations at once. "You there, begone!" shouted a gruff voice.

"Hold, fool," said someone else. "It's a messenger in the king's colors."

They didn't know who he was. Fury burned the edges of Tobeszijian's patience. He flung back his cloak to reveal his breastplate and pushed back his mail coif to reveal his face and the gold circlet upon his brow. "The king bids you open," he said.

The sun was not yet up, but the distant sky was now streaked with rose and white. The storm clouds of yesterday had broken up, showing patches of blue sky.

He saw them stare and heard someone swear a terrible oath.

"It *is*!" a voice said insistently.

"It can't be."

"I saw his crest, you fool! And his crown."

Another head appeared over the crenellations, helmeted properly, unlike the others.

"Your majesty!" this man said, sounding astonished. "What marvel is this? How come you here without—"

"Open," Tobeszijian said impatiently. "Or must I beg like a knave?"

"At once, majesty!"

They scurried to pass the word. The ritual was thrown aside. He heard echoing booms on the other side and a flurry of swift orders. Slowly, ever so slowly, the huge gates began to creak open.

It took several minutes for them to move, but as soon as there was enough space for his horse to squeeze through, Tobeszijian spurred his mount forward. His shoulders brushed the wood surface on either side. The grinding creak of the hinges and the groan of the ropes echoed in the close darkness, accompanied by the ring of his horse's iron shoes on the stone pavement.

He rode under the guardhouse, ducking his head slightly and aware of the guards crouching on the planks of the floor above his head, trying to peer at him through the cracks.

Emerging into the light filling the stableyard, he squinted and blinked, drawing rein before a red-faced captain wearing his fur hat cocked jauntily and saluting with a flash of crimson gloves.

"Your majesty!" he cried, then bowed low.

"Up, man!" Tobeszijian said sharply. Behind him, he was aware of orders cracking out and the heave and groan of the winch working the gate. He kept his gaze on the captain, who straightened, his face still flaming red. The captain would not meet his eyes.

"The court, has it gone?" Tobeszijian asked. "I did not see the queen's banner. Where has she moved residence?"

"I—is there no one else attending your majesty?" the captain asked.

Tobeszijian glared at the fellow, wondering why he acted so confused. "I believe my questions should be answered before yours," he said in quiet rebuke.

The captain's face drained of color. He knelt on the snow-dusted cobbles. "Forgive me, sire!"

Behind Tobeszijian the massive gates shut with a boom that made his horse shy. The locking bars slammed into place. Tobeszijian's heart thudded with them. His mouth tightened, and his hands were fists around his reins. It was another trap, and this time it had him.

A part of his mind still couldn't believe it, continued to deny all that was happening. The rest of him faced it with bleak pragmatism.

He did not glance back, although he sensed the guards forming behind him in an undisciplined knot of spectators. Did they expect him to whirl around and order them to release him?

Without another look at the captain, who remained crouched on the cobbles, Tobeszijian rode on into the stableyard proper.

By now, servants, hastily dressed and blowing on their hands to warm them, were stumbling out from the stables. A pair of serfs gawked at him with their mouths hanging open, then busied themselves with building a fire in the yard, well away from the wooden barns and piles of hay. Snowdrifts mounded in the corners and covered a cart resting on its traces. Steam rose from the shuttered windows of the stables, telling him the four-legged occupants inside were warm beneath their strapped-on blankets. He could smell the combined fragrances of horseflesh, grain mash, and straw. Out here, the customary mud and muck of the stableyard was all frozen clean. Everything looked exactly as it should, but it was all horribly wrong.

They stared at him as though he had returned as an apparition.

Several of the serfs cringed back into the shadows, crossing their fingers superstitiously behind their backs, and Tobeszijian wondered grimly what they had been told. That he was dead? Was Muncel so certain of his plot's success that he had already announced Tobeszijian's death and moved the court to his own palace? Why not sit in possession here?

Tobeszijian saw at once that whether he was now a prisoner or not, the servants still feared and revered him. Counting on habit and their sense of duty, he gestured imperiously as though he were returning from an ordinary ride. Two stableboys came darting up warily to seize the bridle of the king's stallion. The horse, well lathered and dripping foam, pranced and sidled. His iron shoes struck sparks off the ice-coated cobbles, and when he tossed his head, he lifted both boys off the ground.

A third came running to help, darting in under the half-rearing animal's chin and snapping on a tether that he fastened to an iron ring embedded in the stone.

By then, Tobeszijian had dismounted. His legs barely supported him for a moment, making him cling hard to the stirrup until the world righted again. He heard a voice talking as though from far away, then he blinked and was well again, and the voice sounded loud and practically in his ear.

"Is aught amiss, majesty?" It was the stablemaster, bowing and frowning at him. The man kept glancing behind him as though expecting the rest of the party to come in. "We heard . . . that is, we were told—"

"What news of the queen?" Tobeszijian asked, interrupting him.

The stablemaster looked taken aback. It was hardly his place to inform the king where her majesty had gone to. And yet, no chancellor of the court was stepping forward in greeting. No pages stood by to offer him wine or to take his filthy cloak and gloves. No courtiers had come forth, eager to catch a glimpse of him and perhaps draw the favor of his glance or conversation.

All his life he had been surrounded by attendants, hangers-on, suppliants, dogs, nobles, and the general action and confusion of the court. There was always someone begging for a word with him, always maids and ladies giggling from the windows in hopes of attracting his eye, always minions and servants underfoot.

Yet now it was as though everyone in the place had been spirited away except the guards and these few servants. Tobeszijian felt like a ghost trying to return to the world of reality, only to find himself trapped behind glass, unable to step through.

Angrily he glared at the stablemaster, who had not answered his question. "The queen, sirrah!" he snapped, all patience gone. "Can you answer a simple question, or not?"

He was in many respects a gentle man, a kind man, but when he spoke in that tone men quailed and the world itself seemed to crack. He stood there, a full head and shoulders taller than the shrinking stablemaster, his blue eyes on fire and his chiseled, beardless face set in lines of stone.

The stablemaster took an involuntary step back from him, his eyes darting in several directions as though seeking aid. "Majesty," he said, turning as pale as the shirt band protruding above the neck of his tunic. "I—I—it is not meet that I should relay such news. The—"

"Her banner does not fly. Has she left residence? With what escort and bound for what location?"

The stablemaster gripped his broad, work-calloused hands together and lifted them in appeal. "I—I—we know only that she has fallen ill. A fever, they say. It came suddenly. It was only—"

Tobeszijian's heart contracted sharply, and he swung away from the man, who gasped and fell silent.

"A fever?" Tobeszijian said with his back still to the stablemaster. His voice was sharp. Heat filled his face, and his ears were roaring.

Not Nereisse, he thought with pain too great to bear. *Not my love.*

The stablemaster prated on, but Tobeszijian did not listen. Nereisse was eldin; she could not catch human fevers. She caught no diseases at all. For her to be taken ill could only mean the poison of spellcraft.

He thought of the shapeshifter and its scream of fury when he rode away from it in the forest. He thought of Kuliestka's slashed and mutilated corpse lying in the snow. He thought of Nereisse fevered and alone, with his enemies closing around her.

"Where have they taken her?" he asked, using every bit of self-control he possessed not to shout.

His quiet voice seemed to unnerve the stablemaster further, for the man gave him no answer.

Tobeszijian swung around, his hand going to his sword hilt. "By Thod, must I wring every answer from you? Where is she?"

"I—I know not," the man stammered. His gaze shifted past Tobeszijian in sudden relief.

Warned, Tobeszijian swung around so fast his cloak billowed from his shoulders.

Another officer of the guard stood close by. This one possessed harder eyes than the captain; his face was like a hatchet. Tobeszijian glared at him, noting that the man's cloak was slightly too long for him and that his hauberk fit him ill. The links of his chain mail were of an unfamiliar design. Tobeszijian's nostrils flared. This man was a hirelance, nothing more than a mercenary cutthroat. Tobeszijian's gaze shifted past the man to the rest of the guards. Numbering about forty, including those who stood atop the wall looking down, most were clearly of the same ilk, wearing foreign-made mail under their borrowed surcoats. Only a handful, including the captain, were clearly genuine members of the palace guards, and they had either sold themselves or were under coercion.

Tobeszijian's gaze narrowed and he swung it back to the hirelance before him. He noted the man's narrow skull and saw a hint of fang in the man's thin-lipped smile. A chill of disgust ran through the king. This man was Gantese, and it took every ounce of Tobeszijian's self-control not to draw his sword and hack the Believer in twain then and there.

"I am Bork, your majesty," the hirelance said. His voice was respectful, but his eyes were not. "You will surrender your sword."

The stablemaster moaned.

Ignoring him, Tobeszijian never took his gaze from Bork. "No."

Bork spread his feet in readiness. His face was hard and wary. "This can go hard, or it can go easy. The sword and your surrender."

Forty to one was impossible. But Tobeszijian had no intention of fighting them yet anyway—there were other things to accomplish first. He mastered his outrage at the man's impudence and made no move to obey.

"This fortress is under your control?" he asked.

Bork smirked. "I command it."

A muscle jumped in Tobeszijian's jaw. Otherwise he did not move. "I am the king, hirelance. Your prisoner or not, I do not surrender my sword to the likes of you. When your master comes to face me, he can demand my sword, and to him alone will I give my answer."

Bork did not like his defiance, but Tobeszijian's gaze held the iron confidence of birthright and lineage. He stared the hirelance down, and when Bork's gaze dropped, Tobeszijian knew he'd won temporarily.

"I will ask this again," he said quietly. "Where are the queen and the royal children?"

"Your queen remains in residence, but not for long, we think."

As Tobeszijian's fingers clenched around his sword hilt, Bork showed his fangs in a broad smile. Behind Tobeszijian the stablemaster whimpered in fear, but fell silent instantly as Bork's cruel gaze shifted to him. Tobeszijian never took his eyes off the hirelance, and inside his glove he could feel his ring growing hot. What else had taken possession of his palace? He could not stop his imagination from running wild, wondering if the Nonkind now roamed the hallways and passages freely. Had Muncel forged a complete alliance with Gant? If so, he must be mad.

With great effort, Tobeszijian pulled his whirling thoughts back under control. He was sweating despite the cold morning air. He told himself to keep his royal dignity. He must betray no fear, no rage, nothing to indicate he had lost mastery of himself.

"Now, your majesty," Bork said, his voice as smooth as a serpent's glide. "You will come with us to the—"

"I will see my queen," Tobeszijian said sharply. "If she lies ill, she is in need of me."

Bork opened his mouth, but Tobeszijian said, "What you have orders to do can be done later. I am now within these walls. You guard the only way out."

Bork's eyes seemed to shrink in his face until they were two dark pinpricks, but he protested not.

Tobeszijian turned his back on the Believer, although he half-expected the man to strike. He caught the stablemaster's attention, and the man gaped at him in open fear.

"Yes, your majesty?"

"A fresh horse," Tobeszijian said. "My palace may be emptied, and my friends vanished, but I will not forgo all custom."

It was the king's custom to pause here in his stableyard to change mounts and strip off his mail and armor in exchange for a courtly tunic before riding into the palace grounds. Most of the time he divested himself of his weapons also, handing them over to his squire to be cleaned. The king's squire, a lad named Rustin and the son of Count Numitskir, had not gone on the hunting trip this year. Shortly before their departure, he'd disgraced himself with a slattern who claimed he'd fathered a child on her. Since squires in training to become knights were expected to remain celibate until after they took their knightly vows, the boy had effectively ruined a promising future. In haste to depart, Tobeszijian had told himself he would judge the matter after his return. It seemed now that he would not. He wondered what had become of the boy. For that matter, what had become of his entire court? Would he ever know?

If he allowed himself to feel his shock, he realized, he would not be able to continue. He refused to think beyond his purpose, which burned like a fire coal in his breast. The future might hold his death at the hands of these rabble, but he would not consider that now.

"Let us amend custom today," he said to the stablemaster. "Just the horse."

The stablemaster gulped and nodded, bowing low and backing away to snap his fingers frantically at the boys, who were staring with their mouths open.

"It's been told that you can ride the darsteed," Bork said, and pointed at the opposite side of the stableyard to a round building with a cone-shaped roof of slate. Lights shone from the tiny windows fitted high in the walls. A bugle of fury, muffled by the stone walls, came from inside, along with a series of rapid thuds.

Tobeszijian's nostrils flared. He felt the darsteed's fiery rage reach his senses, and his own pent-up rage and grief responded like fire in his chest. His heartbeat quickened. For a second his blood raced in his veins.

He sent his mind to it: *I am home/home/home/home.*

The creature needed exercise. It had been neglected during his absence, cooped up in there the whole time. He could feel its explosive need.

Soon, he promised it.

The savage fire of its mind came crashing back to him, making him sway slightly in the effort of absorbing it. *Run/run/run/run.*

Soon, he promised it again, and his heart felt as savage as the beast.

The darsteed inside the fortified stall bugled and kicked.

Tobeszijian blinked and broke the contact, realizing that Bork was staring at him in open conjecture.

Bork smiled and gestured at the stablemaster. "Your king would ride his mighty darsteed. It's in need of exercise."

Tobeszijian frowned. Ordinarily he rode the darsteed into battle instead of a charger. The darsteed was a creature from a nightmare, a beast of war and terror. By the laws of tradition, all kings of Nether had owned a darsteed since the days when Nether first defeated Gant and seized the terrifying beasts as prizes. But the creatures were kept locked up and viewed at a safe distance. No Netheran king, until Tobeszijian, had dared to actually ride one. Thanks to his eldin blood, he could control the brute. When Tobeszijian appeared on the battlefield in full plate armor and antlered helm, bearing his two-handed sword and a war hammer, and riding astride a black fearsome creature that breathed fire and roared with all the violence of hell itself, few Kladite raiders could stand and hold their ground. Few Gantese Believers and Nonkind would either.

Yet Bork was trying to provoke him into bringing it out. Tobeszijian wondered if the hirelances had gone inside to look at the beast and if it had injured any of them. Grimly he met the Gantese's eyes. He would use the darsteed, all right, but not yet. Not until the proper time.

"Ride it," Bork urged him. "We have heard of your legend, King Tobeszijian. We would see it for ourselves. No one will bring it out for us."

Tobeszijian said nothing.

He longed for Kuliestka at his side. By now the lord protector would have tried to put an end to these insults, and gotten himself spitted on the end of a sword. Grief rose inside Tobeszijian, twisting painfully, but he choked it down. He must be iron. He must remain every inch a king if he was to keep himself from being shackled and led away in total humiliation to the guardhouse.

"Forgive me, majesty. We dared not take the beast outside while you were gone," the stablemaster said nervously. "Since Vlout died of that head kick, no one can handle it except your majesty."

Tobeszijian frowned, momentarily distracted. "You were told to find a replacement for Vlout immediately."

"I tried, majesty, but—"

Tobeszijian lifted his hand to silence the man.

"Ride it, great king," Bork said, openly mocking him now.

The stableboys came leading up a bay courser fitted with an ornate saddle of silver and a velvet saddlecloth. Rosettes had been braided hastily into its shining black mane, and its dark hooves gleamed with oil. It tossed its fine head and pranced sideways, its delicate nostrils snorting white plumes in the frosty air.

"That's a lady's mount. Not worth a king's backside," Bork said, grinning and showing his fangs. "Let's see the darsteed."

Tobeszijian was conscious of time running out, of his tiny advantage slipping from his fingers. He must turn the tide of this game, and swiftly, before all was lost.

"The queen's health is my concern now," he said coldly. "When I have seen her, I will consider your request."

Bork growled in his throat and moved sharply. Perhaps he meant to strike Tobeszijian, or perhaps he was only making a rude gesture.

Either way, Tobeszijian turned on him and caught his fist in midair, straining to hold it when the Gantese would have pulled free. Bork's eyes narrowed to black dots of evil. He snarled, baring his fangs.

But Tobeszijian's blue eyes blazed right back, and his mind—unskilled but strong—crashed against Bork's. *Back away/back away/back away,* he commanded.

Bork snarled again. The other guards were closing fast, scenting a problem even while the two men stood close to each other, glaring and locked together, their struggle hidden as yet between their bodies.

"When I am at liberty, I will show you the brute's paces," Tobeszijian said, straining to hold the hirelance. His voice grew rough from the effort he was expending. *Back away,* his mind commanded again.

Bork unclenched his fist and stopped the struggle abruptly. His eyes held anger mingled with confusion.

Tobeszijian knew he could not control the Believer, but he could influence him. He pushed again, and saw Bork blink.

The Gantese stepped back. "At your majesty's leisure," he said, and gestured scornfully at the bay, which shook the rosettes tied to its long mane and pawed the ground. "We shall still be here."

Relief came sharp and sudden, like a dagger thrust. Feeling his knees weaken, Tobeszijian turned away and swung into the saddle with all the grace and strength he could exhibit. He rode through the smaller gates on the other side of the stableyard and took the winding road that led to his palace.

Not caring what any of them thought, he spurred the animal to a gallop and didn't look back.

3

THE PALACE GROUNDS sloped uphill, enclosing a small, well-groomed forest of ash trees that bordered either side of the stone-paved road. Spurring the bay courser again, Tobeszijian rode through the trees and glimpsed the small, sleek herd of royal deer nibbling at the still-green grass they'd pawed up from beneath the snow. Their heads flashed up in alarm as he galloped past, and they turned as one, bounding away.

The road dipped, curved through a snow-rimmed stream, and wound steeply up through a stone archway that had once marked a gatehouse and the crumbled remains of the original fortress walls. Ivy now grew over the fallen stones. Frost had burnished the leaves to tawny colors. From this point the road became older, rougher, narrower. The forest grew right up to it on either side. Then abruptly the trees ended, revealing the top of the hill, which was entirely cleared. The palace stood there, silhouetted against the rosy, pearlescent morning sky. The peaks and spires of its roof seemed to stretch to the heavens.

The palace was a magnificent sight that never failed to lift Tobeszijian's heart. Three stories tall, the long, multiwinged palace stood there airily in its setting of snow, sky, and shrubbery. Its pale yellow stone had been quarried from the rocky hills near Lake Charva, and it featured long rows of tall windows. Every window was fitted with actual glass, a luxury so rare and costly it had once threatened to deplete the treasury.

Delicate columns of white marble supported archways over each window. The columns were carved fancifully in the shapes of serpents, lizards, tree branches, and vines. Winged gryphons lunged from the rooftops as waterspouts, and leaping sea-maids with outstretched arms were carved from marble to form the balustrades on either side of the broad steps leading up into the state portico.

Nowhere else in Grov or all of Nether could such a building be found. It was too ornate, too whimsical. It gave the eye no rest. It was as different from the original fortress on this spot as the sun was different from the moon. Yet its ramparts remained strong and practical. Behind it the sheer stone cliffs dropped straight down into the Velga River, creating a natural defense on that side.

Runtha's Folly, some folk called this bizarre yet beautiful palace. Begun by Tobeszijian's grandfather, Runtha I, and completed by his father, Runtha II, the palace's unusual appearance was blamed on the eldin and their unwelcome influence.

For many centuries eldin and humans had coexisted peacefully in Nether, even joining themselves into the Church of the Circle and forming the basis of modern religion now held by half the known world. The Chalice of Eternal Life was held sacred by both humans and eldin, who believed in the same history of the Origins and the same gods. Folk of the eld, however, had magic which the humans did not. They could enter the second world, which humans could not. Eldin and humans found they were usually more comfortable apart, and in general they kept their communities separate.

Less than two hundred years ago, Tomias the Reformer—a monk and visionary believed to be from Mandria, although he claimed no land as his origin—had entered Nether, bringing with him a different branch of the church and a radical system of beliefs. Tomias and the reformers considered the eldin to be part of the darkness and superstition which had held Nether chained for too long. Church magic, held firmly in the hands of the crimson-robed churchmen, was preached to be honorable and true to the Chalice, derived from its sacred power. Eld magic was said to be derived from perversion and secret liaisons with the darkness, a force that would tarnish the Chalice. But any human could enter the Circle and worship the Chalice, bringing it glory, providing he or she came with a true and willing heart. To serve, a worshiper needed only to feel faith. No actual performance or action was required, refuting what had been the former custom of penitence and ritual. Tomias advocated separation and division between humans and the eldin, claiming that the folk of eld had no actual place in the Circle and need not be considered an equal part of it.

Fresh and appealing, this message of reform took quickly in Grov, and from there it spread across the rest of Nether. It became fashionable to deny that the eldin even existed, fashionable to build stone churches and to burn the old paneathas which had stood in wall niches, honoring the old gods, since time began.

But as a young man, Runtha I shook off the influence of the reformers. One day while riding in the forests alone, he was thrown when his horse stumbled. Knocked unconscious, he awakened hours later to find that night had fallen. Surrounding him was a group of eldin with eerie white flames shooting from their fingertips, lighting the clearing without need of lanterns. Although little contact had been made between humans and eldin since the mission work of Tomias the Reformer, he was treated that night to eld hospitality. Runtha I discovered for himself that the eldin were a gentle, merry people with spirits of light and laughter. He made friends with his hosts, who showed him many wonders and visions. Returning a few days later to his frantic and much-worried court, the young king embraced the old ways and set about undermining the stranglehold of the reformed church. He shortened the sermons and permitted townspeople freedom of choice between the reformed church and the old festivals.

Eld groves were preserved by royal decree, and this palace was constructed around the old, dank, original Hall of Kings. A Mandrian was sent for, and he created these formal gardens of clipped yew hedges, leaving only a small copse of natural hust trees on one side, out of sight. There, roses and sea holly were allowed to grow wild in a thicket. Tended by eldin and much loved by the present queen, this magical place became a riot of color in the spring, when the hust trees bloomed in long white racemes that hung to the ground and all sorts of flowers burst from the ground to open crimson, gold, and pink petals. The bees grew drunk and fat with pollen, the fragrance of flowers filled the air, and the wind would blow a wealth of rose petals across the grassy paths.

As his horse came surging over the last steep segment of road, Tobeszijian summoned a mental image of Nereisse his wife, so pale and graceful, walking there in her grove, her wispy draperies catching on branches, fallen petals hanging in her knee-long blonde hair and scattering behind her. He felt a pang inside him as though he'd been pricked.

It was her pain, reaching to him.

Oh, great Thod, he prayed frantically, *let me reach her in time.*

He kicked his horse forward, making it kick up spumes of powdery snow, its iron shoes slipping dangerously on patches of ice.

No one waited on the broad steps to greet him. Few lights shone in the windows. The tall double doors stood closed, with no servants ready to open them. He saw no curls of smoke spiraling from the chimneys on the roof.

He had never, in all his lifetime, imagined the palace could be this deserted. The sight of it, abandoned and empty, pierced his heart.

A corner of his mind raged, wanting specific names and faces, ready to condemn and assign blame. But it was not that easy to separate the tangled skeins of the political web. Who at court was not an enemy of some kind? The lord chancellor, the lord of the treasury, the keeper of the seal, the guardian of the armory, the cardinal of the church, the steward of the household, and yes, especially yes, the king's own half-brother were all problems, siding continuously against him and the policies he tried to set.

Only five years on the throne, Tobeszijian thought grimly, *and my reign is already in grave danger.*

He could blame part of it on the alliances his father had forged shortly before his demise. He could blame more of it on Prince Muncel's ambition and greed. He could blame the rest on the church and its zealot leader, Cardinal Pernal, who wanted no half-eld king on the throne.

Spurring the courser, Tobeszijian sent it scrambling madly up the broad steps to the very doors of the palace. Leaning from the saddle, he pounded on the wooden panels and listened to the echo of his summons fade inside.

No one came.

Dismounting, he shouldered open the heavy door. Inside, the place was shadowy and cold. He drew Mirengard, flung back his cloak to free his arms, and strode swiftly through the rambling palace.

The emptiness drove a wedge of dread deeper into his heart. There had been no looting. The carpets and furniture still filled the rooms. But no living thing stirred. He heard nothing except his own rapid footfalls.

He passed through a set of tall double doors into the icy gloom of the original Hall of Kings. The room was narrow and cramped with age, its arched ceiling blackened by centuries of fire smoke and grime. Windowless and bleak, the room's only illumination normally came from torches kept burning in wall sconces set between long tapestries. The torches did not burn now, not even around the multitiered paneatha. The ancient gilded icons of the gods, their painted images so dim and worn they were nearly unrecognizable, were gone.

Tobeszijian halted there in shock. Lowering the tip of his sword to the sagging wooden floor, he reached forward and touched each bare arm of the paneatha where an icon should have been hanging.

"Blasphemy," he muttered beneath his breath, and looked up.

On the wall, above the crude and age-blackened throne of the First, should have hung a triangular-shaped sword made of black iron, its hilt wrapped with leather, its double edges nocked and jagged from battles fought in the dim beginning of history.

The sword of his ancestors was gone.

He knew then what else he would find missing.

Fear plunged to his vitals. It was as though while he was away, the world had ended. And during this plotting, he hadn't known, hadn't guessed. How could he have been so blind? He stood in the empty Hall and felt lost, as though he'd been dropped into the third world and could not find his way back out.

Drawing several ragged breaths, he sought to calm himself and knelt before the ancient wooden cabinet that stood beneath the wall niche of the paneatha. Opening its doors, he reached inside, found the hidden depression, and pressed it.

With a faint rumble and scrape, a portion of the wooden floor slid aside. Dank air rose into his face. He ran to light one of the torches, using the striker and stone kept always near the paneatha. When the torch was burning bright, popping as its pitch warmed within the twist of straw, he held it aloft in his left hand and gripped his sword with his right. Thus armed, he descended the rickety wooden steps into the yawning darkness below the Hall of Kings.

At the bottom of the steps stretched a cramped chamber with walls of frozen dirt and stone. In the center were double, semicircle rows of stone benches. On the opposite wall stood a crude stone altar with a cauldron overturned next to it. The torchlight flickered over the reliquaries on the altar, showing him the green-patinated bronze bowls intended to hold salt and sacred water, the old bronze knives of ritual, the rods of white ash, the stubs of Element candles, the incense burners, runestones, a small bell, and the dried remains of vines that had once wreathed the altar.

This was the original worship site. The Chalice of Eternal Life had been placed here when the First received it from the gods. For generations the Chalice had been well guarded by Tobeszijian's ancestors. Although Tobeszijian's father had been besieged by church officials to surrender the Chalice to them so that they might display it prominently in the newly completed Cathedral of Helspirin in Grov's center, Runtha II would not agree. The Chalice belonged here, he said. Runtha had argued that the Chalice was not to be worshiped instead of the gods. Its power protected the land and the people of Nether. But that power was not to be channeled by churchmen for the working of miracles designed only to increase numbers of congregants.

The very day following Tobeszijian's own coronation in the Cathedral of Helspirin, Cardinal Pernal had approached him and requested that the Chalice be moved to the cathedral, far from the primitive cave where it had been hidden from the people for too long. He pointed out the arching ceiling of the nave, so high it seemed lost in the misty shadows. He showed Tobeszijian the sanctum and the stand where the Chalice would be displayed, high enough so that all who came inside the enormous cathedral could see it, with narrow slits of windows surrounding it in order that its light might radiate outside the building at night.

That day, Tobeszijian gazed around at the unfamiliar cathedral, with its fine carvings and its statues of saints instead of the icons of the old gods. He noticed the brilliant blue paint and the extensive, elaborate gilding. Oh, there was no doubt the Chalice would be displayed in as beautiful a setting as man could devise, but Tobeszijian felt uneasy. Since childhood, he had kept in his memory the rites and the ancient phrasing of the oath of protection sworn by him and every other king of Nether since the Chalice came into their care. He had responsibilities that were secret, unknown to this powerful churchman in his crimson robes, responsibilities that did not permit the Chalice to be put on public display. For one thing, its power was too strong, needing containment by magical means involving soil, salt, running water, and ash wood.

Like his father before him, Tobeszijian refused the church's request. Cardinal Pernal's face had gone quite white and pinched around the nostrils. His dark brown eyes had blazed with fury that he clearly had difficulty containing. With his mouth set in a tight line, he bowed to his king, and Tobeszijian left him to fume as he wished.

Now, however, as Tobeszijian walked into this small, dark cave beneath his palace, he saw that this first Circle had been violated, and that the Chalice was gone.

Behind the altar, the natural spring which pooled in the ground had been filled in with dirt and stone, choking it. Tobeszijian touched it and felt dampness, but nothing more. He swore softly. Skirting the spring, he walked deeper into the darkness, holding his torch aloft to light his way, although he already knew.

With every cautious step, his heart raged and grieved. Yet he had to look, had to see for himself all that had been done to defile this holy place.

On the back wall rose a pillar of black obsidian, hewn and polished. The Chalice of Eternal Life should have been standing atop that pillar. It was not.

At the base of the pillar, the hearth of Perpetual Fire lay cold. Removing his glove, Tobeszijian thrust his hand into the white, powdery ashes, but there was no lingering ember to cast warmth. The fire had been dead a long while.

"Muncel," he said aloud in despair, "what have you done?"

The silence seemed to mock him. He stepped back, stumbling a little, then turned and fled, running across the chamber and back up the steps into the Hall of Kings. He kicked the trapdoor back into place and flung his torch into a wall sconce with such force it nearly went out. Wrenching himself around, he strode through the rest of the Hall, passing the rows of ancient weapons—some mysterious, others primitive—hanging on hooks as reminders of the past.

Slamming his way through another set of doors, he left the Hall of Kings and strode through a passageway as gloomy and deserted as the others.

More doors. He burst through them and entered a reception gallery of light and warmth so intense it hit him like a blow. A row of windows along the left wall filled the room with morning sunlight. At the far end, he could see a tall stove, tiled with bright colors and radiating a blast of heat that made him realize how cold the rest of the palace had grown.

His anger sank into a deep, secretive corner of his soul, and was replaced by a renewed sense of caution. If the palace was deserted, who had built this fire?

Gripping his sword with both hands and holding it ready before him, he moved down the corridor on quick, quiet feet, trying to still even the faint jingling of his silver spurs. He wanted to call out Nereisse's name, but he held his tongue.

The gallery looked magnificent in the sunlight. Its tall mirrors, even more costly and rare than the glass in the windows, hung on the right-hand wall, reflecting back the sunlight streaming in. The place was all dazzle and glitter, prismed light refracting on the walls and shimmering from the faceted balls of bard crystal hanging on chains of gold from the ceiling.

It was the Gallery of Glass, famous throughout the kingdoms. His passage beneath the bard crystal balls set them swinging lightly, and he could hear them sing in faint little sighs of melody. The gallery had never failed to enchant all who entered it. Dignitaries from foreign lands often came and sat here by the hour, marveling at the dazzling array of light and color and sound. During festivals, it pleased Tobeszijian to allow dances to be held and madrigals to be performed in here. The fine carpets would be rolled up, and the floors polished. Candles would be lit everywhere until the mirrors blazed with their reflection. The ladies would swish and spin about, laughing to see themselves in the mirrors. The jewel-like colors of their gowns glittered like kaleidoscope pieces on the faceted surfaces of the bard crystal balls overhead, while the crystal sang with the melodies, their tunes eerie and soft.

Sweat beaded on Tobeszijian's brow, and he turned at the end of the gallery to climb a broad wooden staircase, carpeted by handwoven rugs sent by the Wandering Tribes in tribute. The carved wooden heads of idealized danselk, covered with paint and gilding, formed the posts on either side of the head of the staircase. Their antlers held candle stubs long since burned out. A draft of the heated air from the Gallery of Glass blew up the staircase, but it did not reach far.

At the top of the stairs, he rounded the corner and nearly collided with an elderly servant of the Order of the Chamberlain. Stooped with age, his straight gray hair cut in a severe bowl shape above his ears, the servant wore a stiff tabard of embroidered livery in the royal colors of burgundy and gold. His collar of servitude was embossed with the royal coat of arms. He held a key in his mottled hands, and worry puckered his old face.

Startled by this encounter, Tobeszijian swung his sword in reflex even as he recognized the servant. He shortened his swing and the mighty blade whistled harmlessly over the old man's head. Cringing to the floor, the servant lifted his hands and wailed in fright.

"Suchin!" Tobeszijian said in profound relief. He sheathed his sword and gripped the wailing servant's shoulder. "Suchin, do you not know me?"

Gasping, the old man lifted his terrified face and unsquinched his eyes. He stared at Tobeszijian, his mouth falling open and his eyes growing rounder and rounder. All the color leached from his face.

"I live," Tobeszijian said firmly, gripping Suchin's shoulder even tighter. "I am flesh, not ghost."

Relief flooded Suchin's face at that assurance. With a sob, he flung himself at Tobeszijian's feet and wept. "Majesty, you have come!" he cried. "At last, you have come."

Tobeszijian gazed down at the old man lying at his feet and wondered why he was still here. Had he been overlooked, or was he one of the betrayers like the captain of the guard and the stablemaster?

But the king had no time for such questions now. "Suchin," he said firmly, "rise and take me to the queen."

Suchin obeyed, sniffing and wiping his nose on his sleeve. Hurrying to keep up with Tobeszijian's long stride, he pointed toward the state apartments. "Sire," he babbled, "what a relief that you have come home. We had given up all hope."

"How does the queen?" Tobeszijian asked. Guilt choked him as he thought of the palace betrayed and invaded, the queen ill, the Chalice stolen, all while he'd been gone on his pleasure, hunting because he felt tired of his responsibilities. Thod's mercy, but he had much to answer for. "Is she better?"

Suchin sighed and shook his head. "We thought it was nothing at first. Princess Thiatereika fell ill several days ago. Her fever was strong, and kept her tossing and crying out."

Thiatereika, his only daughter. Tobeszijian felt as though he'd been struck by a war hammer. Too much was happening. Too much was being taken away. He could hear a wild, queer laugh in one corner of his brain, while the rest of him stared at Suchin in horror.

"Aye, sire," Suchin said. "Only the queen could soothe the child. Then her majesty took the fever too. She would not give way to it, though, but fought it most valiantly, giving all her strength to the child's care. Even when Prince Muncel came, she received him with pride, facing him down while she tried to hold the palace in the name of the king." Suchin's gaze flickered to Tobeszijian's face. "But she could not prevail and was sent to her chambers. She was kept a prisoner inside until the palace was emptied of everyone. Gilda says her grace cried aloud yesterday afternoon and spoke your majesty's name. She did act most peculiar, weeping that you were dead. Then she swooned and was taken to bed. She lies there still."

Tobeszijian frowned, feeling fresh grief wash over him. She'd known of his danger, while he'd been oblivious to hers. He should never have left this year. He'd known better. Thod's bones, but he should have heeded the warning signs and stayed here to guard what was his.

"What does the physician say?" he asked, pausing while Suchin struggled to push open the double doors leading into the queen's chambers.

Suchin looked at him almost fearfully and stepped aside. "There has been no physician to attend her majesty."

Speechless with anger, Tobeszijian stopped halfway across the threshold. He met the old man's eyes, and suddenly his sword tip was pressing Suchin's throat. "What infamy is this?" he shouted. "By whose order was a physician kept from Queen Nereisse?"

Suchin's face went as gray as his hair. His eyes widened with terror, and Tobeszijian pressed the blade deeper into that soft, wrinkled skin. "Her own order, your grace!" the servant said, gasping.

Tobeszijian had been expecting him to say it was Prince Muncel. Stunned, he released the old man, and Suchin sagged against the door, banging it into the wall. His hand trembled as he pointed at the tall bed standing in the center of the room. Sheathing his sword, Tobeszijian walked toward it in a daze of confusion and anguish.

The state bed of the queen was a massive piece of furniture. Each post was as big around as Tobeszijian's waist and carved heavily with runes of blessing and the faces of ancient tree spirits. Since Nereisse had become queen, the ancient timbers of the bed had sprouted with twigs and green leaves, as though roots still fastened the posts to the soil. Some of the serving maids would not go near the bed, not even to strip the linens for cleaning. Others claimed they could hear the timbers groaning during the day, mumbling in the old tongues things no mortals should hear.

Gold velvet hangings, so heavily embroidered they hung stiff, encircled the bed to keep out drafts. They were parted now on the side facing a roaring fire, and Gilda, the old nurse who cared for the royal children, sat there on a stool at the queen's bedside, sponging the queen's hands and face with a damp cloth.

Nereisse's golden hair spread across the pillow. Reaching to her knees when she left it unbound, the tresses were normally thick and luxuriant. They sprang back from her face naturally, requiring no fillet or band to control them, and the curls and waves of her hair were never still but always in quiet motion, as though a soft breeze blew over her at all times. Now, however, no invisible breeze stirred her hair to life. It lay there tangled and limp, darker at her temples, where she was sweating.

Her clear skin was flushed, and her shut eyelids looked bruised and puffy. She was tossing her head back and forth on the pillow, her hands plucking at the fur coverlet. Gilda grasped one of her hands and held it firmly, patting it with the damp cloth, but Nereisse pulled free and murmured urgently, *"Siobveidhne broic kalfeyd edr hahld!"*

The fire flickered abruptly low as though it might go out, and the air in the room seemed to vanish momentarily as if it had all been sucked away. Tobeszijian's hair stood up on the back of his neck, and he could feel the wild prickling across his skin that told him she was speaking with power.

That was forbidden here. She herself had forbidden it, saying it was not safe within the walls, with so many people about. Power, channeled through the eldin tongue, was for the outdoors, where it could be unleashed with force.

Gilda looked up at Tobeszijian's arrival, and tears glistened in her rheumy eyes, trickling down her wrinkled cheeks. Her bottom teeth had long ago rotted out, leaving her mouth shrunken, and pulling her chin up nearly to her nose. She might look a crone, but hers was a gentle soul. She had never feared Nereisse or the children who had been born in this bed. She had served as Tobeszijian's nurse, mothering him when his own mother died, and she had stood as his ally during the days when his father took a new, this time human, wife who wanted nothing to do with her royal stepson.

"Sire, my sweet lady lies here poorly," Gilda whispered. "Very poorly." She slid off her stool, making way for him to bend over Nereisse.

Tobeszijian gripped his wife's hands in his. They were burning hot. She tossed her head, spilling the cloth Gilda had left across her brow. Tobeszijian stroked the queen's forehead, trying to ease the furrows which creased it. He kissed first her hot lips, then her shut eyelids, then the pointed tip of each delicate ear.

"My beloved," he whispered, grieving for her. She had the smell of death on her skin. She was so hot, his icy queen, so unnaturally hot. Usually Nereisse's skin was as cool to the touch as polished marble. He kissed her again, but her eyes did not open. He felt afraid. "Nereisse," he said in desperation, "I've come safely home."

At last her eyes did drag themselves open. They were blue-gray, tilted at the corners, and they stared at him without recognition. *"Kalfeyd edr hahld!"* she said.

He felt his hair blow back from his brow as she said the words, felt their force. Danger, she was saying. There is danger.

"Nereisse," he said, stroking her cheeks, wanting her to know him. "It's Tobeszijian, come home to you. Look at me, beloved. Hear my voice."

But she tossed in his arms, crying out feverishly, then clutching her stomach with whimpers of pain.

"Help her!" he said to Gilda frantically. "Send for the physician—"

"No!" Nereisse gripped his wrist, pulling herself up off the pillows. Her eyes stared into his as though she saw a stranger. "Keep away!"

"Nereisse, I'm here," he said, pushing her hair back from her face.

She tried to bat his hand away. "No!"

"Hush, beloved. I will not hurt you. Gilda," he said sharply to the old woman, who had not moved, "do as I have commanded!"

"The physician's gone, like all the rest," Gilda said. "There's only me and Suchin left. We hid, or they'd have taken us away too."

Tobeszijian, still trying to soothe his flailing wife, stared at Gilda. Although he had many questions, he knew this wasn't the time. Again he tried to ease Nereisse down, but she was still fighting him.

"Nereisse, it's Tobeszijian, your husband," he said. "You know me. I've come home."

This time she responded to his voice. Her eyes, so wild and frantic behind hanging wisps of hair, glared at him. "You're dead. I parted the veils of seeing, and you were dead."

"No," he said softly, stroking her hair. "I escaped."

"Saw you," she panted. "Saw the Nonkind surrounding you. Saw them rend you. How you fought, my beloved. You fought so fiercely and well, but you were alone and there were so many of them—"

"No, Nereisse," he said, trying to silence her. "I am here, safe with you."

She groaned and clung to him, weeping now. "It cannot be true," she said. "I saw so clearly."

"It almost happened," he told her. "Almost, but they could not trap me. Now you must rest and get better."

He laid her down upon her pillows, but she still clung to his hand, her blue-gray eyes frantic. "It is not safe here for you. The churchmen will capture you. The court has gone. Everything is gone."

"I saw," he said grimly, thinking of the deserted palace.

"Muncel—" She shivered, wracked anew with pain.

"Hush," he said. "I am here now. You must rest and get better. We will deal with the other later."

But she seemed not to hear him. "Muncel has claimed your throne," she said, her voice a whisper. "He has moved the court to Belrad, saying the palace here is accursed by eldin magic. The court left yesterday—nay, the day before. Sleds and troikas and wagons. They took all the—"

"Hush," he said, masking his fury. "Let me worry about that. It does not matter as long as you and the children are safe."

Her gaze shifted, and for a second she was his old Nereisse, gazing into his eyes with a corner of her mouth quirked up in something between disapproval and amusement. "Liar," she whispered.

He gripped her slender hand in his and kissed it to hide a rush of tears. "No," he said, closing his eyes as her fingers swept across his face. "I will make war. Muncel will rue this infamy. He cannot steal my kingdom like a common thief."

"Then flee now," she said, shivering. "Find your allies and loyal liegemen who will raise an army for you. Do not linger here, for they lie in wait for you, intending to take you prisoner. They would dare try you as a common—"

"Never mind," he said, not wanting to tell her he was already a prisoner. But not for long, he vowed. He would crush Muncel. As soon as he raised an army, he would ride on Muncel's holding. Belrad, the fortress he had given Muncel with impulsive generosity. Although he owed Muncel nothing, he had been generous to his half-brother. And this was how Muncel repaid his kindness.

Nereisse shivered more violently, closing her eyes.

Worried, Tobeszijian glanced at Gilda. "What can be done?"

"Nothing," Nereisse gasped out before Gilda could answer. She opened her eyes to stare up at him. "It is spellcraft, this poison. You must stay away from me before you catch it."

She released his hand, drawing back when he would have touched her.

"I cannot catch it," he said.

"You are half eld. It could harm you."

He frowned. "What happened, Nereisse? They told me Thiatereika caught it first. Is she—"

Pain and grief creased her face. "Better," she said hoarsely, her breath coming short and fast. "I drew it from her body."

He understood. In saving the child, she had infected herself. "Then we shall draw it from you."

She shook her head. "Nay, husband. Had there been a *sorcerelle* here when I first took it, perhaps. Not now."

He bowed his head in overwhelming sorrow, gripping her hand again, then holding it even tighter when she tried to pull away.

"The poison was meant for Faldain," she said. "It came in a sweet, baked in the shape he loves best. One sweet, brought only for him. I was preoccupied, not paying attention, or I would have sensed it at once."

"Your majesty was not even in the room," Gilda murmured.

Tobeszijian glanced at the old nurse, and her sad eyes met his. "I did not know, sire," Gilda whispered guiltily. "How could I guess anything was amiss? Except I sent to the kitchens for no such treat. Nor did I recognize the page who brought it for my lamb. Our precious princeling gave such a laugh when he saw it, and clapped his little hands. But the princess is ever greedy, no matter how many times I admonish her. She grabbed it off the tray before her brother could touch it. It went straight in her mouth. Seconds later, she was screaming."

He thought of his daughter, only four, with her mother's grace and slenderness, already a beauty with long, golden curls. His son was less than two years old, chubby and full of mischief. That anyone would want to harm these sweet innocents sickened him, and stirred his rage anew. "Where are they?" he asked.

"In the nursery," Gilda replied. "Suchin watches over them. I could not bring them in here to watch their lady mother die."

"She will not die," he said firmly, turning back to Nereisse. "She will not."

"Save them," Nereisse said softly, her voice as thin as the springtime wind. "The children—so young." She turned her face away and brushed at it with her fingers. "So hot. So hot. I must find my dear Tobeszijian, who walks this land no more."

He stared at her, feeling helpless and afraid, while Gilda went back to sponging her face. There must be something he could do. Her skin looked like wet ashes. She was breathing harshly, with great difficulty, and another spasm of pain shuddered through her, making her cry out.

"*Kalfeyd edr hahld*!" she said.

A whoosh of energy passed his head, just missing him, and one of the massive bedposts split. Gilda dropped the enameled basin of water and jumped back, making the sign of a circle on her breast. "She'll kill us all, sire!"

"Wait, Gilda. She won't—"

The nurse was already scuttling away. Before she reached the door, however, Tobeszijian caught her around the middle and picked her up, carrying her back, kicking and weeping like a child.

"It missed us both," he said, putting the old crone down and patting her shoulder. "She won't harm us. She *won't.* You've helped her so bravely, Gilda. You must help her still."

The old woman managed to stop her weeping and wiped her face with her apron. "Forgive me, sire. There is nothing to be done."

He paced back and forth at the foot of the bed. "If I could reach the eld folk," he said aloud. But even as he spoke, he knew it was futile. He had the Ring to help him escape and return, but despite that he knew not where to go. The eld folk never stayed in a place long. And Nereisse had already said a *sorcerelle* could not help her.

Still, he would not give up. "The bathing tub," he said in sudden inspiration. "Have the servants fill it with water. Cold water."

Gilda gasped. "You'll kill her."

"She's burning up. We must do something. Gilda, get the tub. Call the pages to help—"

He broke off, only then realizing what he'd said.

The old woman pressed a corner of her embroidered apron to her mouth and wept, rocking herself back and forth.

In the bed, Nereisse moaned and tossed, mumbling incoherently in the eld tongue. He felt tears falling down his cheeks. He could not let her leave him.

Instinctively he knew it would take too long for him to go downstairs and find his way to the kitchens, or wherever water was brought from. He hurried to the window and pulled aside the heavy draperies. Immediately cold drafts raced through the room, and when he pushed open the window, brutally cold air poured in. Tobeszijian leaned out, scooping armfuls of snow into the hem of his cloak, and came back inside, slamming the window shut behind him. He carried the snow to the bed and started packing handfuls of it around Nereisse.

She opened her eyes and sighed. "Tobeszijian."

Grateful that she was lucid again, he dropped the snow and gripped her hands, kissing them. "Yes, beloved. I am here."

Grief filled her eyes. "Sorry," she whispered. "All my fault."

He stroked her hot cheek. "What could be your fault? Muncel's ambition and those accursed reformers—"

"No, listen to me," she said urgently. "I was casting with sight, parting the veils of seeing. I was lonely, missing you, missing my own people. It's forbidden, but I wanted to come to you across the—"

"Hush," he said, hiding a shudder of worry. "Never mind now. Come spring I will take you home, and you will see all your family. You will feast and laugh and not feel lonely."

"The evil ones who have joined Muncel saw me," she said, looking past him. Terror filled her face. "I was not careful enough, and they saw me. They heard me. And I heard them. Muncel has made a pact with the Nonkind. This I saw. He has allowed Believers into the kingdom—"

"Gently," Tobeszijian said, his alarm growing. The snow was melting on her skin, darkening her sleeping shift with moisture. She began to shiver, and he drew the furs over her. "It's all right now. I will deal with Muncel."

"No, Tobeszijian, *no*! Nothing is all right. The Nonkind walk among us, by his invitation. They plan to kill you."

His mouth set itself in a grim line. "They will not."

"I wanted to warn you, fearing you would come to harm in the hunt, but they saw me. They would not have struck so quickly, so boldly if not for me."

"Take not their guilt onto yourself," he said. "It is Muncel who is to blame, not you."

"Had you not wed me, the people of Nether would have loved you," she said, weeping. "They would never have given their hearts to Muncel."

He pressed his hand against her lips, silencing her, and

shook his head. Never had he regretted taking her as his wife. He loved her still as he had the first day he saw her dancing in the woods with her companions. She had been singing, wearing a chain of flowers in her hair, which had flowed unbound over her shoulders. Her song was like magic, so pure of note and expressive that he had felt enspelled by it. His gaze would not leave her. And although she had laughed and run, vanishing into the trees, he had pursued her, seeking her among the eldin until she was found. She was a highborn princess in her own right. Had he not been king of Nether, had he not been half eld himself, her parents would have never let her wed him.

"You must guard the children," she said, bringing him back from his thoughts. "Never leave them for a moment. They are in great danger now. They have too much eldin blood for safety. While Faldain is the rightful heir to the throne, Muncel will never leave him be. Even Thiatereika is not safe, for her claim follows Faldain's."

"We are all safe," he said to her, wishing she would stop talking as though he and she were already dead. "Do not worry. I will not let Muncel get away with this. That, I swear to you."

"Swear you will protect the children first," she insisted, her blue-gray eyes searching his. "Swear!"

"By my word and my heart, I will see them safely guarded," he promised. "Now you must sleep a little. As soon as you are better we—"

"Do not wait for me, my love," she said urgently. "Flee with them now. Take them to my . . . The forest will guard them. . . . The forest is friend to them. I can't . . ."

She fell silent then, her eyes closing in exhaustion. Tobeszijian bent over her, kissing her brow. He hoped she would sleep. She must. And he had to find a way to make her better.

"Sire," Gilda said softly, "shall I have Suchin bring the children?"

She gestured as she spoke, and Tobeszijian saw that Suchin had slid open one of the doors to the queen's ornate chambers and was standing there, looking afraid and worried.

"No," Tobeszijian said. "We'll let my lady rest. She seems easier now. The snow has helped her."

"Shall I get more?" Gilda asked.

He nodded and glanced down at Nereisse, who lay quiet and

still. Too still. He did not hear her struggling breathing now. He stared at her, and knew, with a stab of awful certainty.

Swiftly he bent over her, but she lay silent. Her eyes were shut; her head had fallen slightly to one side. In his grasp, her hand had already grown cold.

"No," he said. "Nereisse? No!"

Gilda turned from the window and came hurrying back. One look and she quickly retreated, drawing the circle on her breast. "Oh, your majesty," she whispered.

"No!" Tobeszijian said angrily. He shook Nereisse hard until her head bounced on the pillow. "Nereisse! Nereisse!"

His cry came straight from his wounded heart. She could not answer him, could not smile into his eyes with that little crinkle of her eyelids reserved for him alone. She could not sing to him. She could not laugh and skip across the gardens with the children bounding after her. She could not ride in her troika, bundled in furs, her eyes shining in the starlight and her breath a mist about her delicate nostrils. She could not kiss him and give him the joy of her slender body. She was gone, his Nereisse. Gone forever.

He leaned over her then and wept hard, clutching her to his chest.

It was as though darkness surrounded him. He knew nothing except the weight of her in his arms, and yet already she felt foreign against his chest. For what remained was not his Nereisse, not the quickness and delight of her. All he held was an empty shell, so beautiful yet as worthless to him now as dust. He would gladly see every trace of her beauty gone if only the heart and soul would return to her.

But it could not.

She was dead, and he had lost her forever.

Gilda crept about the chamber quietly, her sniffles muffled, her movements slow. She opened chests and withdrew items, coming back to the bed and gently placing her hand on Tobeszijian's shoulder.

"Let me care for her now, sire," Gilda said softly. "Let me make her ready."

He could not think, could barely hear. Her words made no sense, yet he responded to her soft voice and touch as he had when he was a child in her care.

She took Nereisse from his arms and laid his lady on her pillows. Placing a pristine white linen handkerchief over Nereisse's face, Gilda began dressing her in an exquisitely embroidered court gown.

Tobeszijian stood there in a daze, and a dim corner of his mind recognized it as Nereisse's coronation gown. His eyes burned with fresh tears, and he buried his face in his hands. His mind filled with the memory of how lovely and radiant she had looked that day, her face so piquant and solemn beneath the flashing jewels in her heavy crown. The people had cheered her then, but not warmly. He realized now that he had been so filled with love for her, so certain of her charm and intelligence and value, that he'd never paid attention to the people's lack of enthusiasm. He had believed they would come to know her as he did, and that they would overlook her eldin blood and see only the goodness of her heart.

He clenched his fists against his temples, raging at his stupidity. He had been so blind, so foolish. He had brought Nereisse to this harm. He had taken her from the protection of her own people and brought her here among the bigoted, small-minded humans that were his own subjects. He had made his enemies her enemies, and now they had struck her down.

Her . . . and their children.

For the first time in several minutes he recalled his children's existence. Perhaps some extra sense was trying to warn him, for at that moment he heard a scream in the distance. It was thin at first, then rose to sharp intensity.

He turned around with an oath, and Gilda froze by the bed, where she was carefully folding Nereisse's hands together across the jeweled bodice of the gown.

The scream came again, a piercing shriek that only a terrified child could make.

The grief that fogged him fell away, and he knew that voice as surely as his own. "Thia!" he said.

From the doorway, old Suchin, who was supposed to be watching the royal children, gasped aloud. He turned and ran, while Gilda called out something that Tobeszijian never heard.

He told himself he should have sent for the children the first instant he entered the palace. Now they were in danger, and his heart went wild. He had lost Nereisse. He would not lose his son and daughter as well.

Drawing his sword, he ran from the room.

4

Running from the queen's chambers down the corridor, Tobeszijian passed a series of brightly colored doors. Overtaking Suchin, who was hobbling more than running, Tobeszijian returned to the staircase and charged up another flight of stairs. As he came to the top of the landing and stepped into a smaller, less ornate corridor, he saw a hirelance in helmet and mail struggling with a child he held in his arms. Tobeszijian saw only Thiatereika's tangled curls and kicking legs, but he saw enough.

With a shout of rage, he brandished Mirengard and ran at the abductor, just as a nearby door opened and a second hirelance emerged with Faldain.

Tobeszijian never slowed his charge. His shout had already warned the man holding Thiatereika, but she was kicking and flailing with all her might, screaming at the top of her lungs, and this hampered her captor. He managed only to turn partway around by the time Tobeszijian reached him.

Tobeszijian swung his sword. The great length of steel whistled through the air, and caught the man's upper back. Normally he would have aimed for the hirelance's head, but it would have been too dangerous a blow with Thiatereika clutched tight in the man's arms. Instead, Tobeszijian aimed his sword lower, so that the blade bit deep into the hirelance's back. It cut through his hauberk as if it were cloth and sent tiny links of chain mail flying. The man screamed and dropped Thiatereika as he stumbled sideways. Mirengard had severed his spine, and the man's arms and legs no longer worked. Shrieking, he flopped to the floor, blood streaming from his wound.

Thiatereika darted away from him. With her hands outstretched and her face bright red from screaming, she came straight at her father.

Tobeszijian sidestepped her and spun to meet the second hirelance's charge.

The man had already dropped Faldain on the floor out of his way, and the toddler was wailing lustily.

"My papa!" Thiatereika clutched Tobeszijian around the leg, hampering him.

He parried weakly, and Mirengard was nearly driven right into his face by the other man's blow.

Ducking awkwardly, Tobeszijian scrambled back, disengaging his sword, and parried again—one-handed this time, while with his left he gripped Thiatereika by the back of her gown and lifted her off the floor.

"Climb on my back," he said through gritted teeth, again managing to parry the hirelance's charging attack with one hand. Mirengard was heavy and hard to manage this way. He knew he had only seconds before the hirelance would break through his weak defense. "Hurry, sweet. Play monkey on my back and hold on hard."

Thiatereika grinned at him and climbed him like a tree, swarming across his shoulders and fastening herself to his back. It was a game they often played, with him rolling on the floor like a child himself. Now, she wrapped her little arms around his neck from behind, almost choking him, and sang out, "I'm a monkey from Saelutia!"

Praying she could hang on, Tobeszijian skidded to his knees to duck another blow from the hirelance, and got both of his hands on his hilt. He swung with all the considerable strength and power at his disposal, his muscles flexing beneath his mail. The hirelance swung down his sword to parry the blow aimed at his knees, but Tobeszijian's strength broke the parry and drew blood from the man's legs.

Yelling and cursing, the hirelance stumbled back, and Tobeszijian gained his feet to charge, swinging the mighty Mirengard again and again.

In two more blows, the hirelance's sword shattered. He stared at it and threw it down before he turned to run.

Tobeszijian swung a final time. The hirelance's head went tumbling, slinging blood and gobbets of flesh across the sunny yellow walls. His body crumbled in its tracks, with a great spurt of blood gushing forth from the neck.

Breathing hard, Tobeszijian lowered his blood-splattered sword and pulled in air to the depths of his lungs, then turned around. It had grown deathly silent in the corridor.

He saw his young son standing frozen in the doorway of the nursery. Faldain's thumb was in his mouth, and his pale gray eyes stared solemnly at the corpses. He was too young to understand or to be afraid, but Tobeszijian wiped his sword on a corner of his cloak, sheathed it, and hurried to scoop Faldain into his arms. The boy broke into a wide grin and planted a messy smack on Tobeszijian's cheek.

"Pa!" he said proudly.

Tobeszijian touched his son's black curls, and felt himself undone by the sweet innocence in Faldain's face. He pressed his face against Faldain's tender one, breathing in softness and the smell of little boy. And he thought of Nereisse, lying dead in her chamber, never to kiss this child again, never to soothe him when he cried, or to help him grow up brave and strong in his father's footsteps. Faldain would never know how wonderful she was, or how beautiful. He would never witness her courage or her grace.

Tears burned Tobeszijian's eyes, and he sent up a prayer of thanksgiving that his children had been spared.

"Suchin," he said hoarsely to the servant cowering on the stairs, "get their outdoor clothes. Dress them for a journey."

Still looking frightened, the old man scuttled into the room and began searching through the brightly painted chests and cupboards for small cloaks and smaller boots.

Tobeszijian set both children on the floor. Thiatereika tossed her head, sending her golden curls bouncing on her shoulders, and ran to help Suchin. "I know where everything is," she announced.

Faldain wrapped himself around Tobeszijian's leg and would not turn it loose. When Suchin knelt beside the little prince and tried to pry his hands away so he could put gloves on the boy's hands and boots on his small feet, Faldain let out a mighty screech of rage and clung even harder.

Thiatereika, looking adorable in a cloak of blue velvet trimmed with ermine, her hair now tied back with a ribbon, and dainty fur-lined boots on her feet, went running off into the playroom.

"Thia," Tobeszijian called after her. "Stay here."

"I want my Su-Su," she said stubbornly.

He had no idea what she was talking about, and let her go. Suchin was still on his knees, struggling to exchange Faldain's slippers for boots. The boy was resisting, kicking his feet and turning red-faced with anger.

"No!" he shouted.

Tobeszijian was a man who waged wars, decreed policy, feasted, and hunted. He played with his children more than did many men or kings, but until now he'd had no idea what was entailed in putting clothing on a squirming, rebellious child. To his eyes, it looked as difficult as bridling a wild horse.

"In Thod's name, hurry, man," he said impatiently to Suchin. "They'll need a change of clothing as well."

"Aye, sire," Suchin said breathlessly as he succeeded in getting the second boot on. Faldain rolled onto his stomach and began crawling away as fast as he could.

Tobeszijian let Suchin chase the child and instead went to one of the cupboards and opened it. He pulled out items of clothing at random, surprised at how small they were, and how finely made. Frowning, Tobeszijian looked in vain for sturdy clothing suitable for travel. Had they no hardspun, no leggings, no —

"Here, sire," Suchin said, reappearing with two cups of eldin silver and necklaces of ribbon twisted with gold wire from which pendants of bard crystal hung.

Tobeszijian's frown deepened. "We cannot be hampered by frippery. Sturdy clothing, man! Quickly!"

"They have none, sire." Suchin pressed the cups into Tobeszijian's hands. "But these the queen held important. I'll be quick."

Faldain headed off into the playroom in search of Thiatereika, calling "Ei, ei, ei!" as loud as he could.

Tobeszijian stared, marveling at how quickly they seemed to forget the danger they'd just survived.

The cups he held were of excellent crafting, engraved with flowers and the faces of animals, but they were of no use to him. He tossed them on the floor while Suchin stuffed items into a small cloak that he twisted into an ill-made bundle.

Thiatereika appeared in the doorway, her eyes enormous. "My papa!" she called, whimpering. She was clutching a dirty rag doll to her chest. "Su-Su is scared. My papa, come!"

Suchin hurried over to her, slipping one of the bard crystal pendants over her head and tucking it beneath her cloak. She twisted away from him and stamped her foot.

"My papa!" she shouted. "Come!"

Tobeszijian went to her and put his large hand on her curls. "Hush, sweet. We're going in just a moment."

She shied away from his hand and began to cry, pointing at the other room. Puzzled by what could upset her in there when the dead men in the hallway had not made her blink, Tobeszijian looked inside the playroom.

He saw smoke curling out through the front grille of the yellow and blue tiled stove standing in one corner. The nursery was normally a sunny place, with walls painted in shades of yellow, green, and pink. Painted vines and animals and cherubs adorned the ceiling and climbed down the corners of the walls. Strangely, the air felt icy cold, as though all the windows had been thrown open and the fire in the stove had gone out. But even if the latter had happened, the stove should have continued to radiate stored heat for a long time.

The smoke was still pouring out, curling straight down to the floor and toward the doorway, where Tobeszijian stood, staring at it. It flowed around his ankles, and he felt immediately chilled to the bone. He stepped back quickly, and realized then that it wasn't smoke at all, but instead a black mist that roiled and curled and seemed to be searching for something.

He saw it pause at the doorway near him. Tendrils of the stuff curled up as though exploring, then flowed on through the room in a straight line, aiming itself at the corridor where the corpses lay.

Wide-eyed, Tobeszijian stared at it, suddenly breathing harder than when he'd been fighting. There was more of the mist now, filling the doorway and curling around his ankles again. He retreated a second time, then glimpsed Faldain standing inside the center of the playroom next to the mist. Sucking his thumb, the child stared solemnly at the murky flow of evil.

Tobeszijian's heart lurched in his chest. Pushing Thiatereika back against the wall, he waded through the mist, wincing as his feet seemed to freeze inside his boots. He grabbed Faldain up and carried him out of the playroom. By the time he'd stepped out of the mist again he was shuddering violently, and gritted his teeth to keep from moaning at the pain.

Suchin wailed his prayers and backed against the tall, square bed that the children shared. He drew a circle on his chest with a shaking hand.

The mist flowed through the bedchamber, curling away

from where the silver cups lay on the floor. For Tobeszijian, this confirmed the mist's evil. Nonkind could not cross running water. It could not touch salt or eldin silver, the purest grade possible. He wondered who was directing the mist, and why. Was it Bork, the Believer out in the guardhouse? Or were other Gantese agents lurking in the many passages of the palace?

Dry-mouthed, Tobeszijian realized he could not tarry here much longer. Clearly something out there sensed that Nereisse was dead. She must have been protecting the household, holding these forces back with the last remnants of her waning strength.

Premonition crawled across the back of Tobeszijian's neck, making him shiver. He gestured at Suchin, then caught sight of the bundle in the servant's hands and realized it would not do.

He went to Thiatereika and stripped off her cloak. "That bundle, quickly!" he said.

With a puzzled look, Suchin opened it. Tobeszijian pulled out a gown lined with the softest belly fur of snow-hare. He yanked it down over Thiatereika's head, pulling her arms through the sleeves while she protested in a muffled voice. When her head popped through the neck, she was scowling.

"I can put on my clothes by myself!" she declared.

Not paying attention, Tobeszijian crammed another gown on over her clothing. It was a tight fit, and she fussed about it until Tobeszijian snapped his fingers at her in admonition. He tied her cloak back on and drew up her hood firmly to conceal both her hair and her pointed ears. Her face was streaked with tears, and her eyes looked tired and puffy. Already this morning she'd been through too much. His heart ached with the knowledge that he must submit her to a great deal more.

By now Suchin had succeeded in wrestling an extra pair of hosen and another tunic onto Faldain, who was fighting him about the boots again. Tobeszijian helped the old man, holding Faldain still so Suchin could finish dressing him. Suchin slipped the second bard crystal necklace around Faldain's chubby neck and tucked it inside his tunics.

"For luck, little prince," the old man whispered.

"I'm hot, my papa," Thiatereika declared. She waved her rag doll. "Su-Su is hot too. I don't want to wear this—"

Tobeszijian scooped her into his arms along with Faldain,

settling a child on each hip, and headed out, with Suchin crowding his heels.

The mist filled the entire corridor in front of the nursery.

Suchin whimpered with fear. "There is no way to avoid wading through it, sire."

"Wait," Tobeszijian commanded. Juggling children, he drew his sword and plunged the tip of Mirengard into the black mist. The sword blade glowed white and silver. The mist parted, curling swiftly away from the steel. Quickly, Tobeszijian walked through.

Behind him, Suchin cried out and stumbled, then barreled past Tobeszijian. "The evil is with us," Suchin wailed, running toward the stairs. "The evil is here!"

Thiatereika began to whimper, and Tobeszijian glared at the old man. "Be quiet, you fool!" he said.

Suchin fell as silent as if he'd been strangled.

The mist as yet seemed to have taken no notice of the living. It headed for the two corpses lying on the bloody carpet and began to twist and coil about them. When a column of roiling darkness started rising from the back of the nearest body, Tobeszijian's eyes widened in horror.

He could feel the tingle on his skin and the crawly, itching sensation that told him magic was being used. Yet darkness was not supposed to be able to enter the palace like this. There were safeguards and spell locks designed to protect it.

But Nereisse was dead, and the Chalice was gone. What remained to power the spell locks?

He was thinking like a fool, refusing to accept what was being demonstrated before him. He remembered his promise to himself that Muncel would not get away with this. And now in his heart he made it a vow. Muncel would not win. Tobeszijian swore it on the hilt of his sword, on the heads of his frightened children, and on the memory of his dead wife.

When the corpse that still had its head twitched and began to climb to its feet, Thiatereika screamed, and Suchin wailed.

Tobeszijian turned around and headed down the stairs, his children in his arms. He was not going to waste time fighting Nonkind.

The war had begun. He had lost the first skirmish, but Tobeszijian had never lost a war yet and did not intend to now.

"Hush, my children," he murmured to Faldain and Thiatereika. "You must be brave now. You must not cry."

They clung to him in fear, knowing instinctively that everything around them was wrong. Until today he had never heard Thiatereika cry except in temper. His children had known no unkindness, no fear, no distress. And he hated Muncel for ending their innocence so cruelly.

Suchin trotted at his heels, glancing back apprehensively over his shoulder as though he expected the animated corpse to come after them at any minute. "Sire," he said worriedly, his old voice shaking. "Sire, what is to become of us?"

At the bottom of the stairs, Tobeszijian stopped and juggled Faldain in his arms so he could put a hand on the old man's shoulder. "Suchin, you have been a true and faithful servant," he said, gazing down into the old man's tear-shiny eyes. "I free you from service, you and Gilda both. I ask only one last favor of you."

Suchin bowed his head, weeping openly now. "Anything, sire."

Tobeszijian swallowed hard to clear the lump from his throat. "Bury my sweet lady in the grove that she loved so well. Make it a simple resting place, hidden. The eldin will find her when they come, but tell no one else where she lies."

Suchin nodded, still weeping and unable to look up.

Tobeszijian gripped his shoulder harder until the old man raised his eyes. "Thank you," Tobeszijian said, taking the children's bundle from the servant's arms. "Farewell."

He strode away, and Suchin came scurrying after him like a dog that will not be parted from its master. "Wait, sire!" he called. "Will you not come back to us? Is the kingdom truly fallen?"

Tobeszijian's mouth set itself in a grim line. "I go to fight for it," he said. "How it shall come out, I will know not until I can learn who still calls me liege."

Hoisting Thiatereika and Faldain higher in his arms, he strode out, passing the door to his dead wife's chamber with only the slightest falter in his step. *Forgive me, my lady, for leaving you like this,* he thought, and glanced back at Suchin. "Don't let the Nonkind take her," he said.

"No, sire," Suchin said in a small, frightened voice. He stared at Tobeszijian helplessly. "After we do as you have commanded, where will we go? What will become of us? Will you come back?"

Tobeszijian realized the old man thought he was running away, fleeing to save himself. Anger and hurt pierced Tobeszijian, and he whirled around. "Nether is mine!" he said, his voice ringing out loudly. "I do not desert my kingdom; this, I do swear."

"But, sire—"

Tobeszijian turned and strode on, closing his ears to Suchin's cries. His heart was stone now, his temper a fire that had seared him. With every stride through his empty palace his resolve hardened. He knew exactly what to do next, and he did not hesitate.

The bay horse he had ridden to the doors of the palace still wandered about on the portico with its reins dangling. It snorted when Tobeszijian appeared, but seemed glad to be caught. Most of the rosettes braided in its flowing black mane had already fallen off.

Tobeszijian placed both children in front of the saddle and swung up with a soft jingle of his silver spurs. Pulling on his gauntlets against the cold air, he sent the horse plunging down the wide steps and across the grand courtyard, riding past the fountain with its grand basin and cavorting sea creatures carved of stone. The fountain had been shut down, and the water in the basin had pieces of ice floating in it. Tobeszijian gave it not a second glance and touched his spurs to the horse, sending it galloping straight across the orderly plantings between the courtyard and the curving road.

He returned to the stables, where the serfs sweeping the snow off the cobbles fled at the sight of him and stood peeking out from the shadows behind the piles of frozen fodder. Tobeszijian dismounted and pulled his children down off the horse, while a stableboy hurried to hold the bridle.

Tobeszijian glanced at the boy. "Inform the stablemaster that I want the darsteed," he said quietly.

The boy gaped at him stupidly, looking frozen with alarm.

"Now," Tobeszijian snapped.

The boy went shuffling toward the stables, leading the bay horse.

Thiatereika tugged at her father's cloak. "Are we going riding, my papa?" she asked.

He saw a group of hirelances coming from the guardhouse. His stomach tightened.

"Are we going riding, my papa?" Thiatereika asked again. "Are we going riding? Are we?"

"Yes," he said without glancing at her. He felt a sudden fear that his plan would not work.

Faldain had discovered something on the ground and was bending over, spraddle-legged, to examine it. His small, gloved fingers worked busily.

"When are we going riding?" Thiatereika asked him. "Are we going soon? Is that why I have so many clothes on? I'm not cold, my papa. I want to go riding now."

"Yes," he said distractedly, watching the hirelances come. "Very soon."

From inside the round fortified stall the darsteed scented him and bugled. Its thoughts, like smoking brands, came at him: *Run/run/run/run.*

Soon, he answered it with his mind.

Faldain straightened up, staggering to catch his balance, and grinned at Tobeszijian. "Soon!" he crowed.

A little startled, Tobeszijian stared at him, wondering if the child had overheard his thoughts. But by then the hirelances had reached him. They fanned out, surrounding him in a circle of menace.

"Ready to surrender now?" Bork asked him.

The Gantese's small dark eyes stared deep into Tobeszijian's as though trying to read his thoughts, but Tobeszijian steeled himself against any flicker of communication and felt nothing touch him.

From the round stall a series of powerful thuds could be heard. The darsteed grew louder and more frantic.

Tobeszijian let his gaze stray in that direction. "I thought I would exercise the brute. It gets vicious when it's neglected."

Bork's eyes had shrunk to pinpricks of suspicion. He pointed at the children. "What are they?"

Tobeszijian's chin jutted, and his eyes grew cold. "His royal highness, Prince Faldain," he said in a voice like iron. "Her royal highness, Princess Thiatereika."

Hearing her name spoken, Thiatereika turned and skipped over to Tobeszijian's side. She glared up into Bork's hatchet face without fear. "You aren't one of our guardsmen," she declared. "You wear strange boots."

Tobeszijian glared at the man. "You sent some of your varlets to seize my children from their chambers, Bork. With what intent?"

Bork shrugged. "I follow orders."

"They stay with me."

Bork's fangs showed. "In your land, the mothers keep their young close by. It makes them soft and feeble. Is the queen dead now?"

"No," Tobeszijian lied swiftly, conscious of little ears listening to every word. "She sleeps, and I would not have her rest disturbed by these two."

"A king, herding his own young?" Bork asked in astonishment. "You lie."

Tobeszijian's hand slapped against his sword hilt, and several of the hirelances reached for their own weapons. Bork held up his hand to stop them, and sent Tobeszijian one of his thin-lipped smiles.

"You lie," he repeated more softly. "You and I both know it. A king does not do servant's work."

"He might when there are no servants to do the work," Tobeszijian retorted. "The palace is empty, except for one old woman who tends the queen. Or haven't you gone inside yet? I suppose you haven't, for there's been no looting done."

It was Bork's turn to stiffen at the insult. Tobeszijian faced him, steely-eyed and unflinching.

Bork scowled at him. "Surrender your sword. Now."

Tobeszijian reached for Mirengard slowly. Inside, his heart was already knotting with more worry. He would have to fight them, and the children were in the way. Thod's bones, how was he to get them in the clear?

A commotion in the stableyard gave him his answer.

He spun around, the hirelances turning with him, and saw five sweating stableboys bringing the darsteed out with throat poles. The stablemaster and another boy followed, carrying the armored body cloth and special saddle.

The darsteed was a huge, snorting brute. As black as evil, its slitted eyes glowed red. Hot, acidic saliva dripped off its fangs to hiss upon the icy ground. The sweating, frightened boys maneuvered it around, forcing it to go near the mounting blocks.

Inside the stables, the horses must have sensed that the darsteed was out. Several of them whinnied in alarm, and the darsteed slung its head in that direction. It was bred to hunt and attack anything that moved. It lunged in the direction of the barns, but the boys held it in place.

Roaring in fury, it shook its snakelike head violently and slashed out with razor-sharp hooves. The boys screamed in fear, and one of them dropped his throat pole. At once the darsteed charged, but the others managed to hold it back. The beast shot flames from its nostrils, scorching the paving stones. Again it shook its powerful neck and head, shuddering in an effort to throw its handlers off their feet. The boy who'd fallen scrambled back up and darted forward to seize the dangling throat pole. The darsteed slashed at him, but missed. Enraged, it lashed its barbed tail from side to side.

The stablemaster flung the armor cloth over the beast's humped back and fastened it with swift expertise. The cloth clanked with its movements, and the darsteed roared at the saddle, which was being carried closer now. It lunged, and the boys barely held it in check. The darsteed flung up its head and reared high, and the stablemaster hurried to throw the saddle on its back. He reached under the creature's belly for the cinch, missed, and grabbed again.

The darsteed kicked him, and a bloody gash opened in the stablemaster's leg. Crying out, he yanked up the cinch hard enough to make the darsteed grunt, and stumbled back, limping and clutching his leg.

The darsteed's nostrils flared, sniffing the scent of fresh blood. Its lean head followed the stablemaster, and one of the boys shouted a warning.

Faldain squealed with laughter and darted between the hirelances encircling Tobeszijian. Grabbing at the child, Tobeszijian missed, and Faldain escaped.

Seeing his son run straight at the darsteed, Tobeszijian's heart lurched in his chest. "Stop him!" he shouted.

Bork laughed, and none of the hirelances moved to obey Tobeszijian's command.

Horrified, Tobeszijian tried to go after Faldain himself, but Bork blocked his path.

"You said you wanted to go riding with your young," he said with a laugh that showed his fangs. "Now we will see the truth."

Tobeszijian took a step back and sent his mind to the darsteed, touching cool intelligent reason to hot bestiality. The darsteed quieted at once, despite the child's approach. Its mind held resentment, but it was forced to subject itself to Tobeszijian's command.

Still/still/still/still, Tobeszijian told it.

Breathing smoky plumes in the cold air, the darsteed stood motionless, watching Faldain's approach with its red eyes. The child toddled right up to it, well within striking range, and stopped, laughing and reaching up to the creature with innocent, chubby fingers.

"In Thod's name," the stablemaster breathed, watching with horrified eyes. "Hol, you and Rafe try to get him away from that devil's spawn."

"Let his highness be," Tobeszijian forced himself to say calmly while Bork's eyes widened. "After all, this will be his war mount someday. They might as well become acquainted."

"You bluff well," Bork murmured, unable to take his gaze from the sight of child and beast studying each other. "But still you bluff."

"Do I?" Tobeszijian replied through his teeth. He kept his face stony and calm, but inside his heart was thudding with anxiety.

Thiatereika tugged at his cloak. "I can't see, my papa," she said in frustration. "What is Dainie doing with the black horse?"

Tobeszijian lifted her into his arms. "Making friends with it," he said lightly, feeling sweat bead along his temples.

The darsteed was resisting his control. He could feel its hunger, like a clawing thing, and with dismay Tobeszijian remembered it had not been fed properly for many days now. Faldain was the perfect size for a meal.

Oh, Thod, have mercy, he prayed.

Giggling as though conscious that he was the center of attention, Faldain glanced around at his audience, moved closer, and held up his hand again to the beast looming over him.

The darsteed lowered its head, its red eyes focused on nothing but the child.

Still/still/still/still, Tobeszijian commanded it.

The beast bared its fangs, letting acid drip, hissing, around

Faldain. The child stretched up on his toes, unafraid, and patted the darsteed on the end of its snout.

"Horsey, go ride!" Faldain announced.

A sigh of awe passed through the onlookers. Tobeszijian pushed his way through the hirelances with Thiatereika in his arms. His legs felt like wood, but he forced himself to act the part, calmly walking right up to his son and the beast that wanted Faldain as its prey. Tobeszijian knew he would have to pay a price for this obedience. The darsteed would feed, and very soon now, no matter how much Tobeszijian tried to control it.

"Pet the darsteed, Thiatereika," the king said lightly.

She reached out and gave the creature's leathery neck a single pat before he whisked her out of reach. By then he'd gripped Faldain's arm and pulled him off the ground, spinning and kicking almost under the very nose of the darsteed, which hissed and slavered as little shudders ran through its body. Its tail was lashing from side to side in warning.

Tobeszijian could feel its fury building, and knew his control would not last much longer.

"The bridle, stablemaster," he said quietly.

But the stablemaster had sunk down on the cobbles a safe distance away, blood still streaming from his leg, while some of the other servants tried to tend his wound. The boy who'd helped carry the saddle stepped forward with the simple bridle in his hands. It had no bit, and was merely a headpiece with reins attached.

"Be quick," Tobeszijian murmured to him.

The boy nodded, his throat apple jerking up and down as he swallowed. Drawing a final breath, he darted toward the darsteed, which flung up its head in alarm.

With all the control he still possessed, Tobeszijian pressed harder, and the beast lowered its head. The boy fitted the bridle on, tugging the check strap swiftly into place, and stumbled out of the way.

By then Tobeszijian had both children on the darsteed's back. He mounted in a swift, fluid motion. Gathering the reins, he let a part of himself flow into and become one with the darsteed.

He wanted to feel it attack.

The darsteed's blood boiled through Tobeszijian's veins. His own fury raged back into the darsteed. Impatience filled Tobeszijian, an impatience and anger that he no longer tried to govern. With a flick of his hands, he gestured to the stableboys.

"My children," he said with the last ounce of what remained inside him as a man, "hold on tight no matter what happens."

Inside his glove, the Ring burned hot around his finger. Tobeszijian's heart was thudding faster and faster.

The stableboys released the nooses on the throat poles, and Bork stepped forward.

"You ride it and show us your legend," he said with a sneer. "Then your games are over, king, and you go to the guardhouse as our prisoner."

Tobeszijian spurred the darsteed and slipped his control from the beast's mind.

Feed/strike/go, he commanded.

With a bugle of rage, the darsteed bounded straight at Bork, who had time only to gape in dawning terror before the creature's fangs ripped out his throat, then tore off his head and swallowed it in a gulp.

Tobeszijian spurred it again, and the creature leaped and bellowed and thundered across the stableyard toward the small still-shut gates.

Someone shouted behind him, but Tobeszijian did not listen.

He was concentrating inside, reaching into the heat of the Ring the way his father had taught him long ago. And when he felt the inner flash of white fire as the Ring drew him into its power, Tobeszijian tightened his arm around his children, and spurred the darsteed harder. With a roar, it bounded into the second world with a speed that made Tobeszijian's sweat-soaked hair blow back from his face. All around him was blinding light and a deafening roar of sound.

Chalice, he thought with all his might, forcing himself to concentrate and remain focused. *To the Chalice.*

And to the astonished onlookers remaining in the stableyard of Nether Palace, King Tobeszijian and his children vanished on that fearsome beast of hell into thin air as though the gods had snatched them from this world and taken them far away.

Only a fading shower of golden sparks remained behind to glow upon the hoof tracks etched into the paving stones.

5

FOR TOBESZIJIAN, THE passage through the second world was too swift and confusing to evoke fear. In a terrible silence in which his own voice made no sound, Tobeszijian saw only gray swirling mists and the shadows of things he did not understand. All he knew was that he and his children were still galloping through this nonplace on the back of the darsteed. The beast ran with all its strength, its powerful muscles bunching and thrusting, but if it roared those sounds were silenced. If the children cried, Tobeszijian could not hear them. Looking down at them, clamped together within the tight circle of his arm, he saw them only dimly, as though they were shadows. There was no color in this strange, ghostly place that seemed washed in shades of moonlit gray. There was no sense of time. Nothing lived or moved except them. He perceived an emptiness so profound it frightened him.

Belatedly he remembered he must keep his destination clear in his mind, or else they would be lost here in the second world forever, prey to its many dangers.

Chalice, he thought.

With a great pop of sound, they leaped back into reality, with its noise, smells, and overwhelming kaleidoscope of colors. Disoriented and shaken, Tobeszijian reeled in his saddle, while his children wailed and the darsteed reared and lunged at something moving before it.

Just in time, Tobeszijian regained his senses and realized the moving object was a woman, gowned in vivid blue with a purple girdle and a crimson-lined cloak. Screaming as she backed away from the attacking darsteed, she tripped on the hem of her long skirts and fell. The darsteed lunged at her, its pointed teeth snapping. Cringing and screaming, the woman brought up her hands helplessly to shield herself.

Tobeszijian hit the darsteed with his mind: *Stand/stand/stand/stand.*

The darsteed's head whipped back and around. Its eyes glowed red madness at Tobeszijian. For an instant he thought he could not withstand the hot, molten fury raging inside the beast, but with all his will he held firm. Kicking, the darsteed bugled its frustration and lashed its barbed tail from side to side. But it obeyed him and stood as he commanded.

Sobbing, the woman scrambled away, and others in the crowd helped pull her to safety.

Tobeszijian saw that he was in a stone church, filled with an ethereal glow of dusty sunlight streaming in through tall, slitted windows. Scaffolding in places showed the place to be still under construction. The air smelled of plaster dust and fresh paint pigments. On the left side, a single tapestry hung between two windows, but empty hooks showed where other tapestries would soon hang. Tobeszijian recognized the new Belrad Cathedral.

Netheran nobles in their finery filled the long, rectangular nave. Tobeszijian recognized many faces, faces which either stared at him in flat defiance or reddened and turned away. For here were gathered his missing courtiers, those who had abandoned his palace and his queen while she lay dying.

A fresh burst of grief and accompanying rage shook him. His hands clenched white-knuckled around his reins, and he could feel his pulse throbbing hard in his throat.

There stood Count Lazky with his wife and grown daughters. There stood Prince Askirzikan. There stood Fortinac, the burly knight exiled from Mandria who had found acceptance here. On her stool, surrounded by frightened attendants, sat the Countess Renylkin, her aged face set like stone, her knobby hands clutching a book of Writ tightly in her lap. Only her eyes gave her away, eyes that stared at him with fear and a trace of wonder.

Tobeszijian could not believe that this countess had turned against him, yet here she was with all the others. She met his gaze proudly, never faltering, although her cheeks turned pink. She had been chief lady-in-waiting to the queen, and her desertion of Nereisse made Tobeszijian wonder in despair how he'd misjudged her character so completely. Indeed, how could he have been so wrong about so many?

In that moment of stunned silence as he faced them, still glowing from a golden light which streamed down his body from the delicate circlet of eldin gold on his brow to the rowels of his silver spurs, Tobeszijian looked every inch a king and more. Even now, travel-stained and drawn with grief, holding his big-eyed children clamped against him like refugees, Tobeszijian eclipsed every other man present. The golden light made the jewels in his sword and dagger hilts glitter even more brightly. His skin shone with the radiance of it, as though he'd passed through the breath of the gods. His ice-blue eyes, clear evidence of his eldin blood, glared with a ferocity that stilled the breath in many throats. His courtiers had run away like wicked children, but Tobeszijian had found them, bursting upon them with a great clap of sound and the acrid smell of magic. Even now, the remnants of whatever spell he'd commanded still flowed from him, the golden light of it dripping to the floor and puddling in a pool of radiance at the shifting feet of the darsteed.

Somewhere in the staring crowd there came a rustle of movement accompanied by a faint clanking sound. A man knelt, bowing his head. Another did the same. And another. The Countess Renylkin moved ponderously off her stool, and with the help of her attendants knelt on the stones before her king. Only then did the abundant folds of her skirts fall, allowing him to see the chain that shackled her ankles.

"My heart to the king!" cried a deep voice that Tobeszijian recognized as Prince Spirin's.

Looking in that direction, Tobeszijian saw the tall, lean prince struggling with someone who was trying to keep him from kneeling. Spirin's fur-cuffed sleeve fell back from his wrist, and Tobeszijian saw that he too was manacled with iron.

"To the king!" shouted someone else.

"To the king!"

But the few voices of acclaim were defiant and isolated. They provoked no general cheering. And although many now knelt, others did not.

Rigid with anger at the insult, Tobeszijian saw more and more glances being cast toward the front of the church. He swept his own gaze in that direction, seeking his enemy.

At the front of the church, high above the altar, a wide window of stained glass depicting the Circle surrounded by the crests of the holy orders—created by men, not by the gods—cast an eerie scarlet glow over Tobeszijian's half-brother, Prince Muncel. Wearing an ermine cloak and a tall, pointed crown glittering with jewels, Muncel sat on a gold throne with black velvet cushions, a beyarskin rug separating his embroidered velvet shoes from the cold stone floor. Balanced across his knees lay the sheathed triangular sword of black iron, the antiquated sword that Solder First had carried into battle before he met the gods and was given the kingdom, the Ring, the Chalice, and later Mirengard.

Cardinal Pernal and another ecclesiastical figure sat on either side of Muncel, richly attired in long robes of crimson and purple. They were there for support and confirmation, or perhaps as guards. Gazing at his half-brother in cold speculation, Tobeszijian wondered how much of this evil plot had spun from Muncel's greedy heart. Or was he just a puppet of the church?

Across the distance, Tobeszijian and Muncel locked eyes, pale eyes to dark. The astonishment and growing fury in Muncel were so strong that Tobeszijian felt them. Although he could not reach into the minds of men the way he could those of animals, he knew that his half-brother hated him more than ever and intended to wrest the very kingdom from his hands. This religious ceremony here in the Belrad Cathedral was one more trap among many. Muncel could not strike Tobeszijian openly in the royal palace, but by stealing the Chalice and bringing the courtiers to Belrad, he had lured Tobeszijian onto his own property. If Tobeszijian attacked him here, Muncel could claim he was merely defending himself.

Such legal trickery and cowardice sparked new anger in Tobeszijian. He thought of Nereisse, who had never harmed a living soul, now dead and abandoned in an empty palace, dead by Muncel's order. Grief and rage burned Tobeszijian's throat, and he struck at Muncel with all the strength of his mind.

The prince's face turned gray. He cried out sharply, and fell back in his chair. The gaudy Crown of Runtha slipped forward over his brow and fell into his lap.

Cardinal Pernal was a plump, jowled man with the countenance of a kindly uncle beneath his fringe of white hair, and the rapacious heart of a vulture. At Muncel's collapse, Pernal jumped to his feet. While the other churchmen bent over the swooning Muncel, grabbing the crown before it could roll to the floor, Pernal raised the jeweled circle that hung on a gold chain around his fat neck and cried out in a voice that rang through the church:

"Go back, creature of the darkness, to whence you came!"

The darsteed screamed and reared beneath Tobeszijian, striking out with its deadly hooves, so that people shouted in fear and crowded even farther away from it.

"Go back!" Pernal shouted. "By the power of the Chalice, I command you to go."

Tobeszijian glared at him and spurred his darsteed forward to the altar. Tall and broad-shouldered, with the golden light burnishing his mail and breastplate and his burgundy cloak flowing from his shoulders over the scaled rump of his unworldly mount, the king rode through the nave like a god himself. His blue eyes held the light of battle and righteousness. Pernal's words of repudiation were only sound, lacking power, for he did not command the Chalice, nor did he have true belief. His words were for show, to impress the terrified people watching and drawing shaky circles on their breasts for protection.

Cutting across Pernal's chanting, Tobeszijian said loudly, "I am your king! The only darkness here lies within the hearts of the traitors before me."

His voice rang off the stones and echoed in the corners. As he spoke he stripped off his gauntlets, and the Ring of Solder glowed brightly on his finger, casting its own nimbus of power about his hand. "Let the people of Nether hear my accusations. Muncel, you have defiled the holy first circle. You have stolen the Chalice for your own gain. You have murdered one who was innocent—"

Muncel roused himself from his swoon and thrust himself to his feet, wild-eyed and red-faced. "Who? Your eldin whore?" he shouted, half-hysterically. "Your pagan ways have cost you, Tobeszijian. The people want to follow the Reformed Church. They want to follow me. See? Here they are. Your rule is over."

"I am king!" Tobeszijian said, his deep voice twice as powerful as Muncel's reedy tones. "And all here know it. I wear the true crown, the crown of the First. I wear the Ring, given to the First by the gods. I carry Mirengard, which cannot be touched save by the hand of the true—"

"Pagan idols," Muncel broke in contemptuously. "The very symbols of the old darkness, which we would leave behind."

"The way you smashed and defiled the royal paneatha?" Tobeszijian demanded.

Muncel lifted his head with a proud smile. "The old ways are gone. We look to the future."

"A future based on deceit, murder, and theft," Tobeszijian said.

"There has been no theft!" Muncel shouted angrily. "Only a return to honor for the Chalice of Eternal Life."

"Is that why you defiled the first circle and stole the Chalice?" Tobeszijian asked, keeping his voice loud enough that all the people might hear. "Is that why you stole the sword of the First? Is that why you hold it now?"

"The Chalice belongs to all the people!" Muncel shouted. "It belongs in a place of glory, where it can be seen and worshiped. This sword is my birthright, I, who am the *true* son of Runtha the Second. As is the throne—"

"Wanting a thing does not give you the right to it," Tobeszijian said. He pointed at Muncel, hating him for his betrayal, his cowardice, and his lies. "I accuse you before the gods and the people of Nether!" he cried. "Let the curse of the defiler be upon you and yours for all time. You have broken the circle of trust and honor. Let all here know it."

Muncel's head whipped around. "Guards!" he called.

"Wait, my lord," Pernal said in alarm. "Let there be no fighting in this holy place."

"The usurper must be seized," Muncel said in fury. "I'll have his tongue ripped out for his—"

"The Chalice will drive him out," Pernal said. He headed for the altar, where the Chalice stood centered on a square of pristine white linen. Tall, slender, and made of a glowing white metal only the gods could forge, the Chalice of Eternal Life filled this end of the church with its own kind of radiance.

Pernal reached for it, but just as his plump hands closed around its stem, Tobeszijian drew Mirengard and spurred the darsteed forward. Light flashed off the blade of his sword, and in vengeance for the defilement of his own place of worship, he sent the darsteed bounding up the two steps onto the dais where the altar stood.

Shouting words that Tobeszijian did not understand, Pernal

lifted the Chalice with both hands as though to ward him off, but the cardinal had no understanding of how to wield the Chalice's power. That power was coiled about Tobeszijian's finger, channeled through the Ring, which flashed on his hand with increasing brightness.

"Pernal! Take heed!" Muncel was shouting, but Pernal was still chanting his prayer and did not pay attention to the prince's warning.

The darsteed lunged and struck, its fangs biting a corner off the altar and slinging wood and splinters in all directions. Furious, the darsteed spat and snorted fire. The altar cloth blazed immediately, sending up black smoke and the stench of charred flax.

Looking alarmed, Pernal stumbled back from the fire with the Chalice still in his pudgy hands. "Guards!" he shouted. "Drive this creature out!"

But the guards who clustered in the shadows behind the ranks of ecclesiastical officials did not run forward to confront the darsteed as it hissed and lashed its barbed tail about.

From the day he had been named official heir to the throne, Tobeszijian had been trained secretly in his responsibilities in caring for the Chalice, in mastering the power of the Ring, in protecting the people from disaster should either item be mishandled. Now, drawing on the immense power of the Chalice, Tobeszijian spoke two soft words of command.

A shudder passed through the building, making some of the pillars holding up the lofty ceiling sway. A piece of scaffolding fell, crushing the unfortunates who were trapped beneath it. Fear ran through the crowd, but it was Pernal who screamed most loudly and shrilly. Dropping the Chalice, he stumbled back, moaning and cradling his hands, which were now black and smoking.

An unseen force responded to Tobeszijian's command, filling him with a violence that made him sway in the saddle. With all his strength, Tobeszijian forced himself to control it, drawing on everything his father and Nereisse had taught him. Yet although he had summoned only a tiny measure of the Chalice's power, it was incredibly strong, threatening to overwhelm him. He understood then the terrible danger of what the Chalice could do, and was afraid of unleashing too much of it.

"Strike what is false!" he shouted.

The power coiled through his body, filling his heart until he thought the muscle would burst from the strain. Then white fire, blinding bright, flashed down the length of his arm, sending sparks bursting from the Ring of Solder, and thrumming through his hand. The white fire built there, then shot down the length of his sword. A force greater than his own will aimed Mirengard before white fire shot from its tip and sent the altar exploding in a rain of flames, splintered wood, and ashes. Fire from it caught the hem of Pernal's fine robes.

Yelling in fear, the cardinal rolled and beat at the flames, but Tobeszijian paid the man no heed. Forcing the bucking darsteed around, he thrust the tip of his sword inside the Chalice where it lay on the floor, and lifted it.

"No!" Muncel shouted, trying to rush forward despite the restraining hands of his counselors. "It was given to men, Tobeszijian! You and your tainted blood have no right to it!"

Tobeszijian glared back at him. "Until this evil is cleared from Nether and the hearts of its people are cleansed again, the Chalice will be seen no more. The taint comes from you, Muncel, you and your bigotry!"

"Seize him now!" Muncel ordered the guards.

They rushed forward, trying to surround Tobeszijian, but he let the darsteed strike as it wished, driving the men back. Sheathing his sword, Tobeszijian handed the Chalice to Thiatereika. "Hold tight to this, sweet," he said, while her small face tipped back to look at him solemnly. "Do not drop it, no matter what."

"I won't, my papa," she promised in a tiny voice.

Faldain patted it. "Pretty."

"Sacrilege!" Pernal shouted, howling as the flames continued to burn him despite all efforts to put them out.

With pikes, the guards charged again. Tobeszijian spurred the darsteed right at them, breaking through their attack, and galloped down the aisle of the nave. He lifted the Ring. *Chalice, to safety,* he thought.

And for the second time, the Ring of Solder filled him with heat and a flash of white fire, drawing him into the second world with a rush that made him dizzy. The Cathedral of Belrad and the evil men within it were left staring openmouthed in fear and astonishment at the faint sparkles of light left trailing in the air.

• • •

This time the journey through the second world was long indeed, so long that the grayness and silence began to twist and confuse Tobeszijian's mind. Afraid, he gripped the rim of the Chalice with his bare fingers, while Thiatereika continued to clutch it tightly against her chest. The white light of the Chalice glowed brightly, even here in this place of nothing, and Tobeszijian drew comfort from it, telling himself to have faith.

They exploded back into reality with a jolt that shook Tobeszijian's bones and made Faldain cry. Patting the child to comfort him, Tobeszijian felt his own shoulders sag with weariness. He could not remember when he'd had aught to eat or drink. He'd ridden the hunt hard yesterday—was it only yesterday?—then traveled all night without rest, and now he was drawing on tremendous reserves of energy both to control the darsteed and to channel the Ring's power. He was a man young and strong, but he knew he was nearing his limits.

Fighting off a wave of exhaustion, he sat slumped in the saddle and looked around.

He did not recognize this country at all. No snow lay on the ground, which was littered with fallen leaves. Woods surrounded them, thick and impenetrable. The sky above was bleak and gray. He could smell snow in the air, and felt a biting chill that cut through his cloak and clothing. The weather was about to turn, but as yet this land had known only the lightest bite of frost. The trees were still heavy with foliage, only now starting to turn yellow or bright scarlet. Leaves fell in steady drifts, landing on his shoulders, curling for a moment in Faldain's dark hair before being brushed aside by the cold wind.

The darsteed, lathered and steaming, stood still with its head down as though weary too. Its mind pushed against Tobeszijian's, with more need than anger: *Food/food/food/food.*

Sighing, Tobeszijian dismounted, wincing as his stiff muscles protested. He reached up and pulled his children down into his arms. Faldain's cheeks were wet with tear tracks, and he was whining softly in the way of young children who are too tired. Thiatereika's intelligent blue eyes looked around in open curiosity, but she was also silent. The absence of her usual barrage of questions betrayed her fatigue.

Stepping back, Tobeszijian released the darsteed to hunt,

wondering if he was a fool to let it go. The creature's head snapped up, and it hissed at him ferociously before galloping into the trees and disappearing. Tobeszijian did not watch it go. His mind remained in the lightest possible contact with it, as if connected by a long, long leash. He hoped he could order its return when he needed it.

"My papa, I want down," Thiatereika said, squirming in his arms.

He set her on the ground with relief, taking the Chalice from her, and she turned her hooded head this way and that to study their surroundings.

"What's that?" she demanded, pointing at the cave's mouth.

They'd stopped in what looked to be a shallow ravine, with a thin rivulet of stream running down its center and a rocky, heavily wooded hillside rising sharply on one side. The cave was set into the hill, its mouth half-overgrown with briars and shrubs whose leaves had turned a brilliant yellow.

"That," Tobeszijian said quietly, "is where we are going to hide the Chalice."

Although he'd kept his words low and soft, his voice seemed to ring and echo slightly among the trees. Uneasily, he looked around, trying to sense if anything or anyone was watching. His senses told him nothing was, but he did not like this place. The woods were too quiet. The smells of soil and trees and game were unfamiliar to him. He was not in Nether, but somewhere far away. He did not feel safe here.

Faldain rested his head on his father's shoulder and sucked his thumb, heavy and quiet now. Thiatereika stared at the cave until Tobeszijian took his first stride in that direction, then she ran straight for it.

"Thia, wait!" he said in alarm.

She stopped in her tracks, much to his relief, and he caught up with her.

"We must be careful," he said, not wanting to scare her. "Always approach a cave with caution. You never know what might be living in it."

Her blue eyes widened. "A beyar?" she whispered.

"Beyar," Faldain mumbled sleepily against Tobeszijian's cloak.

At that moment, the king realized what he smelled, and why

he felt so uneasy. A cold feeling of alarm sank through him. He wished he had not let the darsteed go hunting.

Putting down Faldain, who immediately wailed and reached up his arms, Tobeszijian spent several moments comforting the child, until his gray eyes grew heavy and closed. Sighing, Tobeszijian set the Chalice next to the sleeping child and made Thiatereika sit beside her brother. Taking off his cloak, he spread it across them. "Both of you stay right here," he commanded softly.

"I want to see the cave," she said, her voice thin and tired. "I want to see beyars."

"Let me look first," he told her.

"Will it come out and eat us?" she asked. "Is it going to eat us right now? Gilda says that beyars take people into their caves and eat them all winter. It's winter now, isn't it, my papa? I know it's winter because the wind is cold, although there's no snow here. Will it snow here, my papa? Will this beyar keep us in there and eat us?"

He wished, suddenly, that a beyar was all they had to worry about.

"No, Thia," he said sternly. "There is no beyar here. I will look inside while you stay here and guard your brother."

"But, my papa, what if—"

He put his finger to his lips and gave her his sternest look. That was enough to silence her, and Tobeszijian drew his sword as he walked away from the children.

By the time he'd worked his way through the briars and approached the mouth of the cave, he was sweating despite the cold wind. The sour, distinctive smell of trolk was stronger here, strong enough to make him dry-mouthed. Holding Mirengard before him, he stepped cautiously forward. He was a man well seasoned by battle. His courage had never been questioned, not even by his enemies. By tradition, the muscles in his arm had been measured when he assumed the throne, and the measuring cord was thereafter placed in the Book of Counting, where any could see that it was as long as the cord that had measured Solder's sword arm. And Tobeszijian was strong in mind as well as arm, strong enough to command a darsteed with his thoughts, strong enough to have stunned Muncel, at least for a while. But to confront a trolk in its own cave was something else entirely. Tobeszijian himself had never fought one, but he'd seen three men band together against a single trolk and lose. The fierceness of the creatures was legendary. He knew that only a fool would venture in here, and yet the Chalice and the Ring had brought him to this place. Mirengard did not shine, and the Ring neither glowed nor felt hot on his finger. Steeling himself, Tobeszijian stepped inside.

The cave was shallow and low, forcing him to stoop. With his hair brushing the ceiling's dirt and cobwebs, he felt a slight tingle pass through his skin and realized he had walked through a protection spell. The trolk scent had been left on this cave, possibly years ago, to keep intruders out. But in fact it was empty and unused.

Relief swept him, and he let Mirengard dip in his hand. He sensed nothing before him in the shadowy darkness. The stones smelled musty and damp. The ground beneath his feet was soft and slightly moist.

Sheathing his sword, he lifted his hand and let the Ring glow slightly, casting its illumination before him. He saw only a small, slightly rounded chamber, entirely natural. No one had hewn the cave in this hillside. At the rear, he saw a V-shaped fissure in the rock wall. It was exactly the right size to hold the Chalice.

Tobeszijian bowed his head, murmuring a prayer of obedience to the will of the gods. Exiting the cave, he gathered up children and Chalice and brought them inside. The Chalice's natural glow of power filled the cave with illumination. Wedging it in the fissure, Tobeszijian wrapped the sleeping Faldain in his cloak and laid him gently on the ground beneath it. Then, with Thiatereika's small hand clutched in his, Tobeszijian went outside to gather stones worn smooth by the stream. He let his daughter carry some of these while he cut straight slim branches from young ash trees and stripped them of leaves and bark.

He had no candles or salt, but he stood the peeled white ash rods in the fissure with the Chalice, crossing them left to right, west to east. He placed the stones in a small circle on the dirt floor, mumbling the holy words of prayer as he did so. Big-eyed and solemn with a child's instinctive sense of occasion, Thiatereika watched every move he made. When he finished placing the soil within the circle of stones and sprinkled some of it on the base of the Chalice, he knelt before it and lifted the hilt of Mirengard in front of his face.

Thiatereika knelt beside him and pressed her hands together. They said the prayer of the First, Tobeszijian's deep masculine voice filling the small cave and her thin, child's voice piping the words after him in counterpoint.

When he'd finished his part, Tobeszijian listened to his daughter stumbling through the final words. A corner of his heart swelled with love and pride at this sign of devotion, already so strong within her. He placed his hand lovingly on her curls and kissed the top of her head.

Then he said, "O Thod, ruler of all, hear our prayers and our hearts this day. We have consecrated this place chosen by the will of the gods. So will we honor it until this time of strife has ended. Hear my plea now, great Thod, and give thy mercy unto these small children of my loins. Protect them from harm in whatever is next to come. *Anon dein eld.*"

"*Anon dein eld,*" Thiatereika echoed beside him. She folded her small hands together and kissed her knuckles as she had been taught. Tobeszijian kissed the hilt of his sword.

Feeling somewhat restored in spirit, he left the children in the cave and went out to hunt. By nightfall, he'd snared some small game. Skinning the small carcasses, he built a tiny fire outside the cave by the stream and cooked them until the meat sizzled with juices and the aroma made his mouth water. He and his children ate their fill. Then he doused the fire and removed all evidence of his presence. He and the children went back into the cave and bedded down together inside the folds of his cloak beneath the gentle radiance of the Chalice.

Within its light he felt safe and secure, although he knew they could not linger here much longer. With the children snuggled asleep against him like puppies, Tobeszijian breathed in the scent of them and caressed the tender skin of their faces. He knew he could not keep them with him in the days to come. For he was facing war, and civil war was always the worst and bloodiest kind. On the morrow he would have to ride to the northernmost reaches of Nether, to seek out the hold of Prince Volvn, his best general and the wiliest strategist in the realm. Volvn's loyalty was sure. *Or was it?* Only yesterday Tobeszijian had planned to enlist the support of Prince Spirin, but the man was a prisoner of Muncel's and in need of rescue himself.

Groaning a little, Tobeszijian clutched his hair in his hands and tried to battle away the overwhelming blackness of his grief. In the past two days he had lost his best friend and his beloved wife. His world had been turned upside down. Tobeszijian wanted to howl like a wounded animal, but as a man he knew he must control the maelstrom of emotions that made his chest ache. He could not think of what had happened, could not remember his dear Nereisse's face, so still and white in death. Instead, he must think of the future, of tomorrow and the next day. He must plan, for to dwell on his loss was to fall into a pit he might not be able to escape.

He had only one more use of the Ring, only one more journey he could take with its magical powers. He must use it wisely and flee to the north. Up by the World's Rim, where the old ways were still honored, he believed he could raise his army. While he would not count on Volvn's loyalty until he stood face-to-face with the valiant warrior, Tobeszijian did not believe that Volvn could be corrupted by Muncel's lies.

From Volvn's stronghold, he would call on the fealty oaths of his nobles and knights, testing to see who was loyal and who had gone over to Muncel. He realized that Cardinal Pernal would try to twist this whole affair into a vicious holy war. With their souls inflamed, men might tend to forget the true issue at stake, which was that Muncel had no rightful claim to the throne he sought.

Tobeszijian reminded himself that he would have to test the eastern holds for treachery. Someone was letting Believers cross into Nether from Gant. If the border fell, Nether would be overrun quickly.

But for now, where to put his young, motherless children? What place held safety for them? Mandria, yes, but it was too far away. Among the eldin, they would have sanctuary, but Tobeszijian understood that if his son spent more than a few months among his mother's people he would be forever changed by their ways and be rendered unacceptable to his future subjects.

Yet perhaps he was already unacceptable. Bowing his head, Tobeszijian recalled days of argument with his counselors, who'd opposed his marriage to Nereisse. It was traditional for the royal family to have a drop of eldin blood in its lineage, but now it seemed there was too much. Faldain was more eld than human.

Tobeszijian clenched his fists. That did not matter. The

throne was his by birth and by right. Someday it would be Faldain's. Nothing else was acceptable.

But what if this conflict took more than a few months to resolve? He wondered if he should foster the children with a noble. Yet who could he trust? Then again, it would be madness to keep the children near him, for if his enemies struck again they must not find him and Faldain together, two targets for the taking.

Over and over his mind worried at the problem. Nereisse would have known what to do. How he missed her wise advice already. Tobeszijian sighed. Give him an enemy to charge and Mirengard in his hand, and he was fearless and perhaps invincible. Give him shadows and intrigue and betrayal, and he needed guidance to know where and at whom to strike.

He rolled over onto his side, too weary to sleep on the hard ground. The cold sank into his bones and made them ache. He had hidden the Chalice in a safe place. His foremost duty as king had been performed. Now he must think about himself and his future. In the morning, he would use the Ring to take him and the children straight to Prince Volvn. There, he would receive counsel. There, he could make decisions as to what to do next.

6

A NOISE AWAKENED Tobeszijian in the dead of night. He awoke with a start, his heart pounding and his senses straining. At first he heard only the soft rumbling of Faldain's snores and Thiatereika's rhythmic breathing. He glanced at the Chalice, and saw it glowing softly within its circle of honor.

The noise came again, muffled and from outside. This time he recognized the darsteed's grumbling snort.

Astonished, Tobeszijian sat upright. He had not called the darsteed back. For it to return on its own was unbelievable. It wouldn't.

Which meant . . .

He flung off his cloak and reached for his sword, kneeling hastily before the Chalice. "Show me my path," he prayed, "and I will take it."

For a moment there was only silence around him, then a voice came into his mind, very clearly and distinctly: "*The children will not be safe in Nether.*"

He blinked, astonished by this communication, and felt sweat beading along his temples.

Thod had heard his prayer and answered him. Swiftly Tobeszijian prostrated himself on the ground. "Great One, I obey," he murmured, then rose.

Dry-mouthed and trembling with awe, he shoved aside his spinning thoughts, telling himself he could not think about the ramifications of this warning now. If the children weren't safe in their own land, that meant the treachery was more widespread than he'd believed possible. Civil war was usually long and bloody. He might find it difficult to regain his throne. But right now he must act quickly, for danger had come.

He could feel it, waiting somewhere out there in the night. It was not close yet, not as close as the darsteed trampling about in the ravine. But it was coming, as though the Nonkind had been set on his trail again.

By whom?

Muncel might be a traitor, but Tobeszijian could not believe his half-brother would embrace the darkness. Something else was at work here, something that Tobeszijian did not as yet understand.

A shiver passed through him. Nereisse's vision of him surrounded by a Nonkind horde might yet come true.

But, no, he would not frighten himself with visions and imaginings.

He scooped up the children, neither of whom awakened. Going outside, he found the night air bitterly cold. The wind was blowing strongly. Now and then he felt a spit of moisture on his face, though whether it was rain or sleet he could not tell.

He did not see the darsteed, but he could smell its hot, sulfur stink. When he heard it rustling among the nearby trees, he called it.

Reluctantly it came, looming suddenly out of the darkness. With its red eyes glowing in the pitch black, it hissed and blew smoke. Its tail lashed viciously, almost hitting him, and he noticed that the saddle was askew and the armor cloth torn, as though the darsteed had been trying to rid itself of both.

Putting the children out of harm's way, Tobeszijian struggled to right the saddle. He had to strike the darsteed's snout twice to keep it from biting him. The stink of its hot breath filled the air, and it snapped and slung its head about as he tightened the cinch.

Breathlessly, Tobeszijian jumped back out of reach, slapping aside another attempted bite. He scooped up the sleeping children without waking them, and started to mount.

A noise in the distance startled Tobeszijian. He froze momentarily in place and strained his ears to listen.

Hissing, the darsteed raised its head and stared intently in the same direction.

The king's heart thumped hard beneath his breastplate. Hearing the distant sounds growing louder as they approached, he frowned and turned his face into the wind, squinting against the sleet now falling. It was not hoofbeats he heard, but something quieter, a rhythmic *pad-pad-pad,* a progressive rustling through thick undergrowth.

Then he saw a flicker of light in the distant trees. Suddenly there came many pinpoints of light, dancing and glimmering through the sleet-torn darkness. Eldin were coming. Relief eased the tension in his shoulders.

The darsteed lifted its narrow head and bugled an eager greeting. Frowning, Tobeszijian stepped back from the creature and sent it galloping into the forest, snorting and grumbling, the empty stirrups bouncing against its sides.

Turning on his heel, Tobeszijian reentered the little cave, wrapped the sleeping children in his cloak, and left them snuggled beneath the pale white glow of the Chalice's power.

By the time he emerged, the eldin had arrived. Shadowy and only half-visible in the sleet-stung darkness, they filled the bottom of the ravine. Some rode astride beyar mounts, with saddles of crimson leather; most were afoot. A few held their left hands aloft like torches. The flames burning from their fingertips created what was known as fairlight. It should have illuminated the stream and the cave's bramble-shielded mouth, but it seemed dimmer now than when he'd first glimpsed it. He could barely see any of them.

Cautiously, Tobeszijian walked downhill to meet their leader. This eld sat astride a ghostly white beyar with a stripe of gray at its throat. Tobeszijian did not recognize him, but clearly he was an individual of importance. He wore mail made of gold links and a sleeveless tunic of velvet lined with lyng fur. Within the hood of his cloak, a thin gold circlet very similar to Tobeszijian's own crown gleamed on his brow.

Tobeszijian bowed to him in courtesy. "Welcome to my camp," he said, using the old tongue.

The eld's eyes were as pale as stone. They studied Tobeszijian coldly. His face was handsome in the way of his people, lacking a beard, with deep lines grooving either side of his mouth. When he pushed back the hood of his cloak, his ears were revealed to be small and elegant, barely pointed at the tips. He wore a heavy gold ring in the lobe of his right ear. It winked now and then, reflecting the dim fairlight around him.

"I am Asterlain, king of these mountains," the eld said. His voice was clear and musical, with the pure ringing tones of bard crystal. But no lilt or laughter filled that voice. He spoke the old tongue with an accent strange to Tobeszijian, who had learned the language from his eldin mother. "I come seeking Tobeszijian, human king of Nether."

"I am Tobeszijian."

Out in the thicket beyond the small clearing, the darsteed stamped and suddenly bugled.

Its loud voice made Tobeszijian jump, and Asterlain's beyar roared in response, rearing up on its hindquarters and swiping the air with its enormous claws before Asterlain brought it back under control.

Asterlain looked at Tobeszijian. "Why have you brought the Chalice of Eternal Life here?"

Ice encased Tobeszijian's heart. If the eldin knew the Chalice was here, who else had been watching his movements? He sensed evil out there in the dark forest, slinking ever closer, and perhaps listening.

Suddenly he trusted nothing, not even these eldin who had appeared so unexpectedly and oddly just as he was leaving.

"I am here to hunt," he lied warily. He moved his hand casually to his sword hilt. "It is autumn. All who know me know of my custom to range far in search of game and sport."

"Nether has prospered long," Asterlain said, apparently ignoring the lie. "Without the Chalice, its prosperity will end."

Tobeszijian frowned. "My kingdom is not yet lost," he said sternly. "Perhaps you have heard of my half-brother's ambitions. They are rumors only. Would I go out sporting if aught were amiss with my throne and kingdom?"

Asterlain closed his eyes and tilted back his face to sniff the air. Tobeszijian felt pressure pushing against his mind, but he held his thoughts closed. Anger burned in his throat and started throbbing in his temples. Never before had any eld dared to force his mind. The insult tightened his fingers on his sword hilt.

After a moment, Asterlain opened his eyes and looked at Tobeszijian once again. His gaze was harsh with frustration. "You lack the skill to protect the Chalice properly. We have come to help you with your preparations."

Asterlain is guessing about the Chalice's being here, Tobeszijian thought. *He is trying to trick me into confirming his suspicions.* Tobeszijian stood frozen, determined to keep every emotion from his face. He no longer believed he was actually facing real eldin. Whoever, whatever Asterlain and his party were, they could not be what they seemed. Although he sensed no taint upon Asterlain, no evil, he could not stop his thoughts from leaping to the next logical suspicion.

Shapeshifters, he thought, his heart racing. Yet were they? Unsure, he swallowed hard. "It is unwise to doubt my word, King Asterlain," he replied at last. "I am here to hunt, nothing more."

The eld king tilted his head to one side, causing fairlight to glint off his gold earring. "You are far from your lands and kingdom. Your rights to hunt here do not exist, save by my leave."

"Then do I ask your pardon," Tobeszijian said. "I have offered you a discourtesy, which was not meant."

"Where is the Chalice?" Asterlain asked impatiently. "Nearby surely, for we sense it. Yet where?"

Tobeszijian frowned, and managed to keep his gaze from shifting involuntarily toward the cave's mouth. Could Asterlain not see the cave? It was not concealed. The briars which grew over it were not thick enough to act as a shield. Had Asterlain not seen Tobeszijian emerge from it in full view?

Yet the eld kept on staring at Tobeszijian, his pale eyes intense with frustration. Tobeszijian remembered how as a boy he'd had an ancient, much-beloved hound that went blind in its old age. Tobeszijian would sometimes play a game of standing absolutely still and silent while the dog sniffed and searched for him. Sometimes the old dog would come right to him, but sometimes he would stand only a few feet away, whining in frustration and unable to find his master.

That's the way Asterlain was acting, as though he were somehow blind to the cave's whereabouts. Obviously he could sense the Chalice's presence, but he could not locate it.

Perhaps, Tobeszijian thought in amazement, the Chalice's own power was concealing it.

From the corner of his eye Tobeszijian gazed warily at the mounted eldin on their beyars. When he did not look directly at them, they seemed indistinct, not quite real. His thoughts brushed toward them, and encountered nothing. They were phantoms only. Illusions. He blinked, his eyes burning, and let his thoughts spin rapidly through several options. He had to find a way to lead Asterlain away from this place. But how?

"Why do you not answer?" Asterlain asked impatiently. "King Tobeszijian, I bid you respond to my questions."

A strange roaring filled Tobeszijian's ears. He could feel the Ring of Solder glowing hotter and hotter on his finger. His heart began to hammer very hard, but some instinct made him keep absolutely still. He said nothing, almost holding his breath, and watched alarm fill Asterlain's eyes.

The eldin king looked around as though he could no longer see Tobeszijian. "King Tobeszijian!" he called again, his voice even louder now. The air shimmered around him, and the fairlight burning from his fingertips went out.

In that instant Tobeszijian smelled the sickly sweet, decayed stench of the Nonkind. He knew then for certain that he was standing in front of a shapeshifter, the most skilled and powerful one he'd ever encountered. His blood ran cold, and he almost drew his sword to attack the creature. But he stayed motionless, telling himself that to hide this way was sensible, not cowardly. He was outnumbered and on foot. He had his children and the Chalice to protect. It was important to get out of here safely, not fight a battle he was certain to lose. If the

Chalice's power was shielding him now, he must work with it as best he could.

Breathing hard, Asterlain hunched atop his beyar. Rage purpled his face and filled his pale eyes with such heat and intensity that Tobeszijian was certain they could drill right through his concealment.

Yet as long as he did not move, Asterlain could not see him. Tobeszijian slowed his breathing as much as he could, feeling the seconds drawing out slower and slower until they were agonizing.

"Ashnod curse this place!" Asterlain said furiously, pounding his fist on his thigh. His voice had changed pitch, deepening and growing rougher in tone. No longer did he speak in the old tongue of the eldin, but instead in Gantese.

Death stench filled the clearing, polluting the air so heavily that Tobeszijian had to swallow hard several times to keep himself from gagging.

Cursing, Asterlain spurred his beyar straight at Tobeszijian, who stood there rooted, his mind spinning with worry. Should he let the beyar ride straight into him? Should he spring aside at the last moment?

Behind Asterlain, the other eldin riders faded into the darkness. The black shadows of night filled the clearing while fairlight vanished and Tobeszijian's lone opponent cursed and searched.

Tobeszijian's fingers were curled knuckle-white around his sword hilt. If he drew now he could slay the beyar and bring down its rider. If he waited it would be too late to step aside.

He stood with his feet rooted to the ground, his heart pounding in his chest, his sweat cold beneath his mail. *Have faith in the Chalice,* he told himself.

By now the beyar was only a pace away from him. It was a massive brute, its shoulder nearly as tall as Tobeszijian's. Asterlain sat hunched astride the shaggy creature as though in pain. Tobeszijian could hear the shapeshifter's harsh breathing.

The hot, sour stench of the beyar mingled with the corrupt smell of its Nonkind rider. Tobeszijian stared at the long broad muzzle of the beast, at its small, ferocious eyes. Its powerful claws scraped and clattered on the frozen ground, and it grunted steadily, making a savage growling noise that tightened Tobeszijian's guts. He knew that the beyar's claws could rend through his mail, slicing him from gullet to groin in a single blow. By then the shapeshifter would be upon him, or something even worse might come.

Stay still, he told himself, feeling the pressure against his mind return. *Stay still.*

With a growl, the beyar came within inches of him, then veered slightly and trotted past, close enough to brush Tobeszijian's side with its shaggy white fur. Asterlain's toe went right past Tobeszijian's elbow, missing it by less than a breath.

He rode onward, calling Tobeszijian's name and cursing him. Turning around, he came back and brushed past Tobeszijian on the other side. Sleet stung Tobeszijian's face and the cold air sank deep into his bones, but he moved not. He might as well have been carved from stone, the steady warmth from the Ring of Solder on his finger giving him just enough courage to endure while Asterlain cast about, circling the clearing yet again.

Then, from inside the cave, came a child's frightened wail.

Asterlain drew rein sharply and wheeled his beyar around. His thin face turned toward the cave, and he listened intently.

Tobeszijian raged inwardly, cursing this creature that hunted him. He wished with all his might that he could warn Thiatereika to be quiet, but his mind could not reach into the thoughts of people.

"My papa!" she wailed, even more loudly than before. "Where are you?"

The sound of her crying filled the air beneath the steady rattle of sleet among the trees. Asterlain hissed to himself in satisfaction and started toward the cave.

"No!" Tobeszijian shouted. He drew Mirengard, and its blade flashed light through the darkness as he ran forward.

Even as Asterlain was turning around in his crimson saddle, Tobeszijian struck with all the strength of his two arms. Mirengard cut Asterlain in half, separating his head and torso from his hips and legs. A foul black liquid spurted out, splattering the beyar's white fur, and the upper half of Asterlain went tumbling to the ground.

The beyar roared and reared up, and Tobeszijian whistled.

Come/come/come/come! he called with his mind.

Cloven hooves pounded over the frozen ground. As the beyar lunged at Tobeszijian with its deadly claws, the black, scaled darsteed burst from the thicket and struck the beyar's side with its razor-sharp forefeet.

Great gashes opened in the beyar's side. With a roar it turned on the snapping, hissing darsteed and the two creatures joined in battle.

Stumbling out of the way, Tobeszijian barely avoided being struck down by the darsteed's lashing tail. With Mirengard still glowing in his hand, he ran up the hill and ducked inside the cave. It was dark. The Chalice's light no longer glowed.

Thiatereika stood just inside the cave's mouth; he would have stumbled right over her had she not been crying.

Stopping in the darkness, with his rapid breathing sounding harsh and loud in his ears, he pulled her into his arms. "Where is your brother?" he asked.

"I had a bad dream, my papa," she whimpered, clinging to him. "I dreamed that Mama was dead."

"Hush," he said, carrying her to the back of the cave, where he collected the sleeping Faldain.

"She was taken by people robed in black, my papa," Thiatereika said brokenly, her voice torn with grief. "They took her away!"

His arm tightened around her. "Stop it," he said sharply. "No one is taking your mother away. You are with me. You are safe."

"I want to go home," she wailed, crying again. Faldain woke up and began to cry too. "I'm cold, my papa. I don't like this game anymore. I want Gilda."

"Gildie!" Faldain said in shrill agreement.

Tobeszijian knew they were little, knew they were cold and tired and frightened, but he spared no more comfort for either of them as he carried them outside into the bitter night. The sleet was falling even harder. The air was so cold it hurt. He paused at the mouth of the cave and pressed the flat of Mirengard's blade against first one side of the opening and then the other.

"In the name of Thod," he intoned, "let this place lie under the protection of the gods."

Down in the little clearing near the stream, the battle between the beyar and the darsteed had already ended. The beyar lay on its side, its white fur now stained dark. The darsteed was feeding noisily, shaking its lean head viciously now and then to tear off another chunk of raw flesh.

Staying clear of the beast while it ate, Tobeszijian put his children down and pulled free of their clinging hands. Both began to cry again.

"Stand there, for just a moment!" he said sharply, his own stress and fatigue making him harsher than he meant to be. "Do as I say!"

Thiatereika fell silent, and Faldain pressed his face against her, whining still.

Tobeszijian dragged the two halves of Asterlain's body over the frozen ground and tossed them in the shallow stream. A scream rose from Asterlain's dead throat, and Tobeszijian jumped back, stumbling and nearly falling on the bank while he struggled to draw his sword.

But Asterlain did not move. While his corpse lay in running water, it could not resume life. And no other dreadful creature rose to take life from his blood.

Tobeszijian stood there on the bank, breathing hard, his eyes staring at the corpse. Gradually he relaxed and let his half-drawn sword slide back into its scabbard. Relief swept him, and he turned away, hurrying back toward the darsteed.

His head was pounding. His muscles remained knotted with tension. He stumbled, squinting against the sleet, and felt as though he'd stepped into mire and was being pulled down by it.

It was only fatigue, catching up with him. He caught himself wiping the sleet from his face, over and over, his palms scrubbing his skin. His breathing was still rapid and harsh. Now and then he heard a little moan catching in the back of his throat.

Mighty Thod, deliver me from the hands of my enemies, he prayed silently, seeking to find strength enough to hang on. He had fought Gant Nonkind and Believers before, but never alone, on his own, lacking the spells of protection.

The fetid smell of death still lingered on the air. Hurrying back to the children, Tobeszijian scooped up Faldain just in time to save him from the darsteed's snapping jaws.

The beast hissed at him, lashing a warning with its tail, but Tobeszijian knew already that it had eaten its fill. It was only protecting its kill now, and halfheartedly at that.

After a couple of tries, Tobeszijian managed to dart close

enough to grab the dangling reins. He pulled the darsteed around, controlling its desire to strike at him.

"No!" Thiatereika shrieked when her father reached for her. She stamped her foot, her small cloak gusting in the wind. "I don't want to ride anymore! I want Gilda! I want to go home."

Ignoring her protests, he picked her up and set her and Faldain in front of the saddle.

The darsteed whipped its head around and bit Tobeszijian in his side, just above his hip. The creature's fangs glanced off the bottom rim of his breastplate, denting the metal but not piercing it. Still, the attack was vicious enough to knock Tobeszijian against the beast's side.

Gasping with pain, he gripped the stirrup to keep his balance while the darsteed bugled with fury and tried to swing away from him.

Desperately Tobeszijian kept hold of stirrup and reins, knowing he could not let the darsteed run away with the children on its back. It would shake them off and eat them. Furious himself, he struck the beast with his thoughts, but its mind was a red-hot mass, unassailable for the first time since its capture.

Astonished, Tobeszijian staggered, nearly losing his footing as he grappled to keep his hold on the reins. The darsteed reared high above him, deadly forefeet striking out. Tobeszijian dodged, and the darsteed yanked away from him. One of the reins snapped in two with a twang.

Tobeszijian feinted and moved with the beast, trying to stay out of striking range without losing his last, tenuous hold on the remaining rein. Drawing his dagger, he dodged another attempt to bite him and struck hard and precisely, plunging his dagger deep into the web of muscle between the darsteed's shoulder and ribs.

The animal screamed and blew fire. Thiatereika was crying now, screaming to get off. Clinging to the darsteed's neck like a tiny burr, Faldain uttered no sound.

"Hang on!" Tobeszijian told them as he dodged the flames. Fire scorched his cheek, and the pain sent him stumbling back. He would have fallen had the darsteed not dragged him. Its frenzied attempt to pull away lifted Tobeszijian back on his feet. Cursing, he fought the animal, which was bleeding heavily and moaning.

But its pain distracted it enough for him to reestablish control.

Stand/stand/stand/stand, he commanded it.

The darsteed snorted and obeyed him. In that moment, Tobeszijian mounted and jammed his feet firmly in the stirrups. The darsteed reared, trying to brush him off under some tree limbs. Thiatereika cried out and nearly toppled to the ground, but Tobeszijian's arm encircled her and her brother, keeping them snug against him. The darsteed tried to rear again, but Tobeszijian jabbed it cruelly with his spurs, startling it into a weak buck instead.

Snorting flames, the darsteed shook its head in fury, but Tobeszijian leaned over and pulled out his dagger from its side. Blood spurted across his hand, burning where it splattered.

The darsteed bellowed in pain and stumbled, but he had control of it now.

Go/go/go/go, Tobeszijian commanded, and the beast lurched into a stumbling gallop.

Struggling to guide it with only one rein, Tobeszijian tried to find his bearings in the darkness. The sleet soaked through his surcoat and seeped between the links of his mail. He felt chilled to the bone. The wet saddle under his thighs made him colder. Tobeszijian pulled up the children's hoods and tried to cover them with the folds of his cloak. The night was too raw for traveling, but even as he caught himself longing to be safe indoors by a warm fire, the wind shifted and his nostrils caught a stink of something rotten.

More Nonkind were coming. He choked a moment in new alarm, then fear iced his veins.

The darsteed bugled eagerly until Tobeszijian forced it to be silent.

In the sudden quiet, Tobeszijian heard an unworldly howl close by, and his heart skipped a beat. He knew the hunting cry of a hurlhound all too well. Thanks to the rebellion of the darsteed, they'd been delayed long enough for the hurlhound to catch up with them.

What next? Tobeszijian asked himself wearily, then shook off his weakness. Fiercely, he glanced at the hillside on his right. The howl had come from somewhere up there. The hurlhound was close enough to reach him in a few minutes. Already his ears picked up the sound of its crashing progress as it descended through the undergrowth.

The darsteed swung around to face the approaching hurlhound, its powerful body quivering eagerly. Tobeszijian's mind sifted rapidly through a dozen possibilities. He had to think of a refuge for the children outside of Nether, and he had only seconds to make a decision. They must be hidden with someone trustworthy enough not to sell them as hostages to a foreign enemy, or even to Muncel. But as a wheeling series of faces belonging to the handful of nobles in Mandria or to the one-eyed chieftain in Klad whom he'd bribed into being a secret ally crossed his mind, Tobeszijian knew that none of them were right. He knew, too, that he could not afford to make a mistake now; he had only a single trip with the Ring remaining to him.

The hurlhound was still crashing down the hillside, so close now he could hear it snarling and snapping. And at that moment, a second one burst from the thicket on his left and charged straight toward him. Tobeszijian shouted in alarm, but the monster yelped and turned aside at the stream, dashing back and forth as though afraid to leap it.

The hurlhound was a monstrous creature, twice the size of the largest dog in Tobeszijian's kennels, with black, scaled skin instead of hair and a broad, blunt head ending in a powerful muzzle of razor-sharp teeth. Its tongue—glowing with eerie green phosphorus—lolled from its jaws. He could hear the creature panting and whining as it paced back and forth along the narrow stream. Its eyes glowed red, and it stank of rotting flesh, so sickly and foul Tobeszijian thought he would retch.

"Dog!" Faldain announced, pointing.

Thiatereika screamed.

At that instant, the hurlhound leaped across the stream and came bounding straight at them with impossible speed. Reaching them, it jumped up as though to drag Tobeszijian from the saddle.

Tobeszijian swung his sword down in a powerful slash and cut off the hurlhound's head in a clean blow. Mirengard was glowing with blinding radiance. He could feel the magical power in the sword humming through the bones of his hand.

Behind him, the other hurlhound reached the bottom of the hill and came roaring at them. Tobeszijian swung the darsteed around to face its oncoming charge, but at that moment the king made his decision.

Gazing at his glowing sword, he thought of the only swordmaker he knew capable of producing something similar to the legendary Mirengard.

Jerking off his glove with his teeth, Tobeszijian let the hurlhound keep coming and concentrated all his heart and mind on his glowing Ring. Its light shone over the pawing darsteed and Tobeszijian's children.

To Jorb, the dwarf of Nold, he thought. *To Jorb!*

The hurlhound reached them, leaping high. Its cavernous jaws opened wide, revealing its glowing teeth and venomous tongue. Its eyes shone red with the fires of hell, and its stink rolled over Tobeszijian like death itself.

But he pushed his fear aside. He held his ground while his children screamed and struggled against the iron band of his protecting arm. Then the power came, tossing them up into the very air. The hurlhound was knocked aside with a yelp, and they were swept into the second world yet again.

7

NOLD WAS A forbidding, unwelcoming country, damp and cold, and it was still tainted by the residue of magic cast in the mighty battles of antiquity. Sparsely settled, most of the land was choked with the Dark Forest—woods so thick no decent road could be built through them. Instead, muddy trails wound through the trees, trails that might take a weary traveler to a settlement or might stop in the midst of nowhere.

It was afternoon, and Tobeszijian rode along such a trail, trying hard to keep his sense of direction despite the weariness buzzing inside his head.

The darsteed was limping badly. Moaning and snorting, the animal hobbled along stiffly, its wound still oozing and raw.

Every time Tobeszijian tried to dismount to spare it, however, the creature attacked him.

He rode it grimly, forcing it to give him the very last of its strength. When it finally went down, he would have to cut its throat and walk to the next settlement. If he could not buy a decent horse, it would be a long trudge indeed all the way home to Nether.

He sighed, feeling bereft without the children snuggled beneath his cloak. Again and again, his mind conjured up his last sight of their bewildered, tear-streaked faces while Jorb held their shoulders to keep them from running after their father.

Tobeszijian frowned. He could not feel easy about leaving them behind. They had no protectors, no guards, no retainers. Even were he gone a month or two—and certainly it would be no more than that—it was an enormous risk to leave them in the sole care of a near stranger. Tobeszijian knew Jorb on a business footing only. The dwarf was a master armorer, and was known for the fine swords he crafted. Twice Tobeszijian had commissioned him to make armor and daggers for him. Jorb coveted Mirengard. Whenever he talked to Tobeszijian, his gaze would stray to the sword, and his thick fingers—strong enough to crack walnuts—would flex and stretch as though they ached to slide along that shining blade.

Like all dwarves, Jorb was temperamental and sly. He struck hard bargains, but once a dwarf actually gave his word, he would stay true to it. Jorb had demanded Mirengard in exchange for hiding the children.

It was an impossible bargain. Tobeszijian could not hold his throne without the sword, and Jorb knew that. The dwarf had used his unreasonable demand to leverage a fat purse of gold, the jeweled ring from Tobeszijian's smallest finger, his silver spurs, and the cups of eldin silver belonging to the children. Clutching his booty and chuckling to himself, the dwarf had ducked his bearded chin low and scuttled back into his queer hut built in the base of a vast tree trunk, with a stone-lined entry and an iron-banded door. Smoke curled out through a hollow limb overhead, making the tree almost look like it was on fire.

Jorb popped outside a few minutes later and gestured. "Well, bring 'em in. Bring 'em in!" he said.

There had been time only for a swift glance round at the cramped interior. It was swept clean, with every humble possession in its proper place. Tobeszijian knew that Jorb was accounted to be rich and prosperous, as he was much in demand for his skills at the forge. No doubt the dwarf kept his gold strongboxes and treasures down deep in the ground, concealed in mysterious tunnels and burrows. Still, the place was far from suitable for the children of a king. With the blessing of Thod, perhaps they would not have to stay hidden here long.

Tobeszijian had ridden away this morning with the cries of Faldain and Thiatereika echoing in his ears. He knew he must set his face toward war, yet he felt unmanned and guilty. He despaired of ever being reunited with his children.

Soon, my precious ones, he'd promised them silently. *Soon I shall return for you.*

Thiatereika had run down the road in his darsteed's wake, crying out, "My papa, come back! My papa! My papa!"

The heartbreak and terror in her voice had nearly destroyed all his resolve. Although he'd intended to turn around and wave, he kept his back to her, hearing her voice growing fainter and fainter as he kicked the darsteed into a gallop.

They were safe, he told himself for the countless time.

Hidden and safe.

He wanted to feel relief, but instead his sense of uneasiness grew. Nereisse would have condemned him for leaving them behind, unguarded, in the hands of one who owed him no allegiance. It seemed that her spirit, cold with disapproval, perched on his shoulder.

"What else could I do?" he asked aloud.

Tipping back his head, he stared at the overcast sky. The clouds were massed and dark above the thick treetops. He shivered under his cloak.

He felt as though he had somehow failed. And with that came a boiling surge of anger against Nereisse, who had left him to face these difficulties alone. What right had she to risk her life by knowingly drawing poison into her body to save her daughter? What right had she to take herself from him, just when he needed her most? They could have had another daughter, could have faced the future together, could have . . .

Gripping his hair in his fist, he cried out, making an animal sound of sheer anguish.

He did not understand himself. His fury and resentment bewildered him, and he felt guilty, as though he had somehow betrayed his dead wife by feeling this way. He loved her. He had been enspelled by her from the first moment he glimpsed her in the forest. As for weighing the value of Nereisse's life against Thiatereika's . . . what was wrong with him? Could he resent his own daughter for having lived at the cost of her mother's life?

Was that why he found it so easy to abandon his children in this dark, primitive land?

Fearing that some madness was trying to break his mind, he turned his thoughts toward his next responsibilities. He must work quickly to raise an army and crush Muncel's rebellion. If he didn't return to Nether soon and force his nobles and knights to honor their oaths to him, then he might as well stay here in the forests of Nold, an exile forever. He would not seek assistance from Verence of Mandria yet. Thus far, Verence had proven to be a sound ally, but it was best to handle civil war without the help of neighboring lands, which might decide to conquer rather than assist.

The sky overhead stayed gray and tired. Now and then rain drizzled on him. He brushed past leafy branches and ducked beneath loops of gnarled vines. Keebacks wheeled overhead in the sky, making their plaintive cry. He encountered no other travelers, except once, a group of five dwarves clad in green linsey. Stocky and round-cheeked, their beards woolly and matted, they were each burdened with bulky sacks thrown across their shoulders, sacks heavy enough to bend them double. Their furtive eyes glared at Tobeszijian, then they scattered off the road and into the forest, giving him no chance to ask how far it was to the next settlement.

If he could find a village, he would trade his cloak pin for a horse or even a mule, and set the darsteed loose.

He touched his mind to the beast's, trying to urge it, but the darsteed was too filled with pain and fury to go faster.

A keeback burst from the trees ahead of him, calling *kee-kee-kee.* A stag bounded into the road, stared at him with startled eyes, and leaped back into the thicket in a panic. The darsteed stumbled to a halt unbidden, and let its head sink down. Frowning, Tobeszijian kicked it hard, but it only groaned.

He sat there in the saddle, tired and cold and wet, and knew he had pushed it all he could. Its wound was not fatal, but the beast needed rest and care to mend. Tobeszijian had time for neither. He could not set the creature free in these woods, where it would hunt and attack man, dwarf, or creature alike. Which meant he would have to kill it.

"Not yet," he said through his teeth, thinking of the long walk ahead of him. A king afoot in a foreign land? It was a mockery.

Again he urged the darsteed forward, but it stood there with its snout on the ground and would not respond.

Fury and frustration choked Tobeszijian. He knew he had only himself to blame for the darsteed's injury. Tilting back his head, Tobeszijian lifted his fist to the sky. If only he'd used the Ring to go north to Prince Volvn's stronghold as he'd first intended. If only he hadn't been warned not to take the children back into Nether. It was unfair of the gods to set so strict a limitation on the use of the Ring. Only three tries? When there was need of more?

"Damn you!" he shouted. Drawing his sword, he whacked the darsteed's rump with the flat of his blade.

It hissed and whipped its head around defiantly, but took no step forward.

Again he struck it, shouting curses and wishing he had not let Jorb talk him out of his spurs, but all his efforts to urge the creature on were for naught. The darsteed instead sank to its knees.

Tobeszijian twisted around in the saddle and started to dismount. But at that moment he heard a sudden pop of sound, and a creature black and hairy materialized from thin air to stand directly in his path.

It was half the size of the darsteed, and so lean it seemed almost flat when it turned to the side. A stench of sulfur hung on its fur, and its bony head turned on a long, sinuous neck to bare multiple rows of savage teeth at Tobeszijian.

The darsteed bellowed and reared up with an awkward lunge, nearly unseating its rider. Furious at himself for being caught off guard, Tobeszijian had only a second to wonder why his senses had not warned him a Nonkind was this close before the sylith leaped forward.

As the darsteed lashed out with its sharp hooves and the sylith dodged with a snarl, Tobeszijian drew Mirengard. In the presence of Nonkind its blade glowed as white as the purest flame.

Swinging the sword aloft, Tobeszijian fought to control the darsteed and managed to pivot his mount around just as the sylith sprang up at him. Tobeszijian's blade sliced cleanly through the sylith's thin neck, dropping its head to the ground with a spurt of acidic blood that splattered and steamed in the cold air. He smelled the dreadful decayed stench of it and tried desperately to breathe through his mouth.

The headless body of the monster staggered about, refusing to topple. Bugling a challenge, the darsteed brought its sharp hooves down upon the sylith's head, crushing it. Snorting flame, the darsteed set the sylith's narrow body afire.

A shriek rent the air, fading into the ether as the sylith finally died. Its charred body crashed to the ground and lay still. The reek of burned flesh filled the air.

Mirengard glowed even brighter, and the sword's power flowed down its blade, dripping off the tip and cleansing the foul blood away. Tiny silver puddles shimmered on the trampled ground, and green vines sprouted there, unfurling new leaves despite the frost-laden air. In less than a day the vines would grow over the sylith's charred corpse and conceal it as though it had never been there.

Continuing down his road, Tobeszijian drew in a few deep breaths and wondered what had made the monster attack him alone. Syliths seldom hunted singly. Another one was bound to be nearby. He lifted his face to the damp breeze, questing, but sensed nothing. A shiver moved down his spine, and he kept Mirengard gripped in his hand instead of sheathing it.

Snorting little spurts of flame, its eyes glowing red, its tail lashing viciously behind it, the darsteed trotted a few steps, restive and fiery, before it began to limp again.

Tobeszijian kept it going. Settling himself deeper in the saddle, he maintained a wary lookout. He smelled nothing other than the darsteed's lathered sweat, damp soil, and the half-rotted leaves of the forest, yet he stayed tense and ready.

At that moment, twin shrieks filled the air before him. He reined up sharply, his heart nearly bursting through his breastplate. Just as the darsteed wheeled sideways, two hurlhounds materialized on the road, blocking it. The darsteed, still hot with battle-lust, bellowed and lunged against the reins. Another cry answered from behind. Two more hurlhounds appeared there, cutting him off from retreat.

Tobeszijian swore and spurred the darsteed into the forest, although he knew that with its wounded shoulder it could not outrun this unholy pack.

The darsteed reared, and he glimpsed yet a fifth hurlhound, springing at them from the undergrowth.

Black-scaled and vicious, their eyes glowing red and their fangs dripping death, the hurlhounds closed in. Darsteed and rider fought with hooves and sword, grimly determined to prevail. But two of the hounds bit deep into the darsteed's hindquarters, cutting tendons, and brought it halfway down.

The darsteed screamed with pain, and its agony flooded Tobeszijian's senses even as he twisted in the saddle to hack into one of the hurlhounds. The creature collapsed with a yelp, and its companion snarled and sprang back out of reach.

At that moment, Tobeszijian was struck from the left by the weight of another, which gripped the folds of his heavy cloak in its mouth and tried to drag him from the saddle.

Tobeszijian drew his dagger and struck the hurlhound in the face. His dagger point skidded across its scaled skull and rammed into one of its red eyes. Snarling and yelping, the hurlhound snapped back its head so violently that Tobeszijian's dagger was torn from his hand.

He struck with Mirengard to fend off another attack, but one of the creatures sank its fangs into his leg.

Venom poured into his flesh like fire. He heard himself screaming a wild, senseless mixture of curses and prayers. The darsteed bucked beneath him as it tried to pull its crippled hind legs up beneath it. Wobbling, it threw Tobeszijian off balance, and with a moan let itself sink down, only to thrash wildly again.

The remaining hurlhounds did not let up. One went for the darsteed's throat while another nearly pulled Tobeszijian from the saddle. Streaming blood, racked with agony, he killed it, but more of the creatures kept appearing, making sure he stayed surrounded and outnumbered.

Their dim, bestial minds hammered at his: *Kill/kill/kill/kill.*

And another unholy mind came with theirs, one cold, sentient, and clear: *Where/where/where/where?*

Tobeszijian's mind was bombarded with images of the Chalice, death and decay, rotting bones, moldering intestines, gaping wounds, hot biting joy at killing, and implacable fury mingled with frustration.

He gasped, struggling with all his might to hold his mind shut against the mad hounds and their unseen master. He would not surrender the Chalice. Not even to save himself.

He knew he could not prevail. He was tiring, and he wore no spell of protection to shield him. His wounds burned with such fire he thought he might pass out. Yet the pain goaded him to keep fighting even as the poison sapped his strength. He felt himself weakening fast. His sword arm slowed, feeling increasingly heavy. Tiny gray dots danced in his vision. His spirit and mind remained strong, but his body was dying.

Turning in a tight circle, he struck again and again, beating back the hurlhounds with diminishing strength. The poison in his veins was something dark and tangled, tainted with horrors worse than death. His body jerked, and he fought the need to thrash against whatever burned inside him. He would not give way to it, would not become a part of the evil surrounding him.

"No," he said raggedly, hacking a terrible wound across the neck of a lunging hurlhound. With its head nearly severed from its body, it staggered in a circle and snapped bloody, hissing froth at one of its mates.

Wild laughter suddenly filled the air above the ferocious snarls and growls. Yelping, the uninjured hurlhounds sprang back from Tobeszijian as though obeying a silent command. Those bleeding with wounds froze in their tracks and abruptly collapsed.

Swaying, Tobeszijian blinked away the dancing dots for a moment and glanced around.

A short distance away, a trio of men mounted on darsteeds emerged from the woods. Their helms were plain and black. Their hauberks were made not of chain mail, but instead of thinly sliced disks of obsidian stone, coating their bodies like the darsteeds' scales. Gloved and spurred, with long broadswords of black steel hanging at their sides, they stared at Tobeszijian in silence. He saw their eyes glow red and unnatural through the slits in their helms. When they breathed, the stone disks of their armor made faint clacking sounds, and smoke curled forth from their nostrils. The damp air reeked of sulfur and death.

One of the three held a cage that swung freely on a chain. Within the cage writhed something misty and formless. Smaller than a man, it lengthened itself and then shrank, always in flux. It was colored the same sickly gray hue as wood fungus, and it was far more to be feared than any of the other Nonkind present. It was horribly, completely evil.

A soultaker.

Tobeszijian's breath froze in his lungs. Fear rushed through his bowels as though he had suddenly swallowed hot liquid. While syliths and hurlhounds ripped a man's body apart, soultakers came to it, lay on it, and took that which the gods granted to men and not to beasts.

On the battlefield, from afar, Tobeszijian had witnessed soultakers feeding on their victims. He had heard the screams that mortal throats should never make. He had seen afterward the soultakers rise into the air, writhing, bloated, and colored brightly by the life and essence of what they'd consumed. He had seen the corpses rise and follow commands, their dead white faces staring with eyes that no longer saw, their slack mouths sagging open, their clutching hands outstretched to attack the living troops that often fled in disarray. Tobeszijian had seen soultakers sit on the shoulders of these walking corpses, like riders on their mounts. And he had sometimes witnessed soldiers of the darkness such as these opening cages to unleash soultakers within.

Fury and fear tangled with desperation in his throat. That thing would not take him, he vowed grimly. It would not eat his soul and then use his rotting body to harm others. Whether dead or alive, he'd become no eternal prisoner of the Nonkind, doomed for all eternity.

Tobeszijian fought off his swimming dizziness and drew himself erect. Streaming with blood from his wounds, his lungs aching for air, he gripped Mirengard with both hands and raised it in challenge to the Nonkind soldiers. The sword glowed a blinding white, as did the Ring of Solder on his finger. Frowning, Tobeszijian reached deep inside his faith, drawing on the power of the sword and Ring.

"In the name of Thod," he said in a voice that rang out in the silence, "begone, foul demons, and let me pass."

"Surrender the Chalice and you may pass." The voice that

answered him was gravelly and strangled, almost too hoarse to be understood.

Tobeszijian lifted his head higher. He never parleyed with the Nonkind, never discussed their terms. His father had warned him to refuse any request, simply and straightforwardly, and to keep refusing. For to be drawn into conversation was to give their evil minds time to find a way of tricking him.

He met the fierce red eyes of the soldiers. Around him the hurlhounds panted and watched, their fangs dripping saliva that hissed and steamed.

"Surrender the Chalice," the hoarse voice commanded again.

"No," Tobeszijian said, forcing his voice to sound strong and firm while his heart thudded beneath his breastplate. The poison was burning even hotter inside him now, making him shiver and sweat. He wanted to drop to his knees and cry out for mercy. That desire was so foreign and false that he felt appalled, then realized their minds were trying to force his compliance. "No!" he cried.

"Surrender," the soldier in the center of the trio said.

Through Tobeszijian's mind writhed whispers of *Surrender/surrender/surrender/surrender.*

"What makes you think I have the Chalice?" Tobeszijian countered. "I am a common traveler, on my road. You are mistaken."

Rasping, terrible laughter filled the air. "King Tobeszijian, you have become a liar and a coward. Without your armies and your spells, you stink of fear."

Tobeszijian stiffened, but inside he was horrified by the truth of what the Nonkind had said. Never before had he known any cowardice in himself. Never before had he broken from his training. Never before had he been as afraid as he was now.

It was the poison, he told himself feverishly. He had to take care and not let its influence work tricks on his mind.

"Surrender the Chalice," the Nonkind said to him.

The command held force now, a force that rocked Tobeszijian back on his heels. He nearly toppled over backward. Catching his balance, he blinked sweat from his eyes and gripped Mirengard desperately. *Protect me,* he prayed to it.

He knew that the Nonkind would hammer at his will and

courage while the poison sapped his strength. He would have to fight until the hurlhounds tore him apart. Then the soultaker would defile him, taking his thoughts and knowledge, and imprisoning his spirit forever. The location of the Chalice would be known to them, and all would be lost—not just his life and his kingdom, but the very world of truth, mercy, and good.

"Thod have mercy on me," he prayed aloud. Mirengard glowed even brighter, until the blade was a shining flame. He did not want to die, but he could not give these creatures what they wanted.

Tobeszijian shivered and recalled his youth, when his father had taken him far from the palace on a winter's day. In a secret place, King Runtha had made him swear grave oaths of responsibility for the Chalice's safekeeping. Runtha's voice had been solemn and calm as he recited the words. Tobeszijian had repeated them after him, and the words and phrases had echoed strangely in the air around him.

He opened his mouth now to repeat those oaths, but before he could speak the hounds snarled and sprang at him from all sides.

Tobeszijian staggered in an attempted feint, his weakened and bloody body unable to carry through on the maneuver. He struck hard with Mirengard, but a set of poisonous jaws clamped onto his hip from behind, and Tobeszijian cried out as he was driven to his knees.

"No!" he shouted. "May Thod rot you, demon!"

Twisting, he sliced with Mirengard, and the shining sword cleaved the hound in two. The remaining hounds circled him with snapping jaws, but he pivoted on his knees, swinging Mirengard, and they dodged away.

Heartened by their cowardice, Tobeszijian found the strength to stagger back to his feet. The hounds closed in, menace glowing in their red eyes.

Awash with agony, Tobeszijian circled with them. The dancing dots were back in his vision, and his breath sounded ragged and harsh in his ears. Hearing a soft click, he glanced up just as one of the Nonkind soldiers opened the soultaker's cage.

The thing, so pale and formless, slid its pallid tendrils through the opening, and the rest of it flowed out. Writhing, it floated in the air near Tobeszijian, who stared at it in horror and dread.

Thoughts as thin as needles of rain slid into his mind: *Come/come/come/come to me, and I shall eat you, king of men.*

Screaming an oath, Tobeszijian swung Mirengard at it with all his might, but the soultaker sailed upward, and he missed.

A hurlhound struck his back, knocking him down. He heard the ferocious growling as the thing bit his shoulder through his armor, trying for his neck. Shouting, Tobeszijian felt himself lifted by the monster and shaken hard, the way a dog shakes a rat. He felt his neck pop and a dreadful numb sensation spread through him.

In desperation, he looked down and saw Mirengard still glowing white and pure in his bloody hand. He saw the Ring of Solder shining on his forefinger, its power there for the taking, the using. He had spent his three journeys, all that were allowed, but Tobeszijian no longer cared about rules or warnings. He was dying here, defeated and alone. The Ring was his final chance to save himself, to save his soul, to save the Chalice.

Desperately he sent his thoughts into the power of the Ring, finding its center.

He saw the blinding flash, heard the great pop as he was sucked once more into the second world. In the distance he heard howls of anger, as though the hurlhounds were trying to follow him here into this place of gray silence, but this time he went hurtling, hurtling, hurtling as though slung by a catapult. He could not move, could not aim himself, could not command his own body. Instead, he plummeted through the mists of the second world, and flew toward a shining barrier that sparkled and swirled ahead of him. He felt strange tremors in his body, accompanied by a rush of chilling coldness that doused the fire burning his wounds.

Too late he realized he had leaped into the second world without a destination in his mind.

He found himself spinning around and around as though still falling through the air. He seemed to be shrinking, and faintly he heard voices rising and falling in powerful murmurs, voices that seemed to have the power to break all creation if they chose.

Was he going to the third world? Was he now dead like his poor, sweet Nereisse? Would he be reunited with her on the other side of that glowing curtain of light as the Writ promised?

But there was something unfinished. Something that needed doing. Some responsibility he had left behind him.

"You never stick to your duty, boy," his father's voice suddenly boomed at him. "It's duty that keeps a king strong."

"My lord prince, if you will not keep your mind on your studies you will never learn the strategies of rule," his tutor's voice said with a sigh.

"Dear husband, I feel a sense of unease that I cannot as yet explain," Nereisse said on the eve of his departure. "Must you go so far away to hunt this year? Must you be gone so long?"

"My papa! Don't leave me! My papa!"

What had he forgotten? What was there left for him to do?

Spinning in the lost currents of nowhere, Tobeszijian struggled to remember what had been so important to him. He felt shame lingering on his senses, shame for all he'd left undone. It was time he proved himself, time he stuck with his duty.

But hadn't he done enough? He had lost his throne, but he had saved the Chalice from the hands of evil. Was that not duty enough performed?

He found himself at the shining barrier of light. How beautiful and wondrous it was. How brightly it shone. He squinted and thought he could see shapes moving behind it. *The third world,* he thought with a rush of excitement and joy.

He tried to reach out to it, wanting to find Nereisse, wanting to find happiness.

But his duty was unfinished. Had he stayed home instead of going hunting, his enemies would not have had such an easy opportunity to strike against him. Had he chosen his travels more wisely, he might have needed to use the Ring only thrice, as commanded. Had he imprisoned Muncel or exiled him when he first succeeded their father, his half-brother would not have found it so convenient to betray him.

So many mistakes, but this time he would not make another.

The barrier's radiant glow shone across his face. He could feel its warmth, so lovely and refreshing. But when he tried to reach through the light, his hand bounced off something. He could not see the shapes behind it except as motion and color. He could not see Nereisse. He tried to call out, but he had no voice here in the gray void of the second world.

And he knew that he must finish his task before he could pass through. For once in his life he must be the king his father and his subjects had expected him to be. Muncel must not stay on the throne of Nether. The evil that had crept into the land must be driven out. These remained his responsibilities.

Sighing, feeling hollow with regret, Tobeszijian turned back from the gateway to the third world and found himself plunging forever in the gray mists, unable to escape them, his obligations like a chain that held him shackled.

On the narrow road in the forests of Nold, all lay quiet and still. There remained nothing to see of the battle which had raged in King Tobeszijian's final moments except the churned ground and the stripped bones of his darsteed's eaten carcass.

A week or so later, a peddler came wandering along in a drizzling rain, whistling softly to firm his courage there in the gloom of forest. Many tales were told about the legendary Dark Forest of Nold. These woods had seen centuries of evil aprowl, and old battles fought by gods, and long terrors, and darkness, and doom.

The peddler had traveled the length and breadth of Nold often enough to keep him wary but not unduly afraid. Stories were stories. He had a sharp dagger in his belt and a set of good wits. He was a small man, quick of thought and keen of eye.

He paused when he came to the battleground, sensing some lingering disquiet in the air. Doffing his cap, he made a quick sign with his nimble fingers to ward off evil and left the narrow track to tiptoe around the spot where clearly death had struck.

The drizzle stopped and the clouds overhead parted for a moment to let sunshine fall into the forest. In the moisture-laden air, the light sparkled with the soft, magical colors of rainbow.

A wink of something glittering in that beautiful light caught the peddler's eye, and he stopped.

Stooping low, he peered at the ground a long, cautious while. At last, satisfied that no invisible trap of evil had been set there to snare him, he took one quick step onto the torn, muddy ground. He picked up the object and held it aloft.

The ring glittered and flashed in the sunlight. It was finely wrought, its band stamped all around with intricate rune carvings. The top was set with a large oval stone as pale and smooth as milk. He had never seen anything so fine except on the fingers of rich noblemen. Now here, on this lonely road, lay the long bones of a noble's rather large horse, lay also the chewed and tattered remains of a fine leather saddle, lay the noble's fine finger ring; in fact, lay all but the bones of the noble himself.

The peddler grinned to himself at his good luck, and couldn't resist polishing the ring on the front of his jerkin. A fine piece, worthy of a king, he thought.

It would bring him luck. It would bring him a pretty price when he sold it. Not in Nold, of course. The scattered villages and burrows held only rude dwarves willing to buy a few trinkets, colored ribbon, or tea leaves bound up in little bags of coarse cloth, but nothing better. No, he'd not sell this fancy ring until he crossed the border into the rich land of Mandria. He was not an impatient or a greedy man, but when luck came his way he knew what to do with it.

Still grinning to himself, the peddler secured the ring in a safe place inside his clothing. Putting his cap back on, he shouldered his pack and continued on down the road, whistling to himself. Never once did he see the silent shadows which slid forth from among the trees to follow him on his journey.

Part Two

8

15 years later

THE SOUND OF hunting horns—faint at first, then swelling louder—filled the air and silenced the forest. Startled, Dain lifted his head from the shallow pool of water where he'd paused for a drink. He listened intently.

The wailing blat of the horns came again, from his left, the southwest. Dain glanced at the gray clouds scudding low above the treetops, and tried to gauge distance and time. He knew he must be nearly out of the Dark Forest. Rising to his feet, he listened, straining to hear hoofbeats.

Ah . . . yes, crashing like the muted thunder of a distant summer storm. That meant the hunters were Mandrian, for no one in Nold hunted with such noise and fanfare. Most especially not now, when the dwarf clans were at war, their drumbeats throbbing late at night and the smoke from burned-out burrows hanging in the air.

Dain swallowed hard. Never before had he ventured this close to the border. But now was no time to lose his courage. Thia's life depended on what he managed to accomplish today.

Down deep within the knot inside his belly, he felt an ache of fearful despair, but he ignored his emotions and set off at a ground-eating trot, determined to get help for his injured sister.

Dodging and darting through the undergrowth of dense forest, he angled toward the approaching sound of the hunters.

If he was close enough to the border for men to be venturing into the forest, that meant he was nearing settlements and villages, places where he could steal food and perhaps a horse.

Sudden terror, alien and fierce, burst through his mind. With it came a stag that burst from cover and bounded across Dain's trail. The animal passed so close to him that he saw the blood splattering its dusty coat, the heaving flanks, the white of its eye, the dark pink flare within its nostril.

Awash in fear and pain, the creature's mind swept across Dain's, making him stagger to one side and grip a tree trunk for support. Dain closed the stag's senses from his own, shaking his head to clear it.

Seconds later, he heard a deep baying sound that made the hairs rise on the back of his neck. A pack of tall, brawny red dogs came crashing through the thickets and closed in on the faltering stag.

Dain felt the purposeful flick of their minds: *chase/chase/chase/chase*.

He dived for cover, for now the horses and riders were upon him, crashing and blundering through the undergrowth and trees. They were shouting and blowing their horns in great excitement. One rode past Dain so closely he was nearly hit in the face by the rider's spurred foot.

In a heartbeat, they thundered past, kicking up dirt and leaves behind them. He left his cover and followed them, knowing the stag could not run much longer.

Indeed, only a few minutes later the stag went down in a small clearing. The dogs leaped on it with yelps and snarls. For a moment there was milling confusion while the hunters beat off the dogs. Someone shot an arrow into the stag's creamy throat. The noble creature turned its gaze toward its killer for a moment, then its head sank to the ground and it lay still.

Whooping, the hunters surrounded their prey. They were four youths, each about Dain's own age. Richly dressed in velvet cloth and furs, gilded daggers gleaming at their belts, their bows held slack in their hands, they slapped each other on the back and congratulated each other. Three older men in chain mail and green surcoats without crests and one muscular man wearing the crossed-axe crest of a protector stayed in the saddle and watched the proceedings silently.

Dain crept closer, focusing all his attention on the bulging saddlebags of finely worked leather. He could smell food inside—the pale tender bread baked in a puff, wedges of cheese, hanks of cold meat all wrapped in neat waxed-linen bundles. His own hunger was like a living thing inside him, driving him forward, almost making him forget caution.

With his mind, he stilled the nearest horse, turning it around and luring it toward him at the edge of the clearing. Snorting, the handsome animal tossed its head and came forward a few steps, then nibbled at a few blades of grass before coming another few steps closer. Finally it stopped and began to eat in earnest, its reins dragging on the ground.

Dain admired its sleekness, seeing how well groomed and cared for it was. Its splendid leather saddle and cloth alone would bring a fine price. Dain could sell the trappings and the horse for enough gold to support him and Thia for a year. But most of all, he wanted the food in those saddlebags.

Hovering at the edge of the thicket, Dain dared not venture into the open. Keeping a wary eye on the armed men, he crouched close enough to a tangle of briars for the thorns to snag his tattered clothing, and used his mind to lure the horse into coming yet closer.

The young hunters joked and yelped in high spirits. The largest one, with shoulders as burly as a grown man's, passed around a wineskin with a furtive giggle while another boy knelt to dip his fingers in the stag's blood. He smeared crimson streaks across his face, then marked the faces of his companions.

Fascinated despite his sense of urgency, Dain stared at these Mandrian youths, who were his own age and size, yet as different from him as night from day. He had seen Mandrians before, of course. Jorb had done much trade with the nobles, who valued a well-crafted sword. But it was seldom that Dain saw boys of such wealth and magnificence, with such beautiful horses and fine leather tack.

Bold youths indeed, to enter the Dark Forest after game. Dain had heard many tales among the dwarves, tales of the foolish Mandrians who quested in the Dark Forest for the legendary Chalice of Eternal Life or the mythical Field of Skulls, which Jorb said was no place for any common mortal to see. Such searchers often failed to return. The Dark Forest was a mysterious place, full of impenetrable sectors and traps for the unwary. Even the dwarves knew there were parts of the forest where no living creature should go.

But these young hunters laughed and sucked blood from each other's fingers and boasted, each claiming in turn to have shot the arrow which first wounded the stag. The red dogs twisted and circled among them, panting and whining for attention. Dain returned his concentration to the horse, which would not quite venture to the edge of the clearing, despite all his enticements. Perhaps he should risk being seen. If he mounted the horse, he could outrun the others and lose himself quickly in the dense undergrowth. After all, what harm could such boys do him? They were nothing but brave talk and blowing wind. Right now they were discussing whether they should break off the stag's antlers or cut off its entire head. The rich, wasteful fools weren't interested in its flavorful, dark meat or the beauty of its hide.

A corner of Dain's mind urged him to wait out of sight, safe and quiet, until they left with their prize. Then he could help himself to all the venison he could carry. He knew how to build a slow, smoking fire, how to cut the meat into strips and dry it into leathery jerky.

Wait, he cautioned himself.

But the horse was so close. A fleet-footed, strong animal that would carry Thia to a village large enough to support a healer. The Bnen arrow point had snapped off inside her. It festered there, bringing her much pain and fever. Right now she needed tending as much as they both needed food.

Drawing a deep breath, Dain cautiously sent his thoughts in the direction of the four men overseeing their charges.

Look at them, he urged. *Watch what they do. Help them.*

The protector turned his mount to ride toward the hunters, who were now hacking inexpertly at the stag's head. The other men looked that way.

Quick as thought, Dain slipped from cover and went to the horse. Alarmed, it lifted its head from the grass, but Dain soothed it with a thought and swept his fingers gently across the animal's shoulder.

Reassured, the horse bent its head again to eat. Dain drew in scents of warm horse, leather, the boy who'd ridden the saddle, and the ham that was so enticingly close. He gathered the reins and put his foot in the stirrup.

Without warning, the horse squealed in fury and swung away from him. Hopping on one foot, Dain tried to climb into the saddle, but the horse reared, lashing out with its forefeet.

Attack/attack/attack. Its mind was awash with heat. It lunged at him, snapping with huge, yellow teeth. Dain smacked its muzzle and stumbled back, falling in the process.

Across the clearing, the boys stood frozen, staring at him with astonishment. Then the handsomest, best dressed of the lot stepped forward and pointed at Dain.

"A thief!" he called out. "Sir Los, he's stealing my horse!"

With shouts, the armed men drew their swords and came rushing at Dain. He was busy trying to escape from the horse, which sought to trample him, but a shrill whistle from the boy in the blue, fur-trimmed tunic swung the horse away from him. It trotted to its master, and Dain jumped to his feet and ran.

At that moment, two more riders—one clad in chain mail and green surcoat, the other in plain green wool, with a horn slung across his barrel chest and a pointed cap on his head—galloped into the clearing between Dain and his pursuers. The men swore at each other, while the boys ran to mount up. The dogs milled and circled, barking.

"It's an eld!" someone shouted in a shrill voice.

"It's a thief!" said someone else.

"Get him!"

One of the men bore down on Dain, but he ducked to one side, evading the sword swing, and scrambled away. He dived into a briar thicket where the horseman couldn't follow. Burrowing deep, Dain scratched his hands and face and snagged his clothing. Squinting his eyes to protect them, he wiggled deeper into the thicket, his heart pounding too fast, his breath coming quick and short.

There was no time to curse the horse that had turned on him, no time to tell himself he should have just stolen the food and been satisfied. The Mandrians valued their horses the way dwarves valued their treasures. He was in for it now.

"Dogs, *go*!" came the command, and with yelping barks the brutes came after Dain the same way they'd coursed the stag.

Hearing one dog bay over the noise of the others, Dain felt a chill go through the marrow of his bones. He was now their prey, their quarry, and the dogs would run him until they caught him and tore him apart.

With a little sob, he burst clear of the briars on the other side, gaining himself a few seconds of time, and ran for his life.

Dodging and darting on foot, unable to take cover in an underground burrow because the dogs would only dig him out, he ran with all the fleetness he possessed. Dogs and horses drew ever closer, and only his quick wits and sudden changes of direction kept him ahead of them.

His best chance of escape was to head deep into the forest, but his pursuers seemed to know what he would try. They kept driving him the wrong way, pushing him more and more toward the west. He tried to double back and slip between them, knowing that the depths of the Dark Forest would save him. But an arrow hit him, slicing through the meat of his forearm, just below his elbow. The pain came swift and sharp. He stumbled and fell, then rolled desperately back onto his feet while one of the boys shouted, "I hit him! Did your highness see? My arrow caught him."

Clamping his left hand on his bleeding arm, Dain struggled on, but by then a horse and rider blocked his path east. Dain turned west yet again, cursing to himself and wishing he had the powers of a *sorcerel* that would char them to ashes. He called on Fim and Rod, dour gods of the dwarves, to bring a war party of Bnen forth to attack these trespassing Mandrians, but the dwarf gods did not hear the prayers of an eldin boy. No one interceded. No one rescued him. He had only his wits and his nimbleness, and all the while his pursuers kept maneuvering him the wrong way, until the dense thickets grew sparse and the trees spread apart, thinning into open country.

Beyond the edge of the forest, Dain could see a wide, empty marshland—all water and sky. On the horizon, a black rim of trees stood along the opposite side of the river, too far away to offer him any hope. Out there in the open, he could not outrun them. They would hunt him down and kill him without mercy, the same way they'd killed the stag.

For sport, with no need for meat or survival.

He was pagan, with pagan blood. They would not let him go.

With his breath sobbing in his throat, he dropped down into

a briar-choked gully where the horses couldn't go. He doubled back, ducking low to keep himself hidden beneath the short canopy of shtac and perlimon saplings growing thick on the banks. Pushing apart their intertwined branches, the smell of damp crimson and orange-gold leaves thick in his nostrils, he splashed through a trickle of ankle-deep water and ran along its course to throw the dogs off his scent.

Then he dived into a stand of russet-leaved harlberries and crouched low and still, making no sound or movement, not even to breathe deeply while the riders cantered past him, high on the bank of the gully. He was a hare, his clothing the dappled color of bark and leaves, his hair dark, his pale skin dirty enough to blend with the land. Blood from his wounded arm oozed between his fingers. He could smell it, hot and coppery. He feared the dogs would smell it too.

When the riders went past him, he waited a little while, then scuttled out from beneath the bush and went on until the gully ended and he had to climb out.

But ahead of him, blocking the way back into the Dark Forest, was one of the guards, the oldest and wiliest of them, his gaze sweeping the area without mercy, his drawn sword dull silver in his hand.

Dain hissed softly, cursing the man in his heart, and slithered back unseen down the damp, leaf-strewn bank of the gully. He retraced his steps until the gully grew shallow and wide, opening to the bank of marsh. Ahead of him lay open country, a soup of mud, water, and weeds with a river flowing beyond. The boys milled about on the bank with their sleek horses lathered and steaming. The dogs whined and snuffled, casting back and forth for the scent they'd lost.

Careful to stay upwind, Dain crept along behind the boys and angled his way into the marsh unseen.

When he stepped into the water, he nearly yelped aloud. It was icy cold, so cold it burned. He plunged forward as fast as he could without splashing until he reached the freshly cut reeds growing in the water. Shivering and breathing hard, he struggled through them, bruising his feet on the sharp stalks left by the cutters. Reaching some taller, uncut reeds, he crouched there, his head level with their tops. His lungs burned in his chest; his muscles ached with exhaustion.

Clouds as dirty as undyed wool scudded low over the marsh.

No wind blew, but the cold air was numbing enough. With his breath fogging about him, Dain waited a moment, then waded through the knee-deep water even farther into the reeds and crouched again. Constant shivers ran through him, as much from fear as from cold. He clenched his teeth to keep them from chattering. He had to be silent now, as still and silent as the mist lying upon the river that flowed behind him. The wound in his right forearm dripped pale blood into the water. He held his arm beneath the surface in hopes of stanching the bleeding and hiding the smell from the dogs.

The coldness of the water burned his skin and raised huge goose bumps across his body. Sucking in his belly, he bowed his head and let quick breaths hiss in and out through his gritted teeth. His pulse thumped so fast it bruised his throat. His mind was wide open, receiving the crimson bloodlust of the dogs—*chase/chase/chase; kill/kill/kill*—and the flick, flick, flick of men-minds, blurs of thoughts, shapes, and colors he could barely shut out.

A whimper came from between his jaws. He held his breath, savagely starving himself for air. He'd already made enough mistakes today. No need now to lead them right to him because he could not hold his fear silent.

To his right he saw a great levee built of dirt to hold the marsh back. A road paved with stone topped the levee, which curved to accommodate the lazy bend of river. Beyond, trees stood silhouetted against the dirty sky. Spangled in colors of gold, scarlet, and rust, most of them were dropping their leaves. Distant, thin spirals of smoke rose into the sky. A village, he thought, feeling a faint measure of hope. If he could get there, get to the smithy and call himself Jorb's apprentice, he might find refuge of a sort. Most Mandrians were suspicious of strangers, let alone those of his kind, and were inclined to toss those of the bent eye into the nearest horse trough or stream, for despite their priests and large churches, the old beliefs of Mandria claimed that those of pagan blood melted in water.

Dain glanced down at the muddy water enclosing him at the rib line and grimaced. He wished at this moment that the superstition were true. Melting would be a more merciful end than what the hunters planned for him.

He tried to calm himself. Jorb always said no good came of panic. He understood now that he'd tried to steal a war-trained horse, one taught not to let a stranger mount it. Even had he led it into the forest, he could never have gotten on its back without being thrown. It would have been useless for his purposes. Well, the mistake had been an honest one. It was past. He threw it aside and wasted no more thought on self-recrimination.

Only let these hunters go, he thought impatiently, holding his muscles rigid against the shivers which racked him. Let them go before he froze to death in this icy water.

Keebacks perching in a nearby copse of trees on the bank rose with a sudden flurry of wings. Their harsh squawking startled Dain. A cry choked in his throat, and he nearly burst from his miserable hiding place on the force of their instinct.

But he could not run another step. His legs were spent, their muscles cramped and trembling. His stomach felt as though it had been knotted and was being drawn up by slow degrees into his throat to choke him. He crouched lower in the icy water, his gaze on the boys still searching for him among the trees. Although at this distance he could not distinguish their words, he could hear the frustration in their voices as they called to each other.

Dain grinned to himself, feeling his whole body shake. His toes had gone numb. He could barely feel his feet now. Clamping his jaw tight to keep his teeth from chattering, he watched his baffled pursuers and knew they hadn't expected him to actually come out here into the open.

Go away, he thought with all his might. But he was too tired and spent now to focus his thoughts enough to really persuade them.

"A track!" shouted the huntsman. "He took to the water!"

Hoofbeats came thudding across the muddy banks of the marsh. A horse neighed as it floundered belly-deep in water. The dogs' noise changed note, and Dain stopped breathing. He watched the dogs rush to the water's edge, only to leap back. With lolling tongues and waving tails, they barked in his direction as though they could see him in his paltry hiding place. The riders rode back and forth, discussing the matter.

Go away, Dain thought fiercely while the terrible numbness crept up his legs. His strength was waning. He did not think he could hold himself crouched there and still in the freezing water much longer.

Two of the dogs jumped into the water, then scrambled out to shake themselves and whine at their masters.

For an instant the sun broke through the storm clouds to shine upon supple leather, velvets, and fur-trimmed caps. It tipped the hunting spears with gold.

"He's gone to the water, right enough," said one of the men in chain mail. His gnarled voice carried clearly across the marsh. "Morde a day, but he's sly as a vixlet. Yer highness's fine dogs cannae catch scent in yon marsh."

The boy he spoke to snatched off his cap to reveal hair that shone as bright as gold coin. It was the handsome one, the boy whose horse Dain had tried to steal. "I'm aware of that," he said angrily. His voice rang out in a clear tenor, like the song of crystal. "But he's not gone far. He's spilled enough of his cursed white blood to weaken him. I'll wager a gold dreit he's out there in those very reeds now, shivering and trying to cast a spell on us. Thum! Mierre! Attend me, both of you. What say you to it?"

Dain shrank even lower in the water. His eyes were wide and unblinking, focused on nothing save the hunters. His heart thudded harder than ever. Why had fate crossed his path with that of a prince? And gods, this prince guessed his intentions too plainly.

The youth called Thum made no answer to the prince's call, but the other one—burly in the shoulders and moon-faced—kicked his mount closer to his prince. They faced each other at the water's edge, their bodies slack in the saddle while their horses drank. Overhead, the keebacks sailed the skies, crying out their harsh call. In the distance, a bell began to ring, and another hunting horn blew.

"Hear that?" Thum said. "We're being called in."

The others ignored him.

"I say aye, my prince," the boy called Mierre answered. "Our quarry's nearby, all right. The marsh is narrow this way between the road and the river. If he goes on he'll have to swim the river, and I doubt he can do that. Not after the run he's had."

"Cornered," the golden-haired prince said in satisfaction.

"Prince Gavril," Thum said, his voice fine and clear. "It's to be a damned cold wetting, riding into that muck just to fish out a thief. A poor end to fine hunting. Let's leave the wretch to freeze and go back to the hold as we are bidden."

His sensible words gave Dain a trickle of hope.

"No!" Prince Gavril said. "I've not run my horse hard only to go home now. If you're afraid of wet feet, go in and find yourself fire. I'm not finished here."

The boys glared at each other. Even at a short distance Dain could feel Thum's exasperation and Gavril's iron-hard determination.

"He's nothing, the poor wretch," Thum said quietly. "Not worth our trouble."

"He stole from me," Gavril said. "Such an offense cannot go unpunished."

"He was after food, nothing more, I wager," Thum said, refusing to back down. "He looked scrawny enough. Maybe he's a refugee from the clan wars."

Mierre laughed. "He's an eld, you fool, not a dwarf. Or haven't you seen either before?"

Thum's freckled face turned red. "A starving thief is hardly worth a flogging for failing to come in when we are called."

Gavril pointed at him. "You," he said loudly and contemptuously, "are a fool. I fear no flogging. Lord Odfrey would not dare."

Thum's face turned even redder. He bowed low over his saddle, and Dain could feel the force of his angry embarrassment. "As my lord prince says," he replied curtly.

Gavril wheeled his horse away. "You and you," he said to the men, "spread yourselves along the bank. Sir Los, go over there. Mierre, you and Kaltienne stand ready to catch him when I flush him out. Thum, you are excused."

The freckle-faced boy gave his prince a small salute and wheeled his horse harshly around. Spurring the animal with unnecessary force, he went galloping away, his horse's feet throwing up big chunks of mud behind him.

Mierre shrugged his burly shoulders and muttered something to Kaltienne, who laughed unkindly.

Prince Gavril raised a curved horn that he wore slung across his shoulders by a long leather cord. He blew a note that made the dogs howl. It pierced Dain's head. He clapped both hands to his ears in pain, and when the sound faded, taking his agony away, he found Gavril splashing halfway to his hiding place. On the bank, the dogs milled and circled around the legs of the horses, the plumes of their tails waving proudly, while the riders spread themselves along the bank in readiness.

Dain shifted his feet in the water, feeling increasingly cornered. Behind him stretched the expanse of marsh, dotted with reeds and little hillocks of mud that gave way to the channel of the river. Out there, the water ran swift and deep. Dain knew he could not go that way, for the river's current would suck him under in a twinkling should he try to swim it.

Thia, he thought in despair. *Forgive me. I have failed you.*

But Thia was too far away to hear him. Would she wonder when he did not return tonight? Would she surface from her burning fever long enough to worry about him? Would she ever know of her abandonment as she slipped closer to death? Would she have to go into the hands of the gods unshriven and unsung, lacking salt on her tongue to ease her journey into the third world? Would she die without his hand gripping hers, alone in the darkness?

His grief was like an anvil in his chest, holding him down. Dain tried to stay in his hiding place, hoping that if he did not move he would remain unseen. However, the rational part of his mind knew that the uncut reeds provided too thin a cover to hide him for more than a few moments longer. If he jumped up, all would see him. He couldn't outrun the horse, even in the water. No, his only chance was to completely submerge himself in the shallow water and try to crawl to safety.

Breathing . . . He needed a hollow reed, but there was no time to search for one. The reeds growing around him were green. Their centers would be full of a pale, fleshy substance. Fighting desperation, Dain crouched lower in the water.

Gavril rode closer, urging his reluctant horse onward with little nudges of his spurs. By now, Dain could see the boy's white, set face, the dried streaks of blood still on his cheeks. The look of murderous intent in his violet-blue eyes made Dain's blood run cold.

Those vivid blue eyes flashed over him and beyond, searching the marsh, then flashed back. They stared right at Dain and widened. It was as though the curtain of reeds had been swept aside, leaving Dain exposed. Time froze to a standstill in which Dain saw every detail of his pursuer, from the clenched knuckles of Gavril's rein hand, to the golden bracelet of royalty upon his wrist, to the purple stitching on the chest strap of the horse.

Gold and purple . . . colors of the Mandrian king's household. Dain felt small and faint. Even when he'd tried to steal the horse, he hadn't noticed the colors, hadn't paid heed.

I am not your rightful prey! flashed his thoughts.

Gavril winced. "Get out of my head, damn you!" he shouted. He drew a short hunting javelin from his stirrup quiver and hurled it.

Time remained slow, while the fear in Dain swelled like a wineskin. He had to move, had to dodge, had to . . .

The swelling inside him burst. Fear scalded the back of his throat and burned through his chest like acid. The paralysis holding him prisoner broke away, and at the last possible second he flinched aside. The javelin skimmed him harmlessly and thunked into the water near his foot. One end quivered in the air a moment, then the entire javelin sank slowly beneath the water.

Dain gulped in relief along with air.

Gavril glared at him in even greater fury. "Damn you! My next shaft will come at you so hard none of your accursed spells will cast it aside."

He reached for another javelin, but his quiver was empty.

Dain could have bent and seized the weapon now settling into the mud at his feet, but he thought the chase must at last be over. He rose dripping to his feet and held his hands out from his sides in a silent plea for mercy.

Now that his panic had calmed somewhat, all he had to do was *push* a little at Prince Gavril's mind—a man mind, aye, and therefore hard to master, but not impossible—and there would be mercy. He could go free, go on to the village and seek help for Thia there. . . .

Gavril's head jerked. Color flared into his face. "Go free? Run amok in the village? What spell are you casting on me? Begone! Begone, in the name of Tomias!"

As he spoke, half in fury and half in hysteria, his hand raked at his doublet, loosening it. He drew forth a shining, spiraling circle of gold upon a fine chain and brandished it like a weapon. "Get back, demon!"

There was no power in his amulet, but the emotion crackling through the prince was of such intensity Dain backed up a step. The naked fear in Gavril's face faded, to be replaced by a surge of new confidence. He brandished the amulet again, his blue eyes alight with something unpleasant.

"So you do fear some things, monster," he said in a voice of such hatred Dain backed up another step. Gavril pressed the sides of his horse, and the large, snorting creature sidled closer.

Dain's nostrils were flooded with the strong scent of sweaty horse, stronger than Prince Gavril's man scent, stronger than the fishy stench of the mud.

"Bow to the Circle of Tomias, monster. Bow to it!"

Dain had heard the name of Tomias spoken before, but he did not understand why a god should have a man-name. He had seen the man-god's name chiseled on the lintels of village churches. He had heard others call out to this man-god in fear or invoke the name as an oath. But Dain did not live under the power of Tomias. Jorb had taught him to beware the ways of Mandrians and their religion. They took insult quickly, especially from those they considered pagan. Dain had been warned long ago that if he ever spoke Tomias's name in the hearing of a Mandrian, chances were his tongue would be cut out for defilement.

Thus, he could not obey this angry boy's command, even had he wished to, which he did not. There were currents of falsehood and entrapment running through Gavril's voice.

"Bow to this emblem of our holy prophet," Gavril said, "and I shall let you live, though you be a wretched pagan and a miserable thief."

Dain glared up at him, then laughed with harsh disbelief. "You lie."

Pink stained Gavril's pale cheeks, clashing with the dark streaks of blood. He stared, his blue eyes bulging, as though he could not believe Dain's defiance.

"Your prophet has naught to do with this day," Dain said, his tongue curling around the peculiar inflections of the Mandrian language. "You hunt with a full belly and own many horses. Why care you if I take what I need? You are not beggared by it."

Gavril dropped his circle, letting it swing free by its gold chain. He said nothing, but reached for something on the opposite side of his saddle.

Dain stepped back, but he was unprepared for the thin, black blur that came at him. He threw up his wounded arm to protect his face, and the whip snapped across his wound so viciously he screamed.

"Pagan spawn! Monster! I'll be done with you this day," Gavril shouted, whipping Dain's head and shoulders again and again. "I'll crush the life from you for daring to steal from me. There'll be one less pagan alive to taint the air I breathe!"

With every other word a blow cracked down. Dain reeled under burst after burst of agony. He tried to dodge the whip and couldn't. The horse snorted and trampled around him, cutting him off at every turn. Every lash of the whip was a white-hot brand that choked off the breath in his lungs.

Staggering to one side, he slipped and fell into the water. The horse's hooves splashed down just a finger's thickness from his skull.

Dain floundered, trying to get away. His feet slipped in the mud, giving him no purchase. In the distance he could hear a voice shouting in protest.

"Stop it!" one of the men was saying. "My lord prince, that's enough!"

But Gavril either did not hear or he ignored the man. He wheeled his horse around so sharply it reared, and tried to make it trample Dain.

Frantically Dain rolled to one side, swallowing muddy water as he did so, and floundered out of the way as the horse swung around again. Dain groped through the mud for the javelin. Half-stumbling, half on his knees, he scrabbled and searched in desperation. If he could find the javelin, he could defend himself.

The whip caught Dain across the back of his neck, directly on bare skin, with such force his mind went sheet-white, then black. He toppled forward, no more than half-conscious. Dimly he thought that his head must have been severed from his body, which he could not feel.

He hit the water, facedown, and sank like a stone. But the cold water on his cuts awakened a fire so brutal it revived him. He jerked and pushed himself from the water, and his hand found the javelin in the mud. Slinging back his dripping hair and dragging in a deep breath, he coughed up some of the water he'd swallowed.

Somewhere to his left came another shout and the sound of

splashing, but Dain paid that no heed. He rose to his feet, his gaze locked with Gavril's.

"Leave me be!" he shouted, or tried to, but his voice was choked from the water he'd swallowed and came out with little force.

Gavril glared at him. "Why won't you die, damn you? Why do you fight me? You're dead already. Surrender to it!"

As he spoke, Gavril drew his dagger, and the blade was thin and well honed and deadly. Dain recognized in a single, trained glance how tempered it was, how beautifully balanced. He could smell the strength of the metal, and the intent in Gavril's eyes was just as deadly.

Dain shook his head. Inside him came an explosion of rage so hot it charred away his intestines and seared his very bones.

He lifted the javelin.

Alarm replaced the mad fervor in Gavril's dark blue eyes. On the bank, the protector shouted, "Your highness! Come away!"

"I can handle him!" Gavril shouted with a brave gesture. But Dain could see his fright.

It wasn't enough. Dain wanted Gavril to choke on fear, to feel it in his own bile, to scream with it, to have his liver melt to a puddle and all his strength flow out of his body. He wanted Gavril to beg for mercy, to feel his breath come short, to fall off that brute horse and grovel in the mud. But most of all, Dain wanted to ram this spear into the soft part of Gavril's belly, to grind it in until steel grated on spine bone and caught there.

"You dare not strike me," Gavril said. He held up his wrist to make his sleeve fall back and reveal the gold bracelet. "Do you know what this means, monster? To strike at me is to strike at the king, and that is treason punishable by . . ."

Dain stopped listening. In a flash of cunning he realized he must first attack the horse to unseat Gavril. Then he would have Gavril at his mercy.

"Your turn," he said, and lunged.

A whip lashed out from behind him, catching the upraised javelin and flicking it from his grasp. In dismay, Dain watched it go spinning over the reeds and into the water, truly lost now.

He whirled. This time he faced not one of Gavril's companions, but instead a man with lines carved deep in his weathered face and eyes as dark as night. A man in a fur cloak and silver chain, a sword hilt angled beside his hip and rings glittering on his lean fingers.

"Hold this action!" the man said in a voice like thunder. "Both of you stay where you are."

The murderous rage faded from Dain so swiftly he felt hollow and dizzy. For a moment he saw two of this harsh-faced man in his splendid fur cloak. Dain blinked, and there was one again. But the old shortness of breath was back, like a hand constricting his throat. He felt his blood oozing down his arm again, making rapid drips into the water.

Gavril's pale cheeks had turned bright scarlet. "Chevard Odfrey!" he said shrilly. "My lord, you saw! You saw what this creature attempted against my person. You came just in time—"

"Silence, if you please, your highness," the chevard said curtly. His voice was harsh and flat in tone, as though he had no music in him. "I saw a great many things, most of them which you must account for."

The red in Gavril's face paled. "A mere game of hunt and—"

"Game, was it? I saw a defenseless lad hounded and cornered like a water rat for your sport. I saw him thrashed till he fell and heard you screaming like a fiend instead of a prince of the realm. How far did you mean to go with this game?"

The contempt in the man's voice amazed Dain. He realized he was being championed, for reasons he could not understand. His gaze flicked from one angry face to the other, and he wondered if he dared try to break away.

"Chevard, do you criticize me?" Gavril said angrily. "I warned him of my identity and yet he meant to strike me. That's treason, and he must answer for it."

The chevard gestured impatiently, but Gavril stood up in his stirrups.

"It is!" he said shrilly. "Treason most clear! The law is firm."

"Do you expect an uneducated wretch like this to understand the law?" Odfrey countered.

"Ignorance is no excuse for transgression. Furthermore, he is a pagan and would not kneel to the Circle—"

The chevard held up his hand in a gesture that silenced Gavril in mid-sentence.

Amazed at his power, Dain stared up at the man sitting so straight in his saddle. Lord Odfrey was in his middle years, with no gray showing yet in his straight brown hair, but plenty of it in his thick mustache. The rest of his face was clean-shaven, with a hint of bristle to be seen on his lean jaws this late in the afternoon. His nose was long and straight, except for a slight bump where it seemed to have once been broken. His mouth was uncompromising. He wore no mail, and his long doublet and leggings were dark green wool, the cloth woven tight and hard. His boots reached to his knees, and were made of good leather, much scuffed and worn. His mud-splattered spurs were plain brass. Only the crest embroidered on the left breast of his striped fur cloak proclaimed his rank. Even his rings were not fancy; just a plain signet and a dull cabochon set in gold that was his marriage ring. His horse, heavy-boned and strong, stood in the cold water patiently, unlike Gavril's flashy mount, which shied and pawed and pranced constantly.

Lord Odfrey turned his frowning gaze on Dain and studied him for a long moment. Beneath the fierce, unsmiling facade of this man, Dain sensed kindness and a true heart. Some flicker of mercy or compassion lit in the depths of the man's eyes. It surprised Dain, but he immediately tried to take advantage of it.

"I have offended the prince," he said, although no one had given him leave to speak. "But not enough to be killed for it."

"Silence!" Gavril shouted before he glanced back at Lord Odfrey. "Take care, my lord chevard," he warned nervously. "Do not let his gaze enspell you."

Lord Odfrey frowned.

"He is clearly pagan," Gavril said. "Look at his eyes, how colorless and strange they are. Look at his pale blood. He is a monster. He deserves no fairness—"

"The lad is eldin," Odfrey said impatiently. "Or partly so, perhaps, if his black hair is anything to go by. That hardly makes him a monster. As for fairness, honor is not a quality to be shed or worn depending on the circumstances. If this wretch stole from you and you had your servants catch him and beat him for it, that would be justice."

"He did steal!" Gavril said hotly. "My horse, he would have taken—"

"Your horse?" Lord Odfrey echoed in quiet amazement. "It's war-trained, or so you have boasted."

Again Gavril's cheeks turned pink. "It is," he said, clearly taking offense. "Trained by my father's own—"

"Then this lad could not steal it," Odfrey said. "Impossible."

"But—"

"Did he steal anything else?"

"He meant to! My saddle and accouterments. My coat of arms on the saddlecloth is embroidered of real gold. He—"

"Yet he actually took none of these things?"

"Intent is the same as action," Gavril said in a sullen voice. "Even worse, he insulted the Circle and would not—"

"If you coursed him for sport, let your hounds bay for his blood, and whipped him to a bloody pulp because he did not recognize your Circle, it would seem you ask too much of this young pagan."

"He's a thief!" Gavril said furiously. "When I sought to punish him, he defied me. Worse, he insulted me, calling me a liar, and then he tried to harm my person."

Dain glared at Gavril, who was twisting the truth to support his charge. He was a vicious, deceitful worm. Dain despised him for his lies even more than for his cruelty.

Lord Odfrey's stony expression did not change. Solemn and unruffled, he showed little emotion.

"He tried to kill me," Gavril repeated. "You have my word for it, and I am the king's—"

"—son. Yes, I know, your highness. You have reminded everyone in my hold of that fact at least twice a day since you arrived."

"Then you might trouble to remember the fact, instead of mocking and insulting me," Gavril said haughtily.

"Cool your wrath, boy. It's most unseemly in one of your station."

Gavril stared at him, openmouthed and sputtering.

Lord Odfrey met his look of wild astonishment and dawning rage with a grim lack of deference. "If you expect me to believe a tale such as this, you are much mistaken. You sit on a war-trained horse, armed with dagger, whip, and javelins. Do you really expect me to believe an unarmed, half-starved, wounded, and frozen wretch like this eld boy could bring the slightest harm to your royal person? I think not."

Gavril's blue eyes grew very dark and still. "Do you also call me a liar, my lord?"

"I call you a spoiled lowland brat," Odfrey replied. "You flight around my lands with courtier airs and too much conceit in yourself. The king sent you to me for training, and by the blood of Tomias I do not see that task as one of providing you with more flattery and spoiling. You've been here a month, and by now you should know my rules. Did I not expressly forbid you and the others to enter the Nold forest? There is a war in that land, a war that is no concern of ours except in avoiding its dangers. Your safety cannot be guaranteed in such a place."

"I will hunt where I please," Gavril replied. "We were coursing a stag. Would you have us let it go free because of a mere boundary?"

"A stag," Lord Odfrey said. His dark eyes narrowed. "What became of it?"

"We brought it down," Gavril boasted. "Kaltienne took the first shot with his bow and wounded it. My dogs are superb coursers, and we caught up with it as soon as it fell. My arrow finished it. We wear its blood, as you can see."

"Who is packing out the meat?"

Gavril blinked as though puzzled. "The meat is of no importance."

It was Lord Odfrey's turn to redden. His mouth opened, but although a small muscle leaped in his jaw he did not speak. After a moment he snapped his jaws shut and wheeled his horse around so fast he nearly knocked Dain over.

"Huntsman!" he shouted with enough volume that his voice echoed across the marsh. "Take those men and go back for the meat."

"But, m'lord, it's to be dark soon," the man protested.

"You know I will not abide waste," Odfrey said.

"But the dark, m'lord. In Nold, m'lord."

Lord Odfrey growled to himself. "Sir Alard," he said to one of the knights. "Did you leave the arrows in the beast?"

The man had been slouching in his saddle when Lord Odfrey spoke to him, then quickly sat erect. "I'm sorry, m'lord," he said slowly. "In the race after—I didn't think of it—it seemed less important than—"

"Mandrian arrows left bold as day in a carcass not even skinned and butchered. What insult will be taken? What clan owns the land where you brought down the stag?"

All of them, Gavril especially, looked blank. Dain comprehended the reason for Lord Odfrey's disquiet. It was an insult to trespass when hunting game, and a bigger insult to hunt game for sport, not food. It spoke of an arrogant disregard for ownership of land and property. If any dwarf found the stag on land claimed by a clan, great offense would be taken. Dwarves could and did start wars with far less provocation. Would they attack a Mandrian hold for such a reason? Unlikely, especially with the war against the Bnen now raging. But Lord Odfrey understood dwarf ways, and that was unusual for a Mandrian noble. Dain's respect for the man went up a notch.

"Were there clan markings that anyone noticed?" Odfrey asked.

Again, no one answered.

In a quiet voice, Dain said, "Yes, the Clan Nega."

Lord Odfrey whipped around so fast Dain was startled. His dark eyes bored into Dain, piercing hard. "Nega? Not Rieg?"

"Rieg lands are here, near the edge of the forest," Dain replied. "The marsh is your land, yes?"

But Lord Odfrey wasn't listening. "Nega," he repeated. His face grew thunderous and he glared so furiously at Gavril that the prince looked momentarily alarmed, then more defiant and arrogant than ever. "You went that deep into the Dark Forest? Against my orders?"

Gavril pulled on his gauntlets of fine blue velvet stitched to leather palms. He shrugged. "When I hunt, I do not let my quarry go. Willingly."

"There has been fighting reported on Nega lands," Lord Odfrey said, ignoring Gavril's last remark. "You take too many foolish risks. There will be no more of it. What if this eld had gone deeper into the Dark Forest? Would you have coursed him to its very center?"

"If necessary," Gavril answered coolly. His eyes met Lord Odfrey's. "I do not fear the dwarves. Besides, we knew he would try to go east, and we kept him from it. I am not the fool you think me, my lord chevard."

"Then obey the orders you are given."

"It is your responsibility to keep me safe," Gavril said. "I shall do as I please. Your orders offend me."

"Learn to be offended," Lord Odfrey snapped. "There will be no more adventures in the Dark Forest. There will be no hunting of people on my land. If my huntsman has not told you this before, you know it now."

"Is this wretch your serf?" Gavril said icily, pointing at Dain with his whip. "We jumped him in the forest, beyond your boundaries, sir. If he is a monster of Nold, then he belongs to no one and should be fair game."

"He's not an animal. He is not to be hunted," Odfrey said.

"He's a thief and a nuisance. If the villagers see an eld lurking about their fields, they'll be—"

"The villagers and their superstitions are my responsibility, not yours," the chevard said with a snap. "The day's hunt is over for you. Call in your dogs and take yourself back to the hold."

Gavril stared at him as though he could not believe what had been said. "You dismiss me?" he said, and his voice was almost a squeak. "The hunt is for my pleasure. You cannot—"

"I can and I will," Odfrey broke in. "My word is law here. Take care you remember that."

"I never forget any slight done me," Gavril said, and his blue eyes were hot with resentment. He cast Dain a glare as though to blame him for this disgrace. "You," he said in a voice that cut. "If I ever see you on Chevard Odfrey's lands, I shall feed you to my dogs."

"If you set your dogs on another person, I will have them killed," Odfrey said. The iron in his voice held heat now. His dark eyes burned in his weathered face.

"You would not dare," Gavril said, then faltered. His gaze shifted to his clenched hands. "They are my property. Am I to blame if they prefer to take pagan scent? One animal is very like another."

"That is the worst sign of your character yet shown to me."

Gavril blinked. "When I came to Thirst Hold, you admired my dogs. No one in this region owns their equal. Their bloodlines are the best in—"

"There are many handsome things in this world," the chevard said, "but not all of them are good. I have said what I will do if you misuse your animals again in this fashion. You have lived under my roof long enough by now, Prince Gavril, to know that I keep my word. Do not force me to order them destroyed."

Gavril sat his horse as though he'd been clouted hard but

had not yet fallen. His gaze never left the chevard's face, but Dain watched his hands clench and unclench the reins.

"Well?" Odfrey asked. "Am I clearly understood?"

Gavril drew a sharp breath. Dain expected him to insult the chevard and gallop away, for that intent burned bright in Gavril's mind. But Gavril said, "Your words are most clear to me, sir."

"Good."

"I hope, sir, that you will not find displeasure when I write to my father the king and tell him of this day's events."

The chevard did not flinch. "I have never feared the truth, or King Verence's sense of justice. He is always interested in hearing both sides of a matter. By all means write to him, but take care that you present the full truth. I am sure he will find your actions, and your motivations for them, greatly enlightening. Your letter can go in my next dispatch pouch."

Gavril's gaze dropped. He wheeled his horse about and kicked it into a gallop. As he rode away, he splashed water over Dain, who was too cold to care.

Grateful to be free of the prince, Dain edged away a couple of steps, but the chevard's gaze swung to him and he stopped.

Now that it was just the two of them alone, some deep sadness appeared in Lord Odfrey's face. "You are just his size," he muttered as though to himself. "That same way of standing. That same fearless turn of the head. What is your name, lad?"

"Dain."

"You are far from the mountains of the eld folk."

"I come from Nold. I am—was apprenticed to Jorb the swordmaker."

The chevard smiled, and his face transformed from a stern, stony countenance into one gentle and warm. The deep lines that bracketed his mouth were smoothed away. Crinkles fanned at the corners of his eyes. He looked younger when he smiled, far less formidable. "Jorb, the old rascal. I carry one of his swords," he said, indicating the weapon that hung from his belt.

"Yes, lord," Dain said awkwardly. "I saw."

Odfrey's smile faded. "But you say you *were* his apprentice. Not now? Has the trouble reached him too?"

Dain's throat closed in sudden grief. He thought of how he'd returned from his errand three days, no, four past, and found the tree burrow ablaze. The forge was already gone, charred to ashes. Jorb's body was a blackened, twisted thing, hacked and broken by the axe that had felled him, so broken he couldn't crawl away from the fire that had burned him alive along with his home.

Jorb had always been a force in Dain's life, a short, surly, gruff-voiced taskmaster who liked his pipe in the evenings and who would sit watching the stars contentedly, humming along in his basso voice while Thia sang and Dain played accompaniment on a lute. Jorb liked his ale and his food; he was nearly as wide as he was tall. He was hot-tempered and impatient, yet he took infinite pains with the swords he crafted, turning each blade into a thing of rare beauty. And when the steady *tap-tap-tap* of his hammering was done, he would hone and polish, humming to the steel as though to bring it to life. His craggy face would light up and he would smile as he spoke the final words over each creation: "*Kreith 'ng kdag 'vn halh.*"—"This sword is made."

He had taught Dain metals. He had taught Dain his skills but never his artistry. Some days as they worked together in the hot forge, Jorb would sweat and hum without uttering a single word. Other days he would talk endlessly on a variety of subjects, giving Dain the teaching, as he called it. He was father, teacher, taskmaster, friend. Behind the gruffness and stern air of authority he was kind and good, with a fondness for riddles and a love of song.

And now he was dead, dead because of Dain. There was no getting past the guilt or the grief. Each time Dain pushed it out of his mind, the memories came flooding back. He could smell the sickening stench of burned flesh, the smoky stink of charred cloth. He could feel Jorb's sturdy shoulder cupped in his hand, how stiff and wrong it felt. He had dug a grave and spoken the words of passing in the dwarf tongue. He had sprinkled salt over the freshly turned soil and crossed the ash twigs there, but his rites were not enough to cleanse what he'd done or to absolve him of blame.

He frowned, swallowing hard, and found his voice gone. He could not answer Lord Odfrey's simple question. All he could do was glance up, his eyes suddenly brimming with tears, and nod his head.

Regret softened the chevard's face. Looking down at Dain from atop his horse, he said softly, "Dead?"

Again Dain nodded. A sob heaved in his chest, but he would not utter it. His grief was not to be shared with men. It was a private thing. His shame, he would battle alone.

But not just yet.

Mastering himself, he swallowed and struggled to speak. "Please, lord," he said in a choked voice. "I thank you for saving me. Would you also show mercy and save my sister as well?"

"What?"

"My sister. She's hurt. We've come as far away as she can. When the Bnen attacked, they put an arrow in her that I cannot—"

"Where is she?"

Hope filled Dain's chest. He pointed at the forest. "A league away, no more. Not far from where the stag went down. I can show you the spot, lead your men back to it, if you will—"

Odfrey's gaze grew hard and intent. "What know you of the Bnen? How large are their forces?"

"I didn't see them—"

"But there's been talk, surely, in the settlements, and in your friend's burrow. You know Jorb, so you must know members of his family. When did the Bnen attack him? How long ago? Are they moving this way?"

Dain could not answer his rapid-fire questions. His legs felt so numbed by the water he could no longer feel them. Perhaps that was a mercy, for they had stopped aching with fatigue, but he did not feel steady. In fact, as he took a cautious step forward, he thought his knees might buckle beneath him. His arm, wounded by the arrow Gavril had shot at him earlier and now cut by the whip, throbbed with a pain that hurt all the way up to the backs of his eyes. In truth, he hurt all over. And Thia was a league away, hidden in the forest, hurt and in dire need of help. He did not think she would live much longer if the arrow was not taken out. He had tried last night, and only hurt her more. This man was kind. If Dain could only find a way to reach that kindness on Thia's behalf, he knew he could save her.

He reached out and gripped the man's stirrup with his cold hands. "Please help her, for you are a kind and just lord. I only tried to take the prince's horse to get Thia food and help. She needs—"

With a grunt, Lord Odfrey reached around and untied the

cords securing a leather pouch to the back of his saddle. He tossed it at Dain, who caught it clumsily.

"There's food enough to get you home," Lord Odfrey said. "A wedge of cheese and some bread. Now be off with you, lad. No harm will come to you on my land."

"But my sister—"

"There's food enough for her," Lord Odfrey said, already wheeling his big horse around. "Get out of this cold water before you freeze to death. I've a prince to escort and my hold to secure in case the Bnen keep coming west."

Dain stared at him in dismay, knowing he had to do or say something that would change the chevard's mind.

"Please!" he called, splashing clumsily. "May I go with your huntsman? If I bring her to your hold, will your healer give her aid?"

Lord Odfrey barely glanced back. "The huntsman will not be going into the Dark Forest this night. Not with Bnen as near as Jorb's forge. Now get out of the water and build yourself a fire to thaw. You'll freeze if you don't."

Dain opened his mouth to call out again, but Lord Odfrey spurred his horse and rode away, splashing water behind him as he went.

9

IT WAS DARK by the time Dain reached the little burrow where Thia lay hidden. His legs felt leaden, and he was breathing hard. He'd taken no time to build a fire. Running and trotting to keep warm, he'd hoped his clothes would dry on the way. But it was too cold, and they were still damp. The air felt as piercing as needles. When he reached the tiny clearing, he stumbled to a halt at its edge, exhausted but still cautious. Clutching the food pouch in his arms, he ignored the hollow rumbling in his stomach and focused his attention on the clearing.

The forest lay silent and still around him—too still. Dwarf scent came to his nostrils, and he felt the hair on his neck lift. Friendly or hostile, he knew not, but they had been in this clearing within the last hour or so.

He drew in an unsteady breath and reached out with his mind: *Thia?*

Her pain flooded him. Gasping, he broke contact with her, then leaned his shoulder against a tree trunk and drew in several deep, shuddering breaths. He could tell she was worse, much worse. Grief and worry filled him.

He had to do something to save her. She was all he had left. He could not bear to lose her too.

He crossed the clearing, finding it heavily trampled and littered with blackened fire stones and small heaps of still-warm ashes where the dwarves had camped. It was a mercy of the gods that they had not decided to bed here for the night.

On the opposite side of the clearing lay an immense log as thick as Dain was tall. Rotting and half-covered with the vines and brush that had grown up around it, the log must have fallen years ago. Fallen leaves drifted deep against it. Dain dug with both hands, scooping dirt aside until he cleared away the shallow layer of soil that covered a lattice of woven twigs. It was perhaps the size of a fighting shield. Pulling it out of the way, he thrust his head and shoulders into the shallow hole it had covered, and inhaled the damp scent of soil and worms.

"Thia?" he whispered. "I'm coming. Don't be afraid."

He wriggled through the tunnel, his shoulders scraping the sides and the top of his head bumping from time to time. It was barely large enough for him. If he grew as much this year as he had last year, he would no longer fit. Little trickles of the loamy soil fell into his hair and ears, working down his neck and beneath his tunic of coarse-woven linsey.

The tunnel angled up. Dain popped his head up into the hollowed-out center of the huge log. He found Thia lying where he'd left her, wrapped in a threadbare blanket, with leaves packed around her for additional warmth.

It was warm and quiet in here. An array of glowstones resting on small niches chiseled into the wooden walls cast a soft, dim, lambent light. The burrow was snug and dry, though cramped for the two of them. It belonged to the Forlo Clan, to be used by travelers on their road to trade with upper Mandria.

Spell-locked so that only members of Forlo could see its rune markings outside, the burrow was fitted with the glowstones, the musty old blanket, and a mug and a plate Dain had found spun over by spiders when they'd first sheltered here last night. They could build no fire inside the burrow, of course. It was warm enough this autumn night, provided someone wasn't afflicted with fever or shivering in wet clothes.

Lying still, Thia gave him no greeting. He frowned at her before looking to see if leaves were sprouting or sap had beaded up along the wooden walls. Thia's presence, he knew, should be bringing this great log back to life, but he saw no signs of it. He knelt beside her, breathing in her scent, which was mixed with the wood, leaf, and worm odors of the burrow. He smelled life in her, and relief gripped his heart so hard he squeaked out her name.

"Thia!" he said, gripping her hand. It was clammy and cold. "I'm home," he told her, stroking her long, tangled hair back from her brow. "I'm here with you."

She moaned, stirring beneath his touch as though even the gentle sweep of his fingers across her brow hurt her.

"I'm back," he said again. "And look, look at what I have brought. Food for us. Good food. Look."

He dug into the pouch Lord Odfrey had given him, pulling out a generous chunk of cheese, fresh and soft, along with bread made of fine, pale flour and apples newly picked. The food's mingled aromas made his mouth water, and his stomach growled louder than ever.

"Thia, open your eyes and see the wealth of our supper," he said in excitement. "This will give you strength. Wake up, dear one, and see our bounty."

She moaned again, turning her head away.

Dain tossed the food aside and pulled her into his arms, rocking her against him while she lay limp and unresponsive. Her long hair, usually constantly moving as though stirred by a mysterious wind, fell lank and snarled across his lap.

Pain filled his chest, a pain so deep and sharp he thought he could not breathe. Tears spilled down his cheeks as he pressed his lips to her temple.

"Live, dear sister," he pleaded with her. "Please, *please* live."

Once again she stirred. "Jorb?" she asked in confusion.

"He is not here," Dain said, tears streaking his face. He did not want her to think about the brutal attack. She had suffered enough. "Jorb is not here. Open your eyes, and try to eat. You must regain your strength."

She said something so soft he could not understand it. Cradling her against his knees, he broke off a small bite of the cheese and put it against her slack lips.

"Try, Thia," he said, his voice shaking now even though he was trying not to sound afraid. "Please, try."

She lifted her head, tipping it back against his shoulder so that she could gaze up into his face. She smiled, yet her face looked so ghostly and wan in that dim, glowing light she seemed to already have entered the third world, where spirits dwelled.

"Dain," she said, her voice a light, insubstantial sigh. She tried to lift her hand to touch his face, but lacked the strength.

He gripped her fingers, willing his strength into her. Sobs shook his frame, and he bowed his head, unashamed of his tears. He had tried so hard to save her. The alternative was impossible, inconceivable, unbearable.

"Dain," she said again. "I cannot go on."

"Don't say that! Don't give up. We're very close to a hold. We can seek help there. They are kind, these men of Mandria. I met one today who gave me the food. He will—"

"I am dying," she interrupted him.

"No!"

"Dying," she said. "Little brother, don't weep so."

But he could no longer listen. Shaking with grief, he bent over her, holding her tightly in his arms, and gritted his teeth to hold in his cries of anguish. She was all he had. She had been sister and mother to him, his dearest companion. Thia was beautiful, a maiden of slender form and infinite grace. Her blonde hair fell in luxuriant waves to her knees, and in the springtime she liked to wear it unbound with a wreath of flowers upon her brow. Her eyes were pale sky-blue and wise, able to sparkle with teasing merriment or gaze steadily into the depths of someone's heart. When Dain was little, she would rock him to sleep at night, singing snatches of incomplete songs and fragments of rhymes that she said she remembered from the before times. Sometimes, she would spin tales of a fabulous palace that stretched in all directions, a palace as large as the world itself, and filled inside with all the colors of the rainbow. She would weave tales that fired his imagination. She'd defended him from bullies until he'd become big enough to handle himself. She'd taught him manners and honesty and to be gentle with all defenseless creatures. From her, he'd learned woodcraft, how to walk through the forest without disturbing the wild denizens, how to find the pure streams that coursed hidden in thicket-choked gullies, how to tell direction from bark moss and the stars, how to let the wind sing to him, and how to hear what the ancient trees themselves had to say.

He could not imagine a world without her in it. He could not think of a day when she would not be waiting in Jorb's burrow to welcome him and their guardian home, her hair smelling of herbs and her eyes as placid as still water. She had but to sing, and her garden seeds would sprout forth, growing vegetables bursting with intense flavor. She had but to smile and the sun brightened in the sky.

That she should now lie here in this burrow far from home, battered and bloody, her slender body racked with pain from the arrow that had brought her down, spoke of great wrong and injustice. It violated all that was true and good in the world. It was a crime that called for punishment and retribution.

"Thia," he said, moaning her name as he wept over her, "don't go. We'll find a way. You can hold on just a little longer until I carry you to Thirst Hold."

"A hold?" she whispered, and this time she found the strength to smooth back his dark hair from his brow. "A man-place? You would trust men, little brother? Has Jorb taught you nothing?"

"I would indenture myself for a lifetime if it would gain you the help of a healer," he replied.

She smiled, but her eyes filled with sadness. "My papa has been a long time coming. I tried to wait. He told me to be good and to wait for him, Dainie, but I'm so tired."

A sob filled Dain's throat. He clutched her. "Thia!"

"Find our papa," she whispered. "Go home and find him."

Dain frowned bitterly. "Why should I? He cast us out and abandoned us. Orphans, he made us. Jorb is the only father I have known, or would call so."

A tear slipped down her cheek. She opened her mouth to speak, but the sound never came.

Just like that, she was gone.

He didn't believe it at first. He couldn't.

"Thia?" he said, his voice carrying his shock and disbelief. "No!"

He called her name again and shook her hard, but silence was his only answer as she lay dead in his arms. He rocked her, moaning her name, and his tears soaked into her hair.

In Prince Gavril's modest suite of rooms in the west tower of Thirst Hold, a fire roared on the hearth, casting a bounty of warmth and light against the icy drafts. Outside the shuttered windows, the night wind sighed and moaned, but inside Gavril and his two companions sat around a small table, cups of cider in their hands, and plotted their raid on Lord Odfrey's cellars.

"We could wait till the household sleeps and sneak in," Kaltienne suggested. A thin, wiry boy with straight black hair and the eyes of an imp, he grinned impudently and quaffed another cupful of cider. "Wait for lights-out and take ourselves into the cellar while the cook's off watch. He snores enough to conceal any noise we might make. If we each carry out a pair of kegs apiece, it should take us only about forty nights of work to—"

"Hush your chatter," Mierre said gruffly. "Fool's talk is not what his highness wants to hear."

"What other plan have you?" Kaltienne retorted. He laughed. "Oh, I see. Nocturnal raids would interfere with your own plans, eh, Mierre? You've caught the eye of that lusty housemaid Atheine, the one with the mole on her—"

"That's enough," Mierre growled.

Frowning, Gavril drew back from them and reached inside his fur-lined doublet to touch his Circle. Cardinal Noncire, his tutor back at Savroix, had warned him that his fellow fosters might already be well versed in the coarsest habits of carnality. Mierre, bigger than the rest of them, with his bullish shoulders and muscular neck, seemed afflicted with a steady lust that pursued any young female servant in the hold. Several ambitious wenches had offered their wares to Gavril, but he had been warned about that, too. He wasn't going to destroy his piety for a few minutes' release in the grimy arms of some turnip-scrubber.

"Be glad you aren't a Netheran and forced to stay celibate

until you're knighted," Kaltienne said with a sly grin. "I saw you with Atheine behind the barn yesterday morning. Those white legs of hers are longer than—"

With a quick, apprehensive glance at Gavril, Mierre turned on Kaltienne and whacked him hard across the back. Whooping for breath, Kaltienne doubled over. His empty cup dropped from his fingers and rolled across the floor.

Gavril ignored him and glared impatiently at Mierre. The burly foster met his prince's gaze and turned a faint shade of pink.

"I beg your highness's forgiveness," he said. He was large, gruff, clumsy, and unpolished, but he was learning courtly ways fast. Gavril valued him for his strength, his growing loyalty, his ambitions, and his natural shrewdness. Mierre frowned at Kaltienne, who was still wheezing. "Kaltienne never knows when to hold his tongue."

"Pardon is given," Gavril said, but his tone was purposely curt to let them know he wanted no more nonsense. "If we may return to the matter at hand?"

Mierre bent over the crudely drawn diagram of the oldest section of the hold. His sandy hair was thin and brittle, sticking out from beneath the edges of his dark green cap, which he wore tilted rakishly on one side of his head just like Gavril did. "I can try to steal a key, your highness, but there's always a guard posted at the—"

"That won't do," Gavril interrupted. Turning away in frustration, he flung up his hands. "What kind of miser keeps a guard posted on his own cellar? Morde a day, but the chevard is impossible."

By now Kaltienne had his breath back. He straightened with a wince, keeping a wary distance from Mierre. "Damne, Mierre, that hurt like the devil."

"You'll get worse if you don't behave."

Kaltienne snorted. "Behave? Thod's teeth, but you're the one who can't behave. When you—"

Mierre raised his beefy hand in menace, and Kaltienne scooted back his stool. He shut his mouth, but deviltry still danced in his eyes.

Sighing, Mierre returned his attention to Gavril, who had begun to seethe. "Forgive me, your highness. He's forever a fool and a knave."

"No," Gavril said, his tone cutting and contemptuous. "Kaltienne is a child. I shouldn't have included him in this—"

"Your highness!" Kaltienne said loudly, horrified. He jumped off his stool to kneel before Gavril. "Forgive me. I was only jesting. I will do whatever you ask—"

Gavril pointed at him and said sternly, "Hold your tongue."

Kaltienne's face turned pale. He reached out as though to take Gavril's hand in his, but Gavril drew back.

"Say no more," he commanded. "Listen and perhaps I will relent."

Gulping audibly, Kaltienne bowed his head and remained kneeling.

Gavril frowned at him with impatience. He was running out of time, and these boys were not providing the quality of help he wanted. "Get on your feet," he said angrily.

Kaltienne jumped up at once. He opened his mouth, met Gavril's angry eyes, and closed his mouth again with a sigh.

"I don't suppose your highness could just ask Lord Odfrey to return your wine?" Mierre asked quietly.

Gavril gritted his teeth. "I did. Lord Odfrey refused me."

That had been a week ago, and his voice still reverberated with his shock and furious disappointment. No one ever refused *him,* the only son of the king. No one ever denied him what he wished or asked for. Except for Lord Odfrey. At every turn the chevard thwarted him. It was maddening. Worst of all, Lord Odfrey had been given this authority by the king's own warrant. Thus far, one month had passed of Gavril's required year of fostering. Already it seemed an eternity. Thanks to the chevard's obstinance, Gavril had made no progress on his secret quest to find the lost Chalice.

Frowning, Gavril held out his jeweled cup in silence, and his lone manservant hurried forward to fill it. The cider was a thin, brown brew pressed from the Thirst orchards. Gavril considered it a peasant's drink, but Lord Odfrey was as miserly a man as Gavril had ever encountered, worse even than the clerks in the royal countinghouse. The chevard served naught but water or cider at his table, except on feast-days and the king's birthday. Nor would he permit Gavril to drink from the costly and elegant wines, or Klad beer, with its kick to the stomach, or the honeyed mead from the Isles of Saelutia that he had brought with him in a wagon made specially for the purpose. That wagon was now lodged in the chevard's barn, and its sublime contents were all under lock and key inside the chevard's own cellar.

Robbery it was, nothing less. Every time Gavril swallowed the sour, thin cider he felt as though his throat had been scalded by his present guardian's thievery and discourtesy. Gavril had been drinking wine since he was seven. It was his custom in his father's palace to drink rounds with the guardsmen once a month on lastday. Among the men he had the reputation for having a hard head and a hollow leg. Therefore, he felt insulted by Lord Odfrey's assumption that he could not command his cup or that he would hold drunken revels with the other fostered boys in his rooms at night.

Even more important than Gavril's own luxury, however, were the kegs of fine mead that he'd intended to use as bribes. How else was he to win over the secret support of Lord Odfrey's knights? How else could he suborn the loyalty of the steward of Thirst Hold? Or persuade the cook to prepare meals of suitable quality for him alone? Saelutian mead was an elixir of such sweetness and flavor that a single goblet of it could make a grown man reel. Rare and costly, it was powerfully addictive and after a few sips one's palate craved it with an ever-growing fierceness. Using it instead of coin was a subtle ploy that appealed to Gavril. He aspired to statecraft of great subtlety. Cardinal Noncire had taught him that intrigue should always be as soft and quiet as a whisper, forever patient, forever relentless, alarming no one yet accomplishing much.

And Gavril had much to accomplish.

"Your highness," Mierre said, "I could ask the servants whether there is another way down into the lower regions besides the stair that's guarded. I think I could persuade someone to help us."

Gavril swung around, feeling somewhat appeased. At least Mierre was trying to help. "You must not give away our intentions with too many questions."

"I would not," Mierre said.

Kaltienne raised his hand, fairly dancing about with his eagerness to speak.

With a sigh Gavril nodded to him. "Yes?" he commanded.

"There's a privy channel going down the back of the hold

into an underground cistern," Kaltienne said. "There has to be a way to get in through the clean-out door—"

Gavril wrinkled his nose in horror.

Mierre grunted. "You can try it."

Kaltienne's eyes widened. "Not me!"

"Who of us do you expect to do it?" Gavril asked.

Kaltienne clearly had not thought through his suggestion. He grimaced and tugged at his tunic, which was wrinkled and stained with remnants of his dinner. He did not answer, and Gavril wished he had never asked Kaltienne to join this discussion. The boy was a fool, useless in planning anything.

He was, however, fearless and willing to try whatever was suggested to him.

"You," Gavril said to him now, "will steal a key to the cellars. I am sure you can do it."

Kaltienne brightened. "Sure," he said with breezy confidence. "All I have to do is go to the kitchens to see what food I can pick up, and I'll get it then."

"Will you!" Mierre said in loud exasperation. "The cellar key is held by the wine steward. Can you get your hands on his ring of keys? I think not."

"I'll find a way," Kaltienne said stubbornly, flicking a glance at Gavril, who was watching them with a grim smile. "His highness wants me to do this, and I *can*."

Mierre growled. "He'll botch it, your highness."

"And you could do better?" Kaltienne said, his voice tight and angry. The tips of his ears had turned red, and fierce determination shone in his eyes.

Gavril smiled to himself and knew he'd succeeded in gaining Kaltienne's loyalty. Cardinal Noncire said that once you persuaded a man to commit a risky act for you, that man was bound to your side forever. If he attempted to draw back, you could always bring his crime before others.

"I could do better," Mierre said, as stubborn as a bull. He lowered his head and glared at Kaltienne. "I'll ask Atheine to get the keys for us. Better yet, I'll see if she can't distract the guard so that we can slip past. Is that not the better plan, your highness?"

Gavril felt his ears grow hot. He swung his gaze away, refusing to let anyone see his embarrassment. He had been sheltered until now, raised in his father's palace, kept from the roughness of other boys, tutored by an official of the church. He was not opposed to carnality, although the Writ cautioned against impropriety and unnaturalness. In fact, Gavril had carefully laid plans to indulge himself with a woman as soon as he finished his quest. But until he found the Chalice of Eternal Life later this year, he intended to remain chaste.

He swallowed hard, banishing certain images from his mind, and mastered his composure sufficiently to face the other boys again.

Kaltienne was smirking, making lewd faces at Mierre and licking his lips.

Mierre's face held caution. The larger boy was learning to watch Gavril, to gauge his moods, and to please him accordingly. He had boasted of his sexual exploits during their first week here, but after Gavril's scathing denunciation, he boasted no longer.

The silence seemed to unnerve him. Hunching his big shoulders, he ducked his head. "If my plan displeases your highness, I—"

Gavril lifted his hand. "Can this servant girl be trusted?"

"She need not know anything except what I wish for her to do," Mierre said arrogantly. "A gift will make her willing."

Gavril crossed the room and unchained his strongbox. Shielding its contents from the others, he lifted the lid and picked out a pair of coins. Carefully rechaining the box, he walked back to Mierre and held out one of the coins, a large silver dreit.

"Is this a suitable gift for your wench?" he asked.

Mierre's eyes went round and wide. He stared at the coin as though he'd never seen one before. "Damne," he said softly. "It's a fortune."

Gavril put the dreit in the larger boy's hand, pressing it hard against Mierre's sweaty palm. "Give her that." He held up the second coin, another silver dreit. "This, she may have when her work is accomplished."

Mierre's mouth was hanging open now. He gaped like the illiterate, ill-bred, minor nobleman's son that he was. Slowly he took the second coin from Gavril's hand. "It's too much," he said hoarsely. "It will frighten her."

"Will it?" Gavril asked scornfully. "I think not. If she's as lusty a drab as you say—"

"She's no drab!" Mierre said hotly.

Gavril raised his brows, and Mierre seemed to realize he'd just yelled at his prince.

Looking shocked, Mierre bowed at once. "Forgive me, your highness. I—I spoke without thinking."

"This isn't a simple kiss. She is to lure the man completely away from his post. If she can do that, especially to one of Lord Odfrey's knights, she will have earned her money well." Gavril cocked his head to one side and stared very hard at Mierre. "You will not let jealousy interfere, will you?"

"No, your highness!" he said too rapidly. "No. She is only a housemaid, after all."

"Exactly."

"Well, well," Kaltienne said, giving them each a wink. "And maybe you will persude her to look twice in my direction too when she is—"

"Shut up!" Mierre shouted.

A knock on the door interrupted them. Gavril frowned and gestured for silence.

His manservant Aoun went to the door, while Gavril's protector, Sir Los, rose quietly to his feet and stood with his hand on his sword hilt.

Aoun murmured with someone on the other side of the door, then glanced over his shoulder.

"Well?" Gavril demanded impatiently. "Is it that page I asked to keep me informed of all messengers who come? Has a dispatch arrived?"

Aoun bowed low and stepped out of the way.

"No," said a tall, lean figure garbed in a tunic of mallard blue. Thum du Maltie entered and swept off his cap with a bow. "Your highness, I have been sent to escort you to Lord Odfrey."

Astonished and far from pleased, Gavril frowned. "Now?"

"Yes, now."

"But I am occupied," Gavril said, gesturing at Mierre and Kaltienne. "With my friends."

He kept his tone quiet and pleasant, but the insult he delivered to Thum was unmistakable. Mierre puffed out his brawny chest. Kaltienne grinned.

Thum's freckled face turned bright red. He was well mannered, educated, quick of wit and understanding, but obstinate, unwilling to commit his loyalty, and too ready to question the worth of Gavril's orders or intentions. Which was exactly why he had not been included in tonight's scheming. If he learned about the intended raid, he would feel it his duty to inform Lord Odfrey. Already, he'd proven himself a tongue-tattle this afternoon by telling Lord Odfrey where to find Gavril in the marsh.

And Gavril never forgot a slight.

"Your highness is to come at once, if it is convenient," Thum said to Gavril.

"It is not," Gavril said.

"Then I am to wait until your highness is free," Thum said.

Annoyed by this interruption, Gavril frowned. He could play the game and dawdle here in his quarters until the evening came to a close. But Lord Odfrey had a disconcerting habit of seeing through such ploys and dealing with them unpleasantly. There might be extra chores assigned to Gavril tomorrow, or extra drills, or some other unpleasantness done to him under the guise of training.

"Very well," Gavril said to Thum. He pointed at the opposite end of the room. "Wait over there."

Thum bowed and walked silently to the place indicated. He stood next to Gavril's writing table of exquisite inlaid wood and appeared to ignore its litter of reading scrolls, a sloppy pile of perhaps five or six leather-bound volumes that individually reflected enormous wealth, an ink pot of chased silver, fine sheets of writing parchment, a hunk of sealing wax, and Gavril's seal.

Gavril glanced at Mierre and Kaltienne. "Do nothing yet," he said in a low voice, picking up the diagram and folding it in half. "We will talk again tomorrow. You may go now."

They bowed, Mierre looking thoughtful and Kaltienne grinning wickedly. Out they went, and Gavril walked into his bedchamber to idle several moments before the looking glass—a costly possession indeed, and perhaps the largest object of its kind in the entire hold. He straightened his doublet, made sure his linen undersleeves were still white and clean, and tilted his cap even more rakishly over his brow. He buckled on a slim, bejeweled poniard that glittered in the soft-burning lamplight, glanced at his prayer-cabinet in the corner, and decided he would not pray before answering this summons.

His anger was a coal that burned steadily inside his breast. The altercation between him and Lord Odfrey this afternoon could not be forgiven. If the chevard was summoning him to offer an apology, Gavril did not know if he would accept it. He had never disliked a man more than Lord Odfrey, never. He found the chevard stern, unyielding, disrespectful, and unfit to run a hold of this strategic importance. The chevard possessed a high reputation as a lordly knight and warrior. Men across all Mandria respected his battle skills. But Gavril valued subservience more, and Lord Odfrey showed him none.

Cardinal Noncire had cautioned Gavril before he chose Thirst that he would dislike this upland hold. However, the king encouraged Gavril to accept the positioning, wanting him to receive his final training at the hands of a warrior like Lord Odfrey. And besides, Thirst was the closest hold to the Dark Forest, the strongest, most heavily manned citadel guarding the northeast corner of Mandria.

Every day, a small detail of knights stationed themselves at the bridge gate. Any travelers wanting to cross the river and continue east into the Dark Forest had to identify themselves and their business. Any travelers venturing forth from Nold into Mandria had to do the same, plus have all their goods searched and accounted for.

Prior to coming here, Gavril had listened to tales of danger, battles to repress raiders, commerce, adventure, good hunting, and how Thirst stood as a beacon of light and truth against the pagan darkness of Nold and other lands. Gavril had imagined a hold full of traditions and honor, always active, always at the center of intrigue and tremendous adventures. Gavril was determined to use Thirst as his base while he searched for the Chalice. It had been missing for many years, and during that time its legend had only grown.

Nether had once been Mandria's most powerful ally, but now under the rule of King Muncel, Nether was only a shadow land, its fortunes dwindling every year. Gavril believed that the Chalice had been stolen from Nether and concealed for a purpose ordained by Thod. Clearly the Chalice was destined to cast its blessings on another realm. He was determined to find it for Mandria. All his life, Gavril had believed himself destined to do something special, to live a life renowned among kings and men. When someday he succeeded to his father's throne, Gavril believed, possessing the Chalice would make his rule both prosperous and powerful. He would wage war on Nether first, crushing the darkness there. He would annex Klad, driving forth its barbarian peoples, and take its valuable pasturelands for his own realm. Someday, he would be a great king, and his name would resound across the land.

But for now, he was only a young prince, his ranks and titles courtesies, his knight's spurs as yet unearned. He chafed at being in this awkward place, neither a child nor yet considered a man.

He had come to Thirst shining with expectations, eager to begin the destiny promised him in the horoscope castings of the court's astrologer. Gavril had brought his servants, his guards, his books, his dogs, his wines, his velvet hangings, his desk, footstools, weapons, horses, falcons, and prayer-cabinet. He had come expecting to live in the unofficial capital of upper Mandria, centered within its intrigue and activity.

Instead, Thirst was an ancient, crumbling, ill-maintained hold on the edge of a bleak marsh in the midst of nowhere. The villages nearby were tiny enclaves of unbearable squalor and poverty. The serfs acted sullen and disrespectful. Many still held old and forbidden memories of when upper Mandria was another realm, called Edonia, with its own king and armies. The land around Thirst Hold was almost flat, cleared for fields, and fitted with ugly levees and channels to drain marsh flooding in spring and autumn. Hunting was poor, except in the forest. The climate was dismal, cold and damp, and winter had not even set in yet. It was only a few days short of Aelintide, the great feast-day of autumn harvest, with a month beyond that to Selwinmas and what the uplanders called the long cold.

Gavril found Lord Odfrey to be the kind of bleak, humorless drudge he most despised, all duty and work, with no understanding of fashion, fun, or the amenities of a civilized life. The chevard locked up Gavril's wine, confiscated half his books, dismissed nearly all his servants, complained that his dogs ate too much and caused trouble in the kennels, refused to alter his chapel hours for Gavril's convenience, and expected Gavril to run, fetch, and scurry with daily chores like the other bumpkins who had fostered here over the years. The chevard's master-at-arms, Sir Polquin, was a muscular brute lacking manners or respect. Rarely would he allow Gavril to practice the more sophisticated and modern swordplay he had been learning at home. Instead, every day brought the same old boring, outdated drills and practice.

Gavril's own private suite—if two meager rooms could be called a suite—was clearly a storeroom that had been cleared out for his use. Never mind that the other fosters shared a single chamber with only their cots and a chest each to hold their possessions. Born and raised in the great palace Savroix, considered the very heart of all Mandria, Gavril had spent his life surrounded by affluent, luxurious comfort. His personal apartments took up a whole wing of the palace; an army of efficient servants garbed in his personal livery anticipated his every wish. Thirst Hold—considered one of the largest and most affluent upland citadels—was in reality shockingly primitive. Even worse, there could be no quest for the Chalice if Lord Odfrey continued to deny Gavril his mead, plus two of his most valuable books, containing as they did much arcane lore about the Chalice, the Field of Skulls, and the channels of magic which ran through Nold. There could be no quest if Lord Odfrey would not let Gavril enter the Dark Forest. He tried to conceal his purpose by conducting hunts with his dogs and friends, but Lord Odfrey worried about everything, including this present war among the dwarves. Gavril did not fear the creatures. He was a prince of Mandria. He had no quarrel with the people of Nold, and he did not believe the dwarves would harm him.

Destiny had brought him here. If he did not take action soon, he would see his destiny slipping through his fingers, unseized through the blundering interference of Lord Odfrey.

Scowling at his likeness in the looking glass, Gavril brushed his golden hair behind his ears and left his bedchamber. Thum was still standing by his desk, speaking in a low, courteous voice to Sir Los.

Gavril's approach caused their conversation to break off. He snapped his gaze from one face to another, with an annoyance that felt sour in the pit of his stomach. "If you are reduced to page," he said tartly to Thum, "then by all means escort me to the chevard now."

10

GAVRIL AND THUM descended the curl of steps leading down inside the tower to the second floor, where a walkway spanned the distance between the west tower and the central buildings. The night air lay damp and cold on Gavril's shoulders. He wished he'd worn a cloak, but he would not go back for it now. If need be, he could always ask Sir Los—following a few steps behind him—to share his cloak.

Thum shivered as he strode along. His doublet was fashioned of thick welt, but it was not fur-lined as Gavril's clothing was. With his breath steaming from his mouth in the gloom, Thum said, "It's mortal cold out here tonight. Winter's on its way, Aelintide or no."

"Are you cold, Maltie?" Gavril asked in a voice as bored as he could make it. "I hadn't noticed. Look yon." He stopped in his tracks and leaned over the parapet, then tilted back his head to scan the dark sky overhead. "Is the cloud cover breaking? Do you see any stars, Maltie?"

Thum was obliged to halt beside him. With chattering teeth, he said, "Nay, your highness. No stars."

"Some glimmer of light from those windows across the keep must have tricked my eyes," Gavril said with a laugh. "Perhaps it will snow by dawn. Think you so?"

"Nay, your highness. It's mild yet in the season. We've some autumn before us yet."

Enjoying his game, Gavril smiled to himself in the darkness. Keeping Thum du Maltie out here in the cold air in his thin clothes was one way to punish him for this afternoon's defiance. He would find more.

"Explain to me the winters here," Gavril said. "We have but scant snowfall at Savroix, but many have told me upland winters are bitter indeed."

"Aye," Thum said, hugging himself. "Bitter enough."

"Then it will get colder than this?"

"Aye."

"Will the snows come often? Will we be trapped indoors?"

"At times."

Listening to Thum's teeth chatter, Gavril's smile widened. "I have heard there is much hunting that can be done even during the cruel grip of winter. Tell me what you know, Maltie."

Thum, his teeth chattering more than ever and his thin shoulders hunched now as he tucked his hands beneath his arms to keep them warm, responded politely, although his descriptions were terse. Gavril felt slightly uncomfortable, but he held himself against shivering and stood there, not listening to anything Thum said.

Across the keep, sentries walked the ramparts. Torches burned at set points along the crenellations, and now and then Gavril saw one of the sentries pause to warm his hands by the blaze. Beyond the marsh, one of the village churches was ringing a bell, its sound echoing along the waterway. The hour grew late. Gavril felt tempted to keep Thum out here half the night.

"Tell me more," he urged when Thum stopped speaking. "You make the customs of this region come alive for me."

"Gladly, your highness, but Lord Odfrey awaits you," Thum said stiffly.

Gavril made a deprecating gesture. "So he does. I had almost forgotten. Come then."

They walked on, Gavril moving leisurely and Thum crowding his flank. At the opposite end of the walkway, Gavril paused, waiting while Sir Los shouldered forward and pushed through the door first. When his protector gestured that all was clear, Gavril stepped through.

Thum entered last, gasping and shuddering while Sir Los shut the door with a faint boom that echoed through the stark, unfurnished antechamber. While Thum blew on his hands, they walked along a corridor adorned only with weapons hanging decoratively on the walls, down more stairs, through a public room hung with tapestries and massive, unlit candles, and up a flight of stairs,. At the end of another corridor at last they came to a stout door of oak, banded with iron. A sleepy young page waited on duty there, yawning in the torchlight.

Gavril paused several paces away from the door and turned his back abruptly on the idle stare of the page. He met Thum's gaze. "Swiftly. What is this summons about?" he asked in a low, curt voice.

Thum's hazel-green eyes blinked in surprise. "I know not."

"Of course you do. Prepare me. Tell me what Lord Odfrey wants with me."

"I cannot—"

"You mean you will not."

Thum's freckled face began to redden. "No, your highness," he said calmly. "I cannot. I do not know."

"But he sent you. You must have heard him say something of his intentions."

"I was summoned to the chevard and we talked briefly. Then he said I was to escort you here to him," Thum replied.

His answer displeased Gavril. "Yes, you talk often with the chevard, do you not?" he muttered.

"Sir?"

Gavril scowled, and his blue eyes met Thum's hazel ones harshly. "You talked this afternoon, and saw that I was reprimanded."

Thum looked astonished. "Your highness, I did not—"

"Do you call me a liar now, as well?" Gavril broke in.

Thum tried to answer, but Gavril lifted his hand for silence. He shot Thum another glare, and turned away from him.

Striding on, he approached the page, who now snapped to attention, and said, "Admit me."

Bowing, the page pushed open the heavy door. It swung slowly, creaking on its hinges, and Gavril entered Lord Odfrey's wardroom. Glancing back over his shoulder, he said to Thum, "Await me. We are not finished, you and I."

Anger had knotted Thum's brow. He gave Gavril only a sketch of a bow and said, "Indeed, we have not. I will see myself cleared in your highness's estimation or—"

Gavril turned away and walked into the wardroom without letting Thum finish. He glanced around swiftly, with little interest. He had been here before. It was a plain, utilitarian chamber, holding a desk and a locked cabinet, a window shuttered now against the night, a few unevenly burning candles, a miser's fire dying on the hearth in a collapsing heap of coals, and Lord Odfrey's weapons, hanging haphazardly on hooks. Lord Odfrey's mud-encrusted boots stood drying on the hearth. The room smelled of smoke, dog, damp wool, and melting tallow wax.

Gavril's nostrils curled in distaste. The chevard lived like a yeoman instead of a lord.

Lord Odfrey's plain brass cup stood on the desk, weighing down a litter of papers and maps. A worn leather dispatch case lay open on one corner of the desk, its contents half-raked out into view. But of the man himself, there was no sign.

Gavril's brows pulled together. He swung around and pinned his gaze on the page. "Where is the chevard?"

"He will return soon," the boy said, his eyes wary. Gavril had a black reputation among the pages. All of them feared him, which was exactly as he wanted it. "He said if your highness came, I was to bid you await him here."

Gavril could not believe this insult. Again and again, Lord Odfrey dealt him rudeness and discourtesy. To leave, knowing his prince was coming, was a deliberate slight. "And how long am I to wait?" Gavril asked in a voice like silk.

The page backed up a step, his hand groping behind him for the door. "Not long, I believe, your highness. Uh, let me fetch your highness some cider."

And the boy dashed out, slamming the door behind him, before Gavril could ask him anything else.

Fuming, Gavril paced around the wardroom, kicking a leather-covered stool out of his way. He ended up beside Lord Odfrey's desk. Frowning, he glared at it, and noticed the maps half-unrolled atop the general litter of papers. The top map was of Nold.

Gavril caught his breath and glanced over his shoulder at the door. Sir Los stood there. The protector met his gaze in silence.

"Lock it," Gavril said.

Sir Los didn't even blink; he was too well trained for that. Putting a hand on the pull-latch, he said, "There's no key."

"Then hold it. Let no one enter and surprise me."

"Be quick, your highness," Sir Los said. "For I hear the footsteps of someone approaching."

"Morde!" Gavril said. He grabbed up the map, knocking over the cup of cider in the process. Brown liquid sloshed out, staining papers and running off the edge of the desk onto the floor.

Gavril batted the cup off the desk, sending it flying across the room, where it banged against the stone hearth. Swearing to himself, he swiped the sticky cider off most of the papers, and watched ink running and melting together.

Outside, footsteps paused at the door, which then swung

open, only to bang against the solid shoulders of Sir Los, who had braced his feet and did not move aside. "What's this?" Lord Odfrey asked in surprise. "Who blocks my door?"

There was no time to clean up the mess. There was no time to study the map, which was large and exquisitely detailed. Frustrated, Gavril put it down on top of the desk, hiding the wet papers, and sprang away from the desk. At his gesture, Sir Los stepped aside from the door.

Pushed hard from the other side, the door banged violently into the wall. Lord Odfrey stood framed in the doorway, scowling. Rid of his hauberk, and clad instead in a knee-long tunic of old-fashioned cut and leggings of dark green wool, soft cloth shoes on his feet, and a ruching of pale linen shirt showing at his neck, Lord Odfrey looked younger and less formidable. His hand, scarred across the knuckles and wearing only a plain signet ring, tightened visibly on the parchment scroll he was carrying. One of his rangy hounds thrust its slim head beneath his master's hand. Behind him stood Thum and the page, both craning their necks to see inside.

Lord Odfrey's dark eyes narrowed on Gavril. "Your highness has come at last, I see."

He sounded short-tempered and tired.

Gavril lifted his chin. "I was about to leave, thinking I had been summoned in error."

"What error?" Lord Odfrey asked, stepping into the wardroom. His dog gazed up at him in adoration, then lay down near the hearth. "What error?" he repeated. "I sent Maltie to you a full hour ago."

Gavril was in no mood to bear another unjust reprimand. Gritting his teeth, he said, "I have answered your summons. What is it you wish to discuss with me?"

"Little enough now at this late hour," Lord Odfrey said in his gruff way. "First of all, has your highness brought any letters? My dispatches to the king are almost complete. The messenger will ride out at dawn. Your letters can go in his pouch."

Gavril moved uneasily away from Lord Odfrey's desk. He wondered if the cider had ruined those dispatches. If so, if Lord Odfrey questioned him about it, he would blame the page's clumsiness rather than his own.

"Any letters, your highness?"

Gavril started and pulled his thoughts together. "Uh, no. I have not yet found the time to write to my father the king."

Lord Odfrey grunted and shifted impatiently to something else. "I have some questions about your hunt today—"

"Surely we have discussed the matter enough," Gavril broke in. "Your reprimand was clear, my lord. You need not repeat it."

"I have no intention of repeating it," Lord Odfrey said impatiently. "I want to know if you saw any signs of battle while you were in the forest. Any trampled ground? Any signs of warning . . . bits of red cloth fluttering from branches, that sort of thing? Any runes scratched into the trunks of trees?"

"No."

Lord Odfrey sighed, but he did not look relieved. "Did you smell any smoke?"

"No."

The chevard clasped his hands behind him and began to pace back and forth in front of the hearth. If he noticed the cup lying dented in the corner, he did not mention it. Nor, to Gavril's relief, did he approach his desk. "A messenger just came from Silon town downriver. There's been trouble there with dwarf raiders. You were lucky today to leave the forest unscathed."

The brush with danger, however faint and until now unknown, pleased Gavril. He puffed out his chest. "We did not venture far into Nold, but had we encountered any war parties, I assure you we would have fought."

Lord Odfrey snorted. "You'd have had little choice otherwise." His glance shot to Sir Los before Gavril could find a retort. "And you, protector? Did you notice aught while the boys were coursing their stag?"

"I did not, my lord," Sir Los replied respectfully.

"Damne. The eld was more informative than either of you. I should have kept him for questioning."

"It is against law and Writ to keep pagans beneath a roof that houses the faithful," Gavril said.

Lord Odfrey glared at him. "That's as may be," he replied curtly. "But it's upland custom that eldin bring good luck to households that give them shelter."

"Old superstitions should be stamped out when they appear, not encouraged."

"If the dwarves decide to carry their war across our border, we'll have need of all the luck we can find, whether it's church luck or pagan."

Gavril drew in a sharp breath. "That's blasphemy!"

"No, it's practicality—something you need to acquire, my prince. Good night."

Gavril stood there with his mouth open, astonished to find himself dismissed so curtly. "We have not yet finished this discussion," he said.

"There's no discussion here," Lord Odfrey said. He left the hearth and headed toward his desk, but Gavril stood between him and the table, blocking his path. Lord Odfrey stopped and scowled. "I've asked my questions, and you've given me no answers. It's late. Go to bed."

Gavril reluctantly stepped aside, allowing the chevard to pass. Lord Odfrey circled his desk and sat down. He did not notice the spilled cider drying on the floor. And as yet, he had not glanced at the disarranged papers before him.

"I will go now and write my letters," Gavril said. Already he was composing in his head his brief note of complaint to the king. But more important was the longer, more detailed missive he would write to Cardinal Noncire. The church needed to know how shaky the faith was in this godforsaken corner of the realm. "I will have two to send with your dispatches in the morning."

"Not now," Lord Odfrey said. "It's too late. Get yourself in bed. You have drills and chores aplenty on the morrow."

Gavril's annoyance came surging back. "Do you now refuse to send my letters?"

"I do not refuse. You have had ample opportunity to compose them since this afternoon. Your failure to take advantage of your free time has served your highness ill yet again. Your letters can go in next week's dispatches, provided they are written by then. Now, good night."

Gavril opened his mouth to protest further, but Lord Odfrey had already turned his attention to his papers. Frowning, he reached for the map draped across the top of his desk. Gavril lost his nerve at that point and hastily strode out.

Thum was waiting outside the wardroom, yawning and rubbing his eyes. He fell into step beside the prince.

Gavril glared at him. "Go to your quarters. I don't want you."

"Lord Odfrey said I was to escort you back," Thum said, yawning again.

"Why? I need no nursemaid, no spy to report if I go where I am bidden to go."

Annoyance crossed Thum's face. "I'm no spy," he said curtly. "I'm just following orders. Lord Odfrey doesn't explain himself. Your highness knows that."

"I know that your presence annoys me," Gavril said.

"Then forgive me, your highness," Thum replied stiffly. "I but follow orders from the same man as you do."

Heat flared in Gavril's face. He glared at Thum, who glared right back.

"First I am a tongue-tattle, and now I am a spy," Thum said, making no effort to keep his voice down. Outside, across the keep in the chapel tower, the bell began to ring somberly, tolling the call for final prayers and lights-out. Downstairs, servants were extinguishing torches and banking fires, chattering and yawning as they went.

"What next will your highness say of me?" Thum continued, still glaring at Gavril. "Why have I offended you so?"

Gavril stopped in his tracks and turned on the other boy. " 'Offend' is exactly the word," he said through his teeth. "You dare question my authority in front of the other fosters. You dare stand up for an eld in defiance of Writ. You give my whereabouts away to Lord Odfrey so that I am dealt his wrath. And now, you dare speak to me with disrespect. Yes, you offend me, Thum du Maltie. And you are treading on dangerous ground in doing so."

The color leached from Thum's face. His mouth fell open, but it was a moment before he uttered any words. "We—we are all as equals here," he said faintly. "Lord Odfrey said so the first day we came. He said we should forget rank and think of ourselves as comrades and knights in training. We must be warriors together first before we can succeed our fathers and stand in rank—"

"Cease your prattle," Gavril said scornfully, and Thum fell silent. Gavril looked him up and down, sneering at him. "You stand before me, wearing your doublet of cheap fool's finery, the youngest son of an unimportant noble, and dare say to me that we are *equals*? Do you know why I was summoned to Lord Odfrey's wardroom tonight?"

A strange, pinched expression had appeared on Thum's face. Stiffly, he said, "As I said before to your highness, I know not."

"It was a courtesy he extended to me. My letters to Savroix are included in his weekly dispatches. Do you write letters to your family, Maltie?"

Thum's throat jerked as he swallowed. "No, your highness."

"Can you write at all, Maltie?"

"A—a little, your highness."

"Do you realize that I have only to pen a few lines to my father the king, stating my complaints, and your family could lose its warrant of nobility?"

Thum's mouth opened, but nothing came out. He stared at Gavril as though he had never seen him before.

"What offends me also offends my father," Gavril went on. He circled Thum, who stood there rigid and unmoving, then stopped in front of him again. "If you cause offense, is your father not also an offender with you? Hmm? You stand there with your mouth open, Maltie, but you make no answer."

"Please," Thum gasped. "My father has always served the king ably. He wears a chain given to him by the king's own hand. He is loyal with all his heart and soul."

"Geoffen du Maltie is well spoken of at my father's court. But that can change," Gavril said, and saw Thum flinch. "Since you think you can reprimand me, question my orders, and ignore my authority over you, what else do you think? That you are better than I?"

"No, your highness."

"Is it worth it, Maltie? To have your moment of supremacy, to laugh at my expense? Is it worth seeing your father ruined, your brothers brought down with him, your elder sister's impending nuptials called off?"

Tears shimmered in Thum's hazel eyes, but he did not let them fall. Instead, he shot Gavril an imploring glance. "Please, I beg your pardon. I did not mean to offend. I misunderstood, and I apologize. I will not repeat my transgressions. I swear this to you."

"You swear."

"Yes," Thum said, blinking hard. "I give you my—"

"Don't give me your word!" Gavril shouted, and Thum flinched again. "You are neither noble nor knight. You are nothing! Your word is nothing."

Red surged into Thum's face, and his mouth tightened. He dropped his gaze quickly, but not before Gavril saw the fury that flared in his eyes.

Gavril raked him with a contemptuous glance. "No land will you inherit. You will be a common knight in another man's service. In a year I will be named Heir to the Realm. I am as far above you as are the stars above this land. That I have deigned to reside here and be trained in your proximity grants you no favor, no right to familiarity. Your family should have taught you better, for if they believe you will gain them more boons at court, you have destroyed those hopes."

Thum kept his gaze on the floor. He was stiff, barely breathing. He said nothing.

Gavril let the silence hang between them before he said, "There is a way for you to redeem yourself."

Thum's gaze flashed up. "What way?" he asked.

He should have promised to do anything, not question the terms, Gavril thought, frowning at him. "Come to my quarters."

Silence held them until they reached the top of the west tower and entered Gavril's chamber, where the fire cast welcome warmth and candles burned despite the last bell. In the bedchamber beyond, Gavril glimpsed his bed, piled with pillows swathed in clean linen, the heavy fur robe turned back. Aoun was standing beside the bed, holding a pole with a heated warmer on the end of it beneath the covers to warm the sheets.

Sighing, Gavril threw out his arms in a stretch and unbuckled his belt. Tossing his poniard onto his writing desk, he pulled off his cap and loosened the laces of his doublet before he turned around to face Thum, who was watching him with a tense, white face.

"What must I do?" Thum asked.

Gavril yawned, playing him the way a cat torments a mouse. "There is a map of Nold within Lord Odfrey's wardroom. Large. About this size." He held his hands apart. "Drawn on parchment. It's on the chevard's desk. I want that map. You will bring it to me."

Thum frowned. "You mean you wish me to ask Lord Odfrey if you may look at it?"

"No. I want the map. When Lord Odfrey is away, you will enter his wardroom and take the map."

"That's stealing!"

"Is it?" Gavril glanced around and saw his jeweled cup waiting for him on the table. He picked it up, swirled the contents a moment, and drank.

"You want me to steal from the chevard?"

"Stop asking stupid questions. I want you to give me that map of Nold. It's quite detailed. I need it."

"But—"

"How you manage to supply my request is your concern, not mine."

"I won't steal for you," Thum said in outrage. "My honor requires—how can you even ask—"

"Then refuse my request," Gavril said with a shrug, and put down his cup. "Clearly you're too much an uplander to be acceptable at court. My father will be interested to learn that the Maltie family sympathizes with old politics that should have been stamped out long before now."

"You can't accuse Geoffen du Maltie of supporting the division," Thum said furiously. "You can't! It isn't true!"

"My observations are quite clear," Gavril retorted. "I can say what I please, and my father the king will listen."

"No," Thum said, breathing hard. "No!"

"Then get out."

"This is unfair!" Thum said. "You tell me I have offended you by speaking plainly, as I was told to do by the chevard. But I am to steal to regain your favor? What trap do you hold for me?"

"Careful, Maltie. Your tongue is digging a deeper hole for you."

Thum clamped his mouth shut and swung away from Gavril with a muted cry. Rigid and anguished, he lifted his clenched fists in the air. Gavril watched him, smiling to himself. Cardinal Noncire had taught him well how to manage the difficult ones. They always had a weakness. It was simply a question of finding out what that weakness was.

"Go," Gavril said, his voice hard and merciless. "Kaltienne lacks your scruples. He will be honored to serve me by bringing the map."

Thum's shoulders sagged. He turned around as slowly as an old man, and Gavril's chest swelled with satisfaction. Thum was beaten, he thought. He would now serve his prince as docilely as a lamb. Never again would he question orders. For once he took this risk on Gavril's behalf, he would be bound to Gavril forever, bound by his own guilt.

Thum looked up. "I will not steal for you," he said, his voice soft and wretched. "Though you be my prince and will one day be my liege and king, I cannot do this wrong."

Fury swept through Gavril. He glared at Thum and reached to his side for the dagger that was no longer there. "You—"

"But I will copy the map for you," Thum said. "If that will please your highness."

It took Gavril's anger a moment to cool. He stared at Thum through narrowed eyes, realizing that this boy had not broken after all. He was still independent, still defiant. Had the map not been truly important to Gavril's plans, he would have ordered Thum thrown out then and there.

Instead, he mastered his emotions and forced himself to think over the offer. "Can you draw?" he asked.

"Yes, your highness."

"Have you ink or parchment? You cannot write, you said."

"I can write a little," Thum replied. "I can copy whatever is written on the map. You have ink and parchment, there." He pointed at Gavril's writing desk.

"Bring the map here and copy it," Gavril said.

Thum looked alarmed. "I dare not take it from Lord Odfrey's wardroom."

"He will only beat you," Gavril said with a shrug. "But I have the power to destroy your family."

"Thod is who my conscience must answer to," Thum replied, revealing a bedrock faith for the first time.

That alone awakened grudging respect in Gavril. He stared at the other boy for a moment and relented. "Very well," he said. "Take what you need from my desk."

Thum blinked, hesitated, then hurried to the desk and drew forth a sheet of stiff parchment and a pen.

"Take care!" Gavril said sharply enough to make him start. "And do the task quickly. I want the map in my hands tomorrow."

"I have duties all morning, and in the afternoon we are to drill with the master-at-arms."

Impatience filled Gavril. He wanted to choke Thum, or have Sir Los beat the knave for his impudence. Instead, he gave him a stony look and said, "Then you will have to copy it tonight."

"But it's past matins," Thum said. "All lights are to be out. I can't—"

"You have little choice. It's easier to enter Lord Odfrey's wardroom now while the chevard is asleep than tomorrow, when you will be missed if you are absent from your duties. And no doubt Lord Odfrey will be going in and out of his wardroom throughout the day—"

"All right!" Thum said. Sweat beaded along his hairline, making his red hair stick out. He drew in a ragged breath and would not meet Gavril's eyes. "All right. Tonight."

Gavril handed him a fat candle. "Work quickly. And make no mistakes. Put it in my hands by noontime."

Thum looked up briefly, his hazel eyes swirling with a mix of resentment and dislike, then he headed toward the door.

"You need not act like a martyr, Maltie," Gavril called after him. "I have offered you my mercy. You should be grateful for a second chance."

Thum paused and glanced back. His freckled face was stony, and not a dram of gratitude could be seen in it. He left without another word, carrying candle, parchment, and pen.

Sir Los closed the door behind him. "That's one to watch, your highness," he said gruffly. "Some of 'em can't be whipped. They've too much spirit for a heavy hand."

Gavril glared at him. "And who asked for your opinion?" he said icily.

Sir Los shrugged. "My opinion matters, your highness, when I've got to keep someone's dagger out of your back."

"Don't be absurd. He would never strike at me."

Sir Los bowed. "As your highness says. If you are retiring now, I will bid you a pleasant sleep."

"Where are you going?" Gavril asked him, still displeased by what he'd said. "Why are you leaving?"

"Going to watch that boy a while," Sir Los said, pulling his indigo cloak tighter around his heavy shoulders. "See if he goes where he's been bid to go."

Gavril frowned.

"Call it my bad feeling," Sir Los said. "Call it making sure. Good night, your highness. Someday perhaps you'll learn not to be so cruel with his type."

"Cruel?" Gavril said in outrage. "I was putting him in his place. The cardinal taught me how to use all—"

Sir Los smiled lopsidedly, clearly unconvinced.

Feeling a qualm of doubt, Gavril frowned. "You have not permission to question my actions," he said haughtily. "Your opinion has not been asked for."

"No, your highness."

"Thum du Maltie hasn't the courage to cause me trouble," Gavril said. "He's smart enough to know better."

"Aye, that's right enough," Sir Los agreed, taking the liberty allowed a protector. He seldom voiced an opinion, unlike his predecessor, who lectured Gavril constantly, but when Sir Los had something to say he was like a dog worrying a bone. He would not leave it. Sir Los looked at Gavril and tapped his thick, oft-broken nose. "But it might be better to mend your ways a bit and not try everything the cardinal has taught you. There's going to come a day when I do fear your highness will run afoul of someone not smart like Maltie, not smart enough to know he's licked. That's when your highness will find trouble."

"Then you will have to make sure I don't come to harm," Gavril said with false sweetness. He smiled at his protector. "I have no intention of mending my ways."

11

DAIN AWAKENED WITH a start and sat up inside the burrow. He listened intently, trying to identify the sound that had awakened him.

Nothing.

It was time to go. He stretched hard enough to make his spine crack, then bent over Thia, touching her cold face in farewell. He had performed the rites as best he could, putting salt on her tongue and wrapping her tightly in the threadbare blanket. He left her pendant of bard crystal lying on her breast. Even in the dim light provided by the glowstones, the faceted sides of the crystal glittered with muted fire. Her face lay in repose, no longer tormented with pain. Even death could not mar her beauty.

He kissed her cold cheek one last time, his eyes wet and stinging. He hated to leave her, but she was no longer here with him. She had gone into the third world, where her spirit would forever sing.

Wiping his face, Dain forced himself to go.

Emerging from the burrow, he popped his head out of the ground, blowing dirt from his nostrils, and gazed cautiously around. The clearing remained deserted in the cold, gray light of morning. It was raining softly in a light mist that stirred the forest scents of leafy mold, bark, and moss. The forest was silent. Not even a bird chirped. There were no rustles, none of the usual activity among the furred denizens of the woods.

A ripple of unease passed through Dain. He pushed his shoulders through the hole and climbed out. Swiftly, keeping his senses alert, he replaced the lattice and soil over the hole, then covered everything with a layer of golden and russet leaves. He worked methodically to erase all evidence of his recent stay there. When he was satisfied, he scratched out the rune mark of the Forlo Clan and drew another, signifying it was now a burial place.

Fresh tears stung his eyes. Fiercely he pushed himself away from there and melted into the undergrowth, leaving the clearing as fast as his legs would take him. He'd eaten the last of the food, and he needed to hunt if he was to have supper tonight. Beyond that, his future stretched empty and unknown before him. His whole life had changed irrevocably in the past few days.

A distant whooping froze him in his tracks. He listened a moment to the yells, and the hair on the back of his neck prickled. A war party, a victorious one from the sound, was coming his way.

At almost the same moment, the wind shifted, and he caught their scent. Dwarves . . . Bnen, probably. His mind caught something else—men-thoughts, awash with fear.

Dain turned about slowly, absorbing sounds, scents, and that wailing panic from human minds. It was time for him to get out of here.

But he did not run. Instead, he waited to make sure he understood from where they were approaching and how many there might be. Dwarves tended to travel in tight clusters of about half their fighting force, with the rest scattered out ahead, parallel with, or behind the pack. If he wasn't careful, he could cross paths with some of the scouts. Unarmed, he had no chance of surviving any such encounter.

They yelled again, chanting their gruff war songs, and a drum began to beat, close and loud. Dain darted undercover and crouched low, making himself as still and small as possible, hoping his clothing would blend into the colors of the thicket.

A scout passed him, gnarled and short, his powerful shoulders supporting a bloodstained war axe, his cap pulled low upon his craggy forehead, his eyes reddened and glaring.

Seconds later, another scout appeared, only to vanish almost immediately back into the undergrowth.

When a third and fourth scout showed themselves, Dain realized they were converging on the clearing where Thia's burrow was. They had camped there yesterday before going on their night raid. Now, in the cold early morning, they were returning, fierce and satisfied, splattered with blood and gore, many of them bearing loot.

At first Dain was puzzled. There were no clans living this close to the forest's edge. Who had the Bnen attacked?

As soon as the question crossed his mind, he knew. They had raided the Mandrian villages across the marsh. Dain did not understand what had driven them to provoke war, and he did not really care. What mattered right now was that he get himself as far away from here as he could, before they caught him, crushed his skull, and drank his blood in celebration.

But he saw the main pack coming, marching along, singing to the beat of their drums. Their number surprised him. Several war parties had obviously banded together, for there were perhaps a hundred or more dwarves marching in close ranks. Most dwarf clans fought in small groups, making surprise attacks of great fierceness, then retreating quickly with whatever loot they could grab on the way. Seldom did they join forces in any kind of army, for they were too fierce, independent, and hot-tempered to work together for long.

All the same, as Dain watched them march past his hiding place, he couldn't help thinking of the old tales Jorb used to spin in the evenings when the day's work was done. Tales of the great dwarf armies in the time before men, when enormous battles had shook the ground, forming the mountains, when the sounds of dying lifted to the skies and created clouds, when blood ran as rivers, making channels for water to flow thereafter. And it hadn't only been the dwarves who'd fought in antiquity, but also trolk and dire creatures spawned in darkness.

One of the most ferocious of these ancient battles had been the last, when the creatures of darkness were at last driven by the dwarves into the wasteland of what was now Gant. This battle had required all the dwarves to band together. It had taken place in what was now the fabled Field of Skulls. It had been a battle so terrible and long, in which so many had been slain and spilled their blood, that the battleground itself grew saturated and became barren. No trees or grass or any living thing would grow on the site. The bones of the dead were said to be piled so high and so thickly that even long centuries later they made the ground look white. No one who found the place could take a single step without walking on the remains of the dead. Power still resonated on this battlefield, a power too strong for time to dispel. It was said to permeate the bones lying there, and if a visitor took away even a fragment with him, the power residing in that piece of bone would bring him either great luck or terrible misfortune. The blood from this battle had flowed so heavily that it was said to be the origin of the mighty Charva River. Whether or not that was true, few dwarves living today would consider wetting themselves in the Charva, for many believed dead souls were still trapped in the waters of the river. Other legends said that Thod had struck the ground with a mighty blow, thus creating a lake from which the Charva flowed as a natural barrier between Nonkind and the warrior dwarves of Nold.

Dain shook off these thoughts. The ancient days were over. These dwarves marching past him now were only Bnen, murderers of his guardian and sister. He curled himself tighter under the bush, aching with rage and grief. He wanted to jump forth and attack them with his bare hands. He wanted to hurt them, defeat them, kill them.

But he was one against too many. If he tried, he would waste his life for no purpose and they would not pay for their crimes. Somehow, he must find a way of revenge.

That was when he saw the prisoners. Bound and bleeding from wounds, they were pushed along at the end of the pack and guarded by tormenters who jabbed them with dagger points, laughing and jeering at them in the hoarse dwarf tongue. Three men, wearing dark green tunics that marked them as being in Lord Odfrey's service. One of them had a horn slung across his shoulder by a leather cord. Dain recognized him as the huntsman whom Lord Odfrey had ordered into the forest to recover the stag carcass.

The huntsman was weeping in fear, his craggy face contorted. He limped along on a leg which oozed blood with every step, and his captors seemed to delight in shoving him faster.

When the prisoners stumbled past Dain, their fear washed over him with such force he felt stunned in their wake:

Dead/dead/dead/dead.

With an effort, he shut their panic away and knelt there on the damp ground, still watching as the pack marched toward the clearing. He cared nothing about those men or their fate, except that no one deserved to die at the hands of the Bnen. For Thia's sake, for Jorb's, he had to try to help them.

He waited for the rear scouts to straggle in, and when at last he thought it was safe, when he could hear the shouting and jubilation as camp was made, Dain followed them, pausing only to pick up the huntsman's cap which had fallen on the ground.

By the time Dain crept up to the edge of the clearing, the dwarves had chopped down three pairs of saplings and were busy stripping them of their branches. A large bonfire had been built in the center of the clearing. Five dwarves with runes painted in blood on their faces and the fronts of their tunics surrounded the fire, which was crackling and throwing sparks toward the sky. Chanting to the beat of the drums, the five circled the fire, now and then throwing something into it which made fearsome green flashes followed by puffs of white smoke.

Dain froze at the sight of wise-sayers. All the clans of the dwarves had them. But never before had he seen five together. They were working a powerful spell: He could feel the strength of it tingling along his face and the backs of his hands.

Yet dwarf magic could not affect him seriously. He had too much eld blood in his veins. Something inside him stirred, brought to life by their incantations, yet not part of it. He frowned, keeping one eye on the wise-sayers as they chanted and marched, and the other eye on the prisoners, who knelt with their hands bound behind them.

By now the saplings were stripped of their branches, creating six long poles. Each prisoner was jerked to his feet, then two poles were lashed to his back.

Dain had never seen this before, but he believed the Bnen were about to commit *kreg n'durgm,* a terrible, ritualistic torture that supported their darkest magic.

Uneasiness prickled harder inside him. He stared, trying to figure out what they sought to conjure forth from the second world. It had to be terrible indeed, if they were creating such a potent spell to control it.

Whatever it might be, he had no desire to witness it.

Dain felt the temptation to turn aside and flee from this evil, but he did not. His heart stirred with pity for the prisoners, who had stopped pleading for mercy now and stood silent, their eyes huge with fear. But more than pity, he felt anger, felt it growing to a terrible heat that burned his core and spread along his limbs. His heart pounded hard with it, and his breathing deepened and grew harsh in his throat.

How dare they desecrate Thia's burial place with their dark spells. It was not enough to shoot her down as she ran defenseless from her burning home, but now they would defile her burial place with their tainted works.

His anger burned hotter, and Dain gripped the branches of the bush before him so hard the twigs cut into his palms. He noticed no discomfort, however. From his heart a summons was cast forth, a summons such as he had never created before. He hardly knew what he was about; he knew only that this must be stopped.

Come/come/come/come!

His mind spread through the forest, gathering all that was living and calling it to him.

The birds responded first—large, black keebacks and tiny brown sparouns, the blue-gray rackens, and the fierce, crested tiftiks. Circling and swooping from the sky, they flew above the clearing, avoiding the billows of white smoke. Ever more of them converged, crowding the sky overhead, shrieking and cawing and chirping and trilling until the noise was almost deafening.

The drumbeat faltered, and the wise-sayers paused in their incantation to stare upward.

"It comes!" one of them said. "It is a sign. We are heard."

The birds descended to the treetops, jostling and crowding each other for perches, some of them beating each other with their wings and pecking viciously. And still more birds flew in.

"This portent is not of our working," another wise-sayer said. "Oglan! Set a watch. You, Targ, keep the beat going."

The drumbeat resumed, pounding beneath the squawking noise of the birds, but it was not as steady a beat as it had been before.

More birds came, darkening the sky overhead and filling the trees with a rustling, jostling, fluttering cacophony.

Dain closed his eyes, filling himself with his anger, letting it burn forth in his summons, which spread ever wider: *Come/come/come/come.*

"Look!" someone shouted.

And now a vixlet darted across the clearing, her russet fur and banded brush glinting in the firelight. She ran straight toward the bonfire, then stopped just short of it and glanced around. Her dark mask of fur banded her narrow face, and she parted her jaws to reveal long rows of sharp, gleaming teeth. Then she darted away.

Mice scurried out from under leaves, running here and there. Hares appeared, and stags and more vixlets, some mated and running in pairs. Rats came, red-eyed and dangerous, their long whiskers quivering as they sat up on their hindquarters and tested the wind. A muted cough warned of the arrival of a tawny canar, muscles rippling beneath its hide, its sinuous neck turning from side to side as it bared its long fangs and snarled.

Crying out, the dwarves fell back from it, abandoning their prisoners, who began to wail their prayers aloud in terrified voices.

The canar, crouching, came running the rest of the way into the clearing, and the smaller animals that were normally its prey scattered. It moved like silk, its long, lithe body tightly wound and ready to pounce. Snarling, it approached the bonfire, sending the wise-sayers backing away, but it did not go too near the blaze.

A roar on the opposite side of the clearing sent the stag leaping into the air, and the smaller animals darted here and there in fresh panic. A beyar, massive and old, gray hairs glinting in its shaggy black pelt, shuffled into sight. It reared up on its hind legs, massive paws swatting at the air, and roared again.

The canar squalled a challenge, and the two master predators of the forest glared at each other across the clearing.

Murmuring, the dwarves clustered to one side, shaking their heads and looking alarmed. As fierce as the Bnen were, even they did not want to be caught in the middle of this battle.

In the distance, wolves set up a chorus, their eerie cries echoing far through the trees. The canar and beyar ignored them, but the other animals shifted uneasily. A vixlet pounced on a hare, killing it with a swift snap of her jaws. The scent of blood filled the air, and the stag broke loose of Dain's control and bounded wildly across the center of the clearing.

The canar, unable to resist such prey, swung about to leap at the stag's shoulder. The animal, caught in mid-bound, bleated and fell heavily, the canar atop its back. Then, with a roar, the beyar charged, knocking the canar off the stag and sending it rolling into the edge of the fire.

The canar screamed with pain, and the scent of burning fur overwhelmed the scent of blood. Squalling and twisting frantically, the canar rolled itself out of the fire and jumped up, singed and furious, to join battle with the beyar.

The dwarves scattered in all directions, while the wise-sayers shouted at them to come back.

Four of the wise-sayers shouted and argued with each other, but the fifth, the tallest of them, with a long, gray beard and eyes as yellow as the canar's, stood apart, silent as he quested the air with his senses.

"It is the shapeshifters!" shouted one of the other wise-sayers, dodging as the battle came in his direction. "They have come to us like this—"

"No," said the bearded one. He dropped his gaze from the skies above and began to look hard at the forest around him. "We have not reached the dark ones. This is magic not of ours. Someone interferes with us."

As he spoke, he reached into a pouch tied at his belt and drew forth what looked like a black stone, except that it smoked in his hand and seemed on the verge of bursting into flames.

He hurled it straight at the bush which concealed Dain, and struck him hard on the shoulder.

The pain of it broke Dain's concentration, and his mastery over the animals fell. They ran in all directions, heedless of the battle between beyar and canar. Some leaped over the dead stag; others bounded back and forth in wild zigzags, the chaos so complete and unbridled the wise-sayers were forced to flee into the forest with the other dwarves.

Knowing this was his chance, Dain ran into the clearing. A vixlet darted between his legs, tripping him. He staggered to keep his balance, and dodged the rats scuttling purposefully toward the food abandoned along with the other loot. Something bit him, and Dain swore and jumped aside.

A few more strides and he reached the prisoners. Picking up a dagger someone had dropped, he sliced through their bonds, ignoring their cries and pleas for deliverance.

"Quiet," he said, cutting the last of the cords. "Run that way. Run for your lives. Go!"

Pointing, he slapped their shoulders, and they set off in as great a panic as the animals. Above them, the birds rose up in a terrible flock, filling the air with the sound of beating wings. Dain ran too, hearing someone shout behind him and knowing they had only scant moments to reach whatever cover they could find beyond the clearing. In minutes, the dwarves would come after them. Dain knew he could outrun them. But the prisoners were stumbling and blundering along, wasting precious moments glancing back.

"Run!" he called to them. "Run!"

The huntsman cried out and fell. Dain went back to pull him upright. The man's face was the color of a grub. He swayed, and the others grabbed his arms and helped him forward.

Dain started to follow, but something snagged him from behind and pulled him back.

At first he believed he'd been gripped by the back of his tunic. Shouting, he twisted around to strike with the dagger he'd picked up, but there was nothing there.

Astonished, he barely had time to realize this before his arms slammed down against his sides and froze there. He struggled with all his might, trying to break free against his invisible bonds, but his feet were yanked out from beneath him. He fell heavily on his side, and grunted at the impact.

In the distance, he saw the bearded wise-sayer pointing at him, shouting some kind of spell in the dwarf tongue.

Dain stopped his struggles at once, knowing that physical resistance only strengthened the spell. Dwarf magic rarely worked on those of eldin blood. Dain's arms and feet were bound with an invisible rope of power, but it could not hold him for long. He saw the pack of dwarves running toward him, and knew he had only moments to avoid capture.

"Fire!" he said aloud, gathering the energy in his mind. He envisioned tongues of flame burning through the rope of power, and seconds later the spell was broken.

Dain scrambled upright and fled.

Half of the dwarves veered to follow him; the rest continued in pursuit of the Mandrians.

With the huntsman's wounded leg hampering them, the men could not hope to outrun their pursuers. Dain ducked into a heavy stand of harlberries, taking care to crush some of the purplish-green stems. A pungent, unpleasant scent rose into the air. Dain smeared some of the pale sap up and down his arms and across the front of his tunic. The scent would mask his own.

Ducking low, he scuttled behind a log, paused a moment, then doubled back, eluding his pursuers. As fast as he could, he headed after the Mandrians.

They were making too much noise. Even a blind dwarf could follow them without trouble. Their scent hung in the air, mingled with fear and fresh blood. Dain angled to one side of the dwarf pack, well under cover, but as fleet-footed as a young stag. He leaped over a fallen log, ducked beneath a low-hanging vine of muscaug with leaves like burnished copper, and tackled the fleeing men from the side.

He knocked them bodily into a gully that cut beneath a stand of shtac, sending them tumbling with muffled grunts and little cries of pain. Breathless and winded, they all landed in the bottom among drifts of fallen leaves.

Dain sat up first, his ears alert for any indication that they'd been seen. No outcry rose up, but the dwarves were still coming, tracking by scent.

Jerking his tattered sleeve free of the briars which snagged it, Dain clutched one man's arm and clapped a dirty hand across another's mouth before they could speak.

"Hush. Hush!" he whispered fiercely, glaring at each of

them in turn. The huntsman lay facedown in the leaves, not moving. Dain gripped his arm and felt the life still coursing through him. "Make no sound," he said softly. "As you value your lives, do exactly as I say."

Big-eyed and afraid, they stared at him.

He listened again, his senses filtering all sounds and movement beyond their poor hiding place. There was little time. He could think of only one thing to do, and he wasn't sure it would work. His sister had been the spellcaster, not he.

But he was determined to try.

"Pay heed," he said to them, struggling to find the Mandrian words he wanted. "I will hide you and go for help, but you must not move. You must not speak."

"Gods above," one of the men said, the words bursting from him as though he could dam them no longer. "We can't hide here. They're almost upon us."

His companion tried to struggle to his feet, but Dain pulled him down. "Listen!" he said fiercely. "I am eld. I can help you, but only if you work with me. No matter how close they come, they will not see you if you do not move and do not speak. Swear you will do this, and I will help you."

The two men, streaked with mud and dried blood, their hair in tangles, their eyes wide and desperate, exchanged a look, then nodded.

Dain pointed at the unconscious huntsman. "Keep him quiet too."

"Done," said one of the men. "But hurry."

Dain drew his bard crystal pendant from beneath his tunic and held it up. It swung on its cord, glittering with inner fire. Dain forced himself to forget how time was running out, how close the dwarves were. He concentrated all his thought and being on trees, ivy-wreathed trees. He thought of their sturdy trunks, their strong bark, their outstretched branches. He thought of their crowns of gold and russet leaves, their deep roots that secured them to the soil. He thought of the shelter they gave to living things. He thought of how they reached tall to the sky, how they swayed in the wind but did not break, how they cast shade in the heat of summer and rattled bare-limbed in the cruel storms of winter.

Still swinging the bard crystal back and forth so that it began to vibrate with melody, Dain listened to the circulation of sap within the trees around him, listened to the steady rustle of their leaves, listened to the digging and searching of their roots within the ground. He opened his mouth and sang, low and soft, the song of trees.

Somber and muted, the notes of his song filled the gully. The men beside him remained still as he had instructed. Dain opened his eyes and saw them no longer. Instead, two saplings grew in the bottom of this shallow gully, with a fallen log beside them.

Dain lowered his bard crystal and tucked it back beneath his clothing. He sang a few more notes to finish the spell, and felt pleased with his results.

"Stay until I return with help," he whispered. "You are safe here."

One of the saplings shuddered and seemed to bend toward him. The image shivered, and Dain saw the man within the spell again.

"Do not move!" he ordered.

The man froze, and the image of the spell became again a young tree. Dain glared at them. "The spell is weak. Do not destroy it."

They made him no answer, but he could feel their fear and desperation. "I will come back," he promised.

There was no more time to give them additional reassurances. The dwarves had arrived.

Dain swore under his breath and ducked beneath a bush, knowing he should have already fled.

The dwarves tramped past the gully, grumbling to each other in vile humor.

"Gonna rip off their heads," one muttered.

"Stab 'em. Stab their guts," said another.

"Make 'em scream long and hard this time. Went too easy on 'em before."

Dain kept his head down while they went by, barely letting himself breathe and trusting that his clothing would blend into the colors of the perlimon bushes and the shtac. The briars choked the rest of the gully, giving him no place of egress except straight up the side.

He waited until the dwarves were gone. Ever mindful of scouts trailing well behind, he waited longer. Then, cautiously, he emerged from his hiding place and slapped the leaves and bits of bark from the back of his neck.

"Stay still," he warned the Mandrians one last time, and left them.

12

BY THE TIME Dain reached the river, he was panting hard and his legs burned with fatigue. He had stopped only twice to catch his wind. His mouth was drawn with thirst, and despite the cold he was sweating.

Leaving the cover of the forest made him uneasy. He had to force himself to venture out into the open. The road made him suspicious. It was too broad, too open, too exposed. He wondered why such flat, smooth stones had been laid to create its surface, yet as soon as he stepped foot on it he understood. Walking on it was wondrous easy. He had no mud to drag his feet, no ruts to stumble over. When the road curved up onto the top of the levee that held back the marsh, Dain could see far in all directions.

Smoke, too much of it, and too dark for common cook fires, rose above the treetops on the other side of the river. Dain suspected the raided villages must be there. Bells were ringing, at least three of them, from three separate directions, tolling a warning across the land.

Ahead of him loomed the stone bulwarks of the bridge that spanned the river. A gatehouse blocked the road, and the armed guards there watched Dain's approach.

He hesitated, unsure that they would let a pagan such as himself cross into their land. It was certain the Bnen dwarves had not used this road, but he did not have time to hunt a ford across the river.

Stopping, Dain dared not venture into arrow range. He

veered off the road and slid down the levee's steep bank to the water's edge. The gray water swept past him, swift and deep.

"You there!" called a stern voice from above.

Dain looked up and saw one of the guards peering down at him from the wall of the bridge.

"Get away!" the guard yelled at him.

Dain ignored him, and returned his attention to the river.

In the next instant an arrow whizzed past him, close enough to be a warning. Dain stumbled to one side, his heart knocking his ribs.

"Get away!" he was told. "Get back where you belong."

"Aye!" called another. "The souls of our dead are not for the likes of you."

"I'm no soultaker!" Dain shouted back.

He saw one of the guards nock another arrow to his bowstring. Dain backed away hastily, but before the man could shoot, hoofbeats thundered and echoed across the water.

Squinting westward, Dain saw an army of riders crossing the bridge. They rode two abreast. Their war chargers were shod with iron, and sparks flew off the paving stones of the road as they came. The men were clad in hauberks and steel helmets. Most were armed with broadswords, spears, and war axes. Pennants flew in long streamers of color, and a horn blared stridently.

The guards ran to open the gates for Lord Odfrey's army. Clearly they were riding forth to deal retaliation for the Bnen attack. Dain ran up the bank to the road and reached the top just as the wooden gates across the bridge were flung wide and the army cantered through.

The figure at the head of this column wore a shining helmet and breastplate. With his visor down, his face could not be seen, but his surcoat was dark green with a yellow crest of rearing stags, and his cloak was chevroned in strips of dark and pale fur. Lord Odfrey himself rode this day, his figure grim and erect in the saddle, his broadsword hanging at his side.

Dain ran onto the road in front of him. Lifting his arms, he shouted, "Stop! In the name of mercy, Lord Odfrey, stop!"

The chevard drew rein, but even as he slowed, lifting his arm in a signal to the riders behind him, another knight spurred his mount forward, straight at Dain.

This man was not as large as Lord Odfrey. He wore a simple

hauberk beneath his surcoat of green. A crest of crossed axes adorned the front of it, and his cloak was made of dark, serviceable wool.

Disbelieving that this man would ride him down, much less attack, Dain held his ground as the charger, wearing its head plate and armored saddlecloth, galloped straight at him. When the man drew his sword and shouted an oath in Mandrian, Dain realized he was serious.

At the last second, Dain dodged, but he was too late.

The knight protector swatted him with the flat side of his broadsword and knocked him head over heels down the bank of the levee. Unable to stop his impetus, Dain tumbled over and over until he landed with a splash in the marsh water.

The icy shock of the water brought him upright, dripping and sputtering. "Lord Odfrey!" he shouted.

But the men were riding on, heedless of his call.

"Lord Odfrey!" Dain shouted with all his might.

His voice was drowned out in the thunder of the hoofbeats, the clanking and jingling of armor, saddles, spurs, and bridle bits. None of them spared him a glance. Their blood beat hot, and their minds were on war.

He could sense it rolling off them like a stench. Desperate, Dain climbed halfway up the slippery bank, and cast his mind at Lord Odfrey's: *Halt/halt/halt/halt.*

Again the chevard reined up, signaling for the column to pause. Dain ran the rest of the way to the top of the bank.

"Lord Odfrey, your huntsman is in mortal danger!" he called, jumping and waving in an attempt to be seen in the midst of the horsemen. "Lord Odfrey!"

"Let him through," someone commanded.

The riders parted, reining their mounts aside, and Dain trotted through their midst straight to Lord Odfrey. Staring at Dain through the narrow eye slits of his helmet, the chevard sat there on his war charger, which pawed the ground and champed its bit with much head-tossing.

Breathlessly, Dain stumbled to a halt before him. "Lord," he said, gasping between words, "your huntsman and two others were prisoners of the Bnen. I set them free, but they are still in danger. The Bnen are hunting them even now, and the huntsman is wounded."

"M'lord," protested the knight who had knocked Dain off

the road only moments before, "have done with this brat. We've a whole village to avenge."

Lord Odfrey raised his visor, revealing a weathered face both stony and hostile. He kicked his mount forward to meet Dain, who reached out for his bridle.

The chevard circled his horse, and as he passed Dain he drew his spurred foot from the stirrup and kicked him in the stomach.

All the wind left Dain in a whoosh of pain. He doubled over, sinking to his knees, wanting to vomit.

The chevard rode around him in a circle so tight, Dain feared the war charger might trample him. "Never seek to command my wits again," Lord Odfrey thundered at him. "Keep your pagan ways to yourself, boy!"

Clutching his aching stomach, Dain struggled to draw breath. He held up the huntsman's cap mutely.

"What is that?" the chevard asked, but Dain could not speak.

The knight protector rode forward and plucked the cap from Dain's hand.

"What is that, Sir Roye?" Lord Odfrey asked the man.

"Nothing," the protector answered. He flung the cap on the ground. "A piece of cloth."

"That belongs to your huntsman," Dain said, finding breath and strength enough to regain his feet at the same time. "He cannot hide in safety long. You must ride to his aid."

"This is mindless babbling," Sir Roye said impatiently. "Let us ride on, m'lord."

"I owe you my life, lord," Dain called out. "Why should I lie?"

Lord Odfrey frowned. With visible reluctance he beckoned to Dain, who approached him warily and stopped out of reach this time. "You are the eld I saw yesterday."

"Yes," Dain said.

"I sent you back into the forest from whence you came. What do you here and now? We've the Nega dwarves to hunt down—"

"But the Bnen attacked your villages," Dain said in protest.

Around him, a babble of consternation and anger broke out.

"What knows he of the raid?"

"Part of it, most like."

"A spy, he is!"

"Let's carve his bones for the trouble he's caused."

A shout rose up, and Dain's knees locked in fear. He held his ground, however, knowing they wouldn't attack him until Lord Odfrey gave them leave. His life hung on the whim of this stern man towering above him on horseback. Dain never let his gaze waver from Lord Odfrey's dark eyes.

"Your wits are addled," the chevard said. "My huntsman is safe behind in Thirst Hold—"

"Nay, he lies bleeding in the forest," Dain interrupted. "And with him are two men, stalwart and tall. One has hair like wheat. The top of his left ear was cut off probably a long time ago. The other has a nose hooked and broken, with no front teeth. Are they not your men? Who else would they be? I saw your huntsman yesterday. I know his face well."

"Enough of this," Sir Roye said. "M'lord, let us go—"

"Silence," the chevard commanded, and Sir Roye clamped his mouth shut without another word.

Lord Odfrey's dark eyes bored into Dain. "Your clothes are torn worse than last I saw them. There's blood on you—"

"The huntsman's," Dain said quickly. "Not mine."

"How far have you run?"

"A league, hardly more," Dain said with growing impatience. "Come, if you will save them—"

Lord Odfrey lifted his hand. "Boy, my huntsman is not—"

"But he came for the stag killed by those boys. I heard you give him the order to fetch the meat."

"So I did," Lord Odfrey said as though he'd forgotten until now. "But this morn, when the alarm was raised, I left orders for him not to go. It's not safe, with raids coming out of Nold."

Dain shook his head. "The man is in the forest, in desperate need of your help. Where I hid him and the others will not hold long, especially if they . . . It will not hold long. If you mean to save them, you *must* hurry!"

"The chevard must do nothing save by his own will," Sir Roye said to Dain. Within the frame of his helmet he had a face like a wrinkled nut; his features were dark and fierce. Hostility and suspicion radiated from his cat-yellow eyes, and Dain knew that were it not for the chevard's presence, Sir Roye would have run him through with that sword instead of just smacking him with it. Already, Dain had begun to feel a steady ache in his ribs from that blow. Sir Roye leaned down from his saddle and stabbed his finger at Dain. "You don't tell him what to do, ever! Morde a day, but I'd like to slit that pagan tongue right out of your gullet."

Believing him, Dain swallowed hard and fought the urge to back up.

"You're saying these men are in the clearing where the stag was brought down?" Lord Odfrey asked.

"Near to it. Not far past it," Dain said. "I'll show you."

He tried to go forward, but Sir Roye moved his horse to block Dain's path. "It's a smooth trick, this urgent story of men in need of us, but it's naught but pagan lies, m'lord. He wants nothing better than to lead us to certain ambush."

"I tell the truth!" Dain said hotly.

"You're lying, like all your kind."

"Hold your tongue, Sir Roye," Lord Odfrey said with steely anger. "This boy was Jorb the swordmaker's apprentice. He's no stranger, and I think no liar."

"M'lord, this tale has holes abounding in it," Sir Roye said. "The men are in the hold where they should be—"

"Nay!" shouted someone from the rear of the column. "They rode out before first light. Caix here saw them go!"

"Aye," said another voice that was fainter, as though even farther back. "I did, m'lord."

The chevard struck the pommel of his saddle with his gloved hand. "Damne! Did the fools leave before word of the raid came to us?"

Sir Roye drew back, but the other men surrounding Dain stared down at him, silent now, and intent.

"Fools," Lord Odfrey muttered again, but Dain wondered if it was the men he meant, or himself. The chevard scowled at Dain. "Quickly now, tell me what you know. You saw Nocine—the huntsman—and two others—"

"Sir Tilou and Sir Valon," Sir Roye muttered.

Lord Odfrey nodded without taking his gaze off Dain. "Exactly where?"

"They are hiding in a gully beyond the clearing of the Forlo travel burrow," Dain said. "Now my sister's burial place."

Compassion sparked briefly in the chevard's dark gaze, then vanished. "A gully? They can't hide there."

"Not for long," Dain agreed. "The Bnen were about to torture them."

"And how did you rescue them from this war party of dwarves?" Sir Roye asked with open skepticism.

Dain opened his mouth to answer, but Lord Odfrey interrupted. "Never mind. There's no time to be lost—"

"But, m'lord," Sir Roye said in protest. "What about the raid that left fourteen of your villagers dead and their huts afire? What about the Nega who—"

"The Nega would not raid," Dain said hotly. "They never raid. They are—"

"We saw their marks, boy," Sir Roye said. "We have proof."

"A mark is not proof."

"And who else would draw it?"

"The Bnen who did the raid," Dain said, meeting the knight glare for glare. "The Bnen I saw carrying man-loot and bringing man-prisoners. Here lies Nega land," he said, pointing at the curve of forest behind Lord Odfrey, "but the Nega do not winter this far west. They are gone south, to their mines in the Rock Hills."

Lord Odfrey pointed to the cap, which lay on the ground where Sir Roye had thrown it. Dain hastened to pick it up and hand it to the chevard, who turned it over in his hands.

"This is Nocine's," the chevard said. "There is blood on it."

Sir Roye's face crinkled up as he squinted at his lord. "And if this one's a trickster, sent forth to lead us off the trail?"

Lord Odfrey looked at Dain. "Come here, boy."

Dain went to him, as wary as before, and stood next to his stirrup. Lord Odfrey reached down his hand. Hesitantly, Dain started to clasp it as he had seen Mandrians do, but Lord Odfrey gripped him hard just above his elbow. The chevard's fingers were like steel, clamped on to Dain's flesh. Dain struggled to hold back a gasp, and hid the pain he felt from his face.

Lord Odfrey's dark eyes bored into Dain's pale gray ones as though he meant to look inside his very soul. Then he released him so abruptly, Dain staggered back.

"He brings us truth," Lord Odfrey declared.

The men exchanged glances, murmuring to each other. Sir Roye's mouth opened in dismay. "M'lord—"

Lord Odfrey drew his foot from the stirrup, and Dain jumped back out of reach.

"Quickly now," Lord Odfrey said to him as though he did not notice. "Get up behind me."

Dain put his foot in the stirrup and scrambled up behind Lord Odfrey's saddle. He had never ridden such a tall horse as this before. He felt as though he were floating high in the air. The charger shifted beneath him, its powerful hindquarters flexing with strength. Dain clamped his legs tight to hold on with, and Lord Odfrey cast him a glance.

"Don't kick him in the flanks or we'll both be thrown," he said, and wheeled the horse around with such speed Dain nearly toppled off. "Hang on to my cloak and point the way."

Dain gripped the magnificent fur in one hand and slid his other past Lord Odfrey's armored elbow. "There."

Lord Odfrey gathered his reins, but Sir Roye was not yet done.

He spurred his horse to block Lord Odfrey's path. His eyes held distrust and suspicion. "M'lord, consider the risk. If he's leading us into a trap—"

"And if he is not?" Lord Odfrey retorted. "Will I chase blindly through the Dark Forest all day or will I use this guide that Thod has brought us?"

"Thod is leading us in the guise of a pagan?" someone behind Dain said in loud disbelief. "Mercy of Tomias, what next?"

Dain did not glance back to see who spoke, and neither did Lord Odfrey. The chevard's gaze clashed with Sir Roye's. "Will you protest all day, or will you follow me, Sir Roye?"

"If he betrays us—"

"Then you have my permission to draw and quarter him," Lord Odfrey said grimly. He glanced back at Dain, who sat very still and wary at his back now. "That is," the chevard added, "after I take off his head. Still eager to save men who are strangers to you, boy?"

Dain swallowed hard, but he knew he could not waver now, before this challenge. "The Bnen killed my family. If I can bring them harm by leading your men to them, I will." He pointed again. "That way, lord."

The chevard turned his gaze on Sir Roye, who backed his mount out of his master's way. Lord Odfrey spurred his horse, and they leaped away in a gallop.

The horse's mind was a dim flicker of *go/go/go.* Grinning with eagerness, Dain tipped back his head to savor the rush of wind against his face. This was like flying. He jounced along, as high as the tree branches, clinging to the back of the chevard's saddle. The rhythmic thunder of the army's hoofbeats filled his ears.

He pointed the way, and the column of riders arrowed into the Dark Forest as fast as the snarled undergrowth would allow. The horses snorted their white breath and ran tirelessly. Leaves were falling, as golden as bright coins, and the small, furry denizens of the forest fled to their dens at the noisy passage of horses and riders. Always, Dain was questing with his mind, seeking the Bnen raiders.

Some remained at the clearing. The rest were scattered. He murmured this in Lord Odfrey's ear, and the chevard nodded.

"The clearing first," he said.

They crossed a road no wider than a trail that wound through the ever-thickening trees. Although a weak, wintry sun shone this day, it barely penetrated the canopy overhead. Here and there, pale shafts of light pierced down to the springy mold underfoot. Vines looped low from branches, creating hazards of their own. The riders slowed down to a trot, ducking vines and branches, sometimes halting to cut their way through.

"This," Sir Roye muttered behind the chevard's horse, "is why we don't bring cavalry into the Dark Forest."

Dain ignored him, as did the chevard. "There," Dain whispered, pointing at the clearing ahead. His keen eyes, long accustomed to picking out the movement of a quarry from the trembling of leaves, saw a group of the dwarves working to pile something in the middle of the clearing. The bonfire blazed less brightly than earlier. He wondered if the wise-sayers had succeeded in bringing their spell to life. Sniffing suspiciously, he detected no dark magic.

The chevard drew his sword, as did Sir Roye and the riders behind them. "This is their smallest force," the chevard said in a soft voice. "Strike quick and hard. We've more work to do elsewhere."

"My lord," asked a cultured voice from among the men. "What degree of mercy do we show?"

Growls of protest rose up, but a glare from Lord Odfrey silenced them all. "No mercy," he said, and spurred his horse forward.

Behind him rose a howling battle cry such as Dain had never

heard before. It was terrifying and exhilarating at the same time. He realized he was being hurtled into battle without arms or weapons, but at that moment he felt immortal and did not care.

He drew his own dagger, gripping the back of the chevard's saddle with his other hand. Lifting his own voice, he cried out Thia's name, and rode the galloping charger into the clearing for blood and battle, seeking her vengeance.

By the time they burst upon the dwarves, the twenty or so Bnen there had thrown down the loot they were stacking in piles and reached for their war axes. Gathering themselves into a knot with their backs guarded, they tried to withstand the initial rush of the riders, but they were too few.

Lord Odfrey did not swerve around them as Dain expected him to. Instead, he set his charger straight at the enemy and rode right into their midst and over the top of them. Several dwarves were trampled beneath the charger's hooves, their screams blending with the shouts and battle cries of the others. Hearing a skull crunch and shatter, Dain swallowed hard and leaned down to swipe the enemy with his dagger. He missed his mark as the charger leaped sideways. Then there came a great whistling whoosh of air as Lord Odfrey's long broadsword swung and sent a Bnen head flipping in an arc to bounce and tumble on the ground.

Blood from the headless dwarf spurted across Dain's leg, then the charger was on the other side of the clustered dwarves. The horse swung around without any command. Dain noticed that the reins were lying slack on the horse's heavy neck. Both of Lord Odfrey's hands gripped the long hilt of his broadsword. His shoulders bunched with effort as he lifted and swung the sword again.

Another dwarf went down, cleaved in two. From the other side, Sir Roye was hacking and cursing steadily.

The dwarves broke ranks and scattered. In a few minutes, all of them lay dead, even the wise-sayers. One of the knights stirred among the loot with the tip of his spear and brought up a child's rag doll impaled on the end of it.

"These are our raiders, sure enough," Lord Odfrey said grimly. Raising his visor, he glanced around at Dain. "Is this all of them?"

"Nay, there are eighty or so more," Dain answered breathlessly. Brief though it had been, this battle had filled his mind with scenes of shock and slaughter. He wanted more. "They're coming."

Lord Odfrey exchanged a glance with Sir Roye. "Hard to maneuver in the trees. Still, the advantage is ours. Give the orders."

Sir Roye wheeled his horse around and bawled out commands. The knights scattered and rode out of the clearing in various directions. In the distance, a drum began to pound. Dain heard it before Lord Odfrey did. Both of them tensed.

"Ah," Lord Odfrey said quietly. He settled himself deeper in the saddle and gathered his reins. "Lead me to where you left Nocine and the others, boy."

On the way to the gully, they encountered two more attacking parties of dwarves. The Mandrian knights had all the advantages of being on horseback and having spears and broadswords. The dwarves were fearless, ferocious, and used both arrows and axes, hesitating not to attack horses as well as men. But the chargers were trained fighters, rearing and trampling with deadly forefeet.

Both times Lord Odfrey fought his way through, with Sir Roye sticking grimly to his side. Two other knights also rode close, protecting the chevard.

Leaving dead or dying dwarves behind them, they rode on in the direction Dain showed them. Before he reached the gully, however, he knew his spell had failed.

Dismay swept his heart, followed by exasperation. The two saplings that should have been standing in the bottom of the gully were gone. Only the real stands of crimson-leaved shtac remained, along with the briars and the clumps of perlimon laden with bright orange globes of intensely sour fruit. It took a hard frost to ripen perlimon, and even then the fruit was often too tart to enjoy. Dain stared into the gully while the charger pawed the edge restlessly.

"Well?" Lord Odfrey asked in a harsh voice.

"They did not stay," Dain said, wondering what had become of the men. "I told them they would be safe if they—"

He broke off, feeling the knights' suspicion gathering around him like a net.

"No cover to hide in here," Sir Roye said, glaring at Dain with his yellow eyes. "I *told* you, m'lord—"

"Wait," Dain said. He slid off the charger before Lord Odfrey could protest. Ducking beneath the perlimons, Dain slithered down the steep bank of the gully to its bottom, where the log still lay, half-covered with drifting leaves.

He knelt and began to scoop armfuls of them away.

"Boy," Lord Odfrey said.

"He's lost his wits," Sir Roye muttered.

Dain ignored them both. Laying his hand on the log's rough bark, he felt the life force of the man within his spell, a dim, nearly spent force. Dain broke the spell, and there the huntsman lay for all of them to see. Nocine's face had turned gray and sweaty. His mouth hung open slackly, but when Dain pressed his palm to the huntsman's chest, he felt the erratic thud of his heart.

"Morde a day!" Sir Roye swore. "What magic is this?"

Dain turned his head to look up at them. "Only a weak nature spell," he said. "It fools the eyes, nothing more. I told the others to stay still. If they grew frightened and moved, the spell would break."

None of the Mandrians replied. They were all staring at him, with expressions varying from fear, to wary admiration, to glaring suspicion, to stern neutrality.

"He's a—Thod knows what he is," Sir Roye said. "Best to keep well away from him, m'lord."

Lord Odfrey said nothing. In the stony lines of his weathered face, his dark eyes looked sad and far away, as though it wasn't Dain he saw at all.

In the distance came the sounds of more battle. Dain tilted his head to listen, and knew the main force of Bnen were coming.

"Your huntsman lives, lord," he said to the chevard. "And the war party is not far from us."

Lord Odfrey blinked as though coming out of his thoughts. He pointed at the unconscious huntsman. "Sir Alard, take him forth from here. See him safely home."

"Yes, my lord."

The knight spurred his horse down into the gully and dismounted to pick up Nocine and drape him across his mount's withers. Returning to the saddle, he sent his horse scrambling back up the slope to the top and headed away.

Dain climbed up after him and stood there, wondering what

was to happen now. He read the faces of the three remaining men and knew they intended to leave him behind.

In that moment, Dain knew he did not want to part ways. He did not want to go deep into the Dark Forest, searching out others of the Forlo Clan and claiming a home with them. With Jorb dead, the Forlo dwarves owed Dain no claim of kinship. Even if another swordmaker accepted Dain as an apprentice, he knew suddenly, he did not want to spend his life making swords—he wanted to wield them. In the last two days, he had glimpsed a different, much larger world than the one he'd always known. His home and family were gone now. He could do whatever he wanted, go wherever he pleased, make a new life for himself.

"You have served me well, boy," Lord Odfrey said.

"My name is Dain."

"You acted well in saving my huntsman's life. You brought us to the raiders responsible for the attack on my village. For these acts I thank you." Lord Odfrey untied the food pouch from his saddle and held it out.

Dain made no move to take it. "Is food all I'm worth, lord?"

Sir Roye growled, and Lord Odfrey blinked. "You hunger, boy," the chevard said. "But if it's gold you would rather have—"

"My name is Dain, and I want a place in your hold as my reward."

"Nay!" Sir Roye shouted before Lord Odfrey could answer. The knight glared at Dain, his yellow eyes afire. "There can be no pagan in a faithful hold. Morde a day, he would bring ill luck to us all—"

Arrows came whistling through the trees into their midst, a whole volley of them. One skimmed over Dain's shoulder, making him flinch and dive for cover. Several struck Sir Roye's back, bouncing off his armor harmlessly. One hit Lord Odfrey in the face.

There was a spurt of blood, and the chevard reeled back in his saddle. Quicker than thought, Dain jumped and caught him before he could topple off his horse. The charger whipped its armored head around and bit Dain in his side.

The pain made him shout aloud. Doubling his fist, he struck the horse across its tender muzzle. The horse released him, and Dain sucked in a shaky breath against the agony flooding his side. He could feel blood oozing along his skin beneath his tunic, but he dared not look.

He was still holding the chevard up, and the man in his armor weighed so much Dain thought he would sink into the ground beneath him. Sir Roye shouted something and rode around to Lord Odfrey's other side. Leaning over, Sir Roye gripped Lord Odfrey's arm and pulled him upright.

"M'lord!" he was shouting urgently. "M'lord!"

Lord Odfrey groaned. He was still pressing his hand to his face, the arrow's shaft and fletching protruding from his fingers. Blood ran everywhere, soaking into his surcoat and trickling down his armor.

From the trees around them, a harrowing cry rose and drums beat like thunder.

Dain climbed onto Lord Odfrey's horse and straddled it in front of the saddle. He was practically sitting on the horse's thick neck, but he grabbed the reins and said, "Hold on to me, lord."

The chevard was breathing hard, making a faint groaning sound beneath each ragged breath. He swayed and turned toward Sir Roye. "Pull it out," he gasped harshly.

Sir Roye's gaze swiveled from him to the dwarves, visible now as they came swarming from three sides. The other knight, whose name Dain did not know, lifted a horn to his lips and blew on it loudly. In the distance another horn answered.

"Pull it out!" Lord Odfrey ordered. "Damne, do as I command."

Sir Roye's fierce narrow face knotted in consternation, but he reached across and gripped the shaft of the arrow. "If it's in your eye, I'll kill you," he said.

Lord Odfrey shuddered and struck Dain in the back with his fist.

Dain looked at Sir Roye and saw the older man's love for the chevard warring in his eyes with what he knew had to be done. "Pull it out," Dain said.

Sir Roye scowled and gave a quick, hard tug. The arrow came out with a great gout of blood that spurted across the back of Dain's head and shoulders. Lord Odfrey cried out and slumped against Dain, who struggled to sit erect and support his weight.

"They're on us!" the other knight shouted, drawing his sword.

Another volley of arrows flew at them. Dain wheeled the charger around, using the reins as he had seen the other men do. The horse backed its ears and fought him, half-rearing, but the arrows skimmed by without striking Dain. He heard some of them hit Lord Odfrey's armored back and fall to the ground.

Shouting hoarse war cries of their own, Sir Roye and the other knight closed ranks and charged the rush of dwarves, although they were hopelessly outnumbered. Lord Odfrey's horse was still fighting Dain, trying to swing itself around toward the battle.

While he was struggling with it, Dain felt Lord Odfrey lift himself. His visor clanged down, and the man shakily drew his sword, nearly cutting Dain's thigh in doing so.

"Boy," he said, his voice thin and muffled inside his helmet, "have you any magic to stanch this wound?"

Dwarves surrounded the two knights on all sides, and more of them came rushing now toward Dain and Lord Odfrey. Dain was afraid. His heart was pounding so hard he thought it would break his ribs. He believed that Lord Odfrey was going to swoon and fall off the horse at any moment. They had to get out of here.

"Boy," Lord Odfrey said again.

Dain shook his head. "Nay, lord. None."

Lord Odfrey gripped his shoulder with such force Dain thought his bones might crack, then said, "Drop the reins on his neck. Let him fight for us. We'll stand here. We will not run."

The chevard's courage shamed Dain. He dropped the reins as commanded, and at once the brawny charger blew through its nostrils and wheeled around to meet the oncoming dwarves. He reared and struck out with his forefeet, bringing two of the dwarves down.

As the horse landed, he leaped forward. Dain was nearly unseated, but Lord Odfrey leaned forward with the horse, using its impetus as he swung his sword.

A dwarf staggered back, his head half-severed from his neck.

Cruel fingers gripped Dain's left knee and tugged hard, trying to pull him off. He twisted around and stabbed the dwarf's forearm with his dagger. Screaming, the dwarf released him and stumbled back. But two others took his place. Lord Odfrey lifted his sword over Dain's head and swung down, eliminating them both.

Dain heard the chevard grunt with the effort, but his courage and refusal to give up infected Dain with the same fiery spirit. Together they fought, circling as the dwarves tried to surround them. After a while, Sir Roye fought his way back to Lord Odfrey's side, protecting him with great ferocity.

Then a horn blew, and from Dain's left came twenty or more Mandrian knights riding through the trees like vengeance itself. They plowed into the dwarf war party and attacked them from their flank, driving them back while some of the knights forced their way to Lord Odfrey's side, shielding him from further harm.

A few minutes later, minutes that seemed to last an eternity to Dain, sudden quiet descended upon the forest. The dead and dying lay sprawled everywhere, their blood soaking into the ground. Silence held the forest, broken only by the harsh breathing of the survivors, who lifted their visors and showed strained, sweat-soaked faces to each other.

Sir Roye glared fiercely around, then sheathed his sword. He reached out and gripped Lord Odfrey's sword arm. "M'lord," he said, his voice hoarse with fatigue and worry. "It's over. M'lord, let me take your sword."

Lord Odfrey sat there in silence as though he did not comprehend, but at last he let Sir Roye pull his bloody sword from his hand.

"Home," he said in a strained whisper.

Sir Roye nodded to Dain, who gathered up the charger's reins. "Go easy with him, boy."

Dain nodded, coaxing the weary charger into a walk.

Sir Roye rode close on his right. Another knight crowded close on the left.

"Know you the way?" Sir Roye asked. "I'm fair turned about in these infernal trees."

"I know the way," Dain said.

Conscious of the importance of his task, he picked a path over the dead Bnen, his enemies no longer. Deep weariness sagged through him, but he resisted it, refusing to give way to the long shudders that shook him. He had never been in battle before. The smell of death hung thick over the woods, tainting them now. He was glad the Mandrian knights did not joke and laugh as they rode home behind his lead. They talked softly among themselves, but did not make merry. He noticed that several seemed to be praying, making the circle of their faith as they did so. He respected them for that.

Good-bye, Thia, he thought. *Sleep well in your resting place. I go to a new life among men. You would not like it. You would tell me to beware, for men are never to be trusted. But I trust this man. His heart is good, and he has honor in him.*

Lord Odfrey moaned quietly and slumped against Dain's back. Sir Roye gripped his arm, steadying him to keep him from falling, and thus did they ride forth from the Dark Forest, crossing the bridge that spanned the river whose name Dain did not know. The bridge guards stared at them, openmouthed and red-faced with admiration, and closed the gates behind them.

When they reached the opposite bank, the road stretched ahead, leading to a slight rise of ground. There rose the tall stone walls of Thirst Hold, a gray fortress with banners flying against the sky.

Seeing it, Dain shivered slightly. His fear and distrust returned and he knew fresh temptation to return to the forest and make a solitary life for himself. He could journey to the north, to see Nether. He could explore the world.

Yet the world seemed too big just now. He was cold and hungry, and he hurt all over. Surely Lord Odfrey would give him a place here, where he would have shelter and food in exchange for whatever work he would do. He'd sensed agreement in the man's mind before the last attack. For now, that was assurance enough.

The massive gates to the hold stood open by the time the riders reached them. They rode through, someone else taking the lead now. There was a cramped tunnel of stone to pass along, then Dain emerged into a spacious, muddy keep surrounded by walls and buildings of stone. Everything he saw amazed him. He could barely take in half of it.

And people . . . there were people everywhere, thronging the courtyard and milling around past another passageway that led into yet a larger yard. Towers rose above the roofs of the tallest buildings. A few of the windows even glinted with glass. He had never seen so much stone, or so much fodder stacked in yellowing heaps next to barns, or so many chickens running and squawking underfoot, or so many barrels and kegs of food. From the looks of things, the inhabitants of several villages had crowded themselves within the walls of the hold.

How they did clamor, shrieking and calling out questions, cheering and waving their caps when the word went forth that the raiders were dead.

They yelled and stamped their feet and hooted and jumped for joy, pressing closer until some of the knights shoved them back.

"Make way!" Sir Roye shouted impatiently. "Make way for the chevard!"

The cheers did not fade. The common folk seemed not to notice that Lord Odfrey was wounded. They milled and scrambled out of the way heedlessly, until at last Dain and Sir Roye rode through their midst and broke free into a third courtyard, this one paved with large, smooth flagstones. The horses' hooves clattered, echoing off the buildings that towered above.

Broad steps led to a central building, one longer than it was tall and flanked by a tower on either side. Servants swarmed down the steps and came hurrying to meet Dain's horse.

"Fetch Sulein at once," Sir Roye ordered. "His lordship is badly hurt."

"Is he dead?" a voice asked, only to be shushed.

A pair of boys gripped the war charger's bridle, and one of them pulled the reins from Dain's hands. "Who's that?" he asked, staring at Dain.

No one answered him.

Eager hands reached up and lowered Lord Odfrey gently from his horse. With his armor on, he was no easy weight. Six men struggled to carry him up the steps and into the building. Dain could hear dogs barking inside and the commotion of voices.

Weary to his very bones, Dain slid off the horse and walked around it to Sir Roye, who was also dismounting.

The knight bowed his head and straightened slowly as though his joints ached. He pulled off his helmet and pushed back his mail coif to reveal short-cropped gray hair darkened with sweat. His yellow eyes held worry.

"Where now should I go?" Dain asked him. "Can I have the food Lord Odfrey offered me earlier?"

"Food?" Sir Roye repeated. He turned his head around and

focused on Dain as though he'd forgotten the boy existed. He scowled. "Food?"

"Yes, I'm hungry—"

"I don't care if you starve," Sir Roye said, but he cut down the food pouch from Lord Odfrey's saddle and flung it at Dain. "There's your reward. Now be off with you."

Dain clutched the pouch and stood there, determined to get what he wanted. "The lord was going to give me a place—"

"He never did!" Sir Roye broke in angrily.

"I asked—"

"Aye, but he gave no promise."

The two of them glared at each other until Dain finally looked away. Desperately he said, "But I helped you. I led you to the Bnen. I saved the huntsman's life. I fought with—"

"There's no place for the likes of you in Thirst Hold," Sir Roye said. "Get back to where you belong."

"But—"

Sir Roye beckoned to one of the mounted knights still nearby. "See to this," he ordered, then turned away and headed up the steps into the building.

Dain stood there, watching him go, and only then noticed that the stableboys were staring at him with open hostility and fear.

"What is it?" one of them asked.

The other shook his head. "A demon maybe."

"Look at them ears."

"Look at them eyes."

"No! Don't look at its eyes. It'll put a spell on ye!"

The knight backed up his horse. "You boys, see to the chevard's horse. He's fought well today, and he deserves an extra ration of grain."

The stableboys ignored him. "Get it!" one of them yelled. He picked up a dried horse dropping and threw it at Dain. The other boy did the same.

Pelted with manure, Dain turned away from them and ran. The knight shouted after him, and Dain glanced back to see him coming in pursuit, his horse's shod hooves clattering on the paving stones. In the gathering dusk, with the charger snorting scarlet and sparks striking from its hooves, the knight looked like a phantasm from the second world astride a darsteed.

Dain imagined the man picking him up by the scruff of his

neck and riding to the gates of the hold, then flinging Dain into the mud.

Refusing to let that happen, Dain darted out of the paved courtyard and back into the larger enclosure and the melee of villagers. Shoved and jostled, he quickly ducked behind a stack of barrels where no one would notice him. Sinking to the cold ground with a weary sigh, he glanced around warily, watching the knight ride by, the war charger pushing through the crowds with ill temper. When the horse kicked a serf and began to paw and champ its bit, the knight reined up and dismounted.

Another knight in a torn and blood-splattered surcoat approached him on foot. "Masen, what do you out here? Have that brute stabled and see to yourself."

Sir Masen pushed back his mail coif, revealing a sweat-soaked tangle of light brown hair. "Have you seen the eld boy, Terent? The one that rode with us?"

"He's with the chevard, I thought."

"Nay. Sir Roye dismissed him. I have orders to see him thrown out of the hold."

The other knight swore. Dain crouched lower in his hiding place, hardly daring to breathe. He feared that both of them would resume the search.

"It grows late," Sir Terent said. "I'm frozen to the bone. Let's see ourselves to a fire first, then we'll worry about the eld. It's too late anyway for tonight. The gates are closing."

Sir Masen hesitated, but after a moment his friend persuaded him. Together, they walked to the guardhouse and the long barracks beyond it, their spurs jingling with every step. Small boys scampered behind them in obvious hero worship.

Relieved, Dain sank onto his haunches and gulped in several deep breaths. He had a chance now to hide himself well before they hunted him again. Grinning, he delved into the pouch and pulled out a wedge of cheese, which he began to eat as fast as he could choke it down.

Exhaustion dragged at him. He felt stiff with cold and his side ached with every breath. He was terribly thirsty, and his hands were cut and skinned across the backs of his knuckles where they'd been whipped by branches and briars during the wild ride through the forest.

The deepening shadows were cold. The sun sloped low and dropped behind the towering walls. He was in a place of strangers, most of whom would as soon slit his throat as look at him. His one ally lay unconscious, perhaps dying. Although Dain knew Lord Odfrey's mind had intended to make the promise Dain asked for, he had not actually given it voice before the arrow struck him.

Sir Roye was the kind of man who would accept only deed or command, not intention. Dain grimaced and spit at the thought of Sir Roye, then went back to chewing cheese. He didn't care if they all cursed him. He needed somewhere to live through the coming winter. Now that he was inside these walls, he wasn't leaving.

13

FAR AWAY IN lower Mandria, a ponderous carriage halted on a low rise, and the Duc du Lindier pulled aside the leather curtain buttoned over the window. "Look, my dear," he said excitedly.

Pheresa's gloved hands clenched tightly in her lap for a moment, but she allowed none of her discomposure to show in her face. Obediently she leaned forward to gaze out the window. One trailing end of her veil fell from her shoulder and dangled. Ignoring it, she gripped the edge of the carriage window and peered out at her future.

The air was mild and a rainy drizzle misted down, casting the world in shades of hazy gray. She saw that they had halted in a wooded park of pleasing scope. Venerable old chestnut trees, their knotty trunks furred with pale moss, spread broad limbs that nearly touched the ground in places. Autumn-blooming cegnias massed at the base of these trees, their fragrant blossoms vivid pink in hue. A carpet of low-growing blue vineca meandered through the park like a road to enchantment. Perky yellow difelias bloomed in scattered clumps. A stream, lined with rounded stones, rushed and gurgled in a course parallel with the winding road.

"Oh!" she said in delight, forgetting her nervousness. "How lovely. I have never seen a more beautiful vista, yet how natural it looks, as though the gardener's hand was never here."

"Ladies and their flowers," her father said with an indulgent chuckle. "Look beyond, my dear. There is the palace."

Pheresa lifted her gaze to the horizon. Beyond the trees, looming through the mist, sprawled a gray mass of stone and spire. She drew in a sharp breath. "Savroix!" she whispered.

It was the size of a town, much larger than she'd expected despite all the tales she'd been told.

Pheresa blinked at it, trying to take in its size, trying to convince herself that this was indeed to be her new home. For a moment she felt lost and overwhelmed. After all, for the past nine years of her life, she had been incarcerated in the nuncery at Montreuv, cloistered there with other young maidens of the highest birth to be educated in all that was desirable and ladylike. A week past, her father had come for her. He was nearly a stranger, looking tall and thin and impatient. She wondered when his hair had turned gray. When had he acquired his limp? He'd bowed to her hastily, clearing his throat in a way she *did* remember, and announced, "The king wants you to come live at Savroix. Get your things ready, for I am to take you there immediately."

Since then, Pheresa's orderly life had become one of chaos and flurry. She'd been given scant time to pack her belongings. Whisked home, she'd tried to familiarize herself with the house and grounds, as well as the three younger sisters she'd acquired in her absence, but her mother was wild with excitement and kept her busy with fittings for gowns and all the accouterments necessary for a lady of fashion. Nothing was ready. Her trunks at this moment contained several half-finished gowns to be completed by the palace seamstresses. The rest of her things would be sent to her later.

Pheresa did not understand the need for such haste. Normally a calm, well-ordered maiden, she preferred life to follow an established routine. She had expected to remain at Montreuv until spring, at which time she would celebrate her eighteenth birthday. The nuns conducted a small, elegant ceremony for their graduates. Pheresa had looked forward to wearing a gown of pure white, with a diadem of silver in her hair and a bouquet of spring lilies in her hands, while the benediction was pronounced over them and bells rang joyously.

All her life she had known what her future would hold. Her mother was Princess Dianthelle, sister to the king. Her father was the Duc du Lindier, one of Mandria's four marechals and a very great warrior. From birth, Pheresa had been destined to wed the Heir to the Realm. She had met Gavril only once, when she was eight years old and he was seven. They had gone through a trothing ceremony to convey the intentions of their parents, although it was not a binding contract of obligation on either side. All she remembered of Gavril was that he was blond-haired, that he had snatched the best pastries for himself, and that he had kicked her when no one was looking.

In the coming year, when Gavril reached his majority and was knighted, he would be proclaimed Heir to the Realm. Upon achieving that title, he would be free to marry. She expected to attend the ceremonies of his investiture. They would be formally reintroduced. He would court her, and if she pleased him, he would propose.

Pheresa was not a vain young woman, but she knew herself to be beautiful. Her figure was well formed and graceful. Her blonde tresses held a natural tint of red, bleached away carefully with the juice of lemons by her maidservant and kept secret from the nuns. She had three freckles on her nose, which she considered too long and slender; the freckles were bleached with lemons too. Now that she was no longer under the aegis of the nuns, who disapproved of vanity, she planned to powder her nose in the court fashion and vanquish her freckles entirely. Her eyes were wide-set and light brown. She was intelligent, able to read and write, versed in many subjects, and levelheaded. She looked forward to parties and dancing, but she planned also to read and study a variety of topics which the nuns had closed to her inquiring mind.

These had been her plans, but now they were thrown awry. She had not expected King Verence to summon her so abruptly to the palace. She did not understand why she was to live with him now, many months before she should even arrive to meet Prince Gavril. Her cousin was away, being fostered. She could not even become acquainted with him as she would like.

"Well, daughter?" her father asked now, beaming at her. His long narrow face was flushed with excitement. He looked puffed up with pride, and she wished he were not. "Is there no smile? Does the sight of your new home not please you? Savroix, my dear. Savroix!"

Pheresa swallowed a sigh and summoned a wan smile to please him. "Yes, Father, Savroix is certainly impressive. I did not expect it to be so large."

"There's nothing like it in all the world," Lindier proclaimed, and rubbed his hands together. He closed the leather curtain and gave the order for the carriage to drive on. "Not much longer now, my dear, and then you shall be home."

She frowned, unable to hide her distaste.

"Why do you look so?" he asked.

"Do you not find this summons odd?" she replied.

"Odd? Certainly not. It is a great honor extended to you. The king has followed your progress and studies with much interest these past few years. Your conduct and deportment have been reported to him as excellent. He is well pleased and now he is impatient to meet you. What is wrong with that?"

"Nothing," she said hastily. "I am honored by this opportunity to meet the king. But—"

"But what?" Lindier snapped. "Why do you frown so? Why do you quibble? What's wrong with you? Nerves?"

"No, your grace," she said, casting her gaze down at her clenched hands. Slowly she forced her fists to uncurl. "But must I live here now?"

"Why not? It is to be your home. The king wishes to get to know you, both as your uncle and as your imminent father-in-law."

"But that is the problem, Father," she said, meeting Lindier's eyes. "It is too soon. Gavril has not proposed to me yet."

"He will, my dear. He must!"

"But he is not bound to choose me."

"Custom binds him," Lindier said grimly.

"But not law. For me to be installed here in the palace, and waiting for him when he returns next year . . . well, it looks too forward. It looks as though I expect him to—that I am sure he will—that I—"

"Nonsense!" Lindier said heartily. "What is this mincing nicety about? Of course you expect him to propose. We all do."

"But I should not appear to be too confident."

"It is custom," Lindier repeated.

"If I offend his pride, this confidence will prove to be the gravest folly," she whispered unhappily. "I have heard that the prince is hot-tempered and stubborn. If he feels coerced or pressured too hard, he may wish to look elsewhere for his bride."

Lindier snorted and gripped her hand briefly in his. "You worry too much. The boy is young and high-spirited, but he is hardly a fool. One look at you, my dear, and he will be captivated."

She smiled at that. She could not help but be won by her father's flattery; however, as they swept through the imposing gates of the palace and rolled along the long drive, her qualms returned.

Still, the wonders and beauty of the grounds amazed her. Her father pulled aside the curtain so they could look out despite the misty rain, and she gasped at the size of the fountain, which seemed as large as a lake. Cavorting sea creatures and cherubs made of mossy stone spouted jets of water. The size and scale of them astonished her. Beyond the fountain lay gardens of riotous color and formal pattern. The flowers glowed in the gentle rain, the day's dreariness making their hues seem brighter. The walls of the palace towered before her with an immense grandeur of spires and statuary, and as she looked Pheresa's heart began to beat faster.

I shall be the mistress of all this, she thought. It was the king's wish, and surely Gavril was no longer as spoiled and horrid as he had been when he was a little child. Even if she did not like him, she liked Savroix very much.

The carriage halted before a vast sweep of steps leading up to tall doors that stood open. Servants in royal livery were lined up in a double row at attention, and a purple carpet was rolled out between them.

As Pheresa was handed out of the carriage with tender care by her father, she met his excited gaze and smiled fully for the first time. In her mind, it no longer mattered if she and Gavril liked or disliked each other. She wanted Savroix for her own. She would do whatever she had to in order to get it.

Far away at Thirst Hold, Gavril's raid on the chevard's cellars worked exactly as planned. With almost everyone in the hold worried about whether Lord Odfrey would live or die, it proved a simple matter to gain entry. Aoun and another manservant coerced into helping carried out perhaps a dozen kegs of the Saelutian mead and concealed them in an unused storeroom.

Now it was the eve of Aelintide. The servants had been abustle all day, making preparations for tomorrow's feasting and celebration of harvest. Julth Rondel, steward of Thirst Hold, wanted to suspend the feast until Lord Odfrey recovered, but Gavril had insisted the celebrations go on as planned.

After supper ended and while the chapel bell was ringing to call worshipers to eventide mass, Gavril collected Mierre, Sir Los, and a servant to carry a keg of the mead. He set out through the crisp night air, his breath puffing white about his face, his jeweled poniard swinging at his side, his fur-lined cloak keeping him warm.

He crossed the hold, walking at first with the general stream of knights and servants going to the mass to pray for Lord Odfrey's recovery, then splitting off and proceeding onward. He noted with approval the long trestle tables and harvest pole already placed in the stableyard. As he approached the guardhouse, he saw lights in the windows and heard the sounds of comradely singing. Sentries patrolled the battlements in silence, keeping the normal discipline of the hold. Although the raiders had been defeated, the dwarf attack had greatly unsettled the serfs. It had been with difficulty that they were persuaded to leave the safety of the hold yesterday. Those who had been burned out were sent off to make new homes for themselves, each survivor given a sack of essentials such as a cooking pot, a hank of salted meat, a length of new-woven linsey to make clothes, and a Circle to hang over their new hearth. Such largess emboldened them greatly, and most set off without further persuasion, pausing only to touch the door of the chapel with prayers for Lord Odfrey.

Pausing outside the door of the guardhouse, Gavril waited for Sir Los to step ahead of him and pound on the thick wooden panels.

The singing died down, and the door swung open. "What's the word o' the master?" asked a gruff voice from within.

"Nothing," Sir Los replied in his terse way. "His highness requests entry."

The door opened wide, and the knights within rose to their feet, scraping back stools and benches in a great crash of noise.

Gavril drew a deep breath. He was almost trembling inside with anticipation, but he forced his emotions under rigid control. He did not want his excitement misunderstood.

"The knights of Thirst Hold bid your highness enter, with welcome," said the man at the door.

He bowed low, and Gavril stepped inside.

The guardhouse was a round, stout structure, built of brick and stone. One half of it held cells for miscreants and suspicious characters awaiting judgment and floggings. The rest of the building was a single, open chamber filled with tables and benches. The knights ate their meals here. In their off-duty hours they diced, studied war strategies, assembled to hear reports and dispatches of trouble on the border, and dictated letters to scribes.

Seeing one such individual now standing in the far corner, still clutching his pen in ink-stained fingers, Gavril frowned and pointed at the man. "Scribe, you are excused," he said.

The scribe's throat-apple jerked up and down. With a hasty bow, he gathered up scraps of parchment, his inkwell, his leather roll, and his assortment of battered pens. Bowing again, he scuttled past Gavril and his party, and exited out the door into the night.

Gavril glanced around at the silent, respectful faces. One man, Sir Bosquecel, captain of the guard, was conspicuously absent. No doubt he had gone to mass. Having counted on that, Gavril concealed an inner smile of satisfaction.

"Come to the fire, your highness," Sir Terent said. He was the man who had opened the door to them. Balding and ruddy-faced, he gestured toward the hearth, where a modest fire burned amidst crumbled embers and white ashes. "Please accept our hospitality and have a chair. Sir Nynth, pour his highness and these companions a cup of cider."

Gavril allowed himself to be ushered closer to the fire, but he did not sit down, and he did not accept the hastily poured cup offered to him. "Please, sir knights. Allow me to offer you a gift instead." He gestured, and his servant set the keg on the closest table. "Saelutian mead, good sirs," Gavril said proudly, beaming at them. "The best quality, fit for the best knights in service in upland Mandria. Let us drink a toast to your recent success in battle."

Silence fell over the room. Many of the knights looked away. Some frowned at Gavril. Others looked shocked.

Taken aback by their unexpected reaction, Gavril allowed his smile to fade from his face. He stared back at them, his pulse beginning to race inside his collar. "What's amiss?" he asked, and hated it that he had to ask such a question.

In that instant he felt like an unschooled boy in a company of men. He did not like the feeling at all.

When no one immediately replied, he frowned and gestured at the keg. "This gift is both costly and rare, worthy of the valor you displayed against the dwarf raiders. Will you not drink it with me, on this eve of Aelintide?"

Red-faced, Sir Terent drew himself to his full stature, standing head and shoulders above Gavril. He cleared his throat and said with hesitation, "Your highness is most generous. Thanks do we give you for this gift, but we'll not accept it."

Gavril's face was on fire. He did not understand, and there was no chamberlain on hand to murmur a swift explanation in his ear. Social gaffes were unbecoming to princes of the realm. So far no one had dared to laugh at him. Their expressions stayed most solemn. But he held himself rigidly, feeling like a fool and insulted past bearing at their refusal.

When he could master his voice, he said, "May I know why you refuse?"

Sir Terent's eyes held kindness and dismay. Bowing his bald head, he said quietly, "Prayed we have to Tomias the Prophet, asking that Lord Odfrey's life be spared. Gave we our oaths of personal sacrifice. While strong drink is permitted on Aelintide, our vows were made not to partake of it until Lord Odfrey is whole again."

Gavril's head snapped up. His pulse was throbbing in his throat now. His face flamed hotter than ever, and certainty that it was red upset him even more. Someone should have told him about this. Someone would pay for letting him make such a mistake.

"I see," he said, his voice tight. "Forgive me. I meant no disrespect of your oaths. Had I known—"

"But wasn't your highness at morning mass?" Sir Nynth asked, frowning.

"Yes, of course I was," Gavril replied.

"We gave our oaths then," Sir Nynth said.

Gavril swallowed, feeling more a fool than ever. He had heard no such oaths, but then he hadn't been paying attention. Having conducted his private devotionals at dawn in his own prayer-cabinet, he'd spent his time at mass deep in thought, planning this evening. With a scowl, he promised himself that everyone in his service would be punished for letting this happen.

"Perhaps your highness simply forgot," Sir Terent said.

"Or perhaps your highness didn't hear."

These huge, ill-educated oafs were trying to be kind. Gavril wanted to choke. He glanced at the door, ready to plunge outside and escape this nightmare, but for the second time Sir Terent offered him a cup of that dreadful cider.

"Drink with us, your highness, but we'll remain sober if it please you."

"Very well." He could do little else but take the cup. With ill grace he quaffed it, and shuddered at the taste.

Laughing in restored good humor, the knights raised their own cups and drank after him.

"Now then," Sir Terent said, pushing forward the room's only tall-backed chair. "Take our seat of honor and bide with us for a time."

Rough-mannered or not, the offer was a gracious one. Gavril knew it was rare for knights to consort with boys in training such as himself. Ordinarily only those holding the rank of full knight could enter here, much less be invited to stay longer than a few minutes. But although he accepted the honor, and seated himself stiffly in the chair, he was still smarting from his thwarted plans to bribe them. Now he would have to think of a different approach.

"Tell me, Sir Terent," he said. "Do you think the dwarves have truly been routed? Or will there be more trouble?"

"None from that lot!" shouted someone in the back of the room. Others swiftly silenced him.

Sir Terent turned red-faced again. "If there are more Bnen uprisings, there may be trouble all winter. That's what we don't know yet."

"Ah." Gavril leaned forward, thrilled to be discussing strategy. For a moment he almost forgot his own plans. "Have you sent scouts into the forest?"

"The captain's not yet given the order. He may be waiting

till after Aelintide, but more than likely he'd rather get his information right here."

"I don't understand."

Sir Terent grinned and said, "From our eld."

Gavril frowned. "What eld?"

"The young 'un what took us into battle," said Sir Deloit in his thick uplander accent. Grizzled and old, with a puckered scar running through his left eye, he slammed his fist on the table with a grunt of admiration. "Like a gift from Thod, he was, appearing on our road at just the right time. Led us true, he did, straight to 'em. And like a burr did he stick to our lord and master. Naught harmed him, though he be right in the thick of battle. A gift from Thod, he was, all right. It's him we want to ask about dwarf uprisings."

A terrible suspicion began to coil through Gavril's mind. There couldn't be two eldin in the vicinity. Not two young ones. Could there?

Again, he had not been told this gossip. It did not matter to him that he'd been so busy organizing and carrying out the recovery of his stolen wine and mead that he'd paid no heed to anything else. Someone should have informed him.

Leaning back in his chair, Gavril shot a dagger glance in Sir Los's direction. The protector's gaze shifted uneasily, and Gavril's anger boiled higher. Sir Los had known but had not told him. Unforgivable.

Sir Nynth, an ugly dark-haired man with keen eyes, edged closer. "Tell us, your highness. How do we go about taming our eld? Getting him to come forth from hiding and trust us?"

Gavril blinked at him in startlement. "Say you that the eld is inside the hold?"

"Aye," Sir Terent said with a nod.

Gavril clenched his hands upon the chair arms. "What does he look like, this eld?"

"He's about your highness's height, but skinny. Black-haired. Young."

Gavril drew in his breath sharply. "I've seen this pagan before."

The knights exchanged delighted glances. "Does your highness know him? Know his name?" Sir Terent asked eagerly.

"No."

"Sir Bosquecel says he is called Dain," Sir Alard contributed in his soft voice.

"That's not an eldin name," another knight farther back protested. "They're all called by names as long as your arm, names that tangle your tongue right up."

"We're trying to get him to trust us and come out of hiding," Sir Terent explained.

"Are you sure he hasn't left?" Gavril asked. "Perhaps when the villagers departed yesterday—"

"Nay. I saw him slinking past the food cellars like a cat midday," said the one-eyed old knight. "I maybe got only one eye, but it sees sharp. He's still hanging about. We got to catch him, see?"

"Yes, of course you must," Gavril said. "It will not do to have a pagan running freely about the hold."

"Aye, he ought to be brought in and given proper shelter," Sir Terent said with a smile that showed where his front teeth had been knocked out in some past battle. "And thanked rightly for what he did for us. Nocine the huntsman owes the boy his life."

"Nocine?" Gavril echoed.

"Aye. Saved him with spellcraft."

Disapproval sank through Gavril like a stone through water. He stared at Sir Terent with a stern face. "Spellcraft is against Writ."

"Aye, of course," the knight agreed with a casualness that made Gavril determined to write down his name as soon as he returned to his chambers tonight. He was starting to compile lists of such names, ferreting out the unfaithful for Cardinal Noncire's information. Sir Terent leaned forward. "But he is what he is. Can't help it, I figure. Anyway, we want to thank him. Make him our mascot and—"

Gavril shot to his feet, causing Sir Terent to break off. "Make him your what?" the prince shouted.

"Our mascot," Sir Terent repeated.

"He brought us wondrous luck," Sir Nynth said.

Other knights were nodding.

"Aye," Sir Deloit said. "Took us through forest so twisted we couldn't never found our way back out again. But he knew all the ways. Saw trails we didn't see. Sniffed his way through, most like. But he didn't get lost once in all the day. Quick-witted too, he is. If ever we go back into Nold, it's that boy I want guiding me."

Other voices lifted in agreement.

Listening to them, Gavril somehow managed to master his shock and outrage. Uplanders were notorious backsliders, always letting their faith falter in favor of the old ways. Many were lenient toward pagans, just as these knights were tonight. They saw no contradiction between that and their oaths of faithfulness to the Writ.

But beyond that, Gavril was thinking of the qualities the knights kept mentioning about this Dain. He remembered the eld he had hunted only a few days ago, the eld with black hair and eyes of pagan gray, the eld who had defied him and fought back with a fearlessness that now made Gavril wonder. Could this eld be put to his use? If Dain truly knew his way about the Dark Forest, then did he know how to find the Field of Skulls? And beyond that, did he perhaps know where to find the Chalice of Eternal Life? Even if Gavril bribed these oafs into searching the forest for him, it was clear they knew not where to look.

A corner of Gavril's heart warned him against the temptation of using pagans in his service. It was opening the gate to worse temptations. But he felt strong in his faith, and certain that he could withstand whatever might try to turn him from the truth of Writ. Was it sinfully wrong to use a pagan in his search for the missing Chalice?

Gavril envisioned putting Dain in a harness, a collar and chain on his throat like a leashed dog. He would ride through the Dark Forest with Dain trotting ahead of him, hunting the Chalice, leading the way to success.

"Your highness?" Sir Terent said, jolting Gavril from his thoughts.

He blinked stupidly, trying to gather his wits and remember what had been said around him. "Yes?"

"I asked what we should do to catch him," Sir Terent said. "I'm sorry if your highness is too tired. It's just—I thought since your highness has been schooled so much in the Writ and the faith, you might know more about the pagan ways than we do. You might know how to make him trust us."

Gavril hesitated only a second, then he smiled. "Of course. I would be most pleased to assist you."

Sir Terent bowed, his ruddy face showing gratitude.

Sir Deloit banged his gnarled hand on the table. "And I say that we ought to try tolling him out with food. Leave it about, easy like, and he'll come for it. Bound to be hungry by now."

"An excellent idea," Gavril said.

"Then we'll do that," Sir Terent said. He glanced at the other knights with a smile and nod.

"I must take my leave now," Gavril told them. "I will think on this matter and give you what help I can. Perhaps I and the other fosters will try our hand at pursuing him."

As he spoke, he glanced over his shoulder at Mierre, who gave him a quick smile.

"Chasing him is likely going to scare him worse," the old knight started in, but someone put a hand on his shoulder to silence him.

Gavril frowned. He'd had enough advice from that quarter. "Good night to you, sir knights," he said with gracious courtesy. "Good Aelintide as well."

They bowed, chorusing, "Good Aelintide, your highness."

"I will wish you luck, also, in tomorrow's games and melee."

Sir Terent's smile vanished, and again an uncomfortable silence fell over the room. "There will be none."

Gavril stared in fresh surprise. "No contests?"

"Not while our lord lies so gravely ill."

"I see." Gavril felt his face growing hot again. He tried to hide his discomfiture by adjusting the heavy folds of his cloak. "Well, then, let us be glad there is still to be a feast."

He turned to go, and Sir Los hurried ahead of him to thrust open the door.

"Wait, your highness!" Sir Terent called after him.

Gavril turned back to see the knight coming with the keg.

"No," Gavril said, lifting his hand. "Keep my gift."

"We cannot accept it," Sir Terent said.

"You said you will not drink it until Lord Odfrey is well." Gavril forced a smile to his lips, still desirous of addicting the company to this wondrous mead so that their allegiance would thereafter belong to him. "Save it until that time, then drink it in celebration."

Some of the knights lifted merry cheers, but Sir Terent still looked troubled. "Lord Odfrey disapproves of strong drink."

"It's fine mead," Gavril said. "But if you wish, feed it to the swine."

Mierre stepped forward, looking red-faced and shy before the men. "It's not polite to refuse a gift from the prince," he muttered in warning.

Sir Terent, thus crudely informed of proper protocol, blinked and stepped back. "Forgive me," he said in haste. "I meant no offense to your highness."

"None is taken," Gavril said sweetly. "Good night."

He walked out, his small entourage trailing behind him. With every crunching step across the frozen mud of the stableyard, his iron control slipped another notch. Seething, he whirled at last and struck Sir Los in the chest with his fist. The blow banged against Sir Los's hauberk, hurting Gavril's hand, but he was too furious to care.

"You knew," he said in a low spiteful voice. "You knew about the eld and you said nothing. You knew about their oaths, and you warned me not. If I were home in Savroix, I'd have your ears and tongue cut as a reward for such service."

Sir Los stared at him through the darkness. "I am your knight protector. I guard your life with my own. Would you chase the eld yourself and risk being burned or killed with his spellcraft? Better to let the knights catch him. Better for your highness to stay far away from him. He would have done you harm that day in the marsh."

Despite his anger, Gavril knew his protector's words were true. He drew in an angry breath, his chest heaving, then spun about on his heel and strode off without another word.

The others followed him in silence. After a moment he reached out and gripped Mierre by his muscular arm. "You will catch him," he said in a voice like iron. "You will trap him and bring him to me. You and Kaltienne work at this."

"Aye, your highness," Mierre said.

Gavril listened for any sound of doubt or cowardice, but Mierre sounded as confident as always. "You do not fear his spellcraft?" Gavril asked.

"Not much," Mierre said. "My grandsire sometimes had eldin come about the place when I was little. They were always gentle."

"This one isn't," Gavril warned him.

"I'll catch him. Worry not," Mierre said. "Besides, I know how to ward him off, if I have to."

Gavril frowned in the darkness. As he strode into the paved courtyard, he saw that the chapel lights had gone dark. All was still and quiet. It must be late, he knew. He had stayed too long with the knights.

He started to warn Mierre against using the old ways, for such were forbidden, but then he bit his tongue. For once he would look the other way and pretend he did not understand what Mierre meant. *It's for the Chalice,* he assured his conscience.

"Be quick about it, if you can," he said at last. "We have free rein only while the chevard lies ill. If he recovers, we'll be back in chores, unable to come and go as we please."

"Aye, this is better," Mierre agreed with a grin. "Your highness?"

"Yes?"

"What about some of that mead for ourselves? We deserve it, after all we've done."

Gavril spun about and struck Mierre across the face, too furious to govern himself this time. "It's not for you!" he shouted. "Not for anyone but whom I say."

Holding his cheek, Mierre took a cautious step back. His green eyes were suddenly flat and sullen. "I beg your highness's pardon," he said.

Gavril took several ragged breaths before he could haul his temper back under control. "Not the mead," he said at last, his voice more its normal tone. "Never the mead. Is that clearly understood? Never."

"Aye, your highness."

"We'll share wine or ale . . . later. Tomorrow perhaps, if you bring me the eld." Gavril's voice was still unsteady. He turned away from Mierre, appalled by how close he could come to disaster if the wrong people got into that mead. It was no brew for anyone except those Gavril wanted to master. He must take care to keep the fosters well away from it. "I think," Gavril said, "that you had better leave me now."

Mierre bowed and ran off across the courtyard. Gavril lingered a moment, gulping in cold air to clear his head. Sir Los dismissed the gawking servant with a gesture and waited in patient silence.

Finally Gavril turned his steps toward the deserted chapel, where the last of the incense still wafted from the brazier hanging outside the door. Gavril stepped into the shadowy interior, which was lit only by a few votives flickering on the altar. The domed ceiling rose overhead into shadows, its gilding reflecting small glints of candlelight. It was painted with a scene of Tomias the Prophet at the Sacred Well.

Gavril paid no attention to the ceiling painting, which he considered crudely drawn and ill-colored by whatever local artisans Lord Odfrey had employed. His heart was not stirred by the carvings on the altar, for they had a flavor of the old ways. Instead, he focused his gaze on the large Circle of gilded brass hanging above the altar. As always, the sight of the cheap Circle annoyed him. Lord Odfrey, he felt, should spend the money for a Circle of solid gold.

Sighing, Gavril sought to clear his mind. This evening he had been crossed by many temptations. He needed a cleansed heart in order to keep his vows and the path he had chosen.

Genuflecting, Gavril pressed his face against the floor and began to pray.

14

SHIVERING IN THE shadows, his breath steaming about his face, Dain watched the prince enter the small chapel, his elegant, cloaked figure momentarily silhouetted as the door swung open to admit him. The prince's protector followed him, then all lay quiet beneath the hand of darkness. Dain had heard every word of the conversation between Prince Gavril and the larger boy called Mierre. He understood that they intended to catch him.

Sighing, Dain slipped from the courtyard and ducked into the warm, smelly kennels. He snuggled in among the dogs, who licked his hands and chin sleepily. These were not the prince's dogs. Those red brutes were kept kenneled in a separate place.

Dain could have befriended them too, but he had not yet taken the trouble.

Weary and afraid, he made himself a nest in the straw and basked in the warmth of the dogs. Gavril would either hurt him or kill him if he let himself be caught. Dain grimaced angrily in the darkness and vowed not to let it happen. He was determined to stay here through the winter, but he refused to be prey for the cruel prince and his companions.

At dawn, the chapel bell rang loudly, shattering all the natural song in the world. Startled awake, Dain sat bolt upright. The dogs clambered to their feet, shook their coats, and whined in anticipation of their morning meal of raw fish.

Angry at himself for having slept so late, Dain scrambled out of the kennel and ducked into a damp alcove over one of the cisterns. Crouched in there, his back wedged against the clammy stones, he listened while the kennelmaster came shuffling along, hitching up his untied leggings with one hand and scrubbing the sleep from his face with the other.

"Merry Aelintide to you," he called out to the dogs, who barked back gleefully.

Dain whispered the word to himself. Aelintide, the great harvest feast. Now he understood what the frenzied work and preparations had been for.

The past few days, harvesters had been bringing food into the hold, until there seemed to be enough to feed all the world.

Dain had never before seen such bounty. The dwarves were not good farmers. Jorb had sometimes grown a small patch of root vegetables to help them get through the winter. Thia loved tending it, although she preferred flowers to the mundane cabbages, turnips, toties, and fingerlings. She would stand in the patch with a hoe in hand and the sun warming her face. She sang so beautifully that the birds would come and perch on her shoulders, singing with her while bees buzzed amid her flowers in low, droning counterpoint.

But these Mandrians were not like the dwarves. Instead, they farmed large fields. Hordes of serfs hoed and pulled weeds throughout the long growing season, then in autumn they went forth to scythe, winnow, and stack sheaves.

Millers wearing Thirst green took charge of the grain brought to the hold in tall-sided carts. They ground flour and baked bread to be sold back to the villagers. The aroma of baking bread made Dain weak in the knees. With his mouth watering, he had skulked about the ovens yesterday and had even risked plucking out a loaf, which was still baking and only half-cooked. Its crust burned his hands, forcing him to juggle it while he ran back into hiding. When he broke it open, a great cloud of steam hit his face. The dough was gooey in the center. He bit into it and burned his mouth. Thereafter he blew on it and nibbled, blew on it and nibbled, marveling at the texture and whiteness of the bread. He ate it all, and later was sick. But he did not care.

One of the many barns held a herd of cows that were taken outside the hold to a pasture in the morning dawn and brought back in late afternoon. They were milked every day, and plump women in kerchiefs and white aprons skimmed cream, churned butter, and made large wheels of yellow cheese that were wrapped in linen and stored in wooden hoop-shaped boxes stacked in a cool cellar.

Men smoked meats in a place built especially for the purpose. Hams and haunches of mutton were hung from the rafters. Fish was filleted and hung up on wooden dowels to dry over slow, smoky fires. Barrels of salted meat were stacked in storerooms and cellars alongside sacks of brown toties and large purple turnips. Baskets of quince, pears, and apples filled another building lined with shelves to hold them all.

Cider-making went on all day long, filling the air with the fermenting fragrance of crushed apples. Berries were put in huge outdoor kettles and boiled into a frothy, sugary confection later spooned into lidded crocks. Young girls wearing long aprons left the hold at early morn and trudged back at eventide, their aprons full of herbs and grasses that were then chopped, dried, and stored in small clay pots with corks.

Such a flurry of work went on around the preparation and storage of food that Dain began to believe this was all the workers did, year-round. The Mandrians stored up food like the dwarves stored up treasure.

Then late yesterday afternoon the work had stopped. The hold looked abandoned, for everyone seemed to have gone indoors. When the bell rang at eventide, many of the hold folk went to chapel for mass. Foul-smelling incense burned night and day from a smoking brass brazier hung outside the chapel door. Dain did not understand all the rituals of man-religion, but he understood that they were praying for the recovery of Lord Odfrey.

Dain was also worried about the chevard. He could not pray to the dwarf gods for mercy, for they did not govern the chevard's fate. He knew very little about the Church of Mandria, because men-ways were also denied to him. As for the eldin gods, if there were any, he had never been taught their ways and could not call on them either.

Feeling bereft, he prayed instead to Thia's spirit, now living as light and song within the third world. In his mind he talked to her, for he had no one else. In the few days he'd hidden himself here, he'd kept himself out of sight, fearing capture and bodily harm, especially if Gavril caught him. The knights knew he was here, for sometimes they searched for him. Other times they left bits of food lying out, like lures for a trap. Dain was not so easily tricked.

Already he had learned the patterns of the place, when to venture out and when to stay in hiding. The sentries patrolled the battlements and bridge spans between towers. He had to make sure he skulked along the shadows and places where a guard overhead could not see him.

And if he was lonely, at least he did not starve. At night he drank water from the stone horse troughs. Food was easy to scavenge, for the hold folk were wasteful and careless with it. The simpleton goosegirl left out crusts of bread to feed the plump pidges that strutted and cooed along the roofs. Careless stableboys sometimes abandoned half-eaten apples or tossed the cores away. Maidservants carried out buckets of scraps at midday and eventide. This bounty was shared first among the scrawny children who worked at keeping the paved courtyard swept clean of leaves and horse droppings. The scraps they left were then given as slop to the pigs. Once he found the food stores, Dain did not have to rob the pigs. There was so much food, nothing would be missed. He had never seen such bounty in his life.

Now, however, as he crouched with his feet planted on the lid of the cistern and listened to the kennelmaster whistle and talk to the dogs, Dain felt a surge of loneliness so great he almost pushed himself out into open sight. But he held himself where he was, aching in a way he could not explain.

Within an hour or so, the smells of baking filled the air with scents that made his mouth water and nearly drove him mad. Strains of music told him the festival was starting. Curious to see some of it, Dain found himself a vantage point by climbing the drainpipe leading to the stable roof and pulling himself inside a window. There, in the fragrant, yellowed mounds of horse fodder, he could peer out the window and watch the celebration in relative safety.

At first he did not recognize the servants who appeared and mistook them for guests. They appeared in finery that made Dain stare round-eyed. Maids he'd seen wearing tattered linsey gowns, their hair braided loosely down their back, were now transformed by gowns of bright blue, crimson, or green, worn with embroidered kirtles and linen undersleeves. Their hair was combed and braided with ribbons into tight coils about their heads. The men had shed their livery and wore new, brightly hued doublets over their old leggings.

Trestles and boards had already been made into long tables that stretched across the yard. More servants carried out platter after platter of meat, pies, bowls of steaming vegetables, more pies, wedges of cheese, loaves of bread, pastries, yet more pies, and jug after jug of cider to wash it all down.

For Dain, crouched in his hiding place, this feast was the most enticing vision he'd ever seen. Wishing he, too, could be a guest, he drank in the sights and sniffed the wondrous smells. The knights, looking manly and splendid in their vivid surcoats, their beards neatly trimmed and their hair combed back, filed forth from the barracks. Led by the captain of the guard, they sat at one of the long tables, and the servants sat at the other. All the workers, from the sweeps to the stableboys to the milkmaids to the cheese-makers and so on, sat and feasted together, clinking their brass cups in toasts, tossing bones to the dogs, laughing and jesting in good fellowship.

"Merry Aelintide to you," they called out to each other in courtesy. "May Thod preserve Lord Odfrey."

"Amen," came the replies.

They feasted all afternoon, until the shadows grew long and the cows lowed in the barn for milking. Scattering, they threw on smocks to protect their finery and went about their chores, feeding the animals but doing little else.

A short mass was held, then torches were lit and music struck up. They danced and feasted yet more, making merry half the night. Inside the central, long building that Dain now knew as the Hall, lights shone from the windows, and the sound of music rose and fell in strange rhythms that made him long to join in. Leaving the stables, he slinked along in the shadows and peered in some of the windows of the Hall.

He glimpsed house servants wearing garments that outshone those of the outside workers. Torches and candles burned in every room of the ground floor, casting a warm glow of light over furnishings that took his breath away. Dain had sneaked looks inside before, but now the Hall seemed transformed. Gone were the floor rushes; beautiful carpets lay spread out on the floor in their stead. The homely stools and benches had vanished, replaced with chairs of fine woods. In the ample candlelight, the tapestries on the walls were no longer huge, gloomy hangings of cloth, but instead vivid depictions of men and women that seemed to shimmer with life, as though magic was woven among the threads.

One of the boys called fosters came into sight. Peering through the window, Dain stiffened with alarm, but he did not slip away. This one was not Mierre, who was dangerous, or the younger boy who was a fool. Dain did not remember this one's name, but he marveled at the gorgeous doublet and leggings the boy wore. He was tall and thin, his red hair glinting like copper in the candlelight. He wore a thin belt with a fine dagger hanging from it. A ring winked on his finger. He was not a prince, but tonight he looked like one.

All too conscious of his own tattered and filthy rags, his unkempt hair that he cut occasionally with a knife to keep it out of his eyes, Dain shivered in the cold and watched this wealthy boy warming himself before a roaring fire.

Mierre, followed by the fool Kaltienne, walked into the room, carrying two cups. Mierre handed one to the red-haired boy. They spoke together for a moment, with Kaltienne laughing. The red-haired boy looked wary, Dain thought. Clearly they were not friends.

Then the prince walked in, and a flare of heat rose through Dain that made him forget how cold and miserable he was. He glared through the window at the prince, whose magnificence outshone that of the other boys. Gavril wore velvet and fur. His slender white fingers glittered with rings, and the gold bracelet of royalty gleamed on his wrist. His dagger hilt shone with jewels, and the prince's dark blue eyes twinkled in good humor. Lurking in the doorway was the protector, in chain mail despite the festivities, wearing his sword as he guarded the prince the way Sir Roye had sought to guard Lord Odfrey.

Prince Gavril laughed merrily and raised his cup in a toast. "Let us hail Aelintide and the success of all ventures."

Everyone drank deeply, except the red-haired boy, who sputtered at what was in his cup.

"This is wine!" he exclaimed. "Where did you get this?"

"I brought it with me from Savroix," the prince said, draining his cup.

"But I thought it was locked away in the—" The red-haired boy met Gavril's narrowed eyes and broke off his sentence.

"Thum du Maltie, you remain a fool," Gavril said with contempt.

"No one gave you permission to get it," Thum said. His hand was white-knuckled around his cup. "Lord Odfrey said our first day here that men in training do not drink—"

"Lord Odfrey has nothing to say in this matter," Gavril said sharply. "Leave me."

Thum set down his cup and bowed low to the prince. He glanced at the other two boys, and his face turned as red as his hair. In silence, he hurried out of sight.

Kaltienne mocked him, clasping his hands under his chin and capering about, pretending to swoon. "Oh! Oh! I have tasted wine," he cried in a high, falsetto voice. "I am corrupted. My wits are rotted. I am undone."

Mierre laughed robustly, flinging back his head. Picking up Thum's cup, he drained its contents and smacked his thick lips. "Do you think he'll run and tell?"

Kaltienne stopped his antics and glowered, but Prince Gavril shrugged one elegant shoulder. "No," he said. "The Maltie honor will not let him. Now, what have you accomplished today?"

Mierre frowned, exchanging a wary look with Kaltienne. "Accomplished?"

"In searching for the eld!" Gavril said angrily.

"We have been at your highness's heels all day," Mierre said.

"Exactly. Getting nothing done. I want him caught while everyone is too busy to notice what we're doing."

"I looked this morning," Kaltienne said. "But the hold is vast, with passages running everywhere. We could search for days, even months before we—"

Mierre nudged him in the ribs, but too late.

Gavril's face darkened. "You will find him tomorrow. By what means I care not. But you will do it."

"But, your highness—"

Gavril snapped his fingers. "Would you rather I order you to search all night in the cold and the dark?"

The other boys silenced their protests and bowed.

Glaring at them both, Gavril strode away. They followed like whipped dogs.

Outside, in the frosty darkness, Dain's hands curled into fists. He hated the prince, hated him with more passion than he'd felt even against the Bnen. For a moment he was tempted to sneak inside the Hall and confront Gavril. But there was the protector to consider. Dain restrained his impulses and crept away to wait until the last of the revelers grew tired and went to bed. When they finally did, Dain crawled under the tables, scavenging with the cats and a stray dog or two for whatever was left of the feast.

Besting a fierce old tom for a bone with a good bit of meat and gristle still attached to it, Dain gnawed it clean, then broke it between his hands and sucked out the marrow. "Merry Aelintide to me," he muttered.

In the morning, bells rang across the land, echoing from long distances. The chapel bell within the hold rang also, but with a muffled clapper. People appeared soon thereafter, rushing through minimal chores in a slapdash way, then resuming their festivities.

Dain wondered how long the merriment would last. In his experience, when the dwarves feasted long into the night, come the morning after they quarreled and suffered from ale-head. Dain had expected similar behavior, but then remembered that most of the Mandrians had drunk cider the day before, not ale. A few individuals crept about wincing and moaning, but they got scant sympathy.

Still in their finery, people set up a tall pole caped like a man with a huge yellow gourd for a head and a paper crown on its head.

"The king of Aelintide," they sang to it, and danced and made merry all morning.

From comments he overheard and the general air of mild disappointment, Dain learned that the knights had been expected to joust for entertainment, but had refrained out of respect for Lord Odfrey's illness.

The servants, however, made do in the afternoon, with the men playing peculiar games of contest involving the juggling of sticks and leather balls, handstands, footraces, the balancing of eggs on their noses, and other silliness. Their efforts were cheered on loudly by the spectators. The stableboys drew lots and pulled off their tunics for wrestling, until they were sweaty and winded from their efforts. At that time, Prince Gavril and the bull-shouldered Mierre came out and exhibited thinsword dueling.

As he had the day before, Dain watched from the fodder loft of the stables. Despite his dislike of the prince, he couldn't help but be fascinated by the intricate footwork and fancy swordplay. The duel was like a dance, every movement graceful yet potentially deadly. Prince Gavril made a striking figure in the sunshine, his hair gleaming gold, his lean, fit body lithe and quick in comparison to the lumbering movements of his opponent.

"Mierre, hold your arm higher," he would call out, then strike in a rapid staccato of beat, feint, attack.

Mierre parried clumsily. Clearly he'd been given only the rudiments of training. His big hand swallowed the hilt of his thinsword. He had the hands and muscles for wielding a broadsword, not this delicate weapon.

While several of the knights watched from the crowd, the prince circled Mierre and attacked again in a flurry of beautiful moves, ending with a flourish and a solid smack of his blunted sword tip against Mierre's chest. Applause broke out from the spectators, and Prince Gavril bowed with a broad smile before clapping Mierre on his shoulder and speaking a quick word in his ear.

The larger boy bowed and hurried away, and the prince sauntered over to speak to a pretty maid in a blue gown, who curtsied and blushed at his attention.

Some of the knights looked less than impressed by Gavril's

exhibition. One of them took Mierre's thinsword and ran his fingers along its blade, flexing it and shaking his head.

Dain drew back from the window, frowning at his tangle of emotions. He'd never seen a thinsword before today, but suddenly he ached to learn how to use one. He hated the prince, yet Gavril's skill was admirable. Dain shoved the hair out of his face, unprepared for his envy.

The smell of roasted meat suddenly filled the stable, rising above the horse fragrance.

Startled, Dain jumped to his feet in alarm and sniffed the air. He could detect nothing except the smell of the meat and dust from the fodder he'd disturbed. He clamped his hand across his nose and mouth to hold back a sneeze. His mouth was watering, and his stomach growled to fierce, insistent life.

No one was supposed to be in here except the horses; Dain had counted all the stableboys earlier to make sure. He listened hard, but he heard no unusual sounds. When he tried to focus his mind to sweep forth, all he could think about was the meat and how hungry he was.

Last night's scraps, after two days of watching people gorge themselves, was not enough to hold him together.

Outside, music struck up, accompanied by shouts and laughter.

Dain didn't bother to look out the window this time. He was tired of merriment he could not join. His stomach rumbled again, and he pressed his hand against his middle. It had to be a trap. If some of the stableboys or anyone else had ducked in here for private merrymaking, there would be the sound of voices and giggling. Instead, all he heard was quiet, broken by the occasional snort of one of the horses in the stalls below.

Easing over to the window, Dain stared down at the people, who were now lining up to dance. He saw Gavril talking to one of the knights. Thum was also in the crowd, looking shy and talking to no one. Of Mierre and Kaltienne, there was no sign.

Anger touched Dain. So they thought he was some stray animal, stupid enough to be enticed with food. He was hungry, but not yet so desperate he would throw away his freedom for a mouthful of meat.

Refusing to panic, he tried to figure out what he should do.

The first step was clear. He had to get out of this building quickly before he found himself trapped up here in the loft. How they'd located him hardly mattered.

Dain decided he'd better leave the hold completely. His hopes of staying seemed futile and not worth the risk of being caught by Gavril or his minions. He would steal enough provisions to last him well, then journey north into Nether in search of the eldin as Thia had asked him to do.

He was not eager to go there. All his life, Jorb had told him it was not safe for him and Thia to seek their own kind. In the past, eldin had lived scattered through parts of Nold and even in the mountains of upper Mandria. But now, few were sighted. Jorb said most had gone into the wilds of Nether. It was said to be a cold, austere land, ruled by a dour king named Muncel, a land of cruel men and harsh ways, savage and unfriendly. But Dain did not think the eldin were welcome even in Nether. Gossip among the customers and traders who came to Jorb's forge said the eldin had been driven into hiding in the northernmost mountains, as far perhaps as the fjords themselves, and could not be found.

A cheer went up from outside. Dain crawled through the fodder to look and saw a long line of people dancing back and forth around the courtyard. A blushing maiden was standing next to the gourd and pole king of Aelintide. As the line of people passed her, the men bowed and the women curtsied.

"Harvest queen!" they shouted to her.

Dain frowned, no longer interested in their rituals. He heard a shuffle from below, and a quick grunt of exasperation, and knew his time had run out.

He could make larger decisions about where to go later. Right now, he'd better keep his wits focused on the problem at hand.

To the sound of stealthy creaks coming from the simple pole ladder leading to the loft, Dain turned back to the window and thrust his head and shoulders through the small opening, twisting painfully to fit. In his haste, he inadvertently caused the open shutter to bang.

"Hey!" shouted Mierre's voice. "Come this way. I think he's up here!"

Cursing softly beneath his breath, Dain hoped the merrymakers were enjoying their dancing too much to look up and see him. The drainpipe could be seen from the yard. He dared not try to go that way.

With one hand bracing himself on the slate roof tiles, he looked straight down into the narrow space between the stables and the cow barn next to it. If he slipped, he had a long way to fall.

Squinting against the sunshine, Dain pulled up his legs and stood on the sill of the small window. Boosting himself, he scrambled up onto the roof and climbed rapidly, slipping and sliding on the tiles as he went.

Behind him, he heard a frustrated grunt. Mierre's voice called out, "He went through the window. I can't fit."

"I'll go!" said Kaltienne.

"Get after him then," Mierre said. "And if the pagan can fly, see that you do it too. I've no head for heights. I'm going down."

"Coward," Kaltienne taunted him.

"Listen! He's going over the roof. Hear that?"

"How can I not?"

"Hurry!" Mierre ordered in exasperation. "I'll go down to see which way he goes."

By now Dain had reached the iron spire atop the ridgepole of the stables. He crouched there, shivering in the cold wind, and found himself nearly as high as some of the towers. One of the sentries on the wall saw him, gave a shout, and pointed.

Cursing him, Dain slithered down the other side of the roof, crouching low on his haunches and skidding along on his heels. By the time he reached the edge, he was going much too fast to stop. Dain's heart jumped into his mouth, but if he lost his nerve now he would surely fall.

Yelling, he stood up at the last moment and leaped with all his might across the gap between the stables and the next building. He landed on the other roof, lost his balance, fell flat, and began to slide down.

But this building had a ledge of sorts to channel water along the edge of the roof. Dain's toes struck it, and he stopped sliding. He lay there a moment, his sweating face pressed against the slate, and waited for his heart to stop thudding so violently.

Shouts from below sent him scrambling up and over the ridgepole of this building. On the other side, he found a drainpipe and climbed down it as far as he could, then jumped lightly the rest of the way to the ground.

He listened a moment, gauging from which way his pursuers were coming, and ran swiftly in the other direction.

A shout from one of the sentries made him glance over his shoulder. He saw the knight gesturing from his vantage point on the battlements. Dain snarled to himself. Why couldn't they leave him alone? Time to go to ground, and get himself out of their sight.

He dodged around the rear of the storehouse, considered the cellars rowed up behind it, and rejected them as dead ends. The boys were still coming. Dain ran on and stopped worrying about who else might see him. He careened past the simple goosegirl feeding her charges with grain from her apron. Clad in her usual rags, with only a scarlet kerchief tied around her throat for finery, she watched him run by with her mouth open in a large O.

A wall rose up before him. It was the base of one of the towers. Behind him, the boys shouted jubilantly. Dain's determination grew. He ran straight toward the wall and bounded up the kegs stacked there as lightly and surefootedly as a young stag.

Teetering on the very top keg as it shifted and swayed beneath his weight, Dain jumped for the window overhead. His outstretched fingers grazed the bottom sill and missed. The keg wobbled under his feet, and Dain felt the whole stack going. He jumped again, kicking the keg out from under him, and this time his fingers grabbed the sill.

He held on grimly, his fingers aching from the strain. Clawing desperately with his other hand, he managed to pull himself up.

Belly-first, he slid headlong through the window and tumbled onto the spiraled staircase inside. It was a painful landing, and he lay there a moment, gasping for breath. The stone steps felt cold beneath his cheek. The stairwell was gloomy and filled with shadows, its only light coming in through the window.

From outside, he heard Mierre swearing. Dain grinned to himself and sat up shakily. They would be coming in through the door in moments. Pulling himself to his feet, he went upstairs, winding around and around until he came to a closed door.

Grasping the ring, Dain tugged hard, but the door did not

open. It seemed his luck had run out. He was hemmed in, with nowhere to go except down, straight into the arms of his pursuers. Gritting his teeth, Dain tugged again on the ring, using both hands and straining until the gristle in his shoulders popped. The door did not budge. From below, he heard them coming.

Dain bared his teeth, breathing hard and trying to think. But he was trapped, with nowhere to go.

He kicked the door in fury and jiggled the ring again, his desperation rising. There came a click, and Dain paused for a second. He stared at the ring in his hand and slowly twisted it.

The catch clicked, and the door swung open.

Dain eeled through the narrow opening and pulled the door shut behind him. The room beyond was poorly lit, but Dain spared it no glance. Instead, he patted the door, seeking some means of barring it.

"Slide that bolt across, and it will hold firm," said a deep, heavily accented voice behind him.

Dain jumped, his heart nearly bounding from his throat. He whirled around and saw a tall figure in a long, dark robe standing no more than two strides away from him. Dain stared, unsure if this was friend or foe, but then he heard the boys' voices.

Gasping, he slid the bolt into place, locking the door just as their fists thudded against it. They shouted on the other side, but for now Dain was safe from them.

Breathing hard, he leaned his back against the door and ventured a cautious smile at the man watching him.

"Thanks to you," he said in Mandrian. "I—"

"So you are the eld of Lord Odfrey's battle, the one Thirst knights have been boasting about these last few days," the man in the shadows said. His voice had a deep, singsong quality that made Dain shiver. "I have been hoping to see you for myself, and now the gods have brought you to my workroom. Thus, it must be that our destinies are entwined."

Frowning, Dain swallowed. He did not like the voice of this man. He kept hearing something, some timbre or tone that made him think of darkness and smoke. He wished he could see the man's face, which remained hidden by shadows, but at the same time he felt relieved that he couldn't. He wondered what this man was, and feared to learn the answer.

"Yes," the man said, stepping forward with a gliding motion

that did not seem natural at all. "You are going to be very useful for my experiments."

Instinct warned Dain that Mierre and Kaltienne were less dangerous than this man. As he whirled and tried to slide open the bolt, the man spoke a single word, a word Dain did not understand, a word like a puff of smoke.

The smell of fire filled the air, and Dain's arms would not move. He realized he was frozen in place, as helpless as if bound by ropes. Fear rose through him. By some terrible chance, he had fallen into the clutches of a *sorcerel,* a creature who could crisp him to ashes with a mere thought.

Sweat broke out along Dain's forehead. His heart was pounding again, and his mouth had gone so dry he couldn't swallow. He stood there, struggling inside with all his might to break free, and could not move even the tip of his finger.

Someone knocked on the door. "We would enter, Master Sulein," Mierre said boldly. "If you are within, grant us admittance."

Sulein glided to the door beside Dain. This close, Dain could smell the man's scent—something acrid and arcane on his clothing from the potions he concocted in this dimly lit room, but also something else, which emanated from his very skin, as though he ate odd things unknown to most folk.

The knocking came again. "Master Sulein! I bid you let us enter and take the eld."

"Begone," Sulein said. "You boys are forbidden inside my tower."

"But, Master Sulein, we have been chasing the eld, at great risk to ourselves. His highness bade us find him and—"

"This is no toy for the prince to play with," Sulein said. "Begone."

"But—"

"Will you interfere with my work, work which may save the chevard's life?" Sulein thundered. "If I must open this door, toads will you become."

From the other side came the sound of running feet, then silence. Dain stood there, still frozen in place, and swallowed hard.

The *sorcerel* put his hand on Dain's shoulder, and Dain flinched inside as though he'd been branded. "You are much in demand, little eld," Sulein said gently, his voice coiling around

Dain like a serpent. "The chevard wants you. The prince wants you. And I want you." He laughed, a low silky sound. "But it is I who have you. And all the powers that you command. Come to my fire, and tell me your mysteries."

The spell binding Dain's feet was released. He wrenched himself away from Sulein's hand, but there was no escape. Sulein stepped between him and the door, and Dain found he still could not move his arms.

Awkwardly he stumbled back from the *sorcerel,* who herded him across the room. It was filled with a crowded jumble of furniture and objects. Dain was forced toward the end, where a fire burned on the hearth.

"Dain you are called. That is no name of the eldin. I can see that your blood is mixed, but there is little enough of the human in you," Sulein said as Dain halted next to the fire.

Sulein glided closer into the light, revealing himself to be hook-nosed and swarthy of skin, with a frizzy black beard and eyes as bright and beady as a keeback's. He wore a tall conical hat edged in monkey fur, and his long brown robe was stained and discolored in places, as though he often spilled his experiments. No gray showed in his dark hair or beard. No wrinkles carved his face, yet his eyes held all of antiquity in their liquid depths.

Dain glanced at him, then away, afraid to meet those eyes for too long.

"You were Jorb's apprentice," Sulein said. "He was a swordmaker, a dwarf, I am told. How peculiar. Tell me, did he buy you? How did you come to be in his keeping? Or were you living in the Dark Forest for a different purpose?"

Dain said nothing. His face felt hot, as though fevered. His lungs could not draw in enough air. Sulein's questions seemed harmless, and yet he feared to answer them.

"How much did Jorb train you? Did he ever let you work with magicked metal?"

Dain felt a growing compulsion inside him to answer. Setting his jaw, he withstood it and said nothing.

After a few moments, the pressure eased and faded. Sulein raised his bushy brows. "Ah," he said as though making a discovery. "Your powers are strong. Good. I will learn all the more from you."

"There is nothing to learn," Dain said defiantly. He spoke in the harsh dwarf tongue, and laced his tone with contempt.

Sulein cast him a sharp look. "But I shall pick you apart," he said, also speaking dwarf. "I am a collector of knowledge, and you, little eld, are a very great prize indeed."

Dain said nothing else. He could not outtrick a *sorcerel;* he was not going to try. Instead, he concentrated on forcing his frozen arms to move. Sheer strength was not enough. He stopped straining and considered the problem from another direction, ignoring whatever Sulein said to him. After a moment, he began to sing inside his mind. It was hard at first—he was too frightened and angry to concentrate—but after a few moments the song flowed more readily inside his mind. He sang of motion, of the wind, of the swaying branches of a willow by a stream, of the flit and wiggle of fish as they swam, of the strong wings of birds on the air. The spell holding him tight began to loosen.

Feeling hopeful, Dain kept the song going in his mind. Sulein spoke again to him, but he paid no heed.

Sulein gripped him by his shoulder. "What are you doing?"

Dain's arms came free. He spun in Sulein's grip, thrusting the man away. As Sulein struggled to regain his balance, Dain dodged around him, slinging a table between them as he went, so that crockery and bottles crashed to the floor. Dain ran for the door.

He reached it, ignoring Sulein's shout behind him, and drew back the bolt. For a moment his body felt heavy and slow, but the remnants of the song still ran through Dain's mind. He concentrated on that, and the heaviness lifted.

Pushing open the door with a mighty shove, Dain jumped over the threshold and bolted for his freedom, smack into a sturdy barrel chest and a strong pair of hands that seized him by his tunic and shook him so hard his teeth rattled.

"Got you!" said Sir Roye.

Dain kicked him in the shins and ran.

Down the steps he flew, ignoring the heated argument between the two men behind him. His feet skimmed the steps. He kept his fingertips lightly on the wall for balance as he went faster and faster.

At the bottom of the tower, the door leading outside stood

ajar. Dain hit it with his shoulder and careened outside into the sunshine, which made him blink and squint.

The music swirled in the courtyard. People were still dancing and clapping their hands.

Mierre and Kaltienne waited a short distance from the tower door, like two cats crouched at a mouse's lair. Kaltienne saw him first and dug his elbow into Mierre's ribs. "There he is!"

They came at a run, and Dain darted off in the opposite direction. Hurrying past a parked cart resting on its traces, he ducked through the first door he came to, fortunately unlocked, but instead of entering the Hall as he expected, he found himself inside a small walled garden. Badly neglected, it was in serious need of tending. Many of the plants had begun to yellow from nightly frosts. Others, overgrown and sprawled across the paths, needed cutting back. Walkways atangle with weeds led to a central axis where a silent fountain stood encircled by a bench of moss-covered stone. Birds rustled and stirred within the branches of a gnarled old fruit tree in the corner. Flowers with dead blooms rattled in the chilly breeze.

On the opposite side of the gate ran a loggia littered with dead leaves. Dain trotted along this, ducking into the shadows at one end just as the boys opened the gate and peered into the garden.

"Halt!" Mierre said in alarm, thrusting his muscular arm across the opening. "We cannot go in there."

Kaltienne pushed at his arm, without budging it. "But I saw him enter."

"Doesn't matter. We're forbidden to go into the lady's garden."

What lady? Dain wondered, pressing himself deeper into the shadows. He hardly dared breathe.

"He's in there," Kaltienne said with frustration. He tried to duck beneath Mierre's arm, but the larger boy shoved him back.

Kaltienne's mouth fell open. "Have you gone mad? You know what his highness threatened if we failed."

"We've got him," Mierre said firmly. "But we don't go in. Not us. The prince can, if he's brave enough."

"But—"

"I've heard the servants and knights talk about this garden. No one is allowed in here. No one. The chevard's son died here. Mayhap his ghost walks these paths."

Dain, peering cautiously around the edge of the wall, saw Kaltienne turn pale and swallow.

"Ghosts, you think?"

"I know not. But I know the chevard's wrath. If he lives I want none of his temper turned against me. You've had one of Sir Roye's floggings. Do you want another?"

"Nay," Kaltienne said with feeling.

"Nor I. If the eld is hiding in here, he can't get out. We'll block this gate and tell his highness—"

"Quick!" Kaltienne said, clutching Mierre's arm. "Someone's coming. If it's Sir Roye, we're—"

Mierre shut the gate, and Dain heard the sound of something being dragged across it.

Soon thereafter came Sir Roye's gruff voice. "You boys! What are you doing there!"

"Nothing, Sir Roye." Kaltienne's voice sounded innocent.

"You can't go in that garden. Get away from there."

"We meant no harm," Mierre said. "We were just exploring."

"Did you see that damned eld come this way?"

"No, Sir Roye," Kaltienne lied without hesitation.

Dain frowned at such smooth duplicity. It was the experienced liars who never hesitated.

"Morde a day, that fool physician had him and let him go," Sir Roye grumbled.

"Did you really see the eld, Sir Roye?" Mierre asked innocently. "I heard the knights want to keep him chained in the guardhouse."

Sir Roye growled something Dain could not distinguish. "Get out of here, both of you. You're sure you saw no sign of him?"

"Not a hair of his head," Mierre answered. "But we'll gladly join the hunt."

"Then go along and tell Sir Bosquecel he got away. I'm searching Sulein's tower again in case he doubled back."

Their voices faded away.

Fearing trickery, or the return of Sir Roye, Dain let out his breath with a sense of wary relief. He waited until the shadows grew long and cold within the little garden. The music faded in the distance, and with it the sounds of revelry. Only then, shivering, did Dain venture forth into the open. He hurried across the garden and pushed on the gate, but it did not budge. The boys had secured it well, no doubt pulling the cart across it.

Muttering to himself, Dain wondered how long it would be before the prince came to get him. The idea of being Gavril's prey both frightened and infuriated him. Now that he had time to think, Dain realized it might have been better if he'd stayed in Sir Roye's clutches. He'd probably have been beaten and flung out of the hold on his ear, but at least he'd have been safely away from this place.

Instead, he'd let the *sorcerel* panic him and scatter his wits. He'd been so desperate to get away, he'd acted without thinking. Now he was boxed in here, desperate with thirst and cold and hungrier than ever.

He prowled about for some time, hugging himself against the frost-nipped air. There were doors at either end of the loggia, but both were securely locked. Cobwebs were spun over one, showing him it had not been opened in years. The other's lock was rusted and leaves had drifted up against its base. He could find no other exit.

The fountain had apparently been dry for years—not even a drop of rainwater did it hold to quench his thirst. He searched in the gathering darkness beneath the fruit tree, but found only pits lying on the ground, the fruit long since decayed.

For whatever reason, Prince Gavril did not hasten here to claim his prey. Perhaps he was waiting until the dead of night. Perhaps he, too, feared the ghosts that walked here and was waiting until dawn. Perhaps the prince was playing with him, hoping to make him afraid. Dain kicked the ground and wished the demons from the second world's perdition would come forth and strike the prince for his cruelty.

In time, frustrated and miserable, Dain retreated to the dubious shelter of the loggia and watched the windows high above one side of the garden. No lights came on, ever, and he realized that this wing of the hold must be as deserted as the garden itself.

Moonlight rose eventually, shining on the pathways and illuminating the silent fountain. Dain huddled on the cold flagstones of the loggia, too cold to sleep, and watched for ghosts to appear. But none walked here through the long, wretched night.

He stared across the garden, studying the tracery of the tree branches beneath the windows, and realized that his only hope was to climb up and try to break through one of the shutters. He wasn't sure the branches would support his weight that high, but it was the only thing left to try, short of waiting here until he was dragged out by his tormentors.

Blowing on his cold hands and flexing them to ease their stiffness, Dain gathered his courage and determination, and began to climb.

15

IN THE NIGHT, the sound of the gate creaking open awakened Dain. Jerking upright, he scrunched himself deeper into the shadows beneath the fruit tree. The movement sent a stab of pain through his shoulder, which had stiffened since he fell out of the tree on it. Grimacing, he held back a whimper and concentrated on staying still.

The gate creaked again, and he heard the soft but unmistakable sound of wood scraping over flagstones.

They were coming for him at last.

Dain tried to stay calm, but his heart started pounding. His last hope had been to climb out of this trap, but after he fell he hurt too much to try again.

Now, as he listened to the stealthy creaking of the gate and quiet footsteps, he gathered a broken wedge of edging stone he'd found lying in the neglected flower bed and waited for a chance to attack. Depending on how many were coming for him, he might yet find a way to get past them.

The scent of food—roasted meat and cold toties—nearly undid the last of his strength. Dain's mouth watered, and for a few moments his hunger consumed him, raging uncontrolled as though it would drive him forward to surrender, to do anything in exchange for nourishment.

"Hello," called a voice, so soft it was barely above a whisper. "I won't hurt you. I'm a friend."

Dain did not recognize the voice, and he frowned in the darkness. He had no friends here.

"Don't be afraid," the voice said, low and reassuring. "I'm coming in, but I won't hurt you. I have some food. I thought you might be hungry."

Dain closed his eyes for a moment as weakness passed through him and made his body tremble. He was so hungry, so terribly cold and tired. Steeling himself, he dragged open his eyes and bared his teeth in a silent snarl, curling his fingers tighter around the piece of stone. He had his dagger as well, but he would not draw it unless forced to.

The gate creaked again, louder this time, and then Dain heard it snap shut. His brain woke up and began to think more clearly. He realized that had Prince Gavril come to torment him, he would have kicked the gate open and entered boldly. No, this unseen visitor was trying to be quiet, and he seemed to be alone.

Dain sat up straighter, gathering his legs beneath him. If the gate remained unlocked and he had only one individual to overcome, then perhaps he stood a chance of escape.

Watching closely, he saw a shadow move quietly along the garden path. The moon had waned, making it much harder to see, even with Dain's excellent night vision.

His visitor stopped near the fountain. "I will put the food here. Take it when you wish," the voice said. "But there is little time before dawn. The hold will start to stir within the hour. I do not know when the prince will rise, but you should not be here when he comes for you."

Dain said nothing, listening hard, his thoughts spinning inside his head.

"I know you are awake and hear what I say," the voice continued in that same quiet, unhurried, reassuring way. "I am Thum du Maltie, and I bear you no ill will."

Dain matched that name to the freckled, serious face of the boy with red hair. Thum who had tried to stop Prince Gavril from whipping Dain in the marsh. Thum had also refused to drink wine with the prince last night. This was no friend of Prince Gavril's. No trickster.

Warily Dain rose to his feet and peered through the gloom at his visitor. "Why?" he asked, his voice hoarse with cold and thirst.

"They are cruel, the other fosters," Thum said. "They keep you here like a caged animal, with no one to stop them. I thought about telling Sir Bosquecel, but I was not raised to be a tongue-tattle."

Dain swallowed. "You brought food?"

"Are you hungry? You must be, after being shut in all night."

Dain rested his hand on the rough bark of the tree, wondering if he was dreaming this. "You are not my friend, Thum du Maltie," he said. "You know me not. Why do you help me?"

"Does it matter?" Thum asked.

Dain sensed no lies in him as yet, but neither had he spoken the complete truth. "Why? Why help me?"

"The knights are still talking about you. How you came from nowhere to help them with the battle. They said if not for you, Nocine the huntsman would be dead now. They said you saved Lord Odfrey's life."

"Is the lord dying?"

"I don't know," Thum said. "The steward looks very grave. He tells us nothing. Sir Roye barely leaves his lordship's side. He has great fever, and Master Sulein fears for his life because of that."

Dain thought of the *sorcerel* who had nearly caught him yesterday. He did not like the idea of that creature, who dabbled in magical realms best left undisturbed, treating Lord Odfrey. Who was guarding the chevard from being possessed by the darkness? Who was protecting his soul from theft?

"We wouldn't have feasted Aelintide at all if the prince hadn't insisted," Thum continued. "I—I guess such celebrations mean nothing to you, but I think it's wrong—disrespectful—to be making merry while the lord of this hold lies so ill. But Prince Gavril said the harvest feast should be made, in order to show our gratitude to Thod for such generosity. No one but Lord Odfrey dares deny his highness anything. With the chevard so ill, his highness is doing everything he pleases. No one says him nay. No one! It isn't right. Especially with Lord Odfrey so—" He broke off, worry strong in his voice.

Dain bowed his head with regret. Although he hated to hear that the chevard was dying, he closed off the liking he'd begun to feel for the man. He'd lost too much already. He wanted no more grieving.

"Get away from the food," he said harshly.

"What?"

"Back away."

"Oh." Thum retreated from the fountain, his shadowy figure a little more visible than before.

Dain glanced at the sky, which had lightened to a dark gray. In the distance, birds chirped sleepily. Time was running out.

As soon as Thum was halfway between the fountain and the gate, Dain dashed forward and snatched up the small bundle lying on the edge of the fountain. Holding it against his chest, he ran past Thum, heading for the gate and freedom.

Thum crashed into him from behind, gripping the back of Dain's tattered tunic. Dain tried to wrench free, but he would not let go. There came the sound of cloth ripping, and Thum flung an arm across Dain's injured shoulder.

Gasping aloud, Dain staggered and sank to his knees, driven down by the pain.

Thum gripped his arms. "What is it? What's wrong?"

Dain concentrated on breathing through the agony, and didn't answer.

"I did not mean to hurt you," Thum said. "Really, I'm sorry."

Snarling, Dain pushed him away. Thum overbalanced and landed on his backside. Dain expected him to lose his temper and come back fighting, but Thum sat where he was.

"You don't have to run," he said. "I'm going to let you out. In fact, I thought I'd help you get out of the hold if that's what you want. But if you run away, I can't help."

Dain didn't answer. He tore open the wrappings and crammed a chunk of cold meat into his mouth, gulping it down in desperation, barely bothering to chew. The totie was cold and shriveled. Dain cared not. He ate it, coarse, gritty skin and all.

In seconds the food was gone, and some of the terrible ache in the pit of his stomach eased slightly. He thirsted more than ever now, and turned on Thum.

"Do you have more?"

"I—no," Thum said apologetically. "I didn't realize you were so—I should have brought more."

"Must get out of here," Dain muttered to himself. He was

still kneeling on the ground, and felt too tired to move. But with dawn coming, there wasn't much time. He looked behind him and listened to his inner senses.

"It's a risk for me, but I'm determined to help you. Anything to defy his highness," Thum said. Resentment throbbed in his low voice. "He rises early, so we must hurry. If you aren't hurt, we'd better go."

Dain pushed himself to his feet, holding his elbow tight to his side to keep from moving his aching shoulder.

Thum stumbled along the path, heading for the gate. "I have to put the cart back across the gate once we're out. Will you help me?"

Dain didn't answer.

Thum stopped and turned to face him. "Look, if the prince finds out I helped you, I'll be in serious trouble."

Dain told himself not to be a fool. He sensed no lies in this boy, and he could tell that Thum's nerve was beginning to waver. "I will help," Dain promised.

"Aelintide is over, you see," Thum said in relief, hurrying forward. "The villagers will be coming today to conduct business as usual, so the main gates will open after sunrise. If you hide somewhere close to the gates, you can get out during the general coming and going of the throng."

"I can do that," Dain said, liking the plan. It was simple, and simple plans worked best. He slipped outside through the gate behind Thum with the feeling of having escaped a cage.

Thum shut the gate as quietly as he could, then tapped Dain's sleeve, making him jump in the darkness. "You push when I say," Thum whispered.

Dain stood behind the cart and pushed it while Thum picked up the traces and steered. It wasn't far out of position; Dain figured Thum had been able to budge it only so far by himself. Together they moved it back across the gate.

Thum dusted off his hands. "Let Thod keep the prince from ever knowing it was me," he said under his breath.

Dain wondered why he was so nervous. "Can the prince beat you too?" he asked.

Thum uttered a sour little laugh. "Worse than that."

"He can kill you? But would your family not avenge you?"

"It's not like that," Thum explained. "My father sent me here, hoping I'd become a companion, maybe a favorite, of the prince. I'm the youngest son. I have to make my own way in life since I can't inherit land. The prince could give me a start, but I haven't pleased him. We don't get along at all, and I—I—" He broke off, his voice a tangle of anger, unhappiness, and restraint. "I don't like him."

"I hate him."

Thum uttered a breathless little chuckle. "Morde, but it's good to hear someone say that. Treason though it is, I hate him too."

Suddenly friends, they grinned at each other in the shadows. Dain reached out and gripped Thum's hand. "My thanks, Mandrian. I will repay my debt to you."

"You owe me no debt," Thum replied fiercely. "I have done what is right. No reward should come for that."

Elsewhere in the hold, a cock crowed. Dain heard distant sounds of life. The hold was coming awake. He must hide himself again, and quickly. But as he turned away, Thum came after him and gripped his arm briefly.

"My mother says it's good luck to help the eldin," Thum whispered shyly, as though half-ashamed to say it. "We're uplanders, and the old ways are still known to us, even if we now follow Writ. You are nothing evil, and should not be treated so."

Dain understood what he was really asking. "If ever there is luck in my life to bestow, I will share it with you," he said.

Thum stepped back. "How close to the gates can you get? They should open just after morning mass and—"

"I know all the hiding places by now," Dain said, interrupting his advice.

"Then may your path be sure," Thum said.

Dain hurried away from him, melting into the shadows between the next building and the wall. Around him, objects and outlines were becoming distinct shapes. The air lay still and cold, and his breath fogged white about his face.

Hurrying, he circled the courtyard, staying well against its perimeter where shadows remained dark. No sentry saw him and called out. No yawning serf stumbled across his path. He slipped past the stables, and paused to break the thin layer of ice on the watering trough. His reflection was a pale, unfocused shape glimmering in the water's surface. Dain drank long and deep of the ice-cold water. It hurt his teeth but cleared his head.

From inside the stables, he could now hear the horses nickering and shuffling in their stalls. Muffled, sleepy voices spoke. A sudden light glowed from a window. Ducking low, Dain flitted onward.

With much trepidation, he ventured into risky territory—the outermost keep, where villagers were allowed in for daily business, bread loaves were sold, and tribute was brought for display. The barracks windows shone with light. From within the guardhouse came the aromas of boiled pork and heated cider.

The sentries stamped their cold feet on the battlements like men counting the minutes until they were relieved.

Dain took cover behind a stack of crates and settled himself there to wait until the gates opened. A cock crowed loudly, and the smell of wood smoke filled the air. Dain swallowed and buried his face against his crossed forearms, trying not to think about his stomach. Thum's gift of meat and totie had been well intentioned, but of small proportion. Listening to his stomach growl, Dain doubted he would ever eat his fill again.

Perhaps he slept, huddled in that cramped space between the crates and the wall, for it was with a start that he suddenly opened his eyes and found sunlight shining across the keep. The gates stood wide open, and guards watched the flow and ebb of excited villagers coming in to haggle over bread or to inquire about Lord Odfrey's health.

"Did he lose his eye, poor man?" a fat woman with a kerchief tied about her head was asking loudly.

"We prayed mass for him yesterday," another woman, lean and toothless, chimed in.

Others swarmed about, babbling questions and repeating gossip.

Rubbing his face, Dain rose cautiously to his feet and worked out the kinks from his stiff muscles. He blew on his fingers to warm them, then sauntered out from behind the crates and melted into a small crowd of serfs haggling with each other over a brace of squawking chickens held upside down by their feet. Nearby, a scrawny child with a dirt-smeared face held the end of a rope tied around a young shoat. The child's eyes widened at the sight of Dain.

Swiftly he ducked away into the general mill and press of people, his heart pounding fast, his mouth dry with fear. Anyone could look at him and sound the alarm. Steadily, refusing to let himself run, he kept pushing his way through the busy crowd, aiming toward the gate.

Ahead, he saw a wide gap between the crowd and the gates themselves. Alert sentries stood there, armed with swords and pikes.

Hesitating, knowing he could never walk alone between those sentries without being noticed, Dain lost his nerve.

Wheeling aside, he eased into the wake of another group of villagers, then broke off and ducked behind the guardhouse. It had no windows at the rear, and there was a narrow space between it and the wall. Above him, the walkway for the battlements jutted across the space like a roof. The sentries up there couldn't see him.

He halted there, his palm pressed against the rough bricks, and tried to regain his courage.

This was a foul place. The stench told him lazy men used this area at night for their latrine instead of crossing the keep. Dain drew a deep breath, and eased his way forward. When the curved wall of the guardhouse took him out from beneath the walkway overhead, he paused a moment and frowned over the logistics of his problem.

Ahead of him stretched another open space to the smithy, then from there, the area in front of the gates remained clear. While he watched, a stooped man and a slim girl entered, both carrying laden baskets on their hips. They paused inside the gates, and the sentries nudged them on.

Dain drew in his breath with a hiss, realizing the only way he could walk out was if he went disguised.

He scowled, refusing to panic. He could do this, provided he used the crowd sensibly and didn't lose his courage.

Ahead of him, the smithy was opened for business, its large shutters thrown wide. Its fire roared in the circular hearth, blazing orange and hot. Dain heard the smith start working at his craft. The hammer made a steady *plink, plink, plink* noise. Listening to that familiar rhythm, Dain caught a whiff of heated metal. A wave of homesickness washed over him. He missed Jorb with a stab of grief so intense he leaned his head against the bricks and closed his eyes.

Why had he ever come to this foreign place, where he'd forced himself to live like a thief, skulking fearfully and risking his life? He belonged in the Dark Forest. It was time to go home, not wander the world.

But there was no home to return to. The Bnen had burned the forge, where Dain could have tried to continue the work Jorb had taught him. They had burned the burrow. All of it, everything he knew and loved, was gone. It would always be gone, even if he did try to return.

Bowing his head, Dain let his emotions wash over him. Perhaps it was only that he was so tired, so hungry, so cold. He couldn't reason anymore. He needed rest and a place of safety. That's why he kept wanting to go home. He realized it was going to take him a long time to remember that home was forever lost to him. Home was to be found in the hearts of loved ones, and his would never again stretch out their hands in gladness to see him, would never again call his name with laughter in their greeting, would never again stand steadfast at his side, their affection a warmth that fed his spirit and gave him comfort.

The loop of a rope settled around his shoulders without warning. A quick yank tightened it about his upper arms, and Dain was pulled off his feet before he knew what was happening.

He landed hard on his side, grunting at the impact. Instinctively he twisted around, trying to regain his feet, but before he could get up, someone jumped on top of him, pinning his legs while he jerked and struggled to free his arms.

A second loop of the rope went around him. Another hard yank nearly crushed the breath from his lungs. His sore shoulder protested with a stab of pain that left him helpless while he was swiftly trussed.

Fearing that he'd been caught by the prince's minions, Dain kept on struggling.

"Be still," said a harsh voice, "and do not put your eye on me. I'm protected from your pagan spells."

Dain recognized Sir Roye's voice. Surprised, he stopped struggling and Sir Roye finished tying him. With a grunt, the knight stood up, taking his bony knee from the small of Dain's back.

At once, Dain startled struggling again. Desperate and frightened, he knew not what would befall him now, but a glimpse up at Sir Roye's hostile face boded no good for him.

Despite his efforts, Dain realized, he had no chance to pull free. Scrambling to his knees, he paused, his breath rasping loud in his throat.

"Morde a day, but you're a sight of trouble. As sly as a cat, slinking here and there. Why didn't you stay in the garden, where I could have caught you quicker?"

Dain squinted up at Sir Roye, silhouetted against the sunshine. He didn't think the knight really wanted an answer. "And now you're going to give me to Prince Gavril? You'll enjoy seeing him whip me. Or do you intend to kill me on his order?"

The knight punched him in the stomach, and Dain doubled over with an agonized whoop.

Sir Roye took a step closer. "That'll teach you to keep a respectful tongue in your pagan head. I am 'Sir Roye' to you, or simply 'sir'. You call me that, and you watch your tone."

Toppling over, Dain retched up his breakfast and managed to roll himself over away from it. Telling himself there was surely worse to come, he scowled and tried to ignore the burning discomfort in his belly.

"I've done no wrong here," he managed to say. "I am no enemy—"

"You're a damned pagan thief and Thod knows what else. Eating from the winter stores is a crime that merits twelve lashes alone."

Dain stiffened, remembering Prince Gavril's whip all too well. "It's no crime to feed myself."

"And who gave you leave, eh? You answer me that."

Dain glared fiercely up at Sir Roye. "I saved Nocine's life. I led the lord to the raiders. I helped in the battle. If I have eaten a few apples as my reward, is that so wrong?"

"If you're hungry, you go to the kitchens and beg along with the other mendicants. You don't steal, unless you want a whipping or your hands cut off."

Dain blinked in fresh horror. "What is man-law, that it should be so harsh?"

"Nothing harsh about it. The beggared have only got to ask for charity. By the holy law of Writ, such have to be fed. But thieves endanger everyone. We have to keep enough in stores to feed every mouth in this place through winter."

"I thought . . . Would a pagan beggar be fed? Or would I be

beaten for asking?" Dain asked. "Does the Writ of your belief apply to folk like me?"

The knight squinted at him and said nothing. Pursing his lips, he looked away, then pulled a servant's cap from his pocket and bent down to cram it onto Dain's head. It fitted close to his skull, with two long flaps that came down over his ears. "You're too much trouble," he grumbled. "If it were up to me, you'd be drowned and well out of our way."

He pulled Dain to his feet, and said, "But it ain't up to me. Back you come."

"He will kill me," Dain said, planting his feet and refusing to budge. "Let me go, Sir Roye. Do not take me to death."

"What is this babble?" Sir Roye asked in exasperation. "I'm not killing you, yet."

"The prince will."

"His highness has naught to say about this matter," Sir Roye announced. "Now move your feet. I've wasted too much time already tracking you for his lordship."

Dain grinned at him with sudden hope. "Lord Odfrey sent for me?"

Sir Roye's yellow eyes glittered resentfully. "Not like you think, you heathen knave. But he's been calling for his boy—Thod rest the poor lad's soul—and that Sulein thinks you'll do as well for him in his fever."

Down sank Dain's spirits. "So he really is dying. I don't want to see him."

Sir Roye whacked the side of his head. "Hold your tongue. No one asked you what you want. Now move!"

He pushed Dain forward, and Dain went, stumbling every time Sir Roye pushed him. Although Dain half-expected Sir Roye to parade him along in front of everyone, the knight kept away from the crowds and out of sight of the sentries. Together they skulked along, seeking to pass unnoticed, and soon Sir Roye was pushing Dain up a series of steps that led to the battlements. They strode along the walkway, with Dain catching wide-eyed glimpses of the world of field and marsh stretching far beyond the hold's walls.

Before they came to the first sentry, Sir Roye shook Dain hard. "Keep your eyes down. Don't let them see who you are."

Dain bowed his head, staggering along as Sir Roye kept

shoving him. When they came to the sentry, the man saluted Sir Roye and stepped aside.

It was the same with the next sentry, and the next.

Soon thereafter, they passed through a door into a tower, then walked along corridors and passageways, up stairs and down, winding here and there until Dain was greatly confused and had little idea of where he might be inside this maze of stone.

Finally Sir Roye shoved Dain into a long, narrow chamber fitted with drains in the floor and stone channels. A fire burned there, and at one end stood a wooden tub as tall as Dain's shoulder, with steps mounting it.

Sir Roye whipped the cap off Dain's head and untied him. Dain tried to shake some circulation back into his arms, but as he turned around, Sir Roye gripped him with both hands and pulled his ragged tunic over his head before Dain could stop him.

Wincing at the pain in his shoulder, Dain sucked in his breath and tried not to yell.

Despite the fire, the room was cold. Shivering, Dain tried to grab his tunic from Sir Roye's hand, but the knight held it out of his reach.

"Get in the tub," he ordered.

"Why?"

Sir Roye glared at him. "Because you stink worse than the dogs. Because I won't take no filthy, gint-eyed knave to my lord with him lying there fevered out of his poor wits. You wash, and make it quick."

Although he longed to be clean, the idea of a cold bath did not appeal to Dain. He tilted his head at Sir Roye and could not resist saying, "But have you not heard that we eldin melt when we get wet? We are supposed to be but watery elements, formed into a cloud of appearance, and that is why we—"

Sir Roye smacked his head, knocking him backward. "Get in the tub, and cease that heathen chatter of yours."

To Dain's surprise, the water was tepid, not icy cold as he'd expected. He enjoyed splashing about, sluicing off the dirt and filth he'd accumulated in recent days. A servant came with a bucket and emptied some heated water into the tub. Dain laughed at such luxury, and even ducked his head under the water, then surged up, shaking himself like a dog.

Sir Roye climbed the steps and prodded him with a wooden pole. "Out," he commanded.

Dain obeyed, dripping and shivering. A servant wrapped him in cloth and shoved him over to stand before the fire. While Dain dried himself, Sir Roye glared at him thoughtfully.

"What happened to your side?"

Dain glanced down at the bruised and discolored web of skin between his lower ribs and his hipbone. "Oh, the lord's horse bit me the day we fought the dwarves."

Sir Roye grunted to himself and grasped Dain firmly while he prodded the wound. Dain sucked in air between his teeth and fought the urge to shove Sir Roye away, knowing it would only get him struck again.

"Hurt?" Sir Roye asked.

"No," Dain lied, glaring at him.

"Could make a fearsome scar," Sir Roye said. He touched the bruises on Dain's shoulder. "And here?"

"I fell out of a tree last night, trying to escape—I mean, while I was climbing over the garden wall," Dain amended hastily. "I fell off the wall."

"A worse lie has never been spoken," Sir Roye said, but he released Dain and gestured for the servant to hand him clean clothes.

They were very fine, these garments, as fine as Dain had seen Thum, Mierre, and Kaltienne wearing—not as fine as the prince's clothes, but soft and well made. Dain fingered them, awed by such generosity.

"Don't just stand there gawking," Sir Roye said gruffly, scowling at Dain. "Get them on."

"But they are the clothes of a lord," Dain said in protest. "They are too good."

"Aye, they are," Sir Roye snapped. His face turned red, and he scowled more fiercely than ever. "They belonged to Lord Odfrey's son. You're his size, close enough. He had dark hair too. Now get dressed. And when you're through giving his lordship comfort, you can have your own filthy rags back again."

Dain blinked, understanding with a bump of reality that this clothing was not a gift to be kept. His mouth twisted wryly and he tugged on the leggings, keeping his head down to hide his expression. His pendant of bard crystal swung and thumped into his bare chest as he straightened and reached for the doublet to pull it on. The servant handed him a linen shirt instead.

"What do you wear?" Sir Roye asked. "A pagan amulet?"

"Yes," Dain said, his voice muffled as he swiftly pulled the shirt over his head. He yanked the garment down before Sir Roye could reach out and touch the pendant. It was not for the likes of the knight to touch. Now the doublet went on. It fit well enough, except for being a little narrow in the chest and too short in the arms. Pushing back his wet hair from his face and letting it drip down the back of his collar, Dain looked at the knight and shrugged.

"Well?" he asked.

Sir Roye frowned at him, and some emotion—sadness perhaps—touched his yellow eyes. "Aye," he said softly. "I see the resemblance now. Damne."

"I look like the lord's son?" Dain asked. "The one who died?"

"Morde a day!" Sir Roye said in startlement. "Who told you about that?"

"Do I?" Dain asked. For a moment he entertained the wild hope that perhaps Lord Odfrey was his missing father, the man who'd given him and Thia into Jorb's keeping, then never returned for them. But as fast as the thought entered his mind, he dismissed it, knowing it could not be so. "What was the boy's name?" he asked.

"Hilard," Sir Roye replied, lost in memory. "A gentle boy, scholarly. Rather read than ply a sword. But a good horseman. Dependable. His lordship was always short with the lad. Impatient with his faults. Wanted him to be a fighter. Wasn't until the stranguli took him that the chevard learned how much he loved that boy."

"When did he die?" Dain asked quietly, hearing old grief echoing in Sir Roye's gruff voice.

Sir Roye scowled at him. "Five years past. He was about your age and size. Dark-haired. Thin."

"Does grieving last so long?" Dain asked, staring at the man in dismay. "Does the loss never go away, never stop hurting?"

Whatever Sir Roye might have answered was interrupted by the door's slamming open. The page who'd opened the door so forcefully jumped aside, and Prince Gavril strolled in, followed by his hulking, silent protector and a red-faced Mierre.

"See, your highness?" Mierre said, pointing furiously at Dain. "I told you someone let him out of the garden. He has not the power to fly—"

A gesture from Prince Gavril silenced him abruptly. Gavril walked farther into the room, his dark blue eyes narrowed with anger, his mouth tight-lipped. The sunlight streaming in through the narrow windows sparked golden glints from his hair. He wore leggings of the softest doeskin and a long doublet of russet wool with the sleeves slashed to show his creamy linen. His bracelet of royalty gleamed golden on his wrist, and a jeweled dagger glittered at his belt.

"What are you about, Sir Roye?" he asked coldly. "Bathing a pagan while your lord and master lies dying?"

Sir Roye turned to face him like a grizzled old dog. "What I do is not accountable to you, highness."

Prince Gavril blinked at such gruff defiance. For a moment he seemed unable to find words. Then his frown deepened. "Harboring a pagan is against Writ. I ordered his capture as soon as I learned he was sneaking about the hold. He is my prisoner—"

"Did you catch him?" Sir Roye countered.

"I ordered his—"

"But you didn't catch him, did you?" Sir Roye persisted.

Gavril was scowling now. "I need not sully my hand. My order is enough."

"Not in Thirst, it ain't. The chevard rules here, your highness. You're a foster, and your orders ain't taken above his lordship's."

Gavril turned bright red. His eyes flashed to Dain, who was listening to this with enjoyment, and he glared more fiercely than ever. "You have bewitched Sir Roye, and—"

"I'm on the chevard's business," Sir Roye said, cutting across the prince's accusations. "Step aside, your highness. I cannot be detained."

Gavril did not budge. "But what are you doing?" he asked. "Bathing him, giving him clothes above his station, feeding him? These are violations of—"

"I got no time for preaching," Sir Roye said. He walked forward, straight at Prince Gavril, who did not move aside. The weathered old knight glanced at Sir Los, who had his hand on the hilt of his sword. Calmly, Sir Roye stepped around the prince and gestured for Dain to follow him.

Dain obeyed warily, determined not to let Mierre or Sir Los seize him. As he stepped past the prince, Sir Los shifted his stance, but quick as thought Sir Roye stepped into his path, blocking him from Dain, who hurried out the door, his relief mingling with shame over his fear.

"Let's not start something we don't want," Sir Roye said, his dark, craggy face inches from Sir Los's. "You have your orders, Los, but so do I have mine."

"Sir Los!" Gavril cried out.

But the knight protector dropped his hand away from his sword hilt and stepped back.

"Sir Los!" Gavril said in fresh fury.

The large knight said nothing and did not look at his master. Sir Roye gave him a little nod and left the room, emerging into the corridor where Dain waited.

He tapped Dain's shoulder, giving him a small push. "Walk on. You've caused me enough trouble for the day."

"But I did not—"

"You're here," Sir Roye said furiously, keeping his voice low as they rounded a corner and passed out of earshot. "On account of you, I've defied the prince of the realm."

"Lord Odfrey will give me a place here. It was meant to be his promise."

Sir Roye snorted in contempt. "A promise not made."

"He will," Dain said with assurance. "Just as soon as I speak to him and—"

Sir Roye shoved him into the wall to silence him. While Dain straightened himself, trying to catch his breath, the old knight glared and pointed his finger at him. "You'll work none of your pagan wiles on him, hear me? You keep yourself quiet now, and don't speak unless you're spoken to."

"I—"

"Quiet!"

Dain shut his jaws and glared back. He was tired of being shoved and smacked and yelled at. He was tempted to break away from Sir Roye, but the knowledge that Gavril and his minions might pounce kept him where he was. As mean and gruff as he acted, Sir Roye meant protection, even if temporarily.

"Sir Roye!" called an accented voice, one that made the hairs rise on the back of Dain's neck. "Where have you been? Why have you been away so long?"

It was Sulein, the *sorcerel,* coming down the passageway toward them. Garbed in a long robe of crimson and green stripes, his conical red hat perched on his head and his dark beard frizzing wildly around his jaw, Sulein stared at Dain with a smile of dawning delight.

Dain stopped in his tracks and would come no closer, until Sir Roye gripped his arm and forcefully shoved him along.

"It took a bit of doing to get this lad," Sir Roye said, pushing Dain past Sulein, who turned and followed them, gliding along in his unnatural way. "He wasn't where I was told he'd be."

"He escaped the garden, where my vision saw him in hiding?" Sulein asked in surprise. "How?"

Dain kept his mouth shut. He wasn't about to answer any questions that would cause trouble for Thum. Unsure if the *sorcerel* could read his mind, Dain began mentally tabulating the weights of metal and made certain not to look Sulein in the eye.

"How he did it matters not," Sir Roye growled. "He wasn't there. What news of my lord?"

"He came awake for a moment. He sleeps now, but he is very restless. The fever does not abate."

As he spoke, Sulein glided ahead of them, then pushed open a door at the end of the corridor. Guards stood on duty on either side of the door, but no page or other servants loitered about. Although they remained at attention without expression on their stern faces, one of the guards blinked at the sight of Dain, and his eyes widened.

The man did not speak, however, and Dain found himself being shoved into a large chamber kept dark and shadowy by the many shuttered windows. A large fire crackled on the hearth. More fires burned in braziers placed on all four sides of a large, box-shaped bed standing in the center of the room. Heavy curtains of tapestry enclosed the bed, except where some of the panels had been pulled aside.

Dain saw the chevard lying there, propped high on cushions. He wore a dark green robe of velvet over a linen gown. His face was heavily bandaged. Dain smelled the meat poultice and the fevered flesh of the wound beneath it. His stomach turned at other sickroom smells, but with a frown he made himself ignore them.

"Go on, boy," Sulein said quietly, freeing Dain from Sir Roye's grip and shoving him forward. "Go and sit yourself on that stool there. Stay very quiet. You will be where his lordship can see you when he wakes up."

"And put none of your pagan hexes on him while he lies helpless," Sir Roye said.

Dain whirled around and glared at him. "I saved his life. Why would I harm him?"

"Get over there," Sir Roye said, baring his teeth.

Sulein clapped his hands between them. "Hush this. There must be quiet. An atmosphere of peace and serenity. No quarreling. Now, boy. Sit on the stool as I told you."

Dain seated himself on the cushioned stool next to the chevard's bed. Although the fires made the room very warm, the chevard was shivering beneath the coverlet and fur robe. His head turned restlessly on the pillow, but his eyes did not open.

"And you, Sir Roye," Sulein said in reproof. "Why do you fear this boy so? The eldin are peaceable creatures. They understand the natural flow of life forces. They are not evil."

Sir Roye grunted, his fear and worry swirling through him so strongly Dain could sense them. Ignoring the men, Dain leaned toward the chevard, who was turning his head from side to side in pain, mumbling words Dain could not understand.

Grief rose in Dain anew. He missed Thia and Jorb with all his heart. He did not want to be in the room of a dying man. He did not want to worry about the chevard, or even to like him. He had been raised to distrust men and their ways. Men were duplicitous, superstitious, and dangerous, like Prince Gavril. But Lord Odfrey seemed different. He was a fair man, an honest man. It was not right that the Bnen arrows should kill him too.

Dain reached out and curled his fingers lightly around the chevard's hand. Its flesh was intensely hot and dry.

Behind Dain, Sir Roye strode forward. "Take your—"

"Hush," Sulein said. "Be still. This is what I hoped for."

Dain glanced over his shoulder at the two men. Sulein was standing in Sir Roye's path, and the knight's face was contorted in a grimace of worry and anger. Neither came any closer.

Dain relaxed. He already knew the answer he'd sought. The

chevard's blood burned with this terrible fever. His pain was strong. But so was his body strong. He was not yet ready to die.

"Lord," Dain said in his quiet, awkward Mandrian, "I have come to speak with you about your promise. Have you forgotten it? Have you forgotten me?"

"Be quiet, boy!" Sir Roye ordered.

Startled, Dain glanced up, but despite Sir Roye's fearsome scowl, Sulein was beaming and gesturing for Dain to continue.

"Do not stop," Sulein said. "Talk to him. It will help center his mind and bring him from his fever. Tell him anything you wish."

Dain drew in a wary breath, trusting the outraged Sir Roye more than he trusted the *sorcerel.* Yet clearly Sulein understood what he was doing.

Returning his attention to the chevard, Dain was surprised to see the man's dark eyes open and staring at him.

"Hilard?" Lord Odfrey said in a shaky voice.

"I am not Hilard your son," Dain said evenly, ignoring Sir Roye's muted growl of protest. "I am the eldin boy who rode with you when you fought the dwarves of the Dark Forest. Do you remember the battle, lord?"

The chevard frowned, looking lost and witless. Pain shimmered in the liquid depths of his dark eyes. Beneath the thick bandage swathing half his face, his skin was pasty white. "Hilard," he said. His fingers shifted in Dain's grip. "You have come."

"Was your son part eldin, as am I?" Dain asked. "Is that why you are kind to us?"

"No," Lord Odfrey said. His voice was a thin whisper. "I want Hilard."

"He is dead," Dain replied. "You know that, lord."

Lord Odfrey gripped Dain's fingers with momentary strength. "You have come back. I prayed for this, and you have come."

Behind him, Sir Roye moaned and walked over to the window. Bowing his head, he put his hand to his face.

Dain swiftly turned his gaze back to Lord Odfrey. "I am called Dain, lord," he said softly. "I was Jorb the swordmaker's apprentice and fostered son. You saved my life, and I saved yours. Where your son walks today, you are not yet ready to go.

It is not your time. Do not let this wound end your life before its fullness."

The chevard closed his eyes and sighed deeply. He seemed to sleep again, but his fingers did not slacken on Dain's hand.

When Dain tried to pull away, the chevard opened his eyes at once. This time they looked more alert. "Stay with me," he commanded, and sank back into his troubled sleep.

Dain stayed.

For three days, Dain remained in the chevard's room, present whenever the man awakened and called for him. A cot was brought for him to sleep on. Food was served to him on trays. Lord Odfrey's condition slowly improved, and Sulein beamed at Dain in approval.

"Your presence is helping. It is exactly as I wished and expected."

Sulein worked hard. He mixed potions with noxious smells that he poured down Lord Odfrey's throat. He changed the bandage occasionally, scraping off the evil poultice and replacing it with fresh. The wound looked puckered and angry. Dain believed it should be exposed to the air, and the windows opened to let in sunlight, but Sulein kept the place tight and airless, like a stuffy cave. His hands were not always clean when he ministered to the chevard. Dain believed Lord Odfrey lived in spite of Sulein's ministrations.

As for spells, he saw Sulein cast only one, and there was little magic in it. Although Dain had been frightened of the physician at first, he gradually began to suspect that Sulein was not a true *sorcerel* after all but instead only a man trying to be one.

Dain was never alone with the chevard. Sir Roye stood guard over his master like a faithful old dog, and Dain had no opportunities to open the windows or to throw the poultice away. Bored, he ate all the food he could get his hands on and wandered about the chamber, examining its contents without touching or disturbing anything.

Then came the early dawn when Dain was awakened by a slight noise. He sat up and left his cot, going to the chevard's bedside at once on silent feet. Sir Roye was slumped in a chair, snoring. Sulein had gone. The candles were all guttered, and the fires had died to a few crumbling, hissing coals atop heaps of ashes. Meager daylight leaked in around the edges of the shutters.

Dain went to one window and opened it, letting in cold air and dawn's shadowy, gray light.

The chevard lay on his side. His eyes stared, and he did not breathe. Horrified, Dain crept closer. It was dawn, the hour when souls were the least anchored to their bodies. Was the chevard dead?

He did not want to believe it, but already grief was swelling inside his heart. Refusing to let his mind touch death, Dain kept his senses to himself and instead touched the chevard's arm.

The man's flesh was warm and pliant. The chevard blinked, and Dain flinched back. Almost at once, however, he smiled to himself and gripped the chevard's hand.

There was no fever in it. Lord Odfrey's hand was cool and dry. Dain touched his throat and found no fever there either.

Relief filled Dain. Shivering a little in his thin shirt and leggings, he sank onto the stool and faced the chevard's intense stare.

"Is this the Beyond?" the chevard asked softly. "I do not know where I am. Nothing looks as I remember."

"The physician changed your room," Dain replied, his voice quiet to keep from waking Sir Roye. "Most of the furniture is stacked in the passageway outside the door. He said there was an imbalance in the forces and elements that—"

"Is this the Beyond?" Lord Odfrey asked again. He sounded tired, as though he had journeyed a long way.

"If you mean the third world," Dain answered, "no, it is not. You are still in the first world, in your hold, in your personal chamber. Sir Roye guards your rest. If you look that way, you can see him."

"I see an eld boy who reminds me of my son," Lord Odfrey said without moving. "Yet you are nothing like him. Strange."

"What is strange?" Dain asked, yawning despite himself.

"You have the spirit he did not. I could not make a warrior of him. I tried too hard, I think."

"We are what we are," Dain said. "I am not—"

"There is a belief, an old one," the chevard broke in, "that the eldin sometimes carry our souls for us. Or the souls of our loved ones. Carried from the Beyond back into our world so that we can see them for a little while. Is that true?"

Dain frowned. "I know not. I have never heard it."

"You must know."

"I was not raised among my people," Dain said. "I do not know their ways."

The chevard's intense stare never wavered. "Do you carry my son's soul, Dain? Is that why you came here? So that I could see some part of him again for a time?"

Dain's frown deepened, for he felt uncomfortable with these odd questions. "I came out of need," he said simply. "I lost my home and family. I had nowhere to go."

He hesitated a long moment, and the chevard did not interrupt. Finally, the truth forced its way out: "I came to you," Dain admitted, "because I knew you would fight the Bnen and defeat them. I wanted revenge for what they did to my sister and to Jorb."

"Did I give you this revenge?" Lord Odfrey asked. "I do not remember."

"You did," Dain said. He started to add that revenge had brought no comfort to his heart. He still missed Thia and Jorb, still hated the Bnen, still wanted everything put back as it had been. The dead did not erase the dead. But he felt it would be wrong to utter such feelings, and he held his tongue. "You fought them valiantly, lord, and you defeated them."

The chevard rolled onto his back and moaned. "My face hurts like—Where is Sir Roye?"

His voice was growing stronger and more querulous. From his corner, Sir Roye snorted awake and sat upright.

"If you hurt," Dain said, "I will fetch the physician to you."

"Don't want him," Lord Odfrey said. "Want my breakfast. Want to sit up. Roye! Damne, where are you?"

"Here, my lord," Sir Roye said hastily, scrambling to his side. The protector scrubbed at his face with his hands, grinning at his master with a delight that transformed his craggy face. "You're awake. Praise Thod!"

"I hurt and I'm hungry," Lord Odfrey said, pounding the bed weakly with one hand. "Why is it so dark in here? Why has the fire burned out? What stinks? Dain!"

"Yes, lord?"

The chevard stared up at him with sudden horror. "Tell me the truth. Is my face infected with the rot?"

"Not yet," Dain replied. "The stink comes from Sulein's poultice. It needs to come off."

"And what do you know about healing and such arts?" Sir Roye asked him fiercely from the opposite side of the bed.

Dain glared right back. "My sister knew healing. She said a wound should be kept clean and exposed to light and fresh air."

"Hah!" Sir Roye said in derision. "You'd kill him certain, with measures like that."

Lord Odfrey reached up and began tugging at his bandages. "Off with it."

"My lord," Sir Roye said, trying to hold down his hands. "Wait for Sulein to do that. You'll hurt yourself, sure."

"Ow!" Lord Odfrey shouted. Cursing, he finished pulling the bandage away and flung it on the floor.

Then Sulein arrived, gliding forward hastily with his robe unfastened and his conical hat on crooked. "What is this? What is this?" he asked, clapping his hands together.

"Wash this damned stink off me," Lord Odfrey ordered.

The commotion began. A page stuck his head inside the room, staring around with his eyes popping. "He's better! He's alive! Praise Thod!"

The guards looked in while the page went dashing away, shouting down the corridor. Sulein bustled to fill a basin with water and started cleaning the wound. Servants, gawking at their master, came in to build up new fires and light fresh candles. Sulein ordered the window shut, but Lord Odfrey ordered it opened again. All the windows were opened, transforming the chamber with sunlight and fresh air.

From outside, the chapel bell began to ring in celebration, sending up ripples of music such as Dain had never heard.

He retreated from the general confusion, taking refuge in a corner, until Sir Roye noticed him and booted him out. But Lord Odfrey ordered him brought back in.

"I want him near me," the chevard said. "Make a place for him. He is welcome at Thirst, as long as he will stay."

Sir Roye bowed, but he shot a quick, scornful look in Dain's direction. "And what place will he have, my lord? Stable work? Field work?"

"Nonsense." Looking suddenly white and exhausted, Lord Odfrey sank back upon his pillows. "Put him among the fosters. Give him training at arms."

The servants froze in mid-task. Sulein jostled his basin of water. Sir Roye's eyes widened in shock.

"He's pagan, m'lord! It's against—"

"Look at his black hair. Look at his size. He's just starting to grow, damne," Lord Odfrey said. "There's human blood in him too. Under the old law, he can be trained."

Sir Roye opened his mouth, but the captain of the guards came rushing in, his surcoat flapping about his knees, his chain mail creaking. Halting, he threw a salute.

"My lord!" he said briskly.

Sulein straightened. "There are too many people in this room," he said in a loud voice that drove out the servants. "The chevard will live, but he must have rest."

Lord Odfrey ignored everyone but his protector. They stared at each other, their strong wills clashing visibly. Dain looked on, holding his breath in amazement. Training? To be a warrior? To perhaps be a knight someday? To have rank and skills and training, to know adventure and battle? His heart started thumping hard, and he could not breathe for excitement.

"Put him in training," Lord Odfrey said.

"M'lord, I would do your will as always," Sir Roye said with a grimace, "but think of what this means. Remember who is fostered here."

"These matters can be settled at another time," Sulein said, trying to interrupt them. He gestured for Sir Roye to withdraw, but the knight protector did not budge from Lord Odfrey's bedside.

"The prince, m'lord," Sir Roye said.

Dain opened his mouth, wanting to offer a dozen assurances. Wanting to plead. Wanting to say anything that would prevail. But he held himself silent, sensing that at this moment he should not interfere.

"The prince does not choose my fosters," Lord Odfrey said, his voice starting to fail him. He shut his eyes a moment, then fought to reopen them. "I rule this hold by royal warrant. Dain will be fostered here, with full rights as such."

"But he has no sponsor, no one to provide for him. He can't—"

"Damne, Sir Roye, do not argue with me!" As he spoke, Lord Odfrey grimaced in agony and fell back against his pillows again, gasping for breath.

"Now this is enough," Sulein said, pulling the coverlet up across the invalid and placing his hand firmly on the chevard's sweating brow. "You will bring back your fever if you do not rest. Sir Roye, why do you argue with your master's orders? Why do you risk his life by making him so upset?"

Sir Roye looked stricken. He bowed low. "Your pardon, m'lord. I did not mean to—"

"You always have the best interests of the hold at heart," Lord Odfrey said in a thin, tired voice. He tried to smile, but that caused him more pain. "I know this. Thod brought him to me. Let him stay, if he will."

Sir Roye nodded, but he glanced at Dain without acceptance. "Boy, do you have any idea of what training means?"

"Yes," Dain said, his eagerness spilling forth. "To learn arms and—"

"Will you stay, unsponsored, and take the training freehold?"

Dain frowned slightly, unsure of what these terms meant exactly. "If it means I can eat food and not be beaten and learn—"

"If I may speak," Sir Bosquecel said.

Sir Roye turned on him fiercely. "You may not!"

"Sir Roye," Lord Odfrey said in rebuke.

The protector's mouth snapped shut. He glared at the captain, who met his gaze without flinching.

"Speak," Lord Odfrey said wearily.

"If it please you, my lord, I will sponsor the boy."

Sir Roye snorted. "Are you adopting him, Bosquecel?"

"The men will see that he has what he needs in equipment and all else," Sir Bosquecel said.

Dain stared, unable to believe his ears.

Sir Bosquecel smiled at Lord Odfrey. "We would have him as our mascot, my lord."

Sir Roye looked at the captain as though he were a fool, but Lord Odfrey smiled back. "These details will be worked out later," he said, and thrust away the cup Sulein was trying to press to his lips. "No, I do not want that abomination!" he said fiercely. "I want breakfast."

Sulein closed in on him again, and Sir Roye came around the bed to gesture at Dain, who followed him over to the captain of the guard.

"You heard the chevard," Sir Roye said gruffly. He shoved Dain at Sir Bosquecel. "He's yours, man. Get him started."

"Yes, sir."

The captain saluted and wheeled around smartly. Dain followed at his heels, but Sir Roye gripped his arm to delay him a moment.

"Heed this," he said in Dain's ear. "The chevard has given you the chance of a lifetime, far more than the likes of you deserves. Don't you let him down, or it's me you'll answer to."

Dain met his fierce eyes, and knew the threat was no idle one. "I understand," he said quietly with equal determination, and hurried out.

Part Three

16

In a northern valley of Nether, up near the World's Rim, the war of rebellion that had been planned and plotted with such care and hope for months came to an end.

It began at dawn, with the blatting of horns and the yelled battle cries of men. Five hundred rebels, trained and drilled to peak efficiency, were led by General Ilymir Volvn, formerly a prince before King Muncel declared him traitor and confiscated his lands and fortune. General Volvn was the greatest military strategist in the realm, and he took on two thousand of the king's troops this day, his hawk face turned fearlessly toward his enemy, his courage and valor infecting his small force.

He should have won today, for his men were the best of the rebel fighters, better trained by far than the Gantese allies and sloppy conscripts of the king. The rebels had justice on their side.

But King Muncel the Usurper had evil on his.

In the second hour of battle, when Volvn's forces were beginning to prevail, a gateway to the second world was opened, and out poured demons of all descriptions. After that the tide of battle had shifted; then had come the slaughter.

Disbelieving, Princess Alexeika Volvn watched the massacre from her vantage point on the hillside. "No!" she cried. "*No!*"

But there was nothing she could do. Had her father suspected a trap waited for him here, he would not have led his men forth. Alexeika had watched the general pray, had watched him think and plan, had watched him devise strategies, study the ground, and rethink his positions. He had been prepared for everything except the Nonkind, and the scouts had not sighted them in the area before battle commenced.

Foul, dirty dishonor was this. Honorable men and armies did not wage war thus. But then, Alexeika's father was the epitome of an honorable man, while it seemed his foes had forgotten what honor was. It was one thing to go into battle against Gant, with all the demons and horrors Believers tried to unleash on their foes. In such situations, Netheran forces summoned special blessings for sword and armor. They positioned *sorcerels* strategically to help repel the Nonkind monsters. But when Netheran fought Netheran, they fought as *men* and adhered to the acknowledged rules of battle.

With growing horror, Alexeika watched the battle rage. Had her father's men been less valiant, it would have ended almost as soon as it began. Instead, they fought on, impossibly brave, refusing to flee or surrender until there was only a small knot of men clustered around the banner in the center of the field. One by one they were hacked down; then the banner fell.

Seeing that vivid streamer plummet to the ground, Alexeika screamed. Beside her, the old defrocked priest Uzfan gripped her arm and began to mutter prayers. The boys and other women nearby cried out and wept.

"What can we do?" Shelena moaned. "Merciful Olas, what can we do?"

There was nothing, of course. They were only watchers, too far away and helpless besides. Stricken with shock, Alexeika looked on with tears running down her cheeks.

Before midday, the victors galloped off, their banners streaming with pride under the hot sun. They left the gallant rebel forces of Nether lying strewn across the battlefield like abandoned toys.

Shelena and Larisa clutched each other, weeping. The boys stood white-faced with shock.

Alexeika's heart was drumming. She had entered a frozen place where she could feel nothing. Jerking the reins of her pony untied, she mounted and stood up in the stirrups.

From her throat came a scream of rage and grief so loud and

terrible it echoed off the surrounding hills and rolled down into the valley below. The king's forces were just vanishing over the far hillside, but Alexeika waited no longer. She spurred her short-legged pony forward down the long, sloping hill from their vantage point.

"Wait!" Shelena called after her. "Alexeika, it's not yet safe!"

Alexeika crouched low over her pony's rough mane and went tearing down into the valley. She intended to ride straight to the center of the field, to the cluster of bodies lying around the broken banner pole, but her pony—no doubt frightened by the smells of carnage—plunged to a halt at the edge of the field. When she kicked him and lashed his neck with the end of the reins, he reared up and nearly threw her off.

Only then did she come to her senses. Down here in the bright, hot sunlight, she could see how trampled the meadow grass was. Bodies lay where they'd fallen. Blood was splashed everywhere, so much blood. The smell of it in the heat flowed over her senses, suddenly unbearable.

She gagged and leaned over the saddle just in time.

When she righted herself, her pony was shifting and turning under her. The world spun a little. She felt light-headed and cold.

By then Shelena, Larisa, and the five boys had caught up with her. Old Uzfan came straggling behind them, beating his slow donkey with a stick. The beast waggled its long shaggy ears and brayed.

The sound echoed across the silent valley, shocking Alexeika. It seemed sacrilege to hear such a common, defiant sound in the presence of so much death.

"The gods protect us," Shelena murmured, drawing rein beside Alexeika.

Larisa covered her mouth with her hand and began to whimper.

Alexeika herself could find no words. She stared in all directions at these hacked and broken bodies belonging to men who last night had been laughing and boasting round the campfires, working up their courage for today. Right now, she recognized none of their slack faces or dusty, staring eyes. They all looked like strangers, and she was grateful for that. Dazed, she knew that soon the real grief would hit her, and she would find herself crushed as though with a stone.

"All of them," Larisa moaned, rocking herself back and forth in her saddle. "All our brave men." Her broad face contorted, and she began to cry with ugly, gulping sobs. "Thornic! My Thornic! My Dragn. My Osmyl."

Shelena's eyes filled with tears. She tipped back her head to utter the wailing, but Uzfan gripped her arm and shook her hard.

"Stop it!" he said fiercely. "Have you no sense? They will hear us."

Larisa went on sobbing, but Shelena glared back at the old priest. "Does it matter?" she retorted. "My man is dead. So is my heart."

Uzfan gestured at the boys, who had clustered together to stare. Their young faces showed how unprepared for this massacre they were. "Quick. You know what to do. Gather as many weapons as you can. We'll load them on my donkey. Quickly! Just as we planned last night."

Hearing him, Alexeika closed her eyes. Last night, the boys who had been chosen for this task of plundering the dead had believed it would be the enemy's weapons they would gather—not their own.

"Hurry!" Uzfan said, giving one of them a shake. "Would you let the Nonkind have their swords and bows?"

That got the boys moving. Tentatively at first, then with more resolve, they began to pick up the weapons.

While Uzfan got Shelena and Larisa to work, Alexeika's head cleared. She remembered her father's careful instructions, given to her in his final words last night. A lump rose in her throat. She swallowed it, refusing to think of him right now. She had her duty, and she must not shirk it. To do so would be to fail him, he who had never failed her.

Swiftly she dismounted and ground-tied her pony. "Uzfan," she made herself ask, "are there any survivors?"

The old priest lifted his head and closed his eyes. His nostrils quivered, and she could feel the pressure of the power he summoned. Then he opened his eyes and shook his head. His brown eyes met hers and filled with compassion. She understood, and dropped her own gaze swiftly to hide her tears.

"Then we mustn't waste time. The looters will be coming."

Both of the older women turned to stare at Alexeika in shock. "No," Larisa whispered.

"The dead will bring them quicker than usual," Alexeika said.

As she spoke she glanced toward the southeast, where the king's forces had ridden. "Help Uzfan salt as many bodies as you can."

Larisa covered her mouth with her hands and began to cry again, but Shelena faced Alexeika. "There isn't enough salt to go round. We can't sprinkle them all."

Alexeika met her eyes grimly. "Do what you can. Just hurry."

Leaving them standing there, rooted in place, Alexeika turned and hurried away, but she'd barely gone more than five strides before someone came puffing behind her and caught her by the back of her jerkin.

Unlike the other women, Alexeika wore male clothing, with leather leggings and a thin linsey tunic reaching nearly to her knees for modesty. Over it she wore a sleeveless jerkin belted by her twin daggers, with their sharp curved blades and ivory handles. Her long, unruly hair hung in a single thick braid down her back, in the way of the Agya soldiers. She was tall for a maiden, lean and surefooted. She strode boylike. She could swagger and curse and spit and ride. She knew how to handle weapons. And she'd been taught to think like a man, coldly and fearlessly, but to keep her feminine cunning as well.

When the back of her jerkin was grabbed, Alexeika whirled around, her braid flying straight out behind her, and slapped the offending hand away. It belonged to Uzfan, and his bearded old face was scowling with disapproval.

"Where do you go?" he demanded. "We must stay together. This is an evil place. Magic still crosses the air. There is no safety here among the dead."

"I'm going to my father," Alexeika said, her voice as rigid as steel. She would not let herself feel, not now. "I must prepare him."

A piece of her heart kept hoping that old Uzfan was wrong, that a few of these fallen warriors still lived. Her father could not be dead. He could not.

That's what she hoped, although she knew the banner would not have fallen if her father lived. Ilymir Volvn, once a general of King Tobeszijian's forces, and now leader of the rebellion, would be shouting orders at this moment if he still had any breath left in his body.

She could not think of it, not now. Her inner core had a crack across its surface, a crack that would let all her strength shatter inside if she did not take care. No, she must follow her orders. She must not fail him.

"Alexeika," Uzfan said, his voice more gentle now, "the preparations are my task, not yours. Stay here close to the others. I will go to him."

Frowning, she turned her gaze away. Time was running out; she could feel it as though the slipping grains fell between her fingers. His protests only wasted the moments that remained.

"I'm going," she said, and started off again. She walked quickly, picking her way over the fallen men.

It was eerie and quiet, this field of the dead. Her ears still echoed with the recent sounds of battle, the yells of ferocity, the screams of the dying. Foot soldiers vying against mounted cavalry. The odds evened by training and righteous determination. King Muncel was evil, weak, and half-mad. He had opened Nether to the Nonkind, bargained with the demons of Gant, and sold his soul into unholy alliances as a means of keeping his ill-gotten throne. He was a murderer, a liar, and a thief. He had confiscated lands and personal treasuries, plundered the old shrines, and forced the realm to accept the Reformed Church without exception. He had deposed some nobles and driven out officers, condemning to death any who defied him. Alexeika's own mother, once lady-in-waiting to Queen Neaglis, Muncel's foreign-born consort, had died twelve years past on the end of Muncel's sword because she refused to say where her husband and a third of the standing army had fled to.

And so it had begun, the civil war that went on and on, a never-ending wound that bled the vitality from this realm.

Perhaps, with this defeat, this massacre, it had ended at last.

Alexeika walked faster, dragging her hand across her burning eyes. She would not accept that. Her father would never want her to think that way. A battle could be lost, but the war had to continue. That's what he would say.

"Papa," she whispered, her heart aching as she stumbled along. Tears spilled down her cheeks, and she brushed them away.

She tripped over a man's legs and fell, landing hard on her knees and crying out. For a moment, she crouched there, gasping for breath, her emotions raw beneath the control she barely held.

When she tried to rise to her feet, she looked at the face of the man she'd fallen over. It was Count Lanyl Otverya, her father's squire, barely eighteen and still growing his first beard. The visor to his helmet had been torn away on one side. It hung twisted and bloody from the axe blow that had killed him.

Alexeika crawled closer and gripped his sleeve. His breastplate was dented and hacked open by the ferocious blows he'd taken. No shield lay near him; she supposed he dropped it in the charge. The blade of his sword had been shattered, and his dead hand gripped only the hilt.

Kneeling beside him, she bowed her head and wept. Lanyl had been fun, always laughing and playing pranks. His clear tenor voice could sing songs of old so sweetly that grown men wept. He should have led his own army, but his lands had been confiscated too. Deposed of his hold, his title officially stripped away, his parents and siblings imprisoned or dead, Lanyl had escaped the purge with only his father's sword as his inheritance. He'd been so optimistic that one day King Muncel would be knocked from his throne and order restored to this weary land.

Lanyl had been like a brother to her. Gently, Alexeika closed his staring eyes, and in doing so stained her fingers with his blood.

When her tears stopped, she pulled the broken sword from his hand and with the tip of her dagger pried the square, thumb-sized ruby from its pommel. She pocketed the jewel, feeling like a thief. Yet they had to live. They had to eat. They had to keep the fight going somehow.

A sob escaped her. She choked back the rest and pushed herself to her feet, turning away from him while she still could.

Puffing heavily, old Uzfan caught up with her. "Alexeika, wait!" he said, gasping between words. "For the love of Thod, please wait."

She slid her dagger back into its sheath and handed Uzfan the remnant of Lanyl's shattered sword. "Take care of him, please." Uzfan's face blurred through her tears. "I must go to my father."

"Child," he said, "there is no more time. Look yon."

She followed the direction of his pointing finger and saw movement atop the distant hills. She drew in a sharp breath, feeling ice in her veins despite the day's heat. Queer little prickles ran through her skin.

"Soultakers," Uzfan said, his old voice quavering with fear. His hand shook visibly as he lowered it. "They are riding with the looters. I feel them."

She nodded, her mouth too dry for talking. "I, too."

"We must hurry. They must not catch us."

"Lanyl," she said. "Please."

Uzfan sighed and nodded. Taking the broken sword, he murmured the words of protection, then peeled away Lanyl's battered breastplate. He struck swift and hard, staking the boy.

Alexeika had already turned away, unable to watch. She heard the blow, and flinched as though the weapon had passed through her own heart. Now Lanyl was freed, his soul severed from his body. The soultakers would not possess him.

While Uzfan sprinkled salt over the body, Alexeika hurried on toward the center of the field.

"Alexeika, no!" Uzfan shouted. The old priest ran after her, caught her shoulder, and spun her around. "No! The risk is too great."

She glared at him. "And what will protect him? Would you leave him to those—" Her voice failed her. She gestured furiously, unable to say the words.

"I will make a spell and cast it over the entire field," Uzfan said. "But come away. Now, child, while there is time."

"I must give him rites," she said raggedly, refusing to listen. "I must take his sword. The looters cannot have it."

"His sword will lie where it lies," Uzfan said fiercely. His old, dark eyes glared at her from beneath wrinkled lids. "Your father is dead, child. His sword is of no use now. The war is ended."

Rage and protest and grief welled up inside her, building a force she could no longer contain. She slapped him with all her might, rocking him on his feet. Spinning from him, she strode away.

He made no further attempt to stop her, and she was glad. Stumbling and half-running, she forced herself to climb over the mound of dead men entangled together at what had been the last stand. A corner of her mind felt shock that she had dared strike a priest, much less Uzfan himself. But the rest of her was too angry to care.

She shoved and shifted and pushed her way through to where the banner lay trampled, its bright colors now stained and coated with blood-splattered dirt.

Her father lay beneath the broken banner pole, his gloved hand still grasping part of it. The banner boy lay headless and disemboweled beside him.

There was a horrible stink in the air, the stink of Nonkind, a taint that burned her nostrils and made her want to retreat. Shaking her head, she knelt instead beside the man who had sired her, raised her, and loved her enough for two parents.

Prince Ilymir Volvn, general of the king's army, protector of the south. His titles had once been prestigious and many. His victories, his decorations for valor, and his honor had all shone brightly until King Muncel declared him a traitor and stripped him of everything. For years now he had lived with a price on his head, a prince turned outlaw. But his dream of restoring the throne to its rightful king had never dimmed.

Her father had been a tall, lean man with a jutting beak of a nose, bushy gray eyebrows, and a harsh gash of mouth. He was gruff and plainspoken, relentless, and a perfectionist, yet this was the man who had taught her to swim in icy streams during childhood summers, holding her around the middle while she laughed and paddled. This was the man who had braided her hair for her, who refused to let her cut it, who had taught her to dance and given her secret deportment lessons suitable for a lady at court, mincing along in the privacy of the woods while he held up the train of an imaginary gown. This was the man who had given her the set of daggers, taken her to a man who taught her how to throw and handle them without cutting herself. Prince Volvn had trained and tempered her as best he could. Never had he been unkind or unfair, despite his high standards. He wanted her to grow up capable, strong, and able to think for herself.

She had loved him with all her heart. Never again would they walk together under the evening stars, plotting campaigns and strategy. Never again would she feel his strong arm across her shoulders. Never would she hear his gruff voice softened to that special tone spoken to her alone, while he murmured, "My pet, do not be so fierce against Lanyl. He is only a boy in love with you, and therefore a fool."

"My pet," he would say, "put aside your temper and *think.* What is your brain for, except to be used?"

"My pet," he had said this morning just before he rode into battle, "I depend on you if anything goes wrong. Keep Severgard out of the hands of the enemy. Never has it been held by a dishonorable man. Protect it as you would your life, and someday give it to your son."

"Don't say such things!" she protested, full of courage then. Her blood was on fire to be with the men; her heart felt certain they would win. "You'll have a victory today. I know it!"

"Follow your orders, daughter," he said, his voice cracking like a whip. "Promise me you'll follow them."

And now she would have to.

"Oh, Papa," she said. Sinking to her knees beside him, she lifted his visor.

He had never known defeat in his long and distinguished career. His valiant name alone was enough to fill the hearts of men with courage. Five times in the past five years he had led the small rebel forces in skirmishes and battles, and each time they won. But today, he had faced the king's real army, one supplemented with hard-bitten Gantese mercenaries and Nonkind, and he had lacked *sorcerels* to protect his men.

In the distance, the looters now came. She felt the thunder of their approaching hoofbeats shaking the valley floor, but she did not lift her gaze from her father's face.

Although his eyes were shut, he looked stern. Already death had made his face a stranger's. She touched his cheek, but it did not bring him closer or keep him with her. He was gone.

Weeping, she drew her hand back and curled her fingers into a fist. The noise of the galloping horses grew louder.

A hand gripped her shoulder. She jumped, screaming, and whirled around to attack, but it was only old Uzfan. Gasping with relief, she sagged down to her knees again.

"Swiftly, child," Uzfan said. "Use the salt you brought. I have no more in my pouch."

Frowning, she reached for the small, heavy pouch hanging at her belt.

He took it from her, sighing and plucking at his white beard.

"Your father's presence is very strong. They will seek him for the power of his life."

She shivered and swallowed hard, trying not to think of the horrors that awaited his body if she and Uzfan failed to protect him now.

Muttering incantations and prayers, Uzfan began sprinkling the salt across Prince Volvn's body.

Alexeika reached down and pulled Severgard from her father's hand. The great sword had been handed down through seven generations of her family. Long and heavy, it had been forged by a dwarf swordmaker who used magicked metal mined in the Mountains of the Gods. The blade was made of black steel, and runes were carved along it. The hilt and guard were wrapped in gold and silver wire, and a great flashing sapphire was set in the pommel. She struggled to lift it.

Gore was drying on the blade, and its stench was rank and tainted. She wrinkled her nose in revulsion. Nonkind had died today on this blade. She wiped it clean, knowing it would have to be scrubbed with both salt and sand and oiled later.

Tugging off her father's belt, she choked back a fresh sob, but she slid the sword into its scabbard and knotted the ends of the belt together before slinging it across her shoulder.

By now Uzfan had finished with the salt. He poured the last of it on Prince Volvn's tongue.

"Is it enough?" Alexeika asked.

The looters were close enough to see them. In their sinister black cloaks, they yelled and cursed. She could smell their evil, a stink as foul as that which had been on the sword. It made her want to run.

"Is there enough time for his soul to leave?" she asked.

Uzfan shook his head sorrowfully. "Nay, child. His presence is too strong. It does not want to accept failure."

She felt sick to her stomach, but she was her father's daughter. She knew what had to be done.

"Child, shall I—"

"No," she said firmly, swallowing hard. She drew her father's dagger and held it aloft. This was a son's duty to a father who fell in battle. She told herself to be strong.

Uzfan did not argue with her. He pulled off Prince Volvn's helmet and the mail coif beneath it. The hot, dusty wind ruffled the dead man's gray hair. Uzfan tipped back his head, exposing her father's muscular throat.

She crouched, her fingers holding the dagger so tightly her whole hand shook. Tears filled her eyes anew, stinging them. "Forgive me," she whispered, and plunged the dagger through his throat.

Something pale and gossamer-light floated upward from his body. It encompassed her for a second, bringing with it a sensation of warmth and well-being. Then it was gone, his soul, gone to the safety of the third world.

She wept, but there was no time. Shouting at her, Uzfan gripped her shoulder and pulled her upright. She stumbled and started to run, then turned back and grabbed the tattered banner.

"Hurry!" Uzfan shouted.

The riders were too close. She heard them whooping and yelling shrilly. All around her darkness seemed to be descending. A bugling roar of something unearthly made her glance back. She saw a darsteed coming after her, bounding with a stride twice as long as a horse's. Its nostrils blew flame, and next to it ran a hurlhound with fangs bared and dripping yellow poison. It bayed at her, and her heart lurched in fear.

Uzfan shouted, and a great cloud of dust whirled up between them and the riders. The swirling cyclone caused the darsteeds and horses to rear to a halt. Two of the hurlhounds came running on, straight into the cloud. They were swept off their feet and flung high into the vortex.

Alexeika saw the look of strain on the old priest's face and knew he could not hold the spell long. Gripping his arm, she ran with him, pushing him when his old legs faltered. At the far edge of the field, Shelena waited on her pony, holding the reins of Alexeika's frightened mount. Larisa and the boys were already fleeing, the boys beating the heavily laden donkey with sticks to make it run.

Uzfan stumbled and fell, despite her efforts to catch him. She crouched low and pulled him upright.

Dirt streaked his face and coated his beard. He was gasping for air, his face purple with exertion. Behind her came a triumphant cheer as the cloud dissipated and the looters surged through.

Most of them fell on the bodies with a savagery that sickened Alexeika. The hurlhounds tasted salt and fell back with yelps of pain.

"Come on," she muttered to Uzfan, pushing him forward.

She thought the looting might distract the horde enough to allow her and the old man to escape. But the sound of pursuit came again.

Uzfan looked back and murmured something that made her ears ring. A column of fire blazed up behind them, cutting off the pursuers a second time.

The smell of magic filled the air, making Alexeika cough. She urged him on, hoping he did not kill himself with such exertion.

"Hurry!" Shelena called. Her pony was rearing with fear. She barely managed to control it.

When it whirled around beneath her, she flung the reins of Alexeika's pony at her and galloped away. Alexeika lunged forward and caught the reins just in time to keep her own mount from bolting as well.

Talking to the frightened animal, trying to soothe it while it reared and pulled back, she got Uzfan astride it and jumped on herself. Wheeling the pony around, she let it run.

An arrow grazed her shoulder blade, stinging harshly though giving her no serious harm. She glanced back, but the looters did not follow her away from the battlefield. The man swathed in black who had shot at her lowered his bow and gave her a mocking salute, then turned his darsteed around and headed back to the carnage.

The pony ran and ran, over the hill and up the next, until the woods swallowed them and they slowed to a jouncing, weary trot through the cool shade.

"I don't believe it," Uzfan muttered in his beard. "We got away. We got away. Do they not know what they let escape? There must have been no Believers controlling them. They let us get away."

"No," Alexeika said firmly. "You frightened them with your magic. Are you feeling better now? Should I find a stream so you may drink?"

"No," he said, his voice sounding weak and shaky. "Do not stop. We dare not stop."

By the time they reached camp on the banks of the fjord, it was late afternoon. Alexeika could hear the women keening, the sound rising and falling like a brutal wind. She bowed her head, struggling with her own emotions, but she refused to wail and tear her clothing and mourn in the way of female serfs.

The camp was a large one, although it did not contain all the families of the men and boys who had died today. Many had come to join the war, leaving their homes to fight the darkness. But now, those who remained—the old men, the women, the children—sobbed and grieved in their tents or else stood as though turned to stone in the midst of some task, their faces ravaged with sorrow.

A few gathered around as Alexeika drew her weary pony to a halt. They stared at her in silence, watching as she carried her father's sword into her tent.

Draysinko, a man no older than thirty but spared from fighting because of his crippled leg, was waiting when she came finally outside again. She had washed her face and eaten the few bites of food she could choke down. Severgard, now clean and oiled, lay in its scabbard atop her father's cot. Tonight, she would light the Element candles and pray for him the same way he had taught her to mourn her mother, in dignified privacy. Not for her the grieving of the serfs, the women sitting outside their tents and keening for hours or perhaps even days. It was the custom of the peasants to show how much they had respected a loved one by mourning for as long as possible before exhaustion claimed them. Sometimes, Alexeika almost believed they were competing with each other by displaying the most grief.

When she emerged from her tent, an uneasy delegation, consisting of Draysinko, five old men, and two gray-haired court ladies determined to look as stern and regal as ever despite their plain linsey gowns, was waiting politely for her.

Draysinko stepped forward, limping on his crooked leg, and bowed to her. "Your father is dead?" he asked.

Formality required her to make an official announcement. The camp now lacked a leader, and she wondered who would be named to take her father's place. She had filled in during his absences before. He had traveled often to secret meetings with other rebel leaders, trying to raise an army, trying to obtain weapons and armor where and when he could. But this time, the absence would be permanent.

Her heart ached, and she swiftly turned her thoughts away

lest she break down. Her father had taught her that a good commander did not betray weakness to his followers.

"Excuse this intrusion," Draysinko said politely, although his eyes looked impatient. "As the daughter of the House of Volvn, you must officially make the announcement."

It irritated her that he sought to instruct her in her public duties. Her head lifted high on her graceful neck. She squared her shoulders.

"Consider the announcement made," she said. "Prince Volvn is dead. The battle was lost."

The men of the little delegation exchanged glances. All except Draysinko removed their caps and bowed to her. She saw tears run down the withered cheeks of Lady Natelitya, but neither of the two older women changed their bleak expressions. They had lost so much in recent years, perhaps they could not feel this most recent blow.

"Tonight," Alexeika said, "I shall speak to the junior auxiliary. We will step up their training. In a month, they should be ready to march on Trebek as—"

"No," Lady Natelitya said. "My husband is dead. My eldest sons are dead. Now my youngest son is dead. You will not kill my grandson as well."

Alexeika frowned. She had not expected opposition, especially not from the fierce Lady Natelitya. "The plans have already been made. My father—"

"—is not here to lead the next skirmish," Lady Natelitya said. "You will not risk the children."

Alexeika drew in a deep breath. "Very well. We will have to send word to the forces at Lolta. We can join them or go to—"

"No," Lady Natelitya said. "It is over."

"But—"

"Over, Alexeika," the woman said. Turning her back, she walked away.

Alexeika stared after her in dismay. She started to go after Lady Natelitya, whose support was important, but Draysinko blocked her path.

"We must talk," he said.

Hope came back to her. She smiled at him and the others who remained. "Then you agree with me that we must continue our strategy? With delays, of course, to recover fighting strength—"

"There will be no more fighting," Draysinko interrupted her.

She could see in their eyes that they were united against her. "Explain," she said sharply.

"The war of rebellion is over," Draysinko announced. "We lost. Today's massacre ends everything."

"No!" she cried. "It cannot. It must not. If you—if we give up now, then everything we lost today was lost in vain. You would make a mockery of their deaths."

"Word has come to us from our friends in Lolta," Draysinko said. "It came too late to stop today's fighting, but there is hope for the rest of us."

"What is this message?" Alexeika asked suspiciously.

"King Muncel offers a royal pardon to all rebels who surrender themselves."

A scornful laugh escaped her. "And you believe this? It's a trick."

"No. It is a chance to live. The messenger from Lolta says some have already accepted the offer. They have not been killed. They are to be serfs in the southeast lands."

Near Gant, she thought with a shudder. "Serfs?" she echoed, disdain harsh in her voice.

"Do not look so unhappy, Princess," Draysinko replied sharply. He had been born a serf, she remembered. "There is hard work, but what is harder than living like this, hand-to-mouth, always in danger of betrayal or capture? It is a chance to make a new beginning. A chance to start over."

"Impossible," she said, shaking her head. "The king seeks to trick us. Tleska, you surely do not believe this offer will be honored?"

The old man she spoke to knotted his face in consternation. He was gripping his cap in his gnarled old hands. They trembled visibly. "We can't go on without the general."

"Yes, we can," she said loudly.

Other people, drawn by their argument, began to gather around.

"We must!" she continued. "One defeat is not enough to stop us—"

"Yes it is!" Draysinko interrupted her. His dark eyes snapped with anger. He looked like he wanted to shake her. "This wasn't just a defeat."

"It was a massacre," Tleska said. "There isn't an able-bodied man left among us."

"Who will hunt for us this winter?" asked a woman from the rear of the crowd. "My Slan was the best with a bow in the camp. Who will feed me and his children now? Who will hunt for the rest of you?"

"I can hunt," Alexeika said proudly. "The older boys can hunt."

"A woman and some children," Draysinko said with a sneer.

She glared at him. "You are not too crippled to learn to shoot a bow. You could fish and—"

"I am not trained for such work," he said, using the argument he always produced to keep from doing his share. He had been a rug-maker in Grov when the purge began. As long as he was only expected to weave cloth, he worked well. Ask him to do anything else, and he shrieked with complaints. "Hear me, all of you!" he shouted to the crowd. "We must face reality. This summer, yes, we can survive in hiding. But come the snows, what will we do?"

"We'll do what we've always done," Alexeika said, astonished by his cowardice. Yes, today had shaken them all. Every time she thought of life without her father, she grew faint and sick inside. Still, he would not want her, or any of them, to give up. "We'll winter in the mountain caves. And we'll go on with what we must do. With what we vowed to do."

"The war is over," Draysinko insisted. "We can have a full pardon if we will surrender."

"Then what did my father die for?" she asked fiercely. "Why did he spill his blood, if not to put a stop to the evil that has taken Nether? He did not fight today so that I could become a Gantese serf."

"Nothing was said about serving the Gantese," said a man quietly.

He was a stranger. She guessed he must be the messenger from Lolta. Even as she sized him up, noting the lean body in mismatched chain mail, the scar on his cheek, the shiftiness to his eyes, and the worn but serviceable sword in his scabbard, Alexeika reminded herself that they should move camp as soon as he left. She did not like the looks of him. Nor would she trust anything he said.

Alexeika looked at the bleak and frightened faces turned to

her. "There's another thing you haven't thought through," she said. "Will you accept the Reformed Church and renounce the old ways?"

That shocked them. Murmurs arose in the crowd. Several women flung their aprons over their heads and began to whimper. Young children, big-eyed still from the news that they had no fathers or brothers, stood huddled together in clusters, watching their mothers panic.

"Nothing was said about that," Draysinko admitted. He turned to look at the messenger, as did everyone else.

The stranger shrugged. "Heard nothing about it."

"You know it will be required," Alexeika said. "That's the trick, isn't it? By law, a serf is required to follow the beliefs of his master. Will you kneel to the Reformed Circle? Will *you,* Draysinko? Will *you,* Tleska? Boral? Tomk? Ulinvo?"

No one answered her. She noticed old Uzfan walking toward the rear of the crowd. Pale and weary, he leaned heavily on a wooden staff.

Drawing in a breath, Alexeika pointed at the priest. "Here is our Uzfan. Remember that he was defrocked by the reformers because he would not leave the old ways. His brethren were beheaded."

Uzfan nodded. "She speaks the truth. The Circle was once a theology of tolerance, embracing old messages and new. No longer is this true. You have lost your kinsmen today in this terrible tragedy. Take care you do not lose your gods as well."

Alexeika looked at the messenger, her eyes filled with challenge and distrust. "You've delivered your message," she said. "Go back to Lolta."

The man bowed to her. "I will tell them of the defeat."

She frowned, biting her lip, but there was no way to stop him. It was the truth, the dreadful, unflinching, harsh truth. Unbearable, and yet they had to bear it.

As the man mounted his horse and rode away, she squared her shoulders with an effort and faced the people again.

"We must grieve first," she said. "Let us give ourselves time for that before we make any hasty decisions. In the morning, we'll move camp and then we'll—"

"Why?" demanded Larisa. "Why should we move?"

"For safety," Alexeika replied. "We have always done so after a messenger comes to us."

"But who will strike the tents?"

"We can," Alexeika said.

"It's nearly nightfall," Tleska said sadly. "We can't march in the dark. Our hearts are too heavy."

"No, of course we will not march tonight," Alexeika agreed, masking her sigh. "I said we'll break camp in the morning. At first light."

"But how will my da's ghost know to find me if I move away?" asked a little girl. She was missing her front teeth and had a spattering of freckles across her nose.

The wailing resumed, with women turning away, wadding their aprons in their hands. Children scurried after them, clutching folds of their skirts and crying too.

Dismayed, Alexeika felt weary to her bones. Grief had exhausted her. She wanted no conflict now, but Draysinko and the other men still stood there before her, looking indecisive. She could think of only one other way to raise their spirits and bring back their courage.

"Let us not forget why we fight," she said. "Uzfan, when night falls, will you cast the prophecy about our true king once more?"

The old priest shook his head wearily. "Nay, child," he said. "Not this night. You cannot rouse the hearts of people until their sorrow is spent."

She would have argued and cajoled him, but he turned and walked away, leaning on his staff. One by one, the others trickled away, until only Draysinko was left.

"The people will not follow you," he said spitefully. "You are not your father. You are no man, despite your leggings and daggers."

"I know what my father would wish me to do," she replied, still astonished by his hostility. Draysinko had always grumbled, but never before had he tried to create open dissension. Perhaps he had not dared to until now. Perhaps he wanted the leadership for himself.

She looked at Draysinko's sour face. "I do not want my father's death to be in vain."

He frowned. "We will choose a new leader tomorrow."

"We'll choose when we reach our new camp. In a few days."

"And who finds this new camp?" he asked with a sneer. "You?"

She opened her mouth to say she could, but he turned away. Frowning and feeling troubled, she watched his limping figure a moment, then withdrew into her tent to think.

Her father's presence seemed to fill the small space. Despite the gathering shadows she could see Severgard lying where she'd left it. It was a potent weapon, powered with magic. Who would carry it into battle now?

Sitting down on her cot, she gripped her hair with her fingers and leaned over, her grief mixed with resentment. If only she could have been male. Her father had needed a son to inherit this sword, to carry his name into history, to continue the fight for the true king. She was strong and fearless, but not strong enough to wield Severgard. She could barely lift it, and she knew not how to control its power.

What was she to do? Let these people disperse and surrender? Let the rebellion fall apart? Tell herself she could do nothing except bed a man and bring a son into the world, a son who years from now would perhaps live to carry this sword into battle? Why had the gods given her an agile mind and a strong will, if her loins were all she was good for?

Worst of all, she was disappointed in her people, disappointed by how thoroughly they had been demoralized. It was as though this blow had killed their hearts, leaving them without the will to continue. Was she the only one who raged at the massacre, who vowed in her heart she would never give up, would never surrender, would never accept Muncel the Usurper as her rightful king? She was ashamed of the people she called friends, ashamed and disappointed in them.

Perhaps tomorrow they would regain their courage. But as she listened to the wailing in the tents, she did not think they would. It was hard to lose, devastating to lose, knowing right was on your side, and yet losing anyway.

"Oh, Papa," she whispered through her tears. "What am I to do?"

17

IN LOWER MANDRIA, the palace of Savroix was lit inside and out for an evening summertime festival. Flambeaux atop poles illuminated the garden paths, and richly garbed guests wearing masks as disguises strolled in all directions. Laughter and playful shrieks filled the warm air among the hedges. Lute music played in the distance.

A girl went running by with a merry tinkling of tiny bells sewn to her skirts, her mask slipping and her hair half-unbound. She was pursued by a young man with streaming lovelocks and a short beard. He carried his mask in his hand and was laughing lustily.

"Wicked, wicked!" the girl said. Her words were a rebuke, but her tone was all surrender. She ran on, disappearing into the shadows of the shrubbery, the young man on her heels.

Standing next to a stone statue, Pheresa watched the amorous couple vanish. Although she had lived at court for several months now, she remained shocked by these wanton escapades. King Verence was a kindly, good-hearted man, but what misbehavior he did not himself witness he seemed to take no interest in. Nor did he want anyone carrying tales to him. Therefore, the courtiers did as they pleased as long as they kept decorum in the king's presence. As for Verence himself, he kept two mistresses in opposite wings of the palace, and officious little secretaries with pens and parchment were in charge of keeping the two ladies' schedules apart so that they never met each other.

Pheresa had not been trained to lead such a life as she saw daily at court. Nor could she bring herself to embrace it, despite the joking advice of others. Often, she felt unsophisticated and alone. She had written only once to her mother for advice, but Princess Dianthelle's reply was curt. Pheresa had to make herself admired if she was to succeed. No one could obtain popularity for her.

Pheresa had no particular wish to be popular among courtiers who were idle and heedless of anything except their next pleasure. She was interested in the workings of government and longed to be allowed to sit in on the meetings between king and council. Once, she had requested permission to attend. Her petition had been denied.

Now, her three companions—Lady Esteline, who was Pheresa's court chaperone, plus Lady Esteline's husband, Lord Thieron, and brother, Lord Fantil—observed her round-eyed expression at this evening's festivities and laughed.

"That was the little Sofia you saw running into the shrubbery, my dear," Lady Esteline said, giggling behind her slim hand. "One of the ladies in waiting to Countess Lalieux."

Pheresa blinked. The Countess Lalieux was the king's newer mistress. "I see," she replied, but her voice was clipped.

Lady Esteline laughed harder. "Do not worry," she said gaily. "Sofia and her pursuer are engaged to be married. Such a frown you wear."

Lord Fantil bowed to Pheresa. "Enchanting," he said, showing his teeth in approval. "Such old-fashioned, country notions of propriety. Most young maidens fresh out of the nuncery are eager to embrace all that they see here. Few are as shy . . . and as beguiling . . as you."

Pheresa blushed to the roots of her hair and hoped the shadows concealed her change of color. She looked away from him, feeling his compliments and flattery to be inappropriate.

Lady Esteline laughed again. "Take care, Fantil. This child would rather read the dreary foreign dispatches and harvest accounts than flirt with a handsome man. I think it a grave disservice to teach young maidens how to read. See what comes of filling their minds with such nonsense?"

Lord Thieron threw back his bald head and brayed. The others joined in his laughter. Pheresa smiled to be a good sport. They were always laughing at her and teasing her. She disliked it very much, but she did not know what to do about it. Nor did she quite know how to acquire friends of her own choosing. Her place at court remained tenuous. The king liked her, and she had the honor of visiting him daily for chats and occasional games of chess. But she had no official position here. Niece of the king or not, she had no duties and no importance. Neither of the king's mistresses had chosen to receive her or invite her to join their circle of companions. Pheresa was relieved because as a member of the royal family, she knew she should not recognize either woman. Yet she was lonely. King Verence's wife had died several years ago, and he had not remarried. Pheresa believed he erred in this, for a queen would have curbed the courtiers' excesses and organized their society more productively. But she knew better than to dispense either her opinions or her advice.

The best and most courteous of the older courtiers spoke to her pleasantly, but most of the younger set did not bother with her at all. Pheresa understood, of course. Until she was engaged to Prince Gavril and officially destined to one day be queen, she meant nothing here.

Now, she and her companions resumed their stroll along the garden path, and Pheresa kept a wary eye on how far away from the palace they seemed to be going. From all sides, she could hear furtive rustlings and giggles in the ornate shrubbery. During the day, she adored the gardens and loved walking through their beauty. On evenings like this, however, she would rather have been safe in her own chamber.

Lady Esteline stumbled and gripped the arm of her husband. "Oh, how silly of me," she said unsteadily. "This blighted slipper has come apart. Thieron, you must assist me."

Her husband bent to reach beneath the long hem of her gown. Lord Fantil moved to stand beside Pheresa. She could smell a fragrance on him, something musky and disturbing. Her father had never worn scent. Nor did the king. She did not like the custom.

"Is it easily mended?" Fantil asked politely.

Lord Thieron pulled the slipper off his wife's foot and held it up for inspection in the gloom. "I think not."

"Such a bother," Lady Esteline complained, "and I paid four dreits of silver for these shoes. I shall insist the cobbler refund my money."

"Let us go back," Pheresa said with relief. "The men can help you walk, and I shall—"

"No, my dear. How can you think of spoiling your evening because of my silly slipper?" Lady Esteline patted Pheresa's hand. "You really must see the north fountains by moonlight. They are the most enchanting sight. Fantil, please escort Lady Pheresa there."

"Of course," he said eagerly.

A tiny sense of alarm passed through Pheresa. "The fountains will wait for another occasion," she said, trying to keep her voice light and steady. "I could not leave you like this, my lady."

"Dear child," Lady Esteline cooed. "So sweet of you to worry about me. But I have my Thieron to escort me. Please go on."

"I am a little tired," Pheresa said desperately.

Fantil took her hand and tucked it in the crook of his arm. "Then we shall not tarry long. But the fountains by moonlight you must see, if my sister has decreed it. Come, my lady."

He led her away into the shadows, away from the palace and the flaming torchlight. Pheresa did not want to go with this man. She knew she should not be with him alone, but her own chaperone had put her in his keeping. She did not know how to extricate herself from this situation without making a fuss. People already considered her quaint and old-fashioned. She would be joked at and mocked even more if she took fright and ran away.

The fountains stood beyond the farthest edge of the gardens, with the woodland park behind them. Cascades of water poured down and jetted into the air. Although the moon was only a thin sliver tonight, the effect was a pretty one.

Pheresa stood there, gazing at the sight, and feeling very conscious of how close to her this man stood, of how tightly he kept her arm clasped within his.

"Beautiful," she said. "Now, let us go back."

She tried to turn around, but he held her where she was.

Pheresa frowned. "Please."

"There is no hurry, my lady," he said, and his voice was deep and smooth and assured. "Let us linger a few moments more to savor all that is special here."

From the corner of her eye, she glimpsed another couple nearby. They were embracing in a passionate kiss. Lord Fantil bent over her, and she could feel his warm breath upon her cheek.

She felt trapped, too warm, and a little faint. He meant to kiss her, of that she was certain. His arm had now encircled her back. His fingers splayed across her waist, pulling her closer to him.

"You are a beautiful child," he murmured. "Your skin is so white it glows by moonlight. Your lips are—"

Pheresa had a sudden clear thought of the palace and how

close she stood to jeopardy here. If Fantil compromised her, she would leave Savroix in disgrace. Certainly she would never marry the Heir to the Realm.

With a gasp, she turned her head, averting his lips from hers. He kissed her cheek instead, and she twisted in his hold, giving him a strong push.

He released her at once, much to her relief, and held up his hands. "Now, now, my little dove. What do you fear? Have you never savored a man's ardor before?"

"I do not intend to savor yours," Pheresa said tartly.

"That is unkind. If I have frightened you, I beg your pardon. Please, my lady, there is nothing to fear. It is pleasant, once you grow used to it."

"No doubt," she said, gathering up her skirts and walking around him. He turned to go with her, and she quickened her pace. "But I do not intend to dally here in the moonlight with you."

"Tell me how I displease you," he said, reaching out and gripping her wrist.

She stopped, too furious now to feel afraid. "Release me."

He obeyed, but in doing so he allowed his fingers to stroke her arm lightly. She shivered.

"Am I too ugly or too old for you?" he asked.

Pheresa frowned. Lord Fantil was young and very handsome, as well he knew. His games annoyed her. With a little huff, she started walking again.

"Lady Pheresa—"

"Hush!" she said angrily. "How dare you use my name out here. Do you intend to cause a scandal?"

He did not reply fast enough, and that told her the answer.

She drew in her breath sharply. "I see."

"No, I don't think you do," he replied. "Tarry a moment, and let us talk."

"There is nothing we need say," she told him, walking faster. "I understand this matter perfectly. You have a younger sister, do you not? One reputed to be beautiful indeed."

"Yes," he replied with caution.

"Yes," Pheresa repeated, nodding to herself. Her anger deepened with every step. "A sister whom you would like to marry to his highness."

"My lady—"

"Enough! Do not waste my time with falsehoods," she snapped. "You and Lady Esteline think me unprotected and foolish, too naive to guard myself from ruinous seduction. I fear to disappoint you, my lord, but you have overestimated the power of your charm."

He kept pace with her, but even through the shadows she could see how tense he had become. When he spoke, his voice was as tight and clipped as hers. "Forgive my offense. If you believe my family plots against you, you are completely mistaken. My youngest sister is already betrothed to a young man of worth and fortune. She is no rival to your ambition."

Just short of a flambeau, he stopped on the garden path and faced her, his face and shoulders in shadow. "You quite mistook me. My compliments were sincere, but I assure you they will not trouble you again. Good evening."

With a bow, he strode away, leaving her there alone.

Pheresa stood next to a large shrub with her face and throat flaming hot. Her mind—momentarily so clear and certain—fell into confusion and she did not know what to think. It seemed she had erred again, and in doing so had insulted a man of importance. All the popular ladies at court had admirers, but she had just spurned her first so clumsily she might never attract another. The nuns had taught her how to read and think for herself, but not how to flirt.

Dismayed, she stood there hiding in the shadows until she was certain she would not cry, then slowly returned to the palace.

Far away in Nether, the shadows grew long and darkened inside Alexeika's tent. Eventually, she found a measure of calmness. She thought of the stories her father used to tell her about King Tobeszijian, handsome and strong, with his eld eyes and his thick black hair. When Queen Nereisse was poisoned and the throne overturned, Tobeszijian had acted like the true king he was. He seized the Chalice of Eternal Life from the hands of the churchmen who stole it and rode forth into a cloud of magic, never to be seen again.

The Chalice and Tobeszijian's heirs were missing all these years later. It was rumored Tobeszijian was dead, for everyone felt he would have returned to fight for the throne had he been alive. But his body was never found. Men had searched. Often

Alexeika had seen pilgrims trudging along lonely forest paths or steep mountain passes, their footgear worn to shreds as they searched tirelessly for their lost king.

Uzfan had cast prophecy and evoked visions, saying the king was lost forever, but that his son would one day return.

"King Faldain," Alexeika whispered now. Her heart stirred at the mention of his name. He would be about her age, perhaps a year older, for she was not born until after the troubles in Nether began. Her older sister had died of some childhood illness. Later her mother had been killed. That was when her father came forth from hiding in exile and took Alexeika into his care. That was when he began to actively campaign against King Muncel. There had been war ever since.

If she had anything to do with it, there would continue to be war.

She wondered what Faldain looked like, if he was as strong and handsome as his father had been. Did he have Tobeszijian's black hair? Or was he pale and fair like his eldin mother? Where did he live? Did he know of his heritage? Was he training, even now, in the arts of war so that he could return to avenge his parents and seize the throne rightfully his? Was he worthy of his name? Did he have the character and courage to be a king? Or was he spoiled and shallow?

She sighed, pushing away her speculation. The problem was that the people needed a man of flesh and blood to fight for. They needed to know that their rightful king existed. Until now, they had put their faith in her father and followed his leadership. But without the general, there was little to keep their hopes alive.

If Uzfan would only cast a vision of Faldain, the people might keep going. If they could see their king, they would know him worth waiting for.

She stood up, intending to go to the old priest and persuade him to cast a vision. But as she stepped outside her tent into the soft evening air, she halted. She could not ask again. If Uzfan possessed the strength to conjure up the vision, he would have done it rather than refuse her. It would be unkind to pester him and make him admit he was too weak to perform the task.

The evening breeze felt cool and pleasant. The camp lay quiet now, for most people had withdrawn inside their tents. She realized she hadn't scheduled the night watch, but a shadow moved among the trees, telling her the work was being done anyway.

Out on the fjord, the water lay still and dark. A moon was rising in the sky. She watched it climb the heavens and knew she needed hope as much as the others. Perhaps more.

Well, then, she would use her own insignificant abilities and cast a vision for herself. Her mother had possessed a bit of eldin blood. Alexeika's gifts were small indeed, and seldom used, for when she'd been younger Uzfan's attempts to train her had been unsuccessful and frustrating to them both. Tonight, however, she decided to try. Perhaps, instead of a vision of the king, she would seek a vision of her father.

As long as she lived, she would never forget the sensation of feeling his soul pass from this world into another. It had felt like a benediction, his parting blessing, although he had never been a sentimental man given to emotional displays. Already she missed him so much.

Quietly she walked down the steep bank and untied a small fishing skiff. Climbing in, she paddled her way across the fjord until she was well away from the bank. Shipping her paddle, she let the skiff bob there on the surface, waiting until the water grew calm and still.

The moon's pale sliver hung above her. Stars spangled the darkness around it. The water reflected back moon and starlight. She centered herself until she found a place of peace and acceptance.

Closing her eyes, she concentrated her thoughts on her father, envisioning a mist upon the water. Long ago she had tried to part the veils of seeing, as Uzfan referred to casting a vision. She was never very good at it, but now she tried not to think about old failures. In the past she'd wanted to see her mother, and her mother had not come willingly into sight.

Tonight, however, Alexeika still felt the fleeting touch of her father's soul. She focused on him, feeling the mists of her mind swirl around her, and opened her eyes, waiting with what patience she possessed.

The moonlight glowed deep within the water, shining deeper than she had ever seen it before.

After a time, however, she realized that this was not the moonlight which glowed in the depths, but rather something else.

It rose slowly, slowly to the surface of the water, wavered there, then broke through and lifted into the air. Water and vapor seemed to blend together. The air grew suddenly cold, as though she'd been plunged into winter.

She saw an apparition form and take shape, still glowing from within. It was the figure of a man. Her breath caught, then fled her lungs. This was not her father. Disappointment seeped through her. She saw instead a youth, dark-haired and lanky, his full growth not yet achieved. He stood there, his feet in the mist, his legs straight and coltish, his chest strong, his arms longer than his sleeves. His head was bowed, but then he lifted it and looked right at her.

She sat there openmouthed, unable to look away. How pale his eyes were, glowing with the unearthly light that formed him. His cheeks were lean, his nose straight and aristocratic. His brows were thick dark slashes above his eyes.

He spoke not, and she could not tell if he saw her. Then he lifted his right arm. A sword formed in his hand, both mist and light, a sword whose blade flashed with carved runes. When he swung it aloft, the runes flowed from the blade and sparkled off the tip like shooting stars.

They rained down on her, winking into the water and glowing there like tiny lights.

Tipping back her head, she laughed silently, marveling at the beauty of light and mist and water.

"I am Faldain," her vision said, his voice sounding only in her head. It was a voice young but deepening, with a resonance that echoed long inside her. "Summon me not again. It is not my time to be found."

"We need you," she dared whisper. "Come and save your people."

He swung the sword of mist and light again, this time right at her. The tip pierced her breastbone, and icy fire plunged through her heart. She arched her back with a choked cry.

Then he was gone, the vision fading in a last shower of sparks and starlight. When she recovered her senses, Alexeika found herself huddled on her knees in the bottom of the skiff, doubled over and crying.

She hurt, yet her fingers found no wound where the vision had stabbed her. The mist was gone, and the water lay calm and dark. A cloud had crossed the moon overhead, muting the starlight as well.

With shaking hands, she rubbed the tears from her face. Her teeth were chattering, and she felt so very cold. Whatever she had wanted, it had not been this.

"Alexeika," called a voice softly. It reached across the fjord and brought her from her thoughts. "Child, come back to shore. It is over now."

Startled, she looked at the bank. Uzfan, his long robe perilously close to the water, stood right at the edge, beckoning to her. Behind him clustered what looked like half the camp. The people were silent in the moonlight, which came and went fitfully behind its thin veil of cloud. They stared at her with their mouths open.

Fear touched her, along with embarrassment. What had they seen?

She gripped the paddle, her fingers tight on the polished wood, and felt a strong temptation to go far away into the darkness, never to return.

"Alexeika," Uzfan called again. His voice was gentle, full of understanding. "Come to shore, child. You must be cold."

Yes, she felt as chilled as if it were a winter evening. Overhead, a falling star plummeted through the sky, falling out of sight among the treetops of the distant shore. She shivered and began to paddle slowly to Uzfan.

Her arms felt leaden and stiff. It seemed to take her forever to return, but finally the skiff bumped into the rocks and eager hands reached down to grip it and tie it fast.

Someone took her hands and pulled her to her feet. She stumbled out, feeling as though her mind was not quite connected to her body, and Uzfan gripped her arm firmly.

"Come, child," he said. "Time to rest. Make way for her. Shelena, step aside."

The women and old men parted way before her reluctantly. As she walked between them, they reached out and touched her hair and her clothing, murmuring words she did not quite understand.

Up the hill, as she and Uzfan left the others behind and approached her tent, she faltered and stopped.

"What happened?" she asked, still feeling dazed.

"Come. I will build a fire," the old man said kindly.

Beneath his reassuring tone, however, she heard disapproval.

She frowned. "I don't understand. I wanted to see my father."

Uzfan shook his head and pushed her toward her tent. She stood next to it, watching while he assembled twigs and kindling in a circle of stones and struck sparks into the fluff of shredded bark. A small blaze caught, flaring orange in the darkness.

"Child, child," he said in mild rebuke. "Do you remember none of the lessons I taught you? A soul newly departed cannot be seen. Would you call your father forth from the safety he so barely reached?"

"I miss him," she said, her voice small like a child's.

Uzfan climbed to his feet with a grunt and turned to grip her arms. "Come and sit by the fire. It will warm you."

She sank to the ground, rubbing her chest where she still ached. Uzfan tended the fire, feeding sticks to it as the flames grew hungry and stronger. He kept staring at her with a frown, his eyes shifting away each time she glanced up.

His disapproval seemed stronger than ever.

She frowned. "I did something wrong?"

"Do you think so?" he asked too quickly.

She sighed. She didn't want a lesson. "I don't know. It seemed—I don't know. I've never cast a real vision before. Not like that." She rubbed her chest again. "I didn't know it would hurt."

"Who did you conjure forth?" he asked sternly.

She did not answer. She was suddenly afraid to.

"Child, what you did was very wrong. Think of the danger you have placed yourself in. The camp now knows what you can do."

She shook her head. "I can't. I don't know how it happened. I've tried before, and it never worked. You remember."

"I remember an impatient girl refusing to follow instructions. Did I not warn you never to part the veils of seeing on your own?"

"No."

He snorted. "Then remember it now. Dangerous, child! Dangerous. You must never invoke forces you do not understand or cannot control." He shuddered. "We are too close to the battlefield. Nonkind roam our land, and the darkness is always close. You must never again take such a risk."

"It wasn't malevolent," she said, trying to defend herself now. She felt ashamed, and therefore defiant. "I found no evil—"

"Ah, but evil may find you," he retorted, glaring at her.

She glared back and wanted suddenly to shock him. "It was Faldain," she said. "He told me so."

Uzfan's mouth fell open. He stared at her, his expression altering into one of shock. The stick he held halfway in the fire burst into flames, and still he sat there motionless.

At last, however, he was forced to throw the stick into the fire. Shaking his scorched fingers, he blew on them and stared at her again. "Faldain?" he whispered. "Are you certain?"

"He said that was his name."

"Impossible."

"Why?"

"Because it is. No one knows if the boy even lives, or where he might be."

"He lives," she said with assurance.

Uzfan clasped his hands together. "Great mercy of Thod," he muttered. "How could you find him, an untrained natural—I—I am amazed."

"He said for me not to summon him again. He said it was not yet time for him to be found." Frustration filled her, and she pounded her fist on her knee. "When will he come? If I am to keep people in support of him, he must come soon."

Uzfan reached out and closed his hand over her fist. "Stop this at once. You are not in command of these events."

"Don't you think I can lead—"

"That is not what I'm talking about. Listen to me, child." Uzfan's old eyes, very grave and serious, held hers. "When you want a thing to happen, when you have devoted your life to making it happen, it can be very hard to let events take their course. But you do not control what is to be. You must never again try to force destiny."

"I only wanted to see him," she began, but Uzfan scowled.

"No," he said sternly. "You asked me to give the people a vision of Faldain, and when I refused you set out to defy my wisdom. Is this not the way of it?"

She could not meet his gaze now. Squirming a little, she glared at the fire.

"Alexeika?"

"Yes! I suppose so. I wanted hope for myself. Is that wrong?"

He stared at her. "It is wrong."

Angry, she flashed her eyes at him, then looked away again.

"If he comes one day or if he never comes, it is not for you to decide. You cannot set his path. It is forbidden for you to try. Is that clear?"

"I don't have those kinds of powers—"

"You might! Great Thod, girl, look what you accomplished tonight. Your power unchained and unchanneled, careening everywhere. You are a natural. Your mother's blood gave you what ability you have, but it's erratic, unusable."

"That can't be true," she said in surprise. "Why did you try to train me before if my gifts weren't—"

"To keep you from doing harm to yourself or to others," he said angrily.

"Oh."

"Yes," he snapped. "I felt at the time that it would be unkind to tell you more. You seemed uninterested in learning, and so I let it pass. I see now I was wrong."

"So even if I tried again to do what I did tonight, it might not happen."

"You might set fire to yourself, or nothing might happen at all. Your gift is small and uncontrollable. If you did not bring Nonkind to us, I will be very grateful."

She bit her lip, understanding now why he was so angry. Contrite, she said, "I ask your pardon. I was not trying to do harm. If we must leave camp tonight, then I will—"

"No, no, do not alarm everyone," he said grouchily. "There's been enough trouble for one day. Promise me, child, that you will never do something like this again."

She frowned, feeling sorry, but not yet ready to promise anything. "But he does exist," she said. "He is not a myth. He does live. Somewhere."

"If that is true, then you have endangered him as well. Visions are meant to summon the dead, not those living. You could injure him."

Her eyes widened with alarm. "I didn't mean to. Can you find out where he is?"

"No."

"Then how—"

"Alexeika, I have warned you most strongly. Must I make a spell to take your gift away from you?"

She leaned back, astonished that he would threaten her. "You mean this?"

His gaze never wavered. "I do."

"Did the others see him? Do they know? Do they understand now?"

"They know you have powers, and that can someday endanger you," he said with exasperation.

"No one here would expose me, no more than they would betray you," she said, shrugging off his concern.

"Are you sure of that?" he asked.

"Of course," she said lightly, but the worry in his face gave her pause. She frowned. "Do you think—"

"I do not need to counsel you on who to trust," he said. "This has been most unwise, most unwise indeed. Now, do I have your promise that you will not do such a thing again?"

"Yes," she said in a small voice of surrender.

He grunted and got stiffly to his feet. "Then I shall leave you for the night. You cannot lead people with tricks, Alexeika. That is King Muncel's way, and you know how false he is. Beware your own will. It should never be stronger than your prudence."

She bowed her head under his rebuke. He walked away, grumbling in his beard as he went.

For a while she sat by the fire, until at last the coldness inside her melted away. When she noticed that someone was staring at her from a nearby tent, she threw dirt on the fire, smothering it, and went inside her own.

It was easy to distract herself for a few minutes, packing her possessions and those of her father's that she wanted to keep. It would be a hard job in the morning, getting camp to break.

But when her packing was finished, she had nothing else to do except extinguish the small oil lamp and lie on her cot in the darkness.

Faldain's face swam back into her thoughts. He had not looked like she expected. She wondered when he would come and why Uzfan seemed to think he might never do so. Didn't this young king know who he was and what his responsibilities were? Didn't he care? Surely he'd heard about Nether's misfortunes. Was he trying to raise an army, and if so, from where? Would he enter Nether with an invading force? Would he sell Nether to another realm in exchange for fighting men, the way his uncle had done?

She frowned, fretting in the night, and in time grew angry with the boy she'd seen. If he didn't come, then he was either a fool or a weakling. If he didn't care about his own land and people, then he deserved no throne. In the meantime, she had to find a way to persuade the rebels to carry through the planned attack on Trebek. It was a small but important river town, controlling barge trade between the Nold border and Grov. She had to continue her father's plans. Somehow, even if everyone else turned coward and surrendered, she had to continue.

18

DEEP IN THE night, Dain lunged upright from sleep with a gasp. He felt as though he were drowning in a deep, icy-cold lake. He could not breathe. Water filled his lungs and nostrils, holding him down. In his hand he gripped a sword that flashed with fire. A *sorcerelle* held him enchanted, drawing him forth from the water only to plunge him back in.

Shuddering, Dain rubbed his sweating face with both hands and pulled up his knees to rest his forehead on them. He realized now it had been only a dream. He was safe within the foster sleeping chamber in Thirst Hold, and he'd better take care to make no noise that might disturb the others.

After a time his pounding heart slowed and he began to breathe more normally. It was hot and airless in the chamber. His cot was closest to the window, but the Mandrian custom was to keep windows firmly shuttered at night. If he opened it now to fill his lungs with fresh air, the others might wake up.

Dain had no desire to take a beating from Mierre. As silently as shadow, he slipped from the room, passing Thum's cot, where his friend snored, passing Kaltienne's cot, and finally passing Mierre's. The largest boy was a light sleeper, but Dain made no sound. He had learned early on how to smear goose grease on the hinges of the door so that it could be opened without a sound.

Safely in the corridor, he let out his breath in relief and, barefooted, went padding off outside. He crossed the walkway over to the battlements and leaned his bare shoulder against the cool stone crenellation, gazing outward across the patchwork of light and darkest shadows that marked the fields, meadows, and eventually forest belonging to this Thirst.

It would be morning soon. He sniffed the breeze, aware of an imperceptible lightening of the sky. Down at the corner of the wall, the sentry yawned and resumed his slow walk. The man had not yet noticed Dain, but once he did there would be no challenge. The sentries were used to Dain's nocturnal ramblings. Sometimes he slept on the walkways, or tried to. Usually a sentry roused him and sent him back inside.

No one understood how hard it was for him to sleep inside a building of stone. Although he had lived at Thirst now for three-quarters of a year, he still wondered sometimes what men feared so much that they should build such a fortress of timber and stone to hide within. He found it overwhelming at times to be among so many people, with so many men-minds flicking past his own. He had learned to shut them out as much as possible, but at night it was harder. Sometimes he dreamed their dreams, and that was difficult, if not repulsive.

Tonight's dream, however, had been different. Frowning, Dain rubbed his chest. He still felt unsettled by it, and he hadn't understood it at all. It was almost as though he hadn't dreamed it, but had instead been yanked by magical means into another world and time. If so, why? Who was that maiden on the lake with eyes like starlight, and what had she wanted him to do?

His fingers reached up to curl around his pendant of bard crystal, which wasn't there.

Dain's frown deepened. Angrily he lowered his hand. He kept forgetting he no longer wore it.

Thanks to Gavril and Mierre, who had tormented and teased him on his first day of training. During the break, Mierre and the prince closed in on Dain, and Mierre attacked first. While he and Dain were fighting, the leather cord had snapped, and the pendant went flying into the dirt. Gavril picked it up, exclaiming, "This is king's glass! Where did you get it?"

Pinned at that moment by Mierre, who was sitting on him and twisting his arm painfully behind him, Dain spat out a mouthful of dirt. "That's mine."

"Oh, you stole it, no doubt."

"Didn't."

"I say you did. No one wears king's glass unless they are royalty."

Mierre twisted Dain's arm harder. He grunted, gritting his teeth to keep from crying out, and flailed uselessly with his other hand.

"Mine," he insisted.

"You cannot claim stolen property."

Dain gathered all his strength and managed to break free of Mierre. Sending the larger boy toppling, Dain scrambled up, landed a dirty kick that made Mierre double up and howl, and launched himself at Gavril.

"It's mine!" he shouted, tackling the prince and knocking him down.

Biting and scratching and gouging, the only way he knew how to fight, Dain swarmed Gavril furiously, determined to get his property back. It was all he had of his lost heritage, the only possession his unknown parents had given him. Jorb had warned him and Thia never to lose their pendants, never to show them, never to give them into anyone's keeping. And now, his worst enemy—this arrogant, pompous prince who had already thrown a royal fit at the idea of even being in the same hold with him, much less in training together—clutched his pendant and no doubt intended to keep it for himself.

"Give it back!" Dain shouted. He struck Gavril in the mouth, and pain shot through his knuckles as they split on the prince's teeth. Blood spurted, and Gavril howled. "Give it back!" Dain shouted. Lunging for Gavril's clenched fist, Dain rolled over and over with the prince.

Then they were surrounded by men, who pulled them bodily apart. Bleeding and streaked with dirt, his fine doublet torn,

Gavril pointed at Dain with a shaking finger and gasped, too furious to speak.

Dain glared and lunged for him, only to be held back by the men.

"Now, now, what is all this?" demanded the master-at-arms, Sir Polquin. "This is not the way knights, nobles, and gentlemen conduct themselves on a field of honor."

"He's none of those," Gavril said, his face beet-red with fury. "The dirty little—"

"Now, now, your highness," Sir Polquin broke in. "Dain does not yet know our customs. Let us not lose our temper."

Gavril turned his blue-eyed rage on the master-at-arms. "I shall lose my temper if I desire! He'll die for this! The ruffian attacked me without provocation."

"Liar!" Dain shouted back, struggling against the hands that held him fast. "He is a thief. That pendant is mine. He took it from me."

Sir Polquin's weather-roughened face turned slightly pale. He frowned and scratched his sun-bleached hair, but his green eyes held little mercy when he looked at Dain. "You must never strike his highness or call him a thief or a liar."

"He *is*!" Dain insisted.

Sir Masen cuffed Dain on his ear. Pain flared through his head, distracting him momentarily. "Don't talk back to the master-at-arms, boy."

Sir Polquin beckoned to Mierre, who had dusted off his doublet and now came forward. "And what say you about this? Were you fighting Dain as well?"

"I was showing him how to wrestle, sir," Mierre lied smoothly. "If we must have him with us, we don't want him shaming us by not knowing how to grapple."

The men chuckled, and seemed to accept this lie. Mierre smiled, and his gaze flickered to Dain for one brief, malevolent moment.

Seething, hating them all, Dain set his jaw and glared at everyone. "The pendant is mine," he said. "Prince or not, he cannot take it from me."

"He hit me," Gavril said. "That is a crime punishable by—"

"Come with me," Sir Polquin said. Clamping his hand on Dain's shoulder, he marched him away from the others, off the practice field and out of earshot. "Now," the master-at-arms said grimly, "we're going to have a talk about manners, boy."

"I don't care about manners!" Dain shouted.

"It's against law to strike him. If Sir Los had been here, you'd be dead."

Dain frowned. "But he cannot take my property."

"By right and rank, he can," Sir Polquin told him.

Stunned by this injustice, Dain drew in a sharp breath. "It's mine. It's all I have, all that I own. My father gave it to me. I have nothing else of his, no other—"

"All right, all right. Calm down, boy, and listen to me."

Dain fell silent, but he could not stop fretting. Looking past Sir Polquin's sturdy shoulder, he saw Gavril out there on the field, chatting with the men, laughing at something, his blond hair glinting bright in the sunshine. It was not fair. No matter what man-law or man-custom said, it was not fair, and it was not right.

"Dain!"

Reluctantly Dain turned his attention back to Sir Polquin, who was scowling at him.

"Did you hear anything I said?"

"No," Dain admitted.

Sir Polquin sighed. "Thought as much. Dain boy, heed me. The prince is far above you. He will one day be king, and his word law."

"Pity yourselves," Dain said rudely, "for he will be brutal."

Sir Polquin slapped him. "Never speak thus about his highness again. I'll beat this lesson into you, if I must. To live among us, you must abide by our ways."

Dain's jaw ached from the blow. He straightened himself slowly, resentment still strong inside him. "The prince says I cannot own my bard crystal. He says only royalty may wear it. That is *his* custom, Mandrian custom, but it isn't mine! My father gave it to me. My sister wore one as well. Who is your prince to say I may not have it?"

"I know not what bard crystal is," Sir Polquin said, "but you will respect your betters—"

"King's glass he called it," Dain said.

Sir Polquin opened his mouth, then closed it again. He stared at Dain in bewilderment mingled with a touch of alarm. "King's glass?" he echoed finally. "You wear king's glass?"

Dain shrugged. "Perhaps you think it is worth little. But the trinket is mine, and—"

"Oh, it is worth a great deal!" Sir Polquin said, looking more astonished than ever. "Don't you know its value?"

Now it was Dain's turn to be puzzled. "Its value lies in that my father gave it to me when I was but an infant. Since I never met my father, I have nothing else of his except this small gift."

Sir Polquin whistled, his eyes round with wonder. "Small gift indeed. It's worth a fortune, or so I hear. Naught but the highest born can afford it. And who was your father?"

"I do not know his name," Dain said. "My guardian never told us. I know only that my father rode to Jorb's burrow one day and paid him well to take us in."

"Well, well, Dain boy, it seems we chose you better than we knew," Sir Polquin said with a sudden grin. "Come along now. We're wasting the best part of the day, and there's training to be done."

Dain planted his feet and would not budge. "But what about my pendant? Will you make the prince give it back?"

"Boy, has nothing I've said filled that hollow between your ears?"

Dain frowned. "He cannot take it from me. Prince or not, he has no right."

"Perhaps he doesn't at that," Sir Polquin agreed.

Dain's spirits rose. "Then you agree? I can have it back?"

"I think we'd better take this matter to Lord Odfrey."

"But—"

"Come along!"

In the end, after Sir Polquin took Lord Odfrey aside and whispered long into his ear, after Lord Odfrey frowned, exclaimed, and stared at Dain in astonishment and the beginnings of a smile, and after Gavril was asked to surrender the pendant into Lord Odfrey's keeping, the matter was settled, but to no one's satisfaction.

"He is a pagan nobody, a serf at best, his blood mixed, his parentage unknown," Gavril said sullenly. "He has no right to wear a jewel of this value."

"His father is clearly a noble of high rank," Lord Odfrey replied, turning the piece of bard crystal over and over in his fingers. It whispered faint song in response to his touch. Light prismed and flashed within its faceted depths. "This man must be important enough to wish to avoid the scandal of having a bastard son with eldin blood. That is why you were fostered with Jorb, lad," he said to Dain while everyone stared and began to whisper in speculation. "Now you are fostered here. This pendant," he went on, holding it aloft, "is indeed part of your heritage, and is too valuable to be put at risk. For now, Sulein will keep it safe for you in his strongbox."

"But—"

"It will be safe there, Dain," Lord Odfrey said, his frown and words a warning. "When you are older and more responsible, you will receive it back. Let this matter rest now."

And so the physician who wanted to be a *sorcerel* had it, locked away where Dain could not get it. He tried not to resent such interference. He understood that this was the only way to keep Gavril from taking it completely away from him. And yet, Dain could not help but wonder why the Mandrians talked so much about honor but did not expect it in Gavril, who would one day be their king.

Dain's standing had risen in the hold. Everyone knew him now as a nobleman's by-blow, and he was treated with more courtesy than when they'd thought him simply a stray of no lineage. Dain was not happy to be called a bastard, but the explanation made sense, especially since Jorb had always refused to tell him and Thia where they came from.

Gavril was infuriated that Dain received no punishment for hitting him. But thereafter, he gave Dain a wide berth, refusing to look at him or speak to him, and ceasing to torment him. Rumor spread that the two boys might be cousins. King Verence's younger brother, now dead, had been a roving scoundrel in his youth.

Dain refused to consider any relationship. He believed his father was Netheran, for that much Jorb had said. But if the Mandrians wanted to believe Dain was one of theirs, and if it made them feed him more and treat him better, he was not going to argue. Still, without his bard crystal, he felt bereft and incomplete. He could not wait for the summer to end. For then, Gavril would be leaving Thirst Hold forever. Dain believed that as soon as the prince departed, his pendant would be returned to him.

"A month," he whispered, turning his face toward the dawn, where a corona of gold and rosy pink blazed above the horizon.

Dain sampled the breeze, his nostrils sifting through its myriad scents. "Only a month."

A month hence would fall the king's birthday. King Verence always threw a great festival and invited all the nobles and knights of his realm to participate in a tournament. It was the king's custom to let young men win their spurs by jousting before they joined the knighthood orders. But this year would also mark Prince Gavril's investiture into the knighthood and his coming of age, when he would be named Heir to the Realm. Extra celebrations had been planned accordingly. Gavril himself had been training very hard, practicing privately with Sir Polquin rather than being kept in practice drills with the other fosters.

The less Dain saw of Gavril, the better it pleased him. As for today, he grinned to himself, thinking of his plans, and his ambition. Sir Polquin had organized a contest among the fosters to determine by combat which of them would be allowed to accompany Lord Odfrey to the king's tournament as squire. Only one boy would be chosen. Sir Polquin said that measuring the boys' prowess with arms was the fairest way to determine who deserved this honor. Lord Odfrey had agreed to the contest, and the boys were ablaze with excitement.

Now, as the cocks crowed in the stableyard and the hold began to stir, Dain saw a trail of men carrying boards to the practice field outside the walls. They were setting up benches for the spectators. All the knights not on duty intended to come. Servants who could get away from their duties would be there. Villagers would watch as well.

Dain thought of all this and felt nervous, but at the same time he was eager to show off what he had learned the past few months. He had worked hard, harder than he ever had in his life. If Sir Polquin was not putting him through extra practices to help him catch up with the others, then Sir Bosquecel would come along after hours and teach him some trick of swordplay. Or Sir Nynth would give him extra riding lessons. Or Sir Terent would drill him in the finer points of heraldry. Every day Dain felt as though his head would burst from the strain of having so much knowledge tamped into it. His muscles ached at night, but his young body thrived on all the exercise.

He had grown in sudden spurts that surprised everyone and caused him to need more new clothes. No longer was he slight of build like most eldin. In addition to gaining height, he was growing much broader through his chest and shoulders. Hard muscles rippled through his arms.

The knights teased him, saying he was using a growth spell, but Dain thought it was all the food he ate. He was forever hungry, despite regular meals. The more he trained, the larger he grew. His voice deepened, never cracking and breaking at embarrassing moments the way Thum's did, much to his friend's consternation. Dain learned how to cut his hair so that it was short and neat in the way Lord Odfrey preferred his men-at-arms to look, but long enough to cover the pointed tips of his ears. His pale gray eyes would forever mark him, but despite that the maids of the hold began to throw him sultry looks nearly as often as they eyed the other boys. Every time a serving maid lingered while pouring cider in his cup or brushed herself against his shoulder while setting a laden trencher before him, Thum would dig his elbow sharply into Dain's ribs and snicker.

Dain squirmed with embarrassment, but he was seldom fooled. He could read the girls' intentions. Most of them contained a mixture of fervor, curiosity, and scorn. And for all their pretended boldness, most were afraid of him. He pursued no one and accepted no invitations. For one thing, he felt unsure of himself. Nor did he want Mierre's leavings, or worse, Kaltienne's.

Besides, he had yet to grow a beard, although all the others were trying to sprout scraggling versions of them. Sir Nynth had taken him aside one evening and solemnly explained that until he grew a beard, he would be no man that pleased a woman. Sensing amusement in the other knights when he and Sir Nynth returned, Dain grew suspicious of such advice, thinking it a jest. But when Thum said he had also heard this from his older brothers, Dain decided to believe it.

"Better get ready, Dain boy," said the sentry now, startling Dain from his thoughts. He gave Dain a grin and slapped him on the shoulder. "I've bet money on you. Don't let me down."

Realizing he was going to miss his breakfast if he didn't hurry, Dain smiled back and ran for it.

In an hour, the sun was up bright and hot over the practice field. Dain squinted as he helped Thum buckle on his thick padding. Shaped like a breastplate but instead made of multiple layers of wool felt stitched together, it fit over each boy's chest and back and buckled down the sides with leather straps.

"Too tight!" Thum said with a gasp.

Dain eased out the buckle one notch. "Sorry."

"You have to get it even on both sides or it will slip," Thum said. "Pay attention, Dain."

Dain drew a deep breath and nodded. He was trying, but his excitement was too intense. He felt like he might leave the ground and fly about in all directions. Already buckled into his own padding, he finished strapping Thum in and thumped him on the back.

"Now, you're ready," he said.

Thum grinned, meeting Dain's gaze. For a moment, neither boy spoke, and Thum's freckled face began to turn red. "This is it," he said, his voice cracking.

Dain nodded, his gaze darting across the field, where Sir Polquin and his assistants were setting up the equipment, readying the blunted lances, and counting the padded practice swords. Knights and villagers mingled about. The air was festive, despite the summer heat. Some enterprising urchin was selling pies. The Thirst banners swung heavily in the hot air.

"Dain," Thum said, his voice hesitant, "I wish you luck today."

Reluctantly Dain pulled his attention away from the scene and looked at his red-haired friend. "What? Oh, yes. Thanks."

Thum frowned, and Dain scrambled to remember the rest of his manners.

"And good luck to you as well, Thum."

Some of the ire faded from Thum's face. He looked a little troubled, however. "We can't be friends the rest of this day, I suppose. Not and compete at our best. I wish there could be two squires chosen, not one."

Dain understood what Thum was trying to say. For all his sharp wits, Thum had a soft heart. He spent too much time bemoaning what could not be changed. The four fosters were all desperate to see Savroix, the fabled palace of Mandrian kings. Dain knew that Thum, who had failed to make friends with the spoiled prince, might never see Savroix otherwise in his lifetime. In order to advance, Thum would have to become some knight's squire. If he succeeded in becoming Lord Odfrey's, then he would have a good start at a career.

But Dain also wanted to become Lord Odfrey's squire. He admired the chevard very much. He wanted desperately to please him and make him proud. Dain never forgot that he owed his good fortune to the chevard's kindness. He wanted to repay the man with service. Although the other boys had been training at arms for several years, Dain was determined to shine. He practiced harder and longer than the others. He did not let Mierre's taunts and Kaltienne's teasing stop him from trying again and again until he mastered a skill. He had ability; that was evident to all. He learned quickly. Although he might not understand something as it was first being explained to him, as soon as he saw someone demonstrate the movement, he could quickly imitate it. Already he had become an expert horseman. That was easy, for his mind alone was able to control the horse. As for fighting, he was agile, quick, and inclined to cheat. Again and again Sir Bosquecel took him aside to explain that a knight never cheated in a contest of honor, although in real battle anything was permitted against the enemy.

Dain did not understand this distinction and felt it was a silly waste of time. But he worked hard to please the knights.

He heard a shout from the center of the field. Sir Polquin was gesturing for the boys to come to him.

Thum, still looking worried and on edge, frowned at Dain. Dain's own heart was suddenly pounding. He gave Thum a light shove to start him walking and matched strides with him. From the opposite side of the field came Mierre and Kaltienne.

Dain said, "I want to win as much as you do. But if I cannot win, then I want it to be you."

"I feel the same," Thum said quickly. He frowned at the other boys. "Anyone but them."

"Aye." Dain gave him a nudge. "We'll be friends again, come tonight. Don't worry."

Thum's grim look vanished, and he managed a quick grin before Sir Polquin lined them up and started his inspection of their padding. His assistant followed, handing out padded caps.

Dain hated the cap. It was hot and stank of sweat. Complaining about it got nowhere, however. Sir Polquin warned them that the metal helmets they would wear someday were much worse.

"The rules of orderly contest apply," Sir Polquin said

sternly. "We'll draw lots to see who goes first. We'll start with lances. You have three tries to hit the circle."

As he spoke, he pointed toward the alley, where a red shield with a white circle painted on its center swung at one end.

"If everyone hits that, we'll take off the blunted tips and let you aim your lances through this ring." He held up a circle of brass with a loop of rope already tied to it.

Mierre rolled his eyes impatiently. "Games of children," he said. "Why not let us unseat each other, the real way?"

"Because not everyone has learned that skill as yet," Sir Polquin replied.

"You mean, the stray hasn't learned it yet," Mierre said, flicking Dain a look of contempt. "The rest of us are trained for it. Why should he hold us back? At least let us ride at a quintain, if not at each other."

Sir Polquin's weathered face grew quite stiff, the way it did when he was annoyed. "For those who succeed at lance, we'll go to swords and shieldwork. You'll throw lots again to see how you're paired. There will be three judges for this contest: Lord Odfrey, Prince Gavril, and Sir Bosquecel."

Hearing those names, Dain smiled to himself and lifted his chin higher. He was certain to please two judges out of three. Lancework remained hard for him, but he was good at swordplay, very good. He'd learned something new last week, something he hadn't yet shown to Thum. He intended to hold it back as his ultimate trick. It would be impressive, and he was certain to win.

A commotion in the distance caught his attention. He saw Lord Odfrey riding up on a bay horse that was prancing in response to the excitement and noise. Sir Bosquecel rode beside the chevard, but of Gavril there was no sign.

Sir Polquin looked displeased. "Is his highness going to keep us waiting clear to the midday heat?" Grumbling, he strode away to confer with Lord Odfrey, who leaned down from his saddle and shook his head.

Dain and Thum exchanged glances. Thum sighed and circled his thumb around the tip of his forefinger. Dain grinned. They all knew how Gavril liked to make a big entrance.

"Doesn't care, does he?" Kaltienne complained, wiping sweat off his face. "We bore his highness, don't we?"

"Shut up," Mierre growled. "He's got more important things to do. He won't be coming today."

Even Dain blinked at that, but it was Thum who shot Mierre a startled look.

"Not coming?" he echoed. "Why not?"

"Gone hunting," Mierre said.

"Without his lapdogs?" Dain asked. He was learning to hurl insults the courtly way, using words and a sneer instead of his fists. "How can he manage?"

Kaltienne turned on him, hot-faced. "Listen, you—"

"Keep ranks!" Sir Polquin bawled, returning just in time.

Kaltienne snapped back to his place in line, and they all stood at stiff attention.

"There's been a change," Sir Polquin announced. "Sir Roye will be the third judge, instead of his highness."

Dain grimaced to himself. It was hardly an improvement in his favor. Although he left Dain alone, Sir Roye still disliked him. He told himself the protector was a knight and would judge fairly, but in his heart Dain wasn't so sure.

"Let's get this started," Sir Polquin said. He waved at the stableboys, who led the saddled horses up. They were old chargers, long put out to pasture, their muzzles grayed. But these old warhorses still knew their training. They recognized the festivities, and their ears were pricked with interest.

"Must we ride these old plugs?" Mierre complained.

One of the horses tried to bite him, and Mierre's protest was lost in the general laughter.

"Mount," Sir Polquin ordered.

"Hold up!" Lord Odfrey called, interrupting them.

From the benches, the spectators began to yell and clap, trying to get things started. Lord Odfrey, however, rode across the field and pointed at Dain.

"Come away, lad," he said.

Dain handed the reins back to a stableboy. Not understanding at first, thinking Lord Odfrey was going to give him some private word of encouragement and wishing he wouldn't, Dain walked out to meet the chevard. "Lord," he said, grinning as he squinted up into Lord Odfrey's dark eyes, "I will do my best today. I will show you—"

"Leave the field," Lord Odfrey said. "You won't be competing for this honor."

Dain's smile faded. At first, he didn't believe he had heard correctly, then he stammered, "But, lord, I—"

"You heard my command," Lord Odfrey said in his stern way. "Obey it."

"But—"

"Is there a problem, m'lord?" Sir Polquin asked, hurrying up behind Dain.

"No," Lord Odfrey replied, absently pulling a hank of his horse's mane over to the other side of its neck. "This is a contest to determine my new squire. Dain needs at least another year of training before he can expect such an appointment. He has no place in this contest."

"I've worked hard," Dain said, choked with disappointment. His head was spinning. He couldn't believe that Lord Odfrey was making him withdraw. "I can do it—"

"Sir Polquin," Lord Odfrey said.

The edge in his voice was plain to hear. Sir Polquin put his hand on Dain's shoulder. "You heard his lordship, Dain boy. Off you go."

"But I—"

Sir Polquin's eyes sparked with annoyance. Dain realized belatedly that he was protesting direct orders. That transgression alone proved he was too unskilled to be on the field.

His face grew hot. He shut his jaw, clenching it so hard his muscles jumped. This wasn't fair. He'd worked extra hard to be ready to compete. He should be allowed to try, even if he came out defeated.

But to protest further was to embarrass Lord Odfrey and the knights who'd been trying to train him. Dain knew how he was expected to act. He had to pretend it didn't matter. Had to pretend he didn't care.

Somehow, although his body felt so stiff he didn't think he could bend it, he managed to bow.

"Yes," Lord Odfrey said. "You may watch the contest if you wish, but no later than this afternoon you are to report to Sulein for lessons. It's time we concentrated on improving your mind as well as your muscles."

Dain bowed again, his face on fire. His throat had swelled with anger and resentment. He couldn't protest now even if he wanted to.

"That is all," Lord Odfrey said with a nod of dismissal. His dark gaze snapped to Sir Polquin. "Take down the circled shield. They'll go at unseating each other."

"And if they break their fool necks?" Sir Polquin asked.

"Time to stop coddling them," Lord Odfrey replied mercilessly. "I'll not be squired by an untested sprout."

"Aye, m'lord."

Sir Polquin turned away to start issuing orders. Over by the horses, the boys cheered with new excitement. Babbling with the others as they mounted up, Thum paused briefly to glance Dain's way with a frown, but Dain couldn't bear his pity right then.

Unstrapping his padding and jerking off his cap, Dain carried it over to where the rest of the equipment was stacked and dropped it, then marched himself rigidly off the field.

Sir Terent and Sir Nynth intercepted him, their faces red in the heat. "What's amiss? Why are you leaving?"

"The lord ordered me away," Dain said, his voice tight and hard. He did not want them to see his choking disappointment, how much he cared. "He thinks I am not good enough to compete."

"Morde a day!" Sir Nynth exclaimed, his keen eyes snapping. "Of all the injustice—"

"It's for his squire," Sir Terent interrupted, casting his friend a warning look. "Dain's a bit green for that."

"Aye, and what of it?" Sir Nynth retorted hotly. "I've money bet on the boy."

"Better get it off," Dain said, and pushed away from them, ignoring their calls to come back.

He would not watch the contest. He would not hang about, taking hearty slaps of pity or watching the knights talk about him. This was the first opportunity he'd had to prove that he really could fit in, and Lord Odfrey had taken it away from him.

How had he displeased the chevard? What had he done wrong? If the chevard wanted to punish him, Dain would have rather been flogged than humiliated like this.

Perhaps Lord Odfrey had seen him in practice and believed he was no good.

Dain gritted his teeth, walking even faster, and kicked the dirt in front of him. He *was* good now, and he could be even better. He knew it, knew already how natural and right a sword felt in his hands.

The sentries at the gates looked startled to see him. "What's amiss?" one of them called to him. "Are you ousted already?"

Why explain? Dain scowled at them. "Aye," he replied, and strode on while they laughed and called out commiseration that he didn't want.

He walked across the hold to the innermost courtyard and nearly entered Sulein's tower before he stopped, scowling ferociously at the door leading inside.

Lessons? What kind of lessons? Did the chevard think him so hopeless at arms that he would make a scholar of him?

It all came welling up—the months of hard work, the stress of trying to fit in, the brutality of today's disappointment. Dain kicked the door and spun away. He wasn't going to have anything to do with the stinking old physician. He was tired of following orders, tired of doing what he was told.

He hurried away, wishing he'd gone to the woods instead of coming inside the hold. As he reached the outer keep, however, he found it astir. Prince Gavril was mounting his fancy horse. The red and fawn hunting dogs were out, barking and wagging their tails in excitement. Sir Los was climbing into his saddle, as cheerless as ever. Five other knights assigned to Gavril's protection were milling about as well.

Desperate not to let the prince see his disgrace, Dain dodged out of sight. No one called his name, and after a tense moment he relaxed. He hid until he heard the prince's retinue clatter away.

Hunting mad, Dain thought with scorn. The prince went out at every opportunity. Of late he'd grown even more fanatical, as though he thought that once he returned to Savroix he would never be allowed to hunt again. What did he see in this sport? Dain could not understand it, and had no wish to try. Gavril seldom returned with any game. He seemed only to want to gallop about through the Dark Forest as much as possible. Lord Odfrey had warned him again and again to stay away from there, but Gavril went anyway. The knights had orders to steer him in other, safer directions, but since spring these five men seemed to always be the ones that went forth with the prince. They were a scruffy, shifty-eyed lot, the lowest rank, hardly better than hirelances. To Dain's eye, they seemed more loyal to Gavril than they did to anyone else. Certainly they let the prince have his way and go where he wanted.

Dain shrugged, and ventured out of hiding. He hoped the prince got swept off his horse by a tree branch and broke his arrogant neck.

Across the keep, Dain heard the steady plinking of the smith's hammer. He scowled, indecisive for a moment, but then he turned his steps toward the forge. He did not want to leave the hold right now. He was afraid that if he went off into the forest, he might not return. Though perhaps that was what he should do, leave and not come back, Dain was not yet ready to make that decision. He was too angry and confused to think straight. He knew only that he did not want to be alone—his spirits felt too dark and angry for him to stand his own company. He had no wish to talk to anyone either, but the smith might put Dain to work, as he did sometimes when Dain felt lonely and missed his old life too much.

Sir Bosquecel and Lord Odfrey disapproved of Dain's working in the forge. Such manual labor was beneath his rank, they said. But it was as good a place to find comfort as any. When he regained his calm, Dain would decide whether he should run away.

19

THE SMITH'S NAME was Lander. A Netheran by birth, he'd come down to Mandria years ago to escape the civil war raging in his homeland. A local woman lived with him in the village and called herself his wife, but gossip said they were not churchwed. If Lander had any family back in Nether, he never spoke of them. He would not talk about his past, except to say that he'd been born and raised in Grov, but that it was no fit place to live in now.

He was an excellent smith, especially with simple repairs of hinges and plowshares. He worked inside the hold rather than in the village because he was also a skilled armorer, and the knights kept him busy grinding out the nicks in their sword blades and repairing broken links in their mail. To Dain's critical eye, Lander's skill was finer than most men's, although he lacked Jorb's exquisite artistry. But then, Jorb had surpassed everyone, including the other dwarf master armorers.

On this summer's morn, the forge blazed with the heat of its roaring fire. The air inside shimmered and danced. Shirtless, Lander wore only his leggings and a soot-blackened leather apron. His muscular arms and shoulders dripped with sweat.

Concentrating on tapping out a curve in a horseshoe, he barely glanced up when Dain entered the forge. Not until he plunged the shoe into a bucket of water, sending up a great cloud of hissing steam, did he pause to wipe his streaming brow with his forearm and give Dain a quick, shy smile.

"Hearty morn," he said in his foreign way. His eyes were pale blue, almost as pale as Thia's had been, like mist over a spring sky. The rest of him was bulky and hairless except for a tonsure of red curls around a bald pate. His pale flesh never tanned even in the summertime; his thick torso looked like a chunky slab of stone.

He seemed glad to see Dain as always, but his manner was preoccupied. "That's the last," he said to himself, lifting the horseshoe from the water pail and tossing it with a clank onto a pile of similar shoes. Putting away his set of tongs, he left his hammer lying atop the anvil while he stripped off his apron and wiped his face and shoulders with it. "Thought you'd be in the contest," he said. "Over already, is it?"

"Not for the others," Dain said. He scowled at the fire so he wouldn't have to look at Lander.

"Eh? What? Oh. So that's the way of it."

"I wanted to see the tournament at Savroix," Dain said, although he'd already decided not to talk about it. Lander, however, was safe. He made no judgments, offered no advice.

The smith sighed sympathetically. "So would I like to go."

"You?" Dain asked in surprise. He'd been so wrapped up in his own plans of late, it had never occurred to him that probably everyone in the hold wanted to see the king's tournament. "Have you ever been to Savroix?"

"Nay, not I." Lander smiled in his fleeting way and wiped his sweating face again. "But it would be good to go, if I can find a way."

Dain said nothing, sensing that for once the smith wanted to talk.

"In my homeland I was a master armorer," Lander said proudly. "Not just a smith, making horseshoes and repairing latches, but a fine swordmaker. Here, the knights will let me repair their armor. I am allowed to make new helmets, sometimes a shield, but never more than that. I am foreign-born," he said, striking his chest. "That means they think I cannot make swords for them. Not even daggers. No, they go elsewhere. To the armorer at Lunt Hold sometimes, or to the dwarves. I ask you, boy, is a dwarf not foreign? How can they think this way? But they do."

Dain nodded with sympathy.

Lander cast Dain a sideways look. "You know the dwarf swordmakers."

"Jorb was the best."

Lander sighed. "Aye, they all say so. But now there is no Jorb. So will they let me make them new swords for the tournament? No. But there is a way for me to show them what I can do."

Dain traced his finger along the worn handle of the hammer. He knew better than to pick it up without permission. "Make some swords, I guess," he said, without much interest in Lander's problems. "Show them what you can do."

"Hah! Better idea than that I have." Lander tugged him by his sleeve over to a storage cabinet and pulled out a sheet of grubby vellum. He glanced around as though to make sure no one was watching, and showed the drawing to Dain. "What do you think of this?"

The sword depicted was beautiful. Its long tapering blade was carved with rosettes and scrollwork. The hilt guard made the Circle so many Mandrians wanted, thinking the symbol would shield them from harm in battle, and was carved to look like tendrils of gold ivy. The hilt itself was long enough for a two-handed grip, and wrapped ornately with silver and gold wire.

Dain's brows lifted. He was impressed, and yet a drawing was not a sword.

"I could make this sword," Lander said, tapping the vellum with a grimy fingertip. "I *could*!"

"Do it then," Dain said. He rolled up the vellum to hand it

back, but Lander grabbed it and whacked him across his chest with it.

"There is a way to make it better, to make it wondrous," Lander said. He leaned close enough for Dain to smell his sour breath. His pale eyes flashed with passion. "I need magicked metal."

Dain couldn't help it. He laughed.

Muttering furiously, Lander shoved him away and thrust his drawing back in the cabinet. "I should never show you my dream," he said. "Fool I am."

"No, I wasn't laughing at you," Dain tried to reassure him. "It's just—I thought that was forbidden here. Using magicked metal, I mean."

Lander shrugged. "Mandrians have strange ideas. It is not always good to pay attention to what they fear. I have held some of the great swords. I know how they live in the hand. The difference is like night and day."

"Even if you got that kind of metal," Dain said, thinking the man was crazy to have such dreams, "and even if you made it, no one here could afford such a weapon."

"Hah!" Lander said, beaming and pouncing on him again. "Now you understand. The king's birthday, it is a big occasion. Yes, and this year the king will give his sword to his son for knighthood. It is the custom, yes?"

"I know not," Dain replied, wondering where Lander was going with this. He hadn't come to the forge to be a confidant.

But Lander wasn't letting him go. "Yes, the custom. From father to son goes the sword. Valor is passed from the old hand to the young. But the king must have new sword to replace what he gives away. And so there is a contest among the smiths of the land. The sword that is chosen . . . Well, then everyone in Mandria will know that Lander can make them best. Lander is a master, as good as any dwarf."

Dain nodded and started edging away. "I wish you luck, Lander. Now I had better go before—"

"Wait." Lander blocked his path and leaned down, his pale eyes intense. "You were Jorb's apprentice. That means you know his secrets. You know where he got such metal."

Suddenly wary, Dain drew back. "No, I — "

"Yes, yes." Lander gripped Dain's sleeve and glanced

around to make sure no one was nearby. "Do you know the dwarf called Baldrush?"

Dain frowned, still wary. "Maybe."

"Yes! Yes, you do know," Lander said eagerly. "I will make this worth your while, Dain."

"I won't go to him—"

"Already done," Lander said with pride. He pointed at the two-wheeled cart parked near the forge. "I have been working extra to finish my work so I can leave today. I will meet Baldrush and bargain with him for this metal." Lander grinned, his pale eyes atwinkle with excitement. "Advise me, Dain. You know this Baldrush. Tell me how to make a good bargain with him."

Dain dropped to his haunches in the dwarf way. "Let us discuss his terms, then."

A few minutes later, Dain and Lander sauntered out of the forge. Dain blinked in the bright sunshine, feeling sure Lander would be cheated in Nold. He wanted his metal too much. He had saved forty gold dreits in his strongbox, a veritable treasure. But forty dreits was Baldrush's asking price.

"Too high," Dain said. "Thirty is more than fair. Forty is too much."

"Can you make him take thirty?" Lander asked. "Of course I will pay it all, if I must."

"Don't say that," Dain told him, appalled. "You should tell him thirty is all that you have. And don't sound too willing to pay that. Twenty-five would be better."

"No, no, twenty-five is not fair price," Lander said, shaking his head. "You would have me insult him. Already he does not want to sell the metal to me. If I offer twenty-five, he will say I am cheating him in the man-way, and he will leave."

"Thirty, then," Dain said firmly, believing Baldrush would talk Lander into the full amount.

The smith was nodding at Dain. "You come with me. You make the bargain."

Dain smiled. "I must ask Sir Bosquecel for permission—"

"Run, then!" Lander said eagerly. "Run and do it while I get my tunic and some food for the journey. It is a day and a half by cart to go and as long to come back. The mule is slow. You'll come?"

"If I get Baldrush to take thirty dreits instead of forty, will you give me the difference?"

"You?" Lander asked in wonder. "What would a boy like you want with so much money?"

"I need it to buy a sword of my own."

"Ah," Lander said, nodding. "But ten gold dreits is too much wealth for a boy. Whatever you save me off the asking price, half of it will I give you."

Dain grinned. "Done!"

He spit on his palm and held out his hand. Lander spit on his palm and gripped Dain's fingers in a bone-crushing clasp. They shook on the deal.

"Run and get what you need," Lander said. "And ask the captain for permission. I will not take you against his orders."

But as Dain hurried across the keep into the stableyard, he heard cheers rising from the practice field. Defiance unfurled inside him. He decided not to ask Sir Bosquecel's permission. He wasn't going to ask anyone. He'd tried doing things the Mandrian way, following their endless rules, and he'd ended up being punished anyway. Jorb had always warned Dain to beware men, for they turned and betrayed without warning. Today he'd seen it proven true, and in Lord Odfrey, whom he'd trusted above all others. Now that Lander had presented him with an opportunity too good to pass up, Dain intended to start looking after himself in the ways Jorb had taught him.

Hurrying inside the Hall, Dain ran upstairs, taking two steps at a time, and fetched his cloak, spare footgear, and the blanket off his bed. Rolling these into an untidy bundle, he hurried outside again, dashing past the steward, who stared openmouthed at him.

By the time Dain returned to the keep, Lander had hitched his mule to the cart and was holding the reins impatiently. He had crammed on a wide-brimmed straw hat to protect his bald head from the sun. Dain smelled the pouch of provisions in the back of the cart and hoped Lander had brought enough food.

Lander stared at him. "Where did you go? I thought the captain was at the joust, judging the contest."

"No," Dain said, keeping his lie simple.

"Ready?"

Dain climbed onto the cart seat, and Lander yelled at the mule. They rolled out through the gates past the sentries, who didn't challenge them. Lander and his mule cart were a familiar sight, coming and going frequently.

The sun was hot, beating down on Dain's head without mercy. As the mule struck a steady trot, a slight breeze cooled Dain's face. He smiled to himself, suddenly homesick for the cool gloominess of the Dark Forest, and did not look back at the hold behind him.

Away in the Dark Forest, Gavril placed his hand on the front of his saddle and leaned forward eagerly to peer at the cave entrance.

"Just there, yer highness," Sir Vedrique was saying as he pointed. "Look at the top of the cave. See yon stone with the old runes carved in it? Bound to be one of them old shrines, no doubt of it."

Gavril squinted, trying to see through the greenish gloom. The undergrowth and vines were so thick he could barely see the cave itself, much less any runes carved atop it, but at last he spied a mossy stone. His heart leaped inside his chest, and he felt breathless. This could be it. His quest might end today. His prayers would at last be answered.

He dismounted, feeling light-headed, and pushed his way through his milling pack of dogs. Giving them the command to lie down, Gavril wanted to laugh aloud. Just in time he reined back his emotions, preserving his dignity. He must not set too much hope in this old shrine. He had been disappointed before. For months he'd searched diligently, venturing as deep into the Dark Forest as he dared, wishing always that he could go farther. But today, for some unexplainable reason, he believed success was at hand. The Chalice was here. He could almost feel its holy power. His heart was thudding with anticipation.

When he started up the hillside, Sir Los called out in alarm and hurried after him.

The prince paid his protector no heed as he struggled through the briars and tangled vines. He crowded Sir Vedrique's spurred heels. "Hurry, hurry," he said breathlessly.

They crossed the bottom of a small, shallow ravine with a stream running through it. Partway up the slope was the cave's entrance.

This place was hushed and tranquil, like an outdoor chapel. Even birdsong seemed muted and distant. Sunlight stabbed down intermittently through the dense canopy overhead, gilding leaves and moss in its soft golden light.

The closer they came, the slower Sir Vedrique walked.

Growling with impatience, Gavril tried to push past him, but the young knight flung his arm across Gavril's chest to block his way.

"Nay, yer highness. Can't take too much care with these old places. There's power here still."

"And maybe trolk," muttered one of the other knights.

Gavril scowled and glanced back to see who had spoken. The four remaining knights of his party sat on their horses, huddled together as though they feared this old pagan place. Gavril swung his gaze away scornfully. There was nothing to fear. He pulled out his Circle and let it swing atop his linen doublet.

"What are trolk?" Sir Los asked.

Sir Vedrique paused to send him a snaggletoothed grin. "Old myths, protector. Ain't nothing to fear."

"Hurry," Gavril said. "We can talk later. I am not afraid."

Sir Vedrique frowned. "Wait here, yer highness. Let Sir Los and me go first."

Resenting their caution, Gavril seethed. Impatiently he waited, tapping his fingers on his belt, while Sir Los and Sir Vedrique pushed ahead of him.

At the mouth of the cave, Sir Vedrique took his sword and hacked away much of the thicket growing across it. Then Sir Los drew his weapon and ventured inside. He seemed to be in there forever, while Gavril stood fidgeting, agonized with jealousy. What if Sir Los found the Chalice first? How unfair for him to get the glory when it was Gavril who had prayed daily for the honor.

Realizing what he was thinking, Gavril felt ashamed of himself. Scowling, he turned his back on the cave and struggled to master his feelings.

"Your highness," Sir Los called out.

Gavril spun around and saw the protector emerging. When Sir Los beckoned, Gavril hurried into the cave. It was darker inside than he'd expected, and it stunk with something old and sour. Wrinkling his nostrils, he lifted his hand to his face and tried to breathe through his mouth.

"What is this stink?" he asked. "Has some beast died in here?"

"That's trolk musk," Sir Vedrique said quietly. "Real old. Maybe an old spell lingering on."

"A spell!" Gavril said in horror, then caught himself and swallowed. "Of course. This is a pagan shrine. But the magic cannot harm us if our faith is strong. Sir Los, we need light."

The protector found an old stick lying on the ground just inside the cave. He pulled out his tinderbox and set it alight. In silence, he handed the makeshift torch to Gavril.

Holding it aloft, Gavril walked swiftly through the cave. It was quite small, barely tall enough for him to stand upright, and shallow. Cobwebs hung from the ceiling, and dead leaves had drifted in. As Gavril strode back and forth, his excitement faltered. Why, this old cave wasn't any kind of shrine. It didn't even have an altar, just a circle of scattered stones and some sticks wedged against the back wall.

Scowling, he knelt down to study a stone no bigger than his own head. With his fingertips he traced the carvings there, carvings he could not read and did not wish to. Behind the stone he saw a glint of something, and his excitement leaped high again.

He lifted his torch, and its ruddy flickering light spread over a small, nearly concealed pile of dusty artifacts.

Rusted and tarnished, the basin and ill-assorted collection of cups and vessels which he saw were nothing at all, nothing but junk. Maybe a long time ago, some dwarves had crawled in here and drunk themselves senseless. He tossed down the basin, making a clatter, and picked up a tall, flared vessel. A spider was crawling along its rim. Gavril flicked it away and tapped the cup. It sounded dull. He rubbed it, but its surface was so encrusted with tarnish and grime it couldn't be cleaned.

Disgusted, Gavril flung it down with the rest, and rose to his feet.

"Any of that rubbish useful?" Sir Vedrique asked.

"No," Gavril said. He thought of the Chalice, of how it was said to shine with a glorious power so strong it could fill a dark room with light. It certainly was not here in this filthy lair.

Glancing around one last time, he kicked some of the smaller stones with his toe, accidentally knocking them back into a complete circle. His lip curled with disdain. "This is nothing but a pagan hole, as foolish and empty as their beliefs. Let us go."

Sir Los was standing just inside the entrance. He started to exit first, but Gavril angrily darted out ahead of him.

"Come on," he said. "Let's be away from here. We've wasted enough time."

He started down the hillside, leaving the knights to pick their way more slowly after him. But just as he stepped across the tiny stream, a shout rang out, and dwarves rose up from the thickets, aiming drawn bows at them from all sides.

The dogs leaped to their feet, barking furiously. Fearful for their safety, Gavril shouted, *"Stay!"*

Sir Vedrique also shouted in alarm. One of the knights on horseback drew his sword, but a dwarf loosed a shot and the arrow hit the knight in his throat. He toppled off his horse, which bolted into the forest. The others bunched closer, their hands on their weapons, and swore loudly.

"Move not!" ordered a dwarf with a long brown beard. He looked like the youngest of the company. His eyes were keen and fierce. "Stand where you are."

Gavril halted on the edge of the stream, feeling his pulse thumping hard inside his collar. His mouth had gone dry. Suddenly his mind was filled with all the tales and legends of dwarves he'd heard in his life, tales of how fierce they were, how fearlessly they could fight, how brutally they sometimes tortured their prisoners. He thought of the huntsman Nocine, well now in body after being attacked by the Bnen dwarves last autumn, but not yet restored in mind or spirit. Refusing to be afraid, Gavril shook such thoughts away.

"You there," he called out, ignoring Sir Los's choked warning to be quiet, "put away your weapons. We mean you no harm. Why should you attack us?"

The brown-bearded dwarf stared at Gavril, studying him a long while. The drawn bows did not lower. After several minutes the dwarf shifted his gaze to the other men. "Who is leader?"

The insult infuriated Gavril. He opened his mouth to declare himself, but at the last moment caution held his tongue. If they should guess who he was, they might decide to hold him for ransom. He now understood why Lord Odfrey was always warning him against going too deep into the forest. Gavril had never expected to be caught like this, on foot and unable to defend himself.

Sir Vedrique stepped forward, and a warning arrow skimmed in front of his face. The young knight stopped short and lifted his sword ever so slightly. "Now don't get feisty. What clan are you, eh?"

"We are Clan Nega," the brown-bearded dwarf said. "You are intruding on a sacred place, an old place."

"There's nothing here," Gavril couldn't help but say. He was still full of disappointment. And angry. He wanted only to be gone from this shrine that had mysteriously promised so much and had then withheld what he most wanted. "Nothing is left. Not even an altar."

Several of the dwarves glared and some of them muttered angrily in their heathenish tongue.

"Take care," Sir Vedrique murmured to Gavril, never taking his gaze off the dwarves. "We've made 'em mad enough already."

Gavril had no liking for the reprimand, but his own good sense told him this was no time to argue.

"Ain't no offense intended here," Sir Vedrique said. "We didn't know this place was sacred. We've been hunting boar and thought we might have found a lair."

Some of the dwarves laughed. The scorn in their laughter made Gavril flush. He clenched his fists, annoyed with Sir Vedrique. Why must the knight make them sound like fools?

"You hunt boar on foot?" the brown-bearded dwarf asked, a slow, incredulous smile spreading across his face. "You go into boar dens?"

Sir Vedrique shrugged. "Yon cave stinks so bad, we thought it had to be—"

More laughter came from the dwarves. They chattered together in their barbarous language. Gavril fumed and threw Sir Vedrique a glare. The knight raised his brows in return and shook his head quickly. Gavril clenched his jaw, keeping quiet with an effort.

"We didn't know this was one of your sacred places," Sir Vedrique said. "We apologize if we have offended."

"We apologize," Sir Los said from behind Gavril.

Gavril's scowl deepened. If this tale got back to Thirst Hold, he would be a laughingstock. Hunting boars on foot indeed. He was far from being such a fool.

"Say it, yer highness," Sir Vedrique whispered.

"Say what?" Gavril asked, but he knew.

"Ask them for pardon," Sir Los murmured.

Gavril's back stiffened. He opened his mouth to protest, but the brown-bearded dwarf looked at him sharply. Meeting that astute, suspicious gaze, Gavril swallowed his pride as a prince and a hunter. He said, "I beg your pardon for intruding here."

The dwarf said something to his companions, and the drawn bows were relaxed.

"There is good hunting in Mandria," the dwarf said sternly. "You stay off Nega lands. We want no trouble with men."

Gavril opened his mouth to say he would hunt where he pleased, but Sir Vedrique spoke first: "Aye. We'll not trespass again."

"Then go," the brown-bearded dwarf said. "And come not ever again to this place."

Sir Vedrique gave Gavril a light nudge in the back with the tip of his sword. Furious, his face on fire, Gavril strode over to his horse and climbed into his saddle. He would look at no one. In silence, Sir Vedrique and Sir Los mounted.

"Get that man," Gavril said in a low, angry voice, pointing at the dead knight.

The body was lifted across the withers of one of the horses, since the dead man's own mount had run off. The small party rode away at a nervous trot, the dwarves watching them go.

Gavril still burned with humiliation. As soon as they were safely out of earshot, and the cave and its guardians far behind them, he drew rein and glared at Sir Vedrique.

"How dare you make a fool of me," he said. "You are dismissed from my service."

Annoyance crossed Sir Vedrique's face. He hesitated a moment, then bowed. "As yer highness says."

"It is bad enough that we were caught in such a position," Gavril went on, glaring at all of them now. "How could the rest of you let them sneak up on us like that? Taking us like—"

"We heard naught," one of the knights said defensively.

"That's hardly an excuse," Gavril said. "It's your duty to protect me. And what did you do instead? Sat there with your hands in the air and your mouths open. I'm through with all of you."

"Since you ain't going hunting no more in Nold," Sir Vedrique said coldly, "mayhap it's just as well that we are dismissed. My rump's getting galled from so much riding on this quest of yers."

Gavril gritted his teeth. He wanted to lash out at all of them and tell them just how stupid and worthless they were. But Sir Los was frowning at him in warning. Gavril remembered that these men's allegiance to him was of the lightest kind. They had sworn him no oath as they had to Lord Odfrey. Nor were these the best of Lord Odfrey's men. Of the five ranks of knighthood, these were all at the bottom. The worst paid, they were chronically broke, gambling away what little they earned. If they could be bribed with ale and coinage, their characters were thin at best. Gavril realized suddenly that if he went too far in insulting them, there might be another unfortunate accident here in the forest. Sir Los would die to protect him, but Sir Los was outnumbered four to one.

Sir Vedrique's hostile expression eased a bit when Gavril said nothing else. Slumping in his saddle, the knight pointed at the dead man. "We'd better make ourselves a story."

Gavril frowned. "Story? Why should we explain?"

Some of the men laughed.

Sir Vedrique, however, was not laughing. "If you think Sir Bosquecel will not be asking questions when we bring in a dead man, yer highness needs to think again."

"Then you will explain it," Gavril said. "I need not trouble myself."

"Here!" Sir Vedrique said sharply. "We've come out with you into this damned forest, where none of us are supposed to be. What will I say, that one of us shot *him* instead of a stag we were coursing? 'We made a mistake, Sir Bosquecel. Sorry, and we'll take more care the next time'?"

"Mind your tone," Sir Los growled, but the younger knight went on glaring at Gavril.

"I'll see you're paid extra for your trouble," Gavril said.

"Aye, that goes without saying. As for this corpse—"

Sir Los drew rein abruptly and blocked the path of the rider bringing the dead man. "Bury him here and say he deserted."

Everyone stared at Sir Los, and Gavril's bad temper abruptly cooled. It was one thing to claim he hunted on Thirst land and did not defy Lord Odfrey's orders against exploring the Dark Forest; it was another to conceal a murder, to hide the body and lie about it. Such a lie would have to be kept forever.

Feeling strange and cold, Gavril gripped his Circle. The men stared at him, waiting for him to decide. The dead knight, oaf that he was, deserved more than a hasty grave scratched in the forest. Rites should be said to protect his body at least, but there was no one among them who could do the task. Gavril himself knew the correct prayers, but he had no intention of blaspheming by trying to act as a priest.

This was wrong. Gavril felt he should ride back to Thirst and deliver a frank confession to Lord Odfrey of what he'd done and why. But his quest was private, a deeply personal thing. Lord Odfrey would condemn him for it, would point out all the unpleasant details such as disobedience, unnecessary risk, and now, disaster. Gavril felt that today's crushing disappointments were all he could bear. He was running out of time, and he had failed to accomplished the one objective that could have made him great. Enduring a reprimand from Lord Odfrey would be too much.

He looked up and met Sir Los's eyes. The protector's rounded face gave nothing away. It never did.

"See that it's done," Gavril said harshly.

As he watched the work commence, he knew he was making a mistake. The dead man was of the faithful. He should not be buried out here in secret, in unhallowed ground, certain prey for anything evil that wished to dig him up. Still, the arrow had caught him in the throat. Surely his soul had been released and was now safely where it belonged. Wrong or not, concealment would solve many problems. Desertion was a simple explanation; no motive for it need be supplied.

The knights used the dead man's sword to dig the grave, since the weapon could not be kept anyway and the dulling of its blade did not matter. Gavril sat atop his horse, his dogs nosing his stirrup and whining. How he wished he could ride on and leave this dismal, gloomy forest behind. He would never come back. His dreams and best intentions had been for naught. He had imperiled his conscience for this holy mission, had prayed and sacrificed, and still he had failed.

His quest to find the missing Chalice was over.

20

FOUR DAYS LATER, Dain and Lander returned. The plodding mule drew them along the muddy ruts of the river road, where Dain saw a column of black smoke rising above the trees beyond the marsh. Already edgy, he frowned and nudged Lander in the ribs.

"Look yon," he said.

The smith hunched his shoulders and slapped the reins harder on the mule's rump. His face was haggard from fear and lack of sleep, "Think you the hold is burning?"

Dain shook his head. Already his senses told him that the hold was standing firm. Nor had there been death in the deserted village they now passed through. The killing had happened farther ahead, south of the hold, perhaps where that smoke was coming from. Images of agony and blood flashed through his mind. For an instant he seemed to be elsewhere, as though his spirit had been yanked backward in time to the vicinity of that recent battle. He could even hear the screams of the dying mingling with the shrieks of Nonkind. The very air hung thick with the stench of evil.

Dain shivered despite the sultry heat of the afternoon, and with great effort he wrenched his mind back to the here and now. Thirst knights had fought. Some had died in the four days Dain and Lander had been gone; Dain didn't want to know which ones. Already his heart felt torn with horror and grief over how suddenly and unexpectedly danger had come to Thirst in his absence.

He should not have left. He should have been here with his comrades, fighting alongside them. Instead, he had been off in the Dark Forest, striking bargains that Lander could have made alone.

Dain clenched his fists on his knees, gritting his teeth as the cart wheels jounced over the ruts. He wanted to jump down and race ahead on foot, but at the same time he feared what he might find.

It was a hot, sultry day, the air sticky and close with no breeze stirring. Although the sun shone strong and bright, the world seemed to have stilled itself, waiting for trouble the way small rodents hide under the blades of grass when vixlets hunt the meadow. On the distant horizon, storm clouds were massing. Now and then Dain heard a distant rumble of thunder.

The weary mule slowed down as they passed through the village's abandoned huts. Crude doors stood ajar. Kettles and brooms lay on the ground where they'd been flung down. A half-mended fishing net hung on a pole frame, with the mending cords still swinging by their knotted ends in the breeze.

A noise from behind them made Dain spin around on the cart seat, his hand reaching for his dagger.

"Demons!" Lander shouted, and whacked the mule so hard it shambled forward into a trot.

Nearly overbalanced, Dain gripped the smith's shoulder. "Have care!" he said. "It's just a dog."

Lander glanced back unwillingly, his eyes nearly bulging from their sockets.

The mongrel, spotted black and white with burrs matted in its floppy ears, slunk away between two huts. Its tail wagged nervously against the wall, making a hollow *thunk* of sound.

"A dog," Dain repeated in relief, his heart beating too fast.

Lander gulped in several deep breaths. Perspiration beaded down his face, darkening his fringe of red hair. Hastily he drew a circle on his chest. "Thod is merciful."

Sheathing his dagger, Dain gripped Lander's slack hand and shook the reins to make the mule walk on. "Let's get to Thirst before dark."

Lander mumbled something and gave the mule a halfhearted tap with the whip.

Dain sighed. He'd sweated through his tunic so much it had plastered itself to his back. He wished he was carrying salt in his pockets. When he lived with Jorb he never left the burrow without filling his pockets from the barrel kept standing always at the door, a wooden scoop jammed upright in its center. But while he'd been living at Thirst, he'd lost the habit. Men depended on swords and stout walls to protect them. Right now, Dain and Lander had neither.

At the end of the village grew a copse of trees that blocked a clear view of the road beyond. Dain disliked the place, for the bushes grew close and thick, and he could not see ahead. He smelled no Nonkind, but the flick of men-minds suddenly assaulted his senses. At the same moment, a squad of horsemen in armor burst upon them from the cover of the trees.

Before Dain could draw his dagger, they were surrounded, and a lance tip hovered at Lander's throat.

The smith sat frozen, his face red, his mouth hanging open. He tried to speak, but could only sputter.

Dain sat beside him with his dagger half-drawn. Already he'd noted with alarm that these knights did not wear the dark green of Thirst. Their surcoats were scarlet, and their cloaks black. The eyes of strangers glittered through the slits of their helmets.

"State your name and business here," ordered a gruff voice.

Lander whimpered in the back of throat, and it was Dain who answered: "This is Lander, smith of Thirst Hold. I am called Dain."

"Easily said, but harder to prove—"

"By what right do you question us?" Dain demanded. "Who are *you*? What hold is yours?"

The lance remained at Lander's throat. Dain could feel the smith's rigid tension. His fear hung sour on the air.

The knight who had spoken now dipped his head slightly to Dain. He flipped up his visor, revealing a thin, chiseled face made distinguished by an elegant chin beard and mustache. His eyes were dark brown, and although he did not smile the fierceness had relaxed in his gaze.

"A bold tongue you have, boy," he replied. " 'Tis a pity I can believe you not. Neither of you have the look of Mandria. You wear no livery to mark you as Thirst folk."

Lander pulled back his head, taking his throat a few inches away from the steel tip of that lance, which so far had not wavered. "Livery!" he repeated, sounding offended. "Does a smith wear the tabard of a varlet?"

"Nay, but smiths do not journey far from their forge either," the man replied.

One of the other knights rode up beside him and spoke softly, to his ear alone.

The bearded knight frowned, then nodded and gave Dain a closer scrutiny. "Dain, is it?"

"Yes."

"Are you Chevard Odfrey's foster eld who ran away four days past?"

Dain's chin lifted haughtily. "I am both eld and a foster," he said. "I did not run away."

The knight's gaze grew cold, but he made no response. Instead, he rode alongside the cart and peered down at its cargo. "What are you hauling?"

"Metal for my work," Lander said. His voice was swift, high, and nervous. "There's much to do before the great tournament in Savroix a month from now. A few times a year I go to the dwarves of Nold to buy what I need."

Again they got a sharp look. Feeling the hostility emanating from these strangers, Dain frowned. He did not take his hand off his dagger.

"You've been in the Dark Forest, then," the knight said.

"Aye," Lander said. "And a mortal bad time in getting back. The whole world has turned upside down these past few days. Nonkind everywhere, and all sorts of—"

Dain pinched his side to silence him and glared up at the knight. "By what authority do you question us?" he demanded. "What names do you bear? Who is your liege? What hold do you—"

"Hush," Lander whispered furiously to him. "Cause us no trouble. Curb your tongue, boy!"

Dain ignored him. "What is your name, sir knight?" he called out to the bearded man.

The man seemed momentarily amused. "I am Lord Renald, chevard of Lunt Hold."

Dain stared, realizing belatedly that he should have noticed the quality of the man's splendid armor, the good breeding of his horse, the aristocratic air in his cultured voice. Gulping at his breach of courtesy, Dain bowed awkwardly to the man.

"Your pardon, lord," he said with more courtesy. "But what brings you here to Thirst lands? Have you been fighting the Nonkind?"

"You know there's been a battle," Lord Renald said, frowning.

One of the other knights swore violently. "Aye, he knows it, the sly demon-caller—"

Lord Renald's head whipped around, and the other knight abruptly fell silent.

"Let them pass," Lord Renald said, reining his horse aside.

The lance trained on Lander swung away from his throat.

The riders blocking the road reined their horses aside, leaving the way clear. Lander clucked to his mule, but Dain's suspicions grew. There was much wrong, much he did not understand.

Lord Renald sent Lander a stern look. "Head straight to the hold. Make no stops until you reach the gates. The way is clear, but it's been won at a hard cost."

"Yes, m'lord," Lander said, bobbing up and down with gratitude. "Thank you, m'lord."

The chevard gestured at one of his men. "Go with them. Make sure the boy arrives and is presented to Lord Odfrey with my compliments."

The man inclined his head, his eyes glittering angrily through the slits in his helmet. "Aye, m'lord. Though wouldn't it be faster to take him up behind my saddle and ride straight there—"

"No," Lord Renald said firmly. "Let him return as he left. The affair is not our concern."

"When men die on a field of—"

"Sir Metain, you have your orders."

The knight bowed. "Aye, m'lord."

"If you please, Lord Renald," Dain said in puzzlement, trying to sort out what their exchange meant. "What is—"

"Hush," Lander commanded him, elbowing him. "Hold your fool tongue and let us go."

"But—"

Lander whipped the mule, sending the cart lurching forward. They bounced out from beneath the trees and up onto the paved road. In silence the knights of Lunt watched them go, their black cloaks blending into the shadows of the copse, their red surcoats vivid, like splashes of blood.

Sir Metain came trotting after them, grim and silent on his war charger.

Lander's face burned bright red. "Thod's thumbs," he muttered. "Lord Renald himself, and you speaking up as bold as brass. Morde a day, what will become of us now?"

"I gave him little insult," Dain said, glancing back once more. "I just asked for his name. What right, lord or no, does he have here, stopping us and making his demands?"

"What right?" Lander said, clearly horrified by such a question. "What right? The right of a lord. What do you think?"

"But he is not lord of *this* land," Dain said. "He is not chevard of Thirst. What battle has been done? And why? How did it all happen so suddenly, in the short time we were gone? Did you know there was trouble brewing out here, Lander? Did you go to meet Baldrush despite it?"

"What trouble?" Lander said, but he would not meet Dain's eyes. "Had you heard aught? You live closer with the knights than do I. Why would I risk my life dodging Nonkind and all sorts of demons if I did not have to?"

Dain was not convinced. "Because you wanted this magicked metal."

"*Hush!*" Lander said, glancing back at Sir Metain. He looked at his load, the two special bars wrapped in cloth to hide them from view. "No one is to know about what I'm doing. No one!"

His thick, calloused hand, powerful from a lifetime of wielding a hammer, gripped Dain's forearm and squeezed almost hard enough to crack bones. "Keep quiet about it. Morde a day, what eld has ever had a tongue like yours? Supposed to keep yourself to yourself, you are, not challenging chevards and asking questions."

"But something's amiss," Dain insisted.

"Is it now?" Lander retorted with exasperation. "And what would that be? The fact that we've barely returned with our lives? The fact that some village yon is on fire and every other village we've come to has been deserted or looted or both? What could be amiss? You're daft, boy, daft!"

"You don't understand. I mean—"

"What you mean is that you should be quiet," Lander said. He urged the mule onward.

"Why should we have a guard?" Dain asked, glancing again at Sir Metain. "What did they mean about me being returned faster?"

"So you can be flogged for going without permission, I expect," Lander said.

"That's unfair!" Dain said angrily. "You *asked* me to go with you."

"Aye, I needed your help, not that you gave much."

"How could I bargain well with you looking so keen?"

Lander and Dain glared at each other. The smith was the first to drop his gaze and sigh. "Now, now, no need to quarrel. I gave you your reward, as we agreed. Let's put an end to it. If his lordship's wrathful with you, I can't help. I told you to ask for permission to come with me, Dain. If you didn't get it, then there's naught I can do."

Dain knotted his fists in his lap and scowled at them. He realized now he'd been foolish to hope that his troubles would go away during his absence. It looked like they'd only grown worse.

They rolled on in silence, while the walls of the hold rose ahead of them. To Dain's worried eye, Thirst looked the same as always, although more sentries manned the battlements. The gates were closed, and Lander had to shout for them to be opened.

A guard peered down at them from the wall. "Thod's mercy," he said. "Look at what's turned up."

"Open the gate," Lander said impatiently. "Open and let us safe inside. We've dealt with enough. Open!"

Strain made his voice crack. Dain's own weariness sagged clear to his bones. He was tired from little sleep, since they had to take turns keeping watch through the tense nights, and ravenous, for Lander's provisions had not lasted through the extra day it had taken them to return. They'd avoided every settlement they could and were forced periodically to hide, with Lander quaking and praying beneath his breath while Nonkind rode by. They'd had no trouble going into the Dark Forest and reaching the place where Lander was to meet with Baldrush the dwarf, but coming home had been fraught with problems from the moment Dain first sniffed Nonkind and warned Lander to drive them into cover.

Trolk—the first Dain had seen in years—had come marauding by, a snarling pack. Although marching at a fast pace, they stopped periodically to dig their claws into the bark of trees, and the clacking sound of claws against wood still haunted Dain. Dripping saliva from their yellowed fangs, their tiny stupid eyes peering out from beneath a jutting ledge of browbone, they had hobbled along on their bowed awkward legs with their back hair standing up in hostility. They passed Lander and Dain's hiding place while Dain crouched low, holding the nostrils of the mule and using his mind to control its panic. With its eyes rolled white and its ears laid flat, the mule stood tense and quaking until the band of trolk were long gone. Their rancid stink trailed after them, hanging in the air so thickly Lander gagged on it.

"Never have I seen demons such as them," the smith said, gasping for air.

"They aren't demons," Dain said. "They lived in the Dark Forest before the dwarves claimed it. Long, long ago the dwarf clans joined forces and killed the trolk kings. Now the trolk are few. They roam and dig their lairs, but seldom do they march like this. Not banded together."

He frowned, worried by how unusual it was.

"I care nothing about these puzzles," Lander declared. "I just want to get home to Thirst, with no more trouble."

But they found trouble at almost every turn. Had they been on foot, they could have abandoned the narrow road that wound through the forest and taken the shortest way back, but the cart, loaded with the metal Dain had bargained for at the price of six-and-thirty gold dreits, hampered them greatly. Lander would not consider abandoning it. Each time Dain sensed someone approaching ahead or from behind, they had to pull the cart off the trail and conceal both it and the mule, hiding until the way was clear again. Their journey home lengthened by hours, then by an entire day.

Had Dain not led the mule through the dark for half a night, they would still be on their road, far from here.

Now the sentry on the wall shouted at Lander to back up his cart, leave it by the wall out of the way, and unhitch his mule.

"What?" Lander shouted back. "Are you daft, man? I can't leave this load out here to be stolen."

"Your cart won't fit through the petite-porte, and that's all I am allowed to open," the sentry shouted down.

"Thod's bones," Lander swore. "After all I've gone through, I will not leave my load. Open the main gate!"

Sir Metain rode up beside him and interrupted the argument. "You know these two, sentry?"

"Aye, sir, I do. It's Lander, our smith, and the boy Dain."

"Compliments of Lord Renald," Sir Metain said. His voice was gruff and hostile. "We caught this pair sneaking along the river road north of here. I am to deliver this boy into Lord Odfrey's hands."

"And Lord Odfrey will thank you sweetly," the sentry

replied. "We've searched long and hard for him, at least until the trouble started."

"Open your petite-porte, and let them through," Sir Metain said.

The sentry vanished, his voice bawling the order.

Lander knotted his fists and fumed. "I won't leave my cart. Morde and damne all besides. I won't leave it!"

"Calm yourself," Dain said, eying him with concern. "We'll carry the metal inside. It will be safe."

Lander blinked, and relief brightened his face. "Aye," he said, nodding. "Aye! Of course, of course. That can be done."

He jumped off the cart and ran to the head of his mule. The poor, lathered beast, weary to his very bones, refused to turn aside. His head was pointed toward the gate, and no amount of coaxing, swearing, or use of the whip would induce him to back the cart away.

An ear-splitting screech came from the winch inside the gates. Slowly the narrow gate inside the main one creaked its way open. Dain ran to the back of the cart and pulled out the board gate. He climbed atop the metal bars, shifting the magicked ones first.

Wrapped in cloth, they emitted an inaudible hum that resonated deep inside Dain's mind. He almost dropped them, for there was something repellent about this raw metal, something dark and tainted within the spell that had cast it from ore.

Juggling the bars about so that he could hand them down to Lander, Dain recalled that he had not trusted Baldrush, the dwarf they'd purchased this metal from—no, not at all. There was a strangeness about him that bothered Dain immediately. Baldrush was tall for his kind; his head came nearly to Dain's shoulder. His face was narrow and gaunt. His eyes burned with yellow fire. He had a way of muttering to himself within his beard. He paced about, his fingers clutching and unclutching the air. He was never still. Always he kept moving and twitching, muttering and pacing, his eyes darting this way and that. Even the shift of Lander's shadow on the ground made Baldrush jump.

It was the ore madness, Dain knew. Jorb had warned him of the perils of working too much with magicked metal. Glancing at Lander's red, intense expression now, Dain hoped the smith did not catch the affliction.

"Give it to me!" Lander commanded, grunting with the effort to grasp the ends of the bars. "Careful! Don't let them slip."

Dain was glad to release the bars. He crouched atop the load of ordinary metal, his hands still tingling unpleasantly from contact with the magic, and watched Lander hurry through the petite-porte with his treasure.

Annoyance filled Dain as he realized he'd been left out here to cope with the rest of the load. He saw Sir Metain watching him, and Dain's anger grew.

Defiantly he jumped down. He'd worked for Lander like a serf for four days, all for the two pieces of gold now jingling in his pocket. But he wasn't going to carry all this metal inside, especially not by himself.

Overhead, the sun abruptly vanished behind a cloud, and the sky turned black and violent. Wind gusted up, buffeting Dain, who went to unharness the mule. Lightning flashed, with a deafening clap of thunder that made the mule rear, and rain fell in a torrent.

Soaked to the skin in seconds, Dain pulled off the harness, wincing at the sight of the galled sores on the mule's withers, and tossed the harness into the cart. Great forks of lightning jabbed the sky. One struck the ground out in the marsh. Dain heard the crack and sizzle, saw a tree burst into flames that were extinguished by the pounding rain. The noise of the downpour was deafening. Wind buffeted Dain from all sides. The ground at his feet streamed with water. Already his shoes were sinking into the mud. Sir Metain was shouting at him, gesturing for him to get inside. Squinting and gasping, his hair plastered to his skull, Dain led the mule forward and coaxed him through the narrow gate.

Sir Terent stood there, his ruddy face scrunched and squinting inside its mail coif. "Dain, hurry!" he shouted.

He gripped Dain by the shoulder of his tunic and dragged him inside. Someone else took the reins and led the mule away.

The sudden contrast of shelter after the raging torrent outside left Dain stunned and breathless. He huddled there in the dry, with water dripping from his clothes, while the petite-porte was winched closed again. The cable that controlled it groaned and creaked. Its hinges shrieked from disuse, but at last it slammed closed, and a stout bar was thrown across it.

"What about Lander's metal?" Dain asked.

"It's not going anywhere!" Sir Terent replied. He gripped Dain by both shoulders and shook him roughly. "So you're alive, young rascal. I never thought we'd see you again."

"Lord Renald caught him," Sir Metain said. "I am to take him straight to your chevard."

Staring out at the keep from beneath the portcullis, Dain saw knights running for shelter in all directions. Most wore Thirst green, but some displayed the black and scarlet of Lunt. All of them had on hauberks, their swords hanging from their hips, their cloaks soaking up the rain. They were splattered with mud, mire, and blood, and shouted to each other as they dashed to get out of the rain. Squires and servants milled around, coping with war chargers alarmed by the storm. The confusion meant that these men must have ridden in shortly before Dain and Lander themselves arrived.

Dain sensed the battle fierceness still raging in their minds.

Sir Nynth came ducking under the portcullis into the narrow space of shelter by the gates. He saw Dain and his face brightened momentarily. "Dain!" he said in a mixture of relief and exasperation. "Thod be thanked, and Tomias too. Where in all the three worlds have you been?"

Dain opened his mouth, but Sir Terent stepped between them.

"It's a long story, by the looks of him. Lunt riders caught him."

"They didn't catch me," Dain said indignantly. "Lander and I were coming home. We'd have been back yesterday if not for having to hide from Nonkind patrols. Why have they dared come this far into the open? Did they attack the hold? What's been afire?"

"One of the villages to the south," Sir Nynth replied. His voice was grave. He looked weary and grim.

"Is that Dain?" called out another voice. Sir Polquin came striding up, a mixture of emotions afire in his face. "Where have you been? Morde, the trouble you've caused."

"Save it," Sir Terent growled before Dain could respond. "You better get yourself to the chevard at once."

Dain glanced at Sir Metain. "I don't need him to go with me."

The knight from Lunt scowled, but Sir Polquin interceded.

"This is our business, friend knight," he said. "We'll handle it in our own way."

"You'd better keep a close eye on the creature," Sir Metain said. "If he betrayed you once, he'll do it again."

Dain glared at him. "What? Who have I betrayed?"

He found his answer in the grim faces surrounding him, in the censure and doubt that filled every eye.

"He's been in the Dark Forest," Sir Metain said. "Admitted it to Lord Renald bold as brass."

"We were buying metal," Dain said. He pointed at the gate. "It's right out there. Ask Lander. He wanted me to go with him to do the bargaining."

"You can explain yourself to Lord Odfrey," Sir Polquin said. Both condemnation and disappointment could be heard in his voice.

Dain stared at them in horror. Why did they think he'd brought the Nonkind here? "I didn't—"

"Dain, just go," Sir Terent said.

"But I—"

The knight gave him a shove. "Be off!"

As Dain hurried away, Sir Terent said to the others, "Boys be pretty much the same, whether they be pagan or of the faithful. They don't think. They just go off on adventures at a whim."

"Maybe," Sir Polquin said. "Maybe not."

Sir Nynth shook his head. "I wouldn't want to stand in his shoes while he faces Lord Odfrey."

"Will he?" Sir Metain asked doubtfully, still looking as though he meant to follow Dain out into the downpour. With his hand on his sword hilt, he stood at the edge of the shelter and glowered at Dain, who was hesitating, soaked and miserable, while they talked about him. "Will he go and do as he is bidden?"

"Aye," Sir Terent said. "He will. He's a good boy, our Dain."

"We needed him and his luck with us today," Sir Nynth added.

Dain frowned, forcing himself to turn away, then he was dodging and twisting through the crowded keep. He saw no reason for Lord Odfrey to be angry at him. He'd been gone only a few days. Was he a prisoner here? Had he no freedom to come and go if it pleased him? Lord Odfrey saw little use in him as it was. Why should the chevard care where Dain went or with whom?

But despite his inner defiance, Dain knew very well that he'd broken the rules of the hold by leaving without permission.

He'd had plenty of time to think it over while riding on that uncomfortable cart. He'd been prepared to return with humility, and he'd come to accept Lord Odfrey's decision to withdraw him from the squire contest. He was, after all, eld. Although the men of Thirst Hold might make a pet of him and give him run of the place, he knew he must never forget that he was not equal to the other boys.

Something deep inside Dain's heart burned with anger at that, but he ignored it, telling himself it was the way of the world. He must never forget the lessons about men-ways that Jorb had tried to instill in him. Forgetting led to blind trust, and that left him vulnerable to being hurt. He liked and admired Lord Odfrey very much; he had even respected the man. But Lord Odfrey was what he was. He dealt less hurt than other men, but he was still capable of acting arbitrarily and unjustly.

You are not like the other fosters, Dain reminded himself often during his trip with Lander. *You are eld, and will always be the less for it.*

Had he been a simpleton or born with a humble heart, he thought, his lot in life would have been easier. He would have been grateful for shelter and food. He would have been pleased at the training in arms they'd given him. He would not have wanted more, or been ashamed of his mean estate and questionable birth. He would not wonder why he owned a piece of bard crystal—he and his sister both—and he would never question where he'd come from or why he'd been driven from that place, cast out to struggle on his own. He would not dream of all that his life could be. He would concern himself only with where he walked at this moment, thinking neither behind him nor ahead. He would be content.

Most important, his heart would never ache the way it did right now.

He had counted the knights his friends. He had grown to accept and believe in their rough affection. During the last four days, he had struggled hard to lose his pride and come to terms with Lord Odfrey's decision.

But now, he found that they blamed him for the raiding of the Nonkind and the battle that had been fought. What greater injustice could there be than this?

Fresh anger boiled up inside him. He told himself that if the knights could turn on him this quickly and believe him capable of betraying them to the Nonkind, then he didn't want to be here. He would leave Thirst for good, and Thod smite them all.

21

RAIN CONTINUED TO pour, hammering Dain's skin. Drops hit the ground with such violence they bounced up. Water was flooding the keep, turning it into a bog of mud and manure. Grooms hurried along, leading war chargers with rain-soaked manes and stringy tails, empty stirrups flapping as they trotted by. The villagers had pitched makeshift tents across the keep's expanse. They huddled inside their crude shelters, peering out at the rain, their livestock milling about in everyone's way. Slipping and sliding in the mire, Dain made his way through the small set of inner gates and into the cobbled stableyard beyond.

The stables were jammed with horses. A fodder barn had been cleaned out to shelter more, but it was overflowing too. Others were tied outside these structures, standing with their rumps to the wind, their ears flat with misery. The groom who had passed Dain moments before was now carrying his master's saddle indoors.

As Dain jogged through the rain, squinting, his shoulders hunched up, he saw the Thirst stableboys standing in the doorway, gawking and chewing straws.

One of them pointed at Dain and said something, but just then more lightning clawed the sky, nearly blinding Dain. Thunder seemed to break the world apart.

He cried out, dropping to his knees with his hands clapped over his ears, and saw a jagged fork of lighting hit the banner pole atop the west tower. Sparks and fire flew in all directions, scoring a black mark on the stone. The air was choked with the burned smell of it, and Dain abandoned his idea of going all the way to the Hall.

Fearing that he might be struck by a lightning bolt, Dain glanced at the stables, but the doors were now shut and everyone had vanished.

He looked across at Sulein's tower and headed for it at a run. If the world was ending, he wanted his bard crystal in hand.

The door leading in to Sulein's tower was unlocked. Dain pushed his way inside, gasping with relief as he slammed the door behind him. The interior of the tower lay shrouded in gloom, relieved only by the flashes of lightning seen through the small windows cut in the staircase wall.

Dain leaned against the door to catch his breath and wipe the water from his face. His hair dripped down inside his collar, but he was so wet he hardly noticed. Gripping the hem of his tunic, he wrung it out as best he could, leaving a puddle on the floor, then squelched his way up the stairs in his sodden shoes.

As he climbed, he could smell the peculiar combination of herbs and potions which always lingered here. He felt the resonance of weak magic and half-formed spells which permeated the place. His heart started to beat faster, but he kept going.

He would never find it easy to be near the physician, but if luck was with him today Sulein would be elsewhere, attending wounded men.

It was not to be.

Dain reached the top of the stairs and walked to Sulein's door. No sooner did he grip the iron ring than Sulein yanked the door open.

Standing framed in the doorway, his loose brown robe stained and discolored as usual from the ill effects of his experiments, the physician stared down at Dain with a toothy smile.

"So," he said, "you have returned in a storm of sky fire and thunder. Come inside, eld. Long months have I waited for you to come to me."

Dain opened his mouth, but could say nothing. The hair prickled on the back of his neck. In that moment, lightning flashed outside the windows, and its eerie white light threw strange shadows across the physician's face, as though a skull were gazing down at Dain. He stood there frozen with dismay, every instinct warning him to run from this man who craved the dark secrets of a *sorcerel.*

Sulein's fevered smile faded, and he reached out his hand as though to draw Dain in. "Come," he said again. "There is something you want, is there not? Something that is yours? What will you give me in exchange for it? What eld secrets will you share?"

As he spoke he stood aside and gestured at the interior of his workroom. The place was filled with shadows and gloom, with no lamps or candles lit to illuminate it. Yet suddenly at a wave of Sulein's long-fingered hand a glow of lambent light came from nowhere and fell across a wooden box on one of the tables.

Dain could sense his bard crystal within it, could almost hear it. That Sulein should have possession of it, that he should guard it from its rightful owner incensed Dain so much he forgot his fear.

"Come inside," Sulein said softly, his eyes bright and eager. "Let us bargain."

And Dain stepped over the threshold into his lair.

Outside, the storm ceased as abruptly as it had begun. Aware of the silence, when moments before rain had been pounding on the conical roof of Sulein's tower, Dain blinked and looked around. He drew in a deep breath, and suddenly his mind cleared.

He could tell where Sulein had gripped his emotions, especially his resentment, and where he sought to manipulate him.

Frowning, Dain glanced at the physician without meeting the man's eyes and ran across the room to grip the box with both hands.

"Put it down!" Sulein said in alarm. "You have not my permission to touch it."

Paying him no heed, Dain opened the box. His pendant lay glittering inside upon a scrap of fine cloth, its cord coiled neatly around it. An assortment of other items lay scattered next to it, including a large ring with runes carved on its band. Dain ignored everything but what belonged to him. He picked up the bard crystal, and heard it sing softly within the curl of his fingers.

Soothed by its faint melody, Dain smiled, but Sulein grabbed the pendant from his hand.

"No!" he said firmly. "You may not take it from this place of safekeeping. We will talk first."

Anger swept Dain. He snarled a curse in dwarf and reached for his dagger.

Sulein's intense eyes met Dain's and held them. Neither of them spoke in that moment, and no magic was used. Yet Dain left his dagger half-drawn, his chest heaving with every furious breath as he battled himself.

"You do not wish to draw your weapon against me, Dain," Sulein said quietly, his dark face very serious behind his frizzy beard. "I am Lord Odfrey's man, and no warrior. Would you break the laws of this hold in such a way?"

Dain bared his teeth. "The pendant is mine. I want it back."

"Why?" Sulein asked him. "So you can run away from Thirst for good? You had to return today, of course, for your property. You were foolish to forget it the first time, but then your temper is fierce, I think."

"I did not run away," Dain said angrily. "If you are as wise as you claim you would know this."

"Don't be impertinent," Sulein replied. He placed the bard crystal back in his strongbox and closed the lid.

Dain reached out, but Sulein carried the box across the room and placed it on a shelf alongside numerous bottles and small clay pots.

"No," he said, dusting off his long slender hands and returning. "Let us sit and have our talk."

Dain scowled, prickling with unease, and swung away from him. "What do you want in exchange for my property? I have no secrets to share."

"Oh, but you do. You are a treasure trove walking among us." Sulein smiled. His dark eyes shone through the gloom. "What do you fear, boy? Why will you not answer my questions?"

"I have no knowledge of the dark ways," Dain answered. "I can tell you nothing about them."

Sulein laughed, throwing back his head so far it was strange that his conical hat did not fall off. "Ah, so that is it! I do not seek ways of the darkness or the forbidden. This do I assure you, boy. Have you never studied?"

"Studied what?" Dain asked suspiciously.

Sulein seated himself on a stool. He gestured for Dain to do the same, but Dain remained standing, ready to run for the door if he had to.

"Studied knowledge, for its own sake," Sulein replied, lighting several candles. Their flickering glow reduced the gloom, driving back the shadows.

The room was cluttered as always, filled with stacks of old scrolls that looked so brittle with age they would probably have crumbled to dust if anyone tried to unroll them. A dead vixlet, embalmed and mounted, snarled at Dain from atop the shelves. Its eyes, made of colored glass, reflected the candlelight in an eerie fashion, almost as though the thing were possessed.

"Can you read, Dain?" Sulein asked.

"Of course."

Sulein picked up a scrap of parchment and held it out. When Dain kept his distance, Sulein rattled it impatiently.

"Oh, come, come, boy, what have you to fear? Take the paper and tell me what it says."

Dain stepped closer reluctantly and saw small, strange characters drawn across the page. Anger flared inside him. "Another game!" he said impatiently. "I have no time for this. Give me my bard crystal!"

"No, Dain," Sulein replied softly, his tone quite firm. "Not without Lord Odfrey's order."

"Then I have other things to do." Turning about, Dain headed for the door.

"You lived among the dwarves," Sulein said after him. "Presumably you learned to read and write in runes."

Dain glanced back. "I have orders to report to Lord Odfrey. I cannot dally here, talking of runes and such."

"Lord Odfrey is busy with what has transpired during your absence. I believe he is praying in the chapel now for the souls of the men who died in this day's battle."

Some of Dain's annoyance faded into concern. Some of those dead knights were surely men he'd liked. He wanted to know their names, and yet he dreaded finding out.

"There is a little time," Sulein said. "You know this, or you would not have come here on your way to his lordship."

Dain frowned, but Sulein was right. "Are there many dead?" he asked.

"Since when do you care about the fate of Mandrian serfs?"

Dain's frown deepened. "I meant, are there many dead among the knights?"

"You care for them, then? As comrades?"

"Of course!" Dain said hotly. "What do you think of me? Why does everyone think I had something to do with—"

"You have changed while living here among us," Sulein said. "You have begun to think more like a Mandrian and less like a dwarf."

"I am neither," Dain said flatly.

"That is correct. Were you born in Nether?" Sulein asked.

The sudden change of subject threw Dain for a moment. "I know not."

"*Krogni da vletsna ryakilvn yla meratskya.* Do you understand those words?" Sulein asked.

"No," Dain said, but uneasily. Though the words meant nothing, their cadence had a familiar rhythm and lilt. Thia used to sing a child's song of nonsense words. She taught him to sing it too, but neither of them knew what the words meant. That little song was similar to what Sulein said. Dain felt cold inside. "*Never go into Nether,*" Jorb had warned him and Thia most solemnly. "*Seek not the eldin who live there.*"

"Did Jorb your guardian ever speak to you in Netheran?" Sulein asked.

"No."

"Did he tell you where you came from?"

"I am eld," Dain said harshly. "That is enough to know."

"You are highborn, and you know it," Sulein persisted. "Are you afraid to accept this? Why? It is to your advantage to be educated, to know how to read and write in more than one language. To have knowledge of classical learning so that you can converse with others of your station."

"Station?" Dain repeated. "I have no station except beggar! I am fostered here on charity, with the superstitions of Lord Odfrey to thank. That is all I am."

"Nether has been missing its rightful king for sixteen years," Sulein said. "King Muncel rules there, and it is Gant he allies himself with now, not Mandria. It is said that King Tobeszijian is surely dead, but that his son, the rightful heir to Nether's throne, lives hidden in exile."

"What do I care about Nether?" Dain said impatiently.

"Save that many eldin live there—or used to, before King Muncel drove them out."

Sulein leaned forward, his eyes boring into Dain. "The rightful heir's name is Faldain."

He seemed to be waiting for something. Expectancy hung on him like a cloak.

Dain laughed incredulously. "You jest, surely. Or do you think me a knave stupid enough to believe such nonsense?"

"It is not nonsense," Sulein said. "This is most important. You could be the missing prince."

"I am not," Dain said. "My name is not—"

"Dain and Faldain are names almost identical," Sulein said eagerly. "You are the correct age."

Dain stared at him with pity. What foolishness was this? "Dain is a common suffix to many eldin names," he said. "Faldain, Sordain, Landain, Cueldain . . . What of that? Oh, you paint a pretty dream. I would love to be a king, with a great treasure in my storehouse and the life of a fable, but I am simply an eld, orphaned and without family. I must live where I can, and keep myself alive."

"You wear king's glass," Sulein said, but his voice had dropped to a whisper.

Dain sensed how desperately the man wanted his idea to be true. For an instant Dain allowed himself to dream as well, but it was too impossible. He could not even imagine it. In that unguarded moment, Sulein's usual protections seemed to have vanished. He sat there facing Dain, his hope plain to read in his face. Dain could tell that this man wanted the reward and honor of finding the missing heir to Nether's throne. Sulein might bury himself in this workroom with his studies and his experiments, but he was an ambitious man. He wanted too much.

He wanted from Dain what Dain did not have to give him.

"The pieces fit. Besides, only royalty may wear king's glass," Sulein said.

"In Mandria, yes," Dain said, deliberately making his voice scornful. "But such is not the custom elsewhere. As a man foreign-born, you should know better than to think the custom of one land is the same in all."

Sulein's face reddened. He drew back as though he'd been struck. "Perhaps," he muttered.

"How many refugees have fled from Nether in recent

years?" Dain asked. "Families have been divided and lost. I could belong to anyone. I have proof of nothing."

"Prince Faldain's mother, the Queen Nereisse, was true eld," Sulein said. "King Tobeszijian was half-eld himself. It is allowed in Nether, to cross blood this way. The old gifts of seeing are valued there, unlike here, where the church has reformed much . . . and caused much more to be lost."

"I must go," Dain said.

Sulein jumped off his stool. "You disappoint me. I thought you would have more ambition for yourself."

"To reach too high is to be struck down," Dain said bitterly. "I cannot even vie for the position of Lord Odfrey's squire. How would you make me into a king?"

Sulein drew in a breath, his brow creasing with pity. "Ah, yes. Perhaps it is so, and my ideas are only foolishness. Well, then, talk to me instead of eld magic. You may trust me not to share what you say. I know that it is not always safe to reveal too much knowledge of the old ways."

Dain frowned, backing up a step. "There is no magic."

"I know differently." Sulein picked up a stick and held it out. "If you hold this in your hand, will it sprout leaves and return to life?"

Dain held his hands at his side and glared at the physician. "No."

"I have talked to Nocine the huntsman," Sulein said. "You cast a spell and turned him into a tree to save his life."

"I created a vision, an illusion," Dain protested.

"You have mastery over the animals."

"No."

"You can touch the minds of men, read their thoughts perhaps. Oh, your abilities in these areas are not as strong as mine, but I have studied and practiced many years to learn the art of mind spells, while this you do naturally."

"I am not like you!" Dain said sharply. "I do not—"

"Wouldn't you like to increase your powers?" Sulein asked him. "Wouldn't you like to know how to wield them exactly as you wish, to use them for—"

"No!" Dain said. He hurried to the door, but it would not open. Frustrated, he tugged at it, twisting the ring this way and that, but it was locked. He gave the wooden panel a kick and turned back to face the physician.

"When you learn to put aside your fear, when you learn to open your mind to what you truly are, then you will have a future of limitless possibilities," Sulein said.

"I have no desire to be a *sorcerel,*" Dain said defiantly. "Let me go."

"But you were so eager to come inside before."

"That's when I thought you might give back my bard crystal," Dain retorted. "Keeping my property from me is theft."

Anger touched Sulein's eyes, and the air inside the room grew suddenly cold. "I study, Dain," he said after a long silence. "I guard. But I do not steal. Remember that."

Dain stood there, mute and angry, his blood pounding impatiently in his veins. Sulein's words were all lies and trickery. Nothing he said could be trusted.

Outside, the chapel bell began to ring, tolling the deaths solemnly while thunder continued to roll in the skies.

"I must go," Dain said.

"One last thing, and then you may relieve Lord Odfrey's mind. Come over to the light."

Sulein walked away from Dain, leaving him to follow reluctantly. The physician bent over another piece of parchment, writing on it with a glass pen spun from myriad colors that shimmered in the candlelight.

Putting down his pen, he turned around and held up the parchment in front of Dain. "Read what this says."

This time Dain found himself looking at runes, simple ones, written in the old style. New wariness entered him, for many times the old runes contained spells.

"Well?" Sulein prompted.

"I can read this."

"What does it say?"

Dain said nothing.

"What does it say?"

Dain felt a pressure to respond. Angrily he gestured at Sulein. "Stop that! It will not work on me."

The pressure stopped, and Sulein frowned. "Your obstinance is most annoying. Why can you not cooperate even in such a simple matter as this?"

"Because it's not simple," Dain said. "The old runes have power and spells in them. It—" He stopped in mid-sentence and frowned. A memory bobbed to the surface of his mind, and he sent Sulein a sharp look. "These are the runes carved on the band of the old ring in your strongbox. You want to know what they say, but I thought you could read—"

"No," Sulein responded with visible discomfort. "I speak dwarf. I cannot read their runes. At least not very well. What does this legend say?"

"Where did you get the ring?" Dain asked. "What do you want with an old ring like that?"

"Never you mind. Just tell me what the runes say."

Dain hesitated, tilting his head to one side. "You must give back my bard crystal."

Sulein's eyes grew angry. "You would have me defy Lord Odfrey?"

"The spells you practice and seek to learn in here defy him every day," Dain replied.

"I will not return the crystal to you," Sulein said, lifting his chin. "Not until Lord Odfrey commands me to do so."

"Then I won't tell you what the ring says."

Sulein glared at him a long while. Dain stared right back, a tiny smile playing at the corners of his mouth.

In the end, it was Sulein who broke eye contact, "Very well," he said. "You may have your king's glass back."

Dain held out his hand.

Sulein drew himself up with a huff. "Do you doubt my word? Translate the runes."

Dain said nothing, just went on holding out his hand.

Muttering in his beard, Sulein glided over to the strongbox and took it off the shelf. Dain hurried to him and received his pendant. Slipping it around his neck, Dain reached into the box before Sulein could close the lid and grabbed up the ring.

Holding it aloft, he read its inscription loudly, "Solder's ring!"

The stones in the walls of the tower shook slightly, and the ring's great stone glowed with white light.

Sulein turned pale. "Mareesh have mercy!" he cried in horror. Grabbing the ring away from Dain, he threw it back into the box and slammed the lid shut. "Are you mad, invoking its powers like that? It is not to be touched, never to be touched without the greatest care and protection."

Alarmed by the reaction to what he meant as a joke, Dain stared at the physician. "What, exactly, is it?"

Sulein looked shaken. Clutching the strongbox to his chest, he wiped his face with his sleeve. "It is," he said slowly, "what I hoped it to be. A miracle brought to me by the gods and a peddler who sold it into my keeping for a piece of silver. The Ring of Solder," he said, his voice filled with awe.

Dain expected the walls to shake again, but all was now still. "I told you the old runes have spells in them. If I say it again, will the walls shake a second time?"

"Foolish boy, do not joke about things you do not understand," Sulein admonished him sternly.

"So who is Solder?" Dain asked with curiosity. "Not a dwarf king. I've never heard of him."

"Someday you will know the legend," Sulein said. "If you do not already. You are a tangle of lies before me, but I will unravel all of them to find the truth of what you really are and what you really know."

"I am not this missing king you're looking for," Dain said, hoping he wasn't going to start that again. "Believe me, if I were him, I'd—"

"Go away, Dain," Sulein said, sounding tired. He waved his hand across the surface of the door, and it unlocked with an audible click. "I have much to consider. Now that I know this ring of legend truly exists, I must study its powers and safeguard it properly. It is not a toy to be played with."

Dain stepped around him, heading for his escape, but Sulein gripped him by the back of his wet tunic and held him back.

"Say nothing about the ring," he said fiercely. "Not to Lord Odfrey, not to anyone. Swear this to me!"

Dain frowned at him with equal fierceness. "Then grant me one boon."

"Must you barter over everything?"

Dain shrugged. "Blame it on my dwarf upbringing. I will keep silent, if you will part the veils of seeing. Show me who I really am. Show me my father and mother. Give me my past."

He expected Sulein to jump on this. After all, the physician still wanted to name him King of Nether. But instead Sulein frowned and shook his head.

"No," he said portentously. "Not now. I have other things to study."

In a flash, Dain knew the truth. Fresh anger welled up inside him. "You do not know how," he said, his voice rising in disbelief. "The first level of the *sorcerel*'s art, and you know it not. Are your minor spells just smoke and illusion? How can you reach past—"

He stopped, aware that in his anger he was revealing too much knowledge of his own.

Sulein was watching him like a hawk.

Dain glared back at him, then wrenched open the door and strode out. As he went, he chastised himself for letting his temper and pride get the better of his good sense. Sulein had learned too much today. If not for the recovery of his bard crystal, Dain would have believed himself completely the loser of this battle of wills.

He tucked the pendant even farther beneath his wet tunic, patting his chest in comfort at having it back again. He felt stronger now, more confident against the dark forces beyond the walls of this hold. The crystal had no special powers, no magic other than how it made song. But it belonged to the side of nature unsullied by the Nonkind. If he fell into trouble, the crystal's presence would help him keep a clear head. Besides, it was his talisman, his only legacy. It did not belong in a box, locked away in the darkness of a crazed man's workroom, but here, singing softly against his flesh, a part of his spirit in some way he could not define.

The chapel doors were just swinging open to let out the mass-goers when Dain hurried across the courtyard and into the Hall. Skirting the public chambers, he went upstairs to change into dry clothes.

The chamber he shared with the other fosters was empty at the moment. Relieved, Dain flung open the lid of the clothes chest at the foot of his bed and found a new doublet folded neatly atop his meager possessions. Holding it up, Dain gave it a shake to release the folds, and thought the sleeves looked long enough this time. The cloth was sturdy and well woven, dyed a handsome dark red.

It was an unexpected kindness, this gift. Dain did not know who was responsible for it. New clothes usually appeared mysteriously like this at Thirst Hold, just when his seams were bursting or his sleeves had shrunk halfway to his elbows.

A lump closed his throat, and he crushed the doublet in his hands. He did not want to leave Thirst, he realized. He did not want people here to hate him.

The door opened and the page named Hueh looked in. "Thod above, where is the lamp?" he asked in his piping voice, and hurried to light it. "You're wanted by the chevard at once. He saw you in the courtyard, so you'd better hurry."

Dain nodded and stripped off his wet clothing. Clad in a dry pair of leggings, he went to the washing bucket to clean the mud off his hands. While he was still bent over it, the door opened and someone came in.

"Well, well, so Bastard du Stray has come back," Mierre said. "Why don't you put your head in that bucket and drown yourself?"

Slinging water from his hands, Dain straightened and turned around to see the largest of the fosters standing there with his feet straddled and his thumbs hooked in his belt. Mierre's green eyes were as unfriendly as ever.

Beside him stood Kaltienne, like a sly weasel, eyes darting with malice. "Aye," he said with a sneer. "You should have kept running. No one wants a traitor like you back."

Dain frowned. "I am no traitor."

Mierre stepped forward. "Mayhap we should drown you and put an end to the matter."

Kaltienne laughed in an ugly way and started to circle around behind Dain. Quick as thought, Dain ran to his bunk and picked up his dagger. He faced them both, standing light and ready on the balls of his feet. The weapon glinted in the lamp-light, and his would-be tormentors paused.

"If that's the way you want this done," Mierre said, and drew his own dagger.

Kaltienne said nothing, but he also drew his weapon.

Dry-mouthed, Dain swallowed. He was outnumbered and boxed in by the beds. In the corner of the room, the young page watched openmouthed, of no help at all. Dain wanted to tell him to run for help, but thought doing so would be cowardly. He held his tongue.

Mierre came at him, thrusting hard and viciously with his blade. Dain dodged it, but Kaltienne was hemming him in on the other side, giving him scant room to maneuver. Dain jumped over the narrow bed, going behind Mierre, who turned with him.

Mierre tried to block Dain's blow, but Dain's dagger sliced

his arm at the shoulder, ripping cloth. Blood welled up, and Mierre swore savagely.

He attacked, and Dain skipped out of reach, only to have to dodge Kaltienne's thrust. Watching their eyes instead of their blades, Dain could hear his breath whistling in his throat. His heart was pounding loud and furiously. But at the same time, he was curiously excited and hot. He saw the warning flicker in Mierre's green eyes, but Dain leaped forward to meet the larger youth. Ducking under Mierre's dagger thrust, Dain stabbed at him, only to be knocked back by Mierre's free fist.

Staggering, his ears ringing lightly, Dain shook his head to clear it, and barely evaded Kaltienne's clumsy lunge.

"Damne!" Mierre said. "Get him and let's end this."

Dain's head was up. With shining eyes, he threw Mierre a wild grin. "Did you think I would stand still and let you gut me?"

"Demon!" Mierre lunged at him again, hitting Dain with his shoulder and driving him back against the wall.

Dain grunted at the impact, and just in time pulled up his dagger between them to block Mierre's thrust at his belly.

"Heads up!" Kaltienne shouted in warning. "The prince!"

Mierre straightened at once, backing away from Dain and turning to face the doorway.

Dain, breathing hard, his knees suddenly weak, glanced up and saw Prince Gavril standing there, gazing in at them. Gavril wore a doublet of pale blue linen, the cloth woven in a chevron pattern. His leggings were of the same pale color, and his shoes were of thin supple leather. On his golden hair, he wore an embroidered cap tilted at a rakish angle.

His violet-blue eyes swept the faces of everyone in the room, lingering on Dain a moment before going to Mierre.

"Fighting?" he asked with a lift of his brows. "Is this seemly behavior?"

Mierre's face turned red. "Your highness, it is only the pagan traitor. We want him not in here with us."

"Naturally not," Gavril said.

He smiled at Dain, and it was the coldest smile Dain had ever seen. He knew right then that Gavril would not help him.

The prince stepped into the room and turned his gaze on the wide-eyed face of the little page. "You," he said to Hueh, "get out."

Hueh fled without a word, not even glancing in Dain's direction.

Kaltienne had already sheathed his dagger, remembering the rule against drawn weapons in the presence of royalty. He bowed. "I beg your highness's pardon. We just thought we'd teach the pagan a lesson."

Gavril gestured at the door. "Close that, and then you may continue."

Dain stared at him, feeling his spirits sink. Three against one was not good, and he could not think of a way out of this. Gavril was gloating openly, his blue eyes clearly inviting Dain to plead for mercy.

Dain clamped his jaw shut. He wouldn't do it, not even if they strung his entrails from one side of the room to the other.

Kaltienne hastened to slam the door shut. Mierre grinned, and his green eyes narrowed on Dain.

"You must always deliver lessons in private," Gavril said. "Never in front of silly little pages."

"Where's your protector?" Dain called out, using bravado to mask his fear. "Why not make it four against one?"

They took no shame at his words. Gavril laughed and seated himself on a stool. "Finish this quickly," he said. "It's almost time for dinner."

Mierre's grin widened. He sprang at Dain, who ducked away with a nimbleness the larger youth couldn't match. Mierre was very strong, but not agile. From the corner of his eye, Dain watched for Kaltienne, always sneaking to get at Dain's back like the coward he was.

With Gavril clearly anticipating some good entertainment, Dain felt determined to best both of these bullies, if only to wipe the smug smiles off their faces. He would have preferred to attack Gavril and see blood splatter across that pretty pale doublet, but right now he had to concentrate on Mierre.

Lunging at Kaltienne, Dain slashed viciously with his dagger in the way Sir Nynth had taught him. Moving his arm up and down in a blur of movement, he attacked with force, driving Kaltienne back until the boy stumbled into one of the beds and fell with a cry of fear.

Dain slashed at his exposed stomach and missed, for at the same moment Mierre gripped him by his shoulder and pulled him back. Dain twisted desperately to avoid being impaled on

Mierre's dagger. He felt the tip rake his ribs, bringing a swift burning of pain and the trickle of blood.

Cursing in the dwarf tongue, Dain ducked and spun, plunging his dagger up at Mierre's vitals.

Mierre blocked the thrust with his blade, and for a moment the two weapons locked. They strained against each other until the tendons knotted in Mierre's thick neck and Dain felt his muscles tremble with effort.

Mierre bared his large, yellowed teeth. His green eyes, savage and merciless, glared down into Dain's.

"Finish him! Finish him!" Kaltienne was shouting.

Dain felt himself giving beneath the other boy's greater strength. With all his will and might, Dain struggled to hold firm. Sweat poured down his face, stinging his eyes. His back was bleeding, but the pain fired his determination all the more. He would not give way. He would not.

But Mierre kept pushing him down, and Dain felt his knees shaking and starting to buckle despite all he could do. Once he was forced to kneel, his throat would be level with Mierre's blade, and too easy a target.

A week past, Mierre would not have dared kill him, for Dain was the favorite of the knights. But today, after the battle with the Nonkind, when everyone seemed to be blaming Dain somehow, he wondered if Mierre would even take punishment.

Dain struggled to disengage his dagger, but Mierre had such pressure on his hand, twisting there, that the blades remained locked. Dain's whole arm was shaking now from the strain. His knees failed him, and Mierre drove him down.

"Now!" Kaltienne shouted.

Mierre twisted his wrist to unlock the dagger guards. Already Dain could feel how Mierre intended to draw his arm horizontally, slashing Dain's throat in one clean stroke.

But as Mierre disengaged, Dain lunged at him and with his head butted Mierre right between his legs.

Mierre howled a shrill, piercing cry of pain. Dain overbalanced him, sending Mierre toppling to the floor.

Dain scrambled on top of him and pinned him while a white-faced Mierre, his knees drawn up, clutched himself.

Gripping the front of his tunic, Dain put the point of his dagger to Mierre's throat and lifted his gaze to Gavril.

The prince had risen to his feet, and was staring at Dain with a mixture of fury and horror.

Behind Dain, Kaltienne was shouting, "Foul trickster! Honorless cheat!"

Ignoring him, Dain kept his gaze on the prince. "Well?" he asked, breathing hard. "Is this the lesson you had in mind?"

Red spots burned on Gavril's cheeks. Before he could reply, however, Kaltienne loosed a hoarse cry and launched himself at Dain's back.

Too late, Dain tried to turn to face his attack. Kaltienne's dagger point skidded across his shoulder blade and gouged into the back of his arm.

Pain blossomed there, and Dain's cry was being engulfed by Kaltienne's furious screaming, when suddenly the door slammed open as though it had been kicked and Sir Roye came rushing inside.

"What's all this?" he demanded.

Gavril pointed at Dain and Kaltienne, who were locked in a struggle atop Mierre. "Stop them at once," he commanded. "Sir Roye, I have ordered them repeatedly to stop, but they will not heed me."

Swearing, Sir Roye gripped Kaltienne and heaved him away, sending him sprawling. His bloody dagger went clattering across the floor. Dain barely had time to drag in a short, gasping breath before Sir Roye yanked him upright.

"Thod's bones," he swore, glaring at Dain as though this was somehow his fault. "Are you bad hurt?"

Bleeding and rigid with agony, Dain could not find enough breath to answer. Sir Roye gave Mierre a nudge with his foot.

"You, get up," he said without compassion.

Mierre rolled onto his side and groaned.

By now Kaltienne was floundering to his feet. Glaring, he pointed at Dain. "He's a pagan cheat and traitor! He does not belong in here with us."

"Aye, that's true enough," Sir Roye muttered. He still had his hand on Dain's uninjured arm, supporting him. His yellow eyes glared at them all, then he glanced over his shoulder at Hueh, who was peeping openmouthed into the room. "You!" he ordered. "Collect these daggers and take them out of here. Now!"

"Yes, Sir Roye." The boy scuttled into the room and picked

up Mierre's dagger where it lay on the floor, then Kaltienne's. At last he came to Dain, who alone still clutched his weapon.

The page's head came only to Dain's waist. His face held the roundness of babyhood, despite his six or seven years. Brown curls framed his face. If he had fetched Sir Roye, then Dain knew he owed this child his life.

Seeing Hueh's fear, Dain managed a smile that was nearly a grimace and flipped his dagger over to hand it hilt-first to the child.

The page's eyes brightened, and in that moment hero worship filled his face. He took Dain's dagger and stepped back.

"Fighting in the presence of the prince," Sir Roye was scolding them all. "You know better, all of you. It's forbidden to draw weapons before him. Morde a day, you deserve more than flogging. Your highness," he said gruffly, "where is Sir Los?"

Gavril shrugged. "I gave him leave for the evening. I thought myself safe enough in the Hall."

"Apparently not," Sir Roye said.

"We weren't attacking *him*," Dain said, but Sir Roye shook him so hard he cried out with pain.

"Silence! No one gave you leave to speak. Come on," he said, pulling Dain toward the door. "Out with you. Mierre and Kaltienne, clean yourselves up. And get this room put back to rights."

Not waiting for any of them to reply, Sir Roye jerked a stiff little bow in Gavril's direction and marched Dain out.

As soon as they were in the corridor, Dain tried to explain, but Sir Roye refused to listen. In grim silence Dain was taken to the bathing chamber, deserted now except for two servants trying to mop up spilled water and gather up the towels someone had tossed about.

Sir Roye pushed Dain onto a stool. "Sit."

When he began probing at Dain's cuts, his fingers were far more gentle than his tone of voice.

"Shallow, most of it. Just one spot that's deep. You'll do," he said with gruff relief. Tearing some strips off a towel, he bound Dain up efficiently.

"Thank you," Dain said.

Sir Roye glared at him, his dark weathered face as stern as ever. "I want you in good shape for the flogging that awaits you. Deserting the hold and Thod knows what else."

Dain frowned, anxious to vindicate himself. "I didn't do anything wrong. I just went with Lander to buy sword metal."

"Explain yourself to the chevard," Sir Roye said without interest, tossing the bloody cloths into a heap on the floor. "I'm not your judge."

"Why won't anyone believe me?" Dain asked. "I didn't bring the Nonkind here—"

"Who says you did?" Sir Roye asked sharply.

Dain hunched his shoulders. "Everyone."

"Daft nonsense," Sir Roye said. "The raids came from the south. That's why Lunt Hold sent warnings. Their lands have been raided too."

Relief filled Dain. He smiled at the protector, glad at last to find someone who believed him.

Sir Roye scowled back. "Get yourself dressed and go to his lordship's wardroom."

"Yes, sir," Dain said, still smiling. "Thank you for your help."

Sir Roye refused to meet his gaze. "I do not want your thanks."

"You saved my life."

"The page did!" Sir Roye protested fiercely. "Running to me and bawling like a babe."

"I must thank him too," Dain said.

"You'll report to the chevard, the way you were told to the moment you set foot in the hold. Thod's bones, brawling before the prince. If he chooses to be offended, you're in for it."

"But I—"

"And you can thank whatever pagan deities you pray and blaspheme before that Sir Los wasn't there. He'd have gutted you the moment you drew your dagger. Gods! Have you not learned any sense in all the time you've been among us?"

"They attacked me," Dain began. "I had to defend myself."

"Brawl with your fists, you dolt, when the prince is there."

"I had little choice in the matter," Dain said stiffly, his back rigid with resentment. "I did not start the fight."

"And what does that matter?" Sir Roye said without a trace of compassion. "Sir Polquin has taught you that a knight commands his combat. If honor requires, you move it to a place that's—"

"And if you have no choice?" Dain asked hotly. "If there's no honor shown?"

Sir Roye's single eye was stony. "Honor is *your* responsibility. You don't don it or discard it according to the situation. That's where you will never be one of us, boy."

"I—"

"Enough of this talk. I am no keeper of yours, nay, and no teacher either. You have enough of those, and your head must be made of bone for all the good their work has done."

Dain opened his mouth, but Sir Roye held up his hand for silence.

"As soon as you're done with his lordship, you go collect your gear and report to housekeeping. They'll house you elsewhere than the fosters' room. You never should have been in there in the first place."

His censure stung. Dain looked down, frowning. "I am glad to get away from Mierre and Kaltienne." It was the truth he spoke, but he knew what Sir Roye meant. No doubt the protector thought he should be sleeping in the stables, if even in the hold at all. Glancing up, Dain added, "Could Thum and I share a chamber?"

"Nay," Sir Roye said with a snort of disgust. "Thum, for all his spindly ways, has at least enough sense to stay out of trouble. He doesn't need to mix with the likes of you. None of them do. I told his lordship you'd bring grief to the place and sure enough you have."

"I—"

"Keep your tongue!" Sir Roye said gruffly. "Now jump to, and do as you've been told! I've wasted enough time with you."

Dain sat there on the stool, seething from all the criticism. It was not fair that he should be blamed for first the battle and now this fight with the fosters. Why had Sir Roye bothered to save him if he thought Dain this worthless?

"Boy!" Sir Roye barked. "On your feet like I said. If you feel faint, I'll pour one of the physician's potions down your gullet, but get to moving now. Any more dallying will be an open insult to his lordship, and then I'm within my duty to take you to the flogging block for that if naught else."

Dain gritted his teeth and rose to his feet. His eyes, hot with anger, met Sir Roye's. The protector gave him a stiff nod and walked out.

22

WALKING STIFFLY OUT of the bathing chamber with his wounded arm cradled against his side, Dain nearly collided with Thum, who was hurrying along the passageway.

Thum jumped back from him, holding up his hands to ask pardon. "Dain!" he said anxiously. "Are you much hurt? Hueh said you were bleeding—"

"Some cuts," Dain said grimly. "I will live."

Thum's freckled face lit up with relief. His red hair lay plastered dark and wet against his head; rain had spotted his doublet. He sported a black eye that was healing in several vivid hues, giving his thin, rather serious face a rakish look. In one hand, he carried Dain's new wine-colored doublet.

"I'm glad you're not bad hurt," he said. "From the way Hueh's been telling it, I thought you were carried away swooning and bloody in Sir Roye's arms."

Little Hueh, Dain thought darkly, had been helpful, but the page had better not go embellishing the tale of what had transpired. Dain shook his head at Thum. "Do you really think Sir Roye would be that tender?" he asked with scorn.

Thum grinned. "Had you waited another few minutes, I would have been there to help you fight the oafs."

"Be glad you weren't," Dain said, reaching for his doublet. "You're the only one of us not in trouble. Well, you and Prince Gavril."

"I know." Thum gripped Dain's uninjured arm to usher him back inside the bathing chamber. "Here, I will help you get dressed."

He took the doublet from Dain's hands and threw it over Dain's head. With quick but gentle tugs, he pulled it down over Dain's shoulders. "Tell me if I hurt you."

Dain was gritting his teeth with pain as he twisted his arm to fit it into a sleeve, but he said nothing. The new doublet was roomy and comfortable, large enough to allow for more growth. Pleased with it, Dain smoothed his hand down the front while Thum belted on his dagger for him.

"You're in greater trouble than just the fight, you know,"

Thum murmured quietly, keeping an eye on the servants, who were still cleaning the chamber and clearly trying to eavesdrop. "Thod's mercy, Dain, what made you run away like that?"

"Not you as well!" Dain cried in dismay. "How can everyone think so ill of me? I went with the smith, that's all. If I'd known the Nonkind were going to attack Thirst, I would have been here to help fight."

"They didn't attack Thirst. Who is spreading *that* tale?" Thum replied. "But it was bad enough, by what I've heard. None of us fosters were allowed in the battle, thanks to you and Mierre."

Dain frowned. "What do you mean? Am I to be blamed next for lightning striking the tower? For the sky turning dark? For the rain that's falling? What else?"

"Do not turn your bad temper on me. You asked what's amiss, and I am only telling you."

"I am not angry at you," Dain said by way of apology.

Thum nodded, then sighed gloomily. "What's all the practice and training for, if we're to be kept in the hold with the women and children?"

"Saw you none of the battle?" Dain asked in sympathy.

"Nay, not one blow."

"Who gave such an order, keeping you home?"

"Sir Bosquecel. He said we were lazy, unprepared louts who couldn't bear arms any better than the serfs."

Dain blinked in astonishment. "But that's not true. Nor is it fair."

"None of this is fair," Thum said. "You have no idea of how angry he is. Well, they all are. Squabbles and quarreling in all directions, for days now. And once the Lunt knights came, there's been trouble with them as well. They eat like horses and drink like fish. And gamble? Morde! But it's worst between Sir Polquin and Sir Bosquecel. They blame each other for what happened. It looked like they might come to blows on the practice field the day of the contest, and they are not speaking to each other still."

Dain frowned, trying to make sense of all this. "Because I left the contest?"

"Nay, because of Mierre. Oh, I tell you, Dain, you and he both have caused more upset this week than I could think of to do in a year."

"I wish you would tell your story straight and not jump from one thing to another," Dain complained. "I do not understand what happened."

"Well, and while there was all the trouble over the contest and Mierre, you were discovered missing."

"I left in plain sight with Lander," Dain said defensively.

"Aye, so the guards said. But Lander told no one where he was going, nor did you. Lord Odfrey believed you would not stay with the smith but instead strike out on your own. And then Lord Renald rode in with news of Nonkind raiders. Lord Odfrey sent men out searching near and far for you. He was certain you'd be killed."

"I've been dodging Nonkind all my life," Dain said with a shrug. "He had no need to worry."

"Well, he did, just the same. And so did Sir Terent and Sir Polquin—and all of us."

Dain frowned, feeling bad. "I did not mean for anyone to worry. I was fine."

"Lord Renald was angered that men were spared to search. He said everyone was needed for fighting, even fosters. That's when Lord Odfrey forbade any of us, from the prince down to yours truly, to leave the hold."

Uncomfortable, knowing he'd done wrong to cause them such concern, Dain changed the subject. "Who won the contest?"

"Mierre, of course."

Dain hissed through his teeth. He was not surprised, but the idea of that hulking bully serving Lord Odfrey infuriated him. From now on it would be Mierre who burnished the chevard's armor, Mierre who honed and polished his weapons, Mierre who fed his dogs, Mierre who rode at the chevard's flank along with Sir Roye. Dain had wanted that position with all his heart, for he craved Lord Odfrey's attention. He wanted to repay the man for his kindness this year by serving him better than any squire had done before. But instead it would be Mierre, churlish and lazy, at Lord Odfrey's side. Before today's attack, Dain had always disliked Mierre, but now he hated him as much as he hated the prince. They were two of a kind, cruel and self-centered. How could Lord Odfrey stand to have Mierre in his service?

"And you, Thum?" Dain asked irritably. "Couldn't you find

a way to defeat him that day? I would have had the honor go to you."

"Thank you, but once I was unhorsed by Mierre's lance, that finished me." Thum touched his face proudly. "That's how I came by this."

Dain admired his puffy and discolored eye. "I have never seen a better one. Did it hurt much?"

"No," Thum boasted. "Well, not much. But you should have seen it the first night, swelled out to here. I couldn't open my eye, and Sulein thought I might lose it."

"Like Sir Roye," Dain said, both revolted and fascinated by the idea.

"I'm glad to have my sight as good as ever," Thum said, betraying his relief. "It would be hard to earn my knight's spurs with only one eye. I had no balance while it was swelled so, and I kept bumping into things."

"If you're going to lose an eye, it should be after you're knighted and happen while you're in a great battle," Dain told him. "Not in a small contest with padded weapons."

"Aye," Thum agreed fervently. He placed his hand over his heart. Making a fancy bow, he said in falsetto voice, "And now, dear maiden fair, let me tell you how I came by my scar. Neither in battle nor in king's joust, but only by riding full tilt into my practice opponent's lance like a dolt and unhorsing myself."

Dain laughed. "Unhorsed by the quintain."

Thum laughed with him. "Aye! Mierre is stupid enough to *be* a practice dummy."

Dain puffed out his chest and spun about stiffly in an effort to imitate Mierre, but it made his arm hurt and he stopped the play with a wince.

Thum sobered abruptly. "But you have taken real injury at his hands. Is it true what little Hueh says, that both the blackguards fought you at once?"

Dain hesitated, but he saw no reason to deny it. "Aye," he said grimly. "They did. Pagans deserve no honorable treatment, I suppose."

"Do not say that!" Thum said angrily. He scowled. "The cowards. They are both bad to the heart. The day they leave this hold can't come too soon for me."

"Leave?" Dain echoed in puzzlement. "But if Mierre is Lord Odfrey's squire—"

"But he *isn't*!" Thum said. His hazel eyes danced with more news. "I wish you had stayed to see it. The contest ended, with me on the ground and my mouth full of dirt, and Mierre was declared winner. Sir Terent looked like he'd eaten sour fruit, and Sir Nynth would not applaud."

Imagining it, Dain smiled. "What happened? Did Lord Odfrey refuse to have him? That's wise, for he—"

"Nay!" Thum said. "Let me tell you. Lord Odfrey had his stone face on—you know how he looks at times."

"Aye," Dain said ruefully. "I know very well."

"He stood before us with Sir Polquin and Sir Roye flanking him, and he conferred the offer of squire on Mierre according to the rules of the contest." Thum paused and gripped Dain's arm hard. "Mierre turned him down."

Dain gasped. "What?"

"Aye. Turned him down with cool hauteur, like Lord Odfrey was dirt to him. It's plain he's learned that manner from the prince, but it did him no credit. Sir Bosquecel was furious, and Sir Polquin more so. Everyone witnessed the grave insult to Lord Odfrey, but we could not believe it. Had Mierre refused such an offer from a sentry-rank knight, I might understand. But no one turns down the chance to be a chevard's squire, especially a warrior of such valor and repute as our Lord Odfrey."

Dain frowned, angry on Lord Odfrey's behalf, though relieved as well. Still, it made no sense. "But why would Mierre refuse? Does he think another knight will offer him a better position? Where? Can his father provide—"

"Rumor has it . . ." Thum paused dramatically, his hazel eyes dancing. "Promise you will not spread it, Dain."

"I am the last person in this hold to know about the matter," Dain said tartly. "Where would I spread such news? Speak!"

"Well, the rumor in the guardhouse is that Mierre is hoping to be named Prince Gavril's squire."

"That surprises me not," Dain said. "No one toadies to Gavril more than he does."

"But it's an awful risk."

"Why? Gavril favors him."

"But the prince is not yet knighted. He can take no squire until he has his spurs."

"In a month he'll have them," Dain said. "I see no risk if the prince has promised him—"

"But has he?" Thum asked.

Dain frowned. "Has he not?"

"Nothing has been said officially."

"What has that to do with anything?"

"Dain, don't you understand court politics at all?"

"No," Dain said defensively. "How could I?"

"Oh. When Gavril's knighted, he is going to be named Heir to the Realm. That means the nobles acknowledge him as the official successor to the throne."

"I thought he already was," Dain said.

"Nay."

"He gives himself enough airs."

"Wait until he's knighted," Thum said darkly. "There'll be no holding him back then. But it's certain that his squire has already been chosen and will be the son of a duc or cardinal, someone of the first rank. Gavril is far too important to be squired by an uplander of minor lineage."

Dain thought of Mierre, a young oaf who clearly burned with ambition to better himself. "There's been a promise made between them," he guessed. "And no matter what the custom may be, Gavril does what he wants."

"Not in affairs of state. He can't," Thum argued. "Just as his marriage has been planned for him from birth to his cousin Pheresa. There is no official engagement as yet, for the Heir to the Realm must do his own choosing of a bride. But by custom it must—or at least *should*—be this lady. Everyone at court, especially the king, expects Gavril to ask her."

"I hope she is a hag and her face sours his breakfast every morning," Dain said.

Thum laughed. "Mierre is gambling heavily, but I think he will be the loser by aiming too high."

"So who is going to be Lord Odfrey's squire?" Dain asked.

The merriment dimmed from Thum's eyes and he shook his head. "I know not. It's something no one dares ask him, for the chevard's mood has been dark indeed this week. Why did you leave the contest grounds, Dain? You were right to be angry. I would have been too, but you should have stayed out of courtesy."

Dain stared at his friend, and saw disappointment lurking in Thum's bruised face. He understood then that Thum had wanted him to stay and cheer for him.

Contrition filled Dain. He put out his hand. "I am sorry," he said quietly. "You think me a poor friend."

Thum gripped his hand. "Nay," he said loyally. "Not poor, but sometimes hard to understand."

Dain sighed. "You must teach me how to do better. My ways are not yours. I do not mean to offend you."

"It's Lord Odfrey you must not offend," Thum said.

Dain's eyes flew wide open. "Oh, gods! The chevard! I should have reported to him long ago. If he was angry with me before, I have little chance of appeasing him now."

"Damne, you will have no appeal," Thum agreed worriedly. "I beg your pardon for chattering so long."

Dain headed for the door, and Thum went with him.

"Dain, you look mortal pale in the face. Are you feeling faint?"

"Nay," Dain answered, his courage sinking like a lead weight. "Though I wish I *could* faint and put off this meeting."

"You dare not."

"Better to get it over with." Swallowing hard, Dain wished he'd never left the hold now. Even the two gold pieces in his pocket were not worth all this. His own angry defiance had faded. He understood plainly why Lord Odfrey must be infuriated with him. And the chevard's temper was never easy to face. Dain sent Thum a look of appeal. "Stay with me?"

"Aye," Thum said like the stalwart friend he was. Of course, since he was not in disgrace he had little to fear, Dain reminded himself.

Together they headed for Lord Odfrey's wardroom.

Sentry knights stood on duty outside Lord Odfrey's door. Servants were walking down the length of the passageway, lighting torches that drove back the shadows. The servants cast Dain sharp, speculative looks and whispered among themselves.

His face felt hot. Stiffly, he walked past them, pretending he did not notice.

One of the knights, Sir Blait, held up his hand to stop Dain's approach. "I'll relieve you of your dagger, Dain," he said gruffly.

Dain's throat closed up with embarrassment and anger. Beside him, Thum began to murmur about offense and insult, but Dain elbowed him to be quiet.

In silence, his face stiff and hot, he drew his dagger and handed it over hilt-first.

"Will you take mine as well, Sir Blait?" Thum asked hotly.

Sir Blait was gray-haired and stooped. Since his knees had begun to stiffen and ache he'd been demoted to sentry duty. Sour-tempered and gruff, he looked annoyed by Thum's remark. He said, "Nay, I have my orders. You know better than to spout your mouth where it's not wanted."

Thum's face turned red, but Dain did not want his friend to join him in disgrace.

"Thum," he said, his voice low and firm, "thank you, but perhaps you'd better go to your supper."

"I said I'd stay with you and I will."

Dain shook his head. "This trouble is mine now. Go and eat supper for us both."

Thum scowled and opened his mouth to protest, then understanding dawned in his eyes. It was likely that Dain would get no supper tonight, and Thum could gather enough food to slip to him later. "I will," Thum said. He touched Dain's shoulder briefly as though to give him encouragement, then left.

Sir Blait scowled at Dain and tapped on the door. "He's here, m'lord," he called out.

Lord Odfrey's voice responded, and Sir Blait pushed open the door. Without going in, Dain could see the chevard at his desk, which was piled high with dispatch scrolls, scraps of vellum and parchment, and a heavy book secured with a lock. One of Lord Odfrey's dogs lay snoring softly against the base of the massive wooden desk. The chevard's boots stood by the empty hearth. The chevard himself sat in a pool of golden candlelight that cast shadows across the angle of his cheekbones and the firm jut of his chin. He wore an old-fashioned tunic of dark gray cloth, and from his shoulders down he blended into the shadows. When he lifted his gaze to meet Dain's, his dark eyes looked fathomless.

"Enter," he said harshly. "I've waited long enough."

Dain gave Lord Odfrey a quick, nervous glance. Squaring his shoulders, he winced slightly and stepped over the threshold. Sir Blait shut the door behind him, and Dain felt suddenly short of breath and hemmed in by this small, cluttered room.

It was very warm. No evening breeze blew through the small window, although Dain smelled rain on the air. He also caught the faintest whiff of Nonkind on the chevard's boots. It unsettled him.

Lord Odfrey went back to his writing. In the silence Dain could hear the faint scratching of the chevard's pen across the parchment. Knowing he was being tested, knowing he must not interrupt, Dain swallowed a sigh of impatience and wished he dared sit, for his knees were feeling weak and his arm throbbed. His famished stomach growled while he listened to faraway sounds of lute music and the clatter in the Hall that accompanied supper.

A tall-backed chair, handsomely carved, faced Lord Odfrey's desk. It looked ornate enough for a lord to sit on. Dain dared not touch it. A map lay thrown across its back. A beautiful thing, the map was colorfully illustrated with vivid inks of scarlet and indigo and green. Tilting his head, Dain studied the geography of Mandria, illustrated with splendid meadows, streams where rainbow-hued fish leaped, and an ornate palace topped by a crown that must represent Savroix, seat of Mandrian kings. Nold was drawn much smaller, and bordered by drawings of crossed axes. Many trees were sketched close together to represent the Dark Forest. Nold's ore-rich mountains were not drawn on the map at all, and the four largest dwarf settlements were marked in the wrong places. Klad was placed north of Nold and was a land Dain knew little about. He recognized it by the drawings of tents and herds of horned cattle. A small portrait of a bearded barbarian with small squinty eyes and long braids of blond hair showed Dain the type of folk who must live there. Jorb had told Dain about selling a sword to a Kladite many years ago, but the Kladites seldom ventured beyond their own borders. They were said to eat hardened milk flavored with blood and to count their wealth by how many cows and wives they owned.

Curious to see Nether, Dain leaned forward to look at the rest of the map.

"Where have you been?" Lord Odfrey demanded. His voice was stern and harsh, his tone unforgiving.

Startled, Dain jumped and met Lord Odfrey's dark eyes. They looked almost black with anger. Dain's answer tangled in his throat. It all seemed suddenly too long and difficult to explain. He could not decide where to start or how to say it.

"Dain, I'll not ask you again."

Thus warned, Dain took refuge in defiance. He shrugged. "I was seeing the world."

Lord Odfrey's fist slammed atop his desk, making a candle jump. "Damne, boy! I'll brook none of your flippancy. You've been in this hold since chapel let out, perhaps longer. Why didn't you report to me at once?"

"I—"

"Did you think me unaware of your arrival? Sir Terent sent word from the gates immediately. He should have escorted you straight here himself. No doubt he thought he could trust you to follow orders. Clearly he was wrong."

Embarrassment flooded Dain. "I had—"

A knock on the door interrupted him. Lord Renald came tramping in without ceremony. He still wore his mail and stained surcoat, but had left his helmet and gauntlets elsewhere. With his brown hair curling almost to his shoulders, the chevard of Lunt looked young, hardly more than twenty. He wore no marriage ring on his hand, but a very fine sapphire ring glittered on his thumb. Dain caught himself mentally apprais-ing its value, then looked away quickly.

Lord Renald stared at Dain with a lift of his brows, but it was to Lord Odfrey that he spoke: "So here he is."

"Yes, finally," Lord Odfrey snapped.

There was no gladness in his voice, no relief, no relenting. Dain frowned, and his own anger and resentment came surging back.

Neither man, however, was paying Dain any heed.

"Forgive me, Odfrey," Lord Renald said, frowning. "My man had orders to see him safely into your hands, but he failed."

"Aye, that he did," Lord Odfrey said grimly.

"I have questioned Sir Metain. It seems he thought deliver-ing the boy within your walls good enough. I've dealt with that misconception."

Lord Odfrey nodded while Dain looked from one to the other, still wondering what they were talking about. "It is no fault of yours, Renald," Lord Odfrey said bleakly. "At least you found him and brought him back."

Frowning, Dain tried to protest. "But I was on my way home—"

"Aye, I found the young devil. Jaunting along in a mule cart with a Netheran." Lord Renald shot Dain a look of distrust and suspicion. "What enchantment did he bear, to be able to pass through the river lands without even a scratch, while the befouled ran there, killing as they pleased? Had I known, had I suspected him of being an assassin, I would have—"

"Enough," Lord Odfrey said, lifting his hand.

"Assassin?" Dain said, unable to keep quiet. "Me? But I am not!"

"They've called for him," Lord Renald said, ignoring Dain's outburst. "They want an accounting."

Lord Odfrey scowled in visible exasperation. "Nonsense. It's a ridiculous accusation, and a waste of time. He—"

"It must be done, Odfrey. The vote was just cast for trial."

A bleak, defeated expression entered Lord Odfrey's face. He rubbed his eyes and pinched the bridge of his nose a moment as though fatigued. "The fools play into the prince's hands," he murmured. "Morde! I hoped it would not come to this. A quiet talk here would do as well. Why must he make a huge drama of the matter?"

Lord Renald's face held no expression, but his eyes were not unkind. They flicked to Dain's face, then returned to Lord Odfrey. "Let me take the eld to them. You need not come."

"Take me where?" Dain asked suspiciously, feeling the urge to escape.

Lord Odfrey rose to his feet. "Thank you, but no. Dain is my responsibility. I brought him into the hold last winter. I brought this risk to his highness. I will see the matter through to its end."

"As you wish," Lord Renald said with a slight bow. "Will it damage your standing with the king?"

Lord Odfrey gestured impatiently. "I cannot be worried with that now."

"Best you do think of it. It's unwise to lose the king's friendship."

"We are a long way from court."

"A private messenger from the prince has already been turned back at your gates and prevented from leaving," Lord Renald said. "And how will that be interpreted?"

"Damne!" Lord Odfrey said. "Prince Gavril schemes like a churchman. He has forced this trial on us and now he tries to bring a higher authority into it. Morde a day, if his highness wants a trial he'll have it, but we'll hold to the law on every point. The truth of this will be decided by my knights and yours. No one else, for that is the law."

"Mandrian law for an eld?" Lord Renald asked softly.

Lord Odfrey's face was stone. "There will be no church inquisitor in my Hall."

Dain stared at them both, his mouth open with alarm. He did not yet understand what was wrong or how he could be accused of a crime worth trial and possible inquisitors, but he knew himself to be in dire trouble.

"What has the prince said against me?" he demanded. He thought of this afternoon's attack, while Gavril sat and watched, smiling. A cold chill ran through Dain, and with it came anger, deep and strong. Sir Roye had tried, in his gruff, hostile way, to warn him that more trouble lay ahead. But Dain hadn't expected it to come this fast. "Lord," he said to Odfrey, "please tell me what I stand accused of. A drawn weapon in his presence? But I was already fighting when the prince entered—"

"Say nothing of this to me!" Lord Odfrey snapped. "You will speak to the assembly."

"But I tell you the truth!" Dain said desperately.

"It's too late to appeal to me now," Lord Odfrey said harshly. "You defied me by running away. And now you have attacked Prince Gavril."

"No!" Dain said, horrified. In a flash, he finally understood. Gavril's evil, lying tongue had twisted everything. "Lord, you must listen to me. It was—"

"The assembly will listen to you," Lord Odfrey said, cutting him off. "Master your fear."

"I did no wrong," Dain insisted. "Hueh was a witness to what occurred. Sir Roye as well—"

"Dain, be silent!" Lord Odfrey said. "We cannot settle this now. If you are innocent, then you must prove that to the knights."

Dain stopped his explanations, feeling desperation clawing inside his chest. How could he explain? Who would believe his word above the prince's? Bitterness twisted inside him, and in his mind he could hear Thia saying, *"Trust not men, Dain. They will always turn and betray you."*

Lord Renald set his hand gently on Dain's shoulder. "Better I take him now."

"No," Lord Odfrey said in a voice like iron. There was fear in him, and Dain's sense of alarm grew. If Lord Odfrey was worried about him, then truly he stood little chance.

Lord Odfrey shook his head. "Thank you, Renald, but please go and tell them that I'll bring him in a few minutes." The chevard's gaze swung back to Dain and narrowed. "He must account to *me* first."

"Be not long," Lord Renald advised him. "The more wine they drink and the longer they talk, the more trouble can brew."

"Dain's delay has already done the most harm," Lord Odfrey said bleakly. "More will matter little."

This remark did not seem to impress Lord Renald. "It will be better if he appears of his own accord. If they must come for him, it will look black against him indeed."

He left with that ominous remark.

Dain frowned at Lord Odfrey. "Who will take my word instead of his?" he asked without hope. "Even you do not believe in my innocence."

"How can I when you have defied me so boldly?" Lord Odfrey retorted.

"I was angry."

"Anger maketh a fool," Lord Odfrey said as though quoting someone.

Dain flushed hot. For a moment he wanted to shout curses at the chevard. But when he saw the anguish in Lord Odfrey's dark eyes, Dain's throat choked up and he could not stay angry. He had tried so hard in recent months to gain this man's respect. Now he saw how deeply he had disappointed Lord Odfrey. But Lord Odfrey needed to understand how much he had hurt Dain as well.

Swallowing hard, Dain said, "I wanted to prove myself to you. I wanted to make you proud of me. When you withdrew me from the contest, I was angry, for I wanted to try, even if I entered at a disadvantage."

"But why run away over something so trivial?" Lord Odfrey asked.

"It was not trivial to me."

Lord Odfrey frowned, and for a long moment there was silence between them.

Dain broke it with a sigh. "I will never be a knight, will I?"

Lord Odfrey's brows knotted. "Dain—"

"I am eld. Neither Mandrian nor one of the faithful." Dain shrugged. "When the knights let me sit and listen to their tales in the guardhouse, I felt as though I belonged. When they taught me swordplay, I could forget what I am. But there is no true acceptance for one such as myself."

"Dain, I sought to protect you from harm," Lord Odfrey said, looking upset. "I feared Mierre would hurt you cruelly on the field, and conceal it as a jousting injury."

"Strange," Dain said, unable to believe him. "Mierre's dagger wounded me today, and now that I am accused of a terrible act I did not commit, you believe them, not me. How does that protect me from harm?"

"It will be the knights who judge you, not I," Lord Odfrey said.

That answer was meaningless, for Lord Odfrey still refused to take his side. Dain stared at him, hurt beyond measure.

Someone pounded on the door. "My lord, bid us enter!"

With a start, Lord Odfrey glanced in that direction. "Wait!" he called.

Dain heard an impatient murmur of male voices outside the door, and Sir Blait growling a response. Fear dried Dain's mouth. If he could not sway Lord Odfrey, how could he prove himself to the rest? Would they let Hueh speak on his behalf? Would the child tell the truth, or lie? It took courage to accuse the prince publicly of lying.

I shall do it, Dain promised himself grimly. *Though they cut out my tongue for it, I shall make them hear how infamous their prince is.*

The pounding came again on the door, more insistent this time.

Dain looked at Lord Odfrey in appeal. "Lord, tell me the law I am to be judged by. If I am to defend myself, I must know how."

Lord Odfrey flung his ink pot at the wall. It shattered there, blotching the wall with a huge indigo stain. "Damne! Had you come straight to me, you would have had no opportunity to attack Gavril. I am certain he provoked you, but why in Thod's name were you so foolish?"

"Open your ears to my words," Dain said. "I did not attack

the prince. Not once. Not in any fashion. He came to watch while Mierre and Kaltienne fought me. Sir Roye told me I was wrong to have my weapon drawn in his presence, but was I to sheathe my dagger to avoid offending his highness, and let them stab me?"

Lord Odfrey closed his eyes as though in pain. He drew in a sharp breath and opened them again. "You will swear to this?"

"Aye, of course I will swear to it," Dain said fervently.

"Truth is the only defense you have."

"My word against Gavril's." Dain sighed. "Will Hueh be allowed to speak for me? Will Sir Roye?"

Lord Odfrey's eyes were dark with anguish. He hesitated a moment before he said, "I have sent Sir Roye away. He is delivering a message from me to Geoffen du Maltie."

Dain stared in disbelief. Cold chills ran down his arms. "Why?" he whispered.

"Thod help me, to save his life," Lord Odfrey answered. His face held momentary despair, then it grew harsh again. "The man has been my protector since I won my spurs of knighthood. I will not let him risk his life by calling the prince a liar."

The coldness in Dain spread. "And Hueh?" he asked.

"The child, by law, is too young to speak."

Dain shivered, turned away, and went to stand by the window. He stared blindly outside, his heart pounding heavily. "Then I am doomed."

Lord Odfrey came up behind him. He touched Dain's shoulder, but Dain flinched away.

"Forgive me," Lord Odfrey said quietly. "They are innocents and I cannot let them be harmed by what has befallen you."

"Of course," Dain said bitterly. "As an eld, I am permitted no defense."

"No!" Lord Odfrey spun him around and glared at him. "Damne, boy! I would rather fall in battle than lose you. I lost one son. I do not—cannot lose another."

"I am not your son," Dain said harshly.

"No."

Dain flung up his chin, facing the man. "Would you defend me if I were?"

Lord Odfrey clenched his jaw so hard a muscle leaped there. "In Thod's name, how can I? When I became chevard of Thirst,

I swore to uphold the law of the land. I tried to protect you, but you defied me, ran away, consorted with a foreigner, and have been traveling through Nold at a time when our lands are under fearsome attack. You defied Sir Terent by refusing to come straight to me. I could have protected you then, but nay, you fell into the trap set for you. Now you would accuse me of not defending you. How can I when you have rejected my every effort to protect you?"

Dain listened to him and felt his defiance crumble. His eyes stung, and he turned away, silent and wretched. His mistakes loomed large, and he saw now how wrong he'd been, how unfair he'd been to blame Lord Odfrey for his problems. His own independence and defiance had played into Gavril's hands.

"What, then, can I do?" he asked. "For me to tell the truth will be to accuse the prince of lying. If I do that, will I break another of your laws?"

"Yes."

Dain swore softly beneath his breath. The trap was even worse than he'd thought. Gavril had him from every side. "If I run away, for real this time? If I never return?"

Sorrow creased Lord Odfrey's scarred face. "You will be wanted for life. You can never cross Mandrian borders again, for the king will set a price on your head. If I or any knight here see you, we will be bound by our duty and fealty to seek your life. I do not want that, Dain. Do you?"

"If I remain here and go through this trial, will I die?" Dain asked bluntly.

"I know not. I hope not," Lord Odfrey said with a sigh.

"But you cannot promise me."

"Dain," Lord Odfrey said, his voice serious indeed, "if you wish to escape Thirst, there is a way out, a hidden way known only by me. It was shown to me by my father, and his father before him."

Hope flashed through Dain. He grabbed at the offer like a drowning man. "Where is it?"

"You will go, then?" Lord Odfrey asked.

"What choice have I?"

Lord Odfrey dropped his gaze and nodded. "Very well. I will show you the way."

The knights outside pounded on the door again. "My lord! We must have him. Surrender him to us now!"

"A moment more," Lord Odfrey called back, and strode across the wardroom to the fireplace. He pressed a stone, and a small, concealed door opened in the wall. "Through here. Quickly."

Dain hurried to it and had started to duck into a cramped, musty passageway draped with cobwebs and smelling of mice when a suspicion tickled the back of his neck. He paused, hesitating, and glanced back.

Lord Odfrey scowled at him and gestured for him to go. "Hurry. You have no more time."

"What will become of you?" Dain asked. "If I go, it will be known that you allowed me to escape. What will befall you?"

"Do not worry about me."

But Dain was thinking of what the chevard had said to Lord Renald. "You said I was your responsibility. Will you be punished for defying the prince?"

"No."

"Tell me the truth," Dain said fiercely.

"If you're going, you must go now," Lord Odfrey said with equal fierceness. "It is the only way to save you."

"Will you stand trial in my place?" Dain asked.

Lord Odfrey said nothing. They stared at each other a long moment in the silence, then Dain slowly backed out of the escape passage and pressed the stone to close its door.

"Dain!"

"No," Dain said softly, "I will not run if it means you will be destroyed in my place."

"I have a better chance than you."

Dain shook his head. "You have given me much kindness this year, lord. I will not serve you ill in repayment."

"In Thod's name, you must go!"

Dain turned away from him and resolutely opened the door. He found himself faced by a delegation of six knights, half Thirst men and half Lunt. His heart was hammering again, and from behind him he could feel a wave of despair pass through Lord Odfrey. Dain's knees felt weak, and he was sore afraid, but he forced himself to face the men with his head held high and his gaze steady.

"Take me to your assembly," he said.

23

THE HALL OF Thirst Hold stretched long and narrow, with a high vaulted ceiling spanned by thick wooden beams and hung with Thirst banners of green. The head of a stag bearing immense, spreading antlers was mounted at one end of the Hall; the massive head of a black, snarling beyar was at the other. Tapestries covered the wall on one side of the Hall, while shields interspersed with chevron-patterned arrangements of swords and rosettes of daggers adorned the opposite wall. Long trestle tables littered with trenchers, riddled wheels of cheese, bread crumbs, and platters of picked-over meat bones stretched the length of the room in a double row, leaving an empty aisle that reached all the way to the great hearth at the north end. Large enough to roast an ox, the hearth stood cold and empty this summer's night. Torches set in iron sconces on either side of the chimneypiece flamed vivid red, hissing and smoking and dripping hot pitch.

When Lord Odfrey walked into the Hall, the musicians fell silent and the knights sitting at the tables stopped their chatter. Pewter tankards of Thirst cider banged the tables. Benches scraped back, and the knights rose to their feet.

The chevard had put on a dark green cloak over his gray tunic. The torchlight glittered on his jeweled cloak pin, signet, and marriage ring. Grim-faced, Lord Odfrey strode along straight-backed, with one hand resting lighting on his sword hilt.

Dain followed behind him, feeling the weight of every pair of eyes in the Hall, from Prince Gavril on down to the lowliest page. Next came the six knights in solemn procession.

The knights of Thirst were sober, but the men of Lunt were not. Dain smelled the fermented ale in their cups and on their breath. He read fierce judgment in their gaze. Their minds flickered against his: *guilty/guilty/guilty/guilty.*

At the head table, which was still laden with supper remains, Prince Gavril sat with the priest and Lord Renald. Only Lord Renald had the right to stay seated in Lord Odfrey's presence, but none of them rose.

The torchlight gleamed on Gavril's golden hair. He wore an indigo doublet of silk. His handsome face smirked with triumph, and his slender white hand toyed with the jeweled hilt of his poniard.

Sir Los stood behind his young master's chair, looking stolid and bulky. His expression was stony, his eyes forever watchful.

The priest was a short, swarthy man with a sunburned tonsure and worried, nervous eyes. Wearing his robes, he looked hot and unhappy.

With his own protector standing behind his chair, Lord Renald leaned back, seemingly at his ease, but his dark eyes held a frown. When Lord Odfrey reached the table, Lord Renald rose to his feet and bowed.

Lord Odfrey inclined his head stiffly in return. Their exchange of courtesies made Gavril look haughty and churlish. When the prince continued to sit in Lord Odfrey's presence, a faint murmur of disapproval spread across the room. Gavril seemed to ignore it, but his dark blue eyes flashed with disdain.

Glancing to one side of the Hall, Dain found the worried faces of Thum and Sir Polquin among the crowd. Sir Polquin scowled at Gavril and Thum looked furious.

Lord Odfrey's gaze passed over Gavril coldly and sought out his captain-at-arms. "Who have been chosen judges?" he asked.

Sir Bosquecel, looking stern and official in his mail and surcoat, came forward. "The judges will be Lord Renald, his captain-at-arms, and myself."

Dain blinked worriedly. Lord Renald seemed fairly neutral and open-minded, but Dain had already heard the man warn Lord Odfrey not to risk offending the king. Dain did not think Lord Renald would fail to follow his own advice. The second man Dain knew not at all. Sir Bosquecel had always been kind to Dain in the past, but now he stood rigid and stalwart before Lord Odfrey and did not glance at Dain once. Even if Sir Bosquecel took Dain's side, that left two whose votes were at best uncertain.

Prince Gavril finally rose to his feet. "A representative of the church should also be a judge," he said.

The priest beside him jumped up hastily, looking more nervous than before. "I shall serve as I am called to serve, my lords," he said in a thin, breathless voice.

Ignoring the priest entirely, Lord Odfrey looked at Gavril with scant patience. "Such is not the law."

Gavril flushed, and for a moment hatred for Lord Odfrey gleamed in his dark blue eyes. "It is the custom at court to include the church as a courtesy."

"We are an assembly of warriors, your highness," Lord Odfrey said in a voice like stone. "We will follow law here, not lowlander custom."

The pink flush in Gavril's face darkened at the rebuke, and some of the knights laughed. Gavril glared at them. "Very well!" he said a bit shrilly. "Let us begin."

Sir Bosquecel looked offended by the prince's brusque command. Watching, Dain got a glimmer of an idea. If he could cause Gavril to lose his temper and display to these men his true personality, then perhaps they might believe what Dain had to say. It was a thin plan, but all he had.

The ceremony began with the head table being pushed back and Dain placed in front of it to face the entire Hall.

A herald wearing Thirst livery came forward and cleared his throat. "Lords and knights," he announced, "let it be known that the trial of one eld youth, known as Dain, has now begun. Let truth be spoken by all. Let all hearts be open to receiving the truth, as we are taught by Tomias, servant of Thod the Almighty."

Someone pounded his tankard on the table at the rear of the Hall. "Hang 'im!" the man shouted drunkenly. "Hang 'im in a river tree an' let the keebacks peck out his eyes!"

Lord Odfrey whirled around. "Seize that man!" he roared.

Two Thirst knights strode down the length of the Hall toward the offender.

"Gently," Lord Renald said with an apologetic shrug. "Chances are he's one of mine."

Lord Odfrey was not listening. His fist was clenched at his side and he fumed, "Drunkenness in my Hall. I will not have it."

The knight who was pulled forth to stand on wobbly knees was not a Lunt man, however, but Thirst. With food and ale spilled down his green surcoat, he let his head loll a moment before he waved and flashed a drunken grin. It was Sir Vedrique, assigned to Gavril's company of guards.

Lord Odfrey looked livid. "Get him out!" he ordered. "Secure him in the guardhouse."

"Aye, m'lord."

Sir Vedrique was hustled out, and Lord Odfrey gazed long and hard around the Hall. "If any other man here is drunk, let him admit it now and leave without censure. Stay, and if I learn you have voted in this trial with your judgment impaired, it will be a public flogging."

Two Thirst knights stepped sheepishly from the crowd, bowed unsteadily to their chevard, and left.

A Lunt man also came forward and bowed to Lord Renald. "I fear, m'lord," he said in a slurred voice, "that I am unfit for this occasion."

"You may go," Lord Renald told him.

Gavril stepped toward Lord Odfrey. "I am to blame, my lord," he said lightly. " 'Twas my idea to cheer and reward the men for a hard day's fighting. I did provide ale from my private stores, after Sir Bosquecel granted permission."

Lord Odfrey scowled at his captain-at-arms, who looked deeply troubled.

"I saw no harm, my lord," he said quietly. "Permission was sought the moment we rode in, before this other trouble began."

"I see," Lord Odfrey said, and let it pass.

Dain, however, drew in a sharp breath and glanced at Gavril. How smug the prince looked. He must have planned this all in meticulous detail.

Why? Dain wondered. What had he ever done to warrant the prince's total enmity? Was this retaliation for that long-ago day when they'd scuffled over the bard crystal? Could Gavril harbor a grudge for something that trivial? Or did blind hatred stem simply from bigotry and prejudice? Gavril had gone to great trouble to see him destroyed.

The ceremony continued. A green square of cloth embroidered with Lord Odfrey's crest of leaping stag and his bars of rank was brought forth by a trembling page. He handed the cloth reverently to Sir Bosquecel, who held it up by two corners and draped it across Lord Odfrey's sword as it was drawn.

Dain noticed that tonight Lord Odfrey's weapon was not the usual utilitarian blade that he wore into battle but instead one longer and very old. It was not fashioned of magicked steel forged by dwarves but instead of some metal equally mysterious, ancient in fact, with a resonance that traveled along Dain's senses. He had never seen such metal before, and he could not get a clear look at it with the cloth draped across the blade, but he closed his eyes and listened to the hum of it.

"*I am Truthseeker,*" it said within the hum. Great power flowed inside the blade. Long ago, many battles had it fought. Images of blood and death mingled with war cries in tongues that Dain had never heard before. He shuddered and opened his eyes as the draped sword was pointed straight at his heart, then turned sideways and laid at Dain's feet. Gold wire was wrapped around the two-handed hilt and a row of fiery emeralds studded the straight edge of the guard. Glittering and gleaming, Truthseeker lay on the floor in humility, but even the cloth could not mask its greatness.

Wide-eyed with awe, Dain stared at Lord Odfrey, and his entire image of the man changed to something new. Of what lineage was this man that he owned a sword made of god-steel? Such ancient weapons were legendary, more myth than fact in these times. Jorb had sometimes spoken of god-steel wistfully, wishing he could touch some of it, just once, in his lifetime. In the olden days, dwarves and other treasure-hunters had scavenged the Field of Skulls in hopes of finding such a weapon among the fallen. To see a sword of this kind, here and now, obviously well preserved and handed down from generation to generation, so astonished Dain that he could not remain silent.

"Truthseeker is—"

Lord Odfrey's gaze snapped to his in warning. As Dain broke off what he'd been about to blurt out, the chevard said in a soft, grim voice, "My ancestral sword is named aptly. And if you are found guilty, it will take your life."

Dain gulped, but Lord Odfrey was already turning away from him. Standing alone, Dain met the eyes of the assembly and told himself that doomed or not he would see the truth told tonight, would hold to his honor and show them eld courage.

The six knights who had escorted Dain here from Lord Odfrey's wardroom now knelt in a semicircle before him. One by one, each man drew his sword beneath a plain cloth and laid the draped weapon on the floor before him. The three judges stood facing Dain on his right; Lord Odfrey, Gavril, and Sir Los stood facing him on his left.

At the rear of the Hall some of the wounded knights hobbled

in with assistance. Four other men were carried on wooden boards, with Sulein hovering in attendance. A loud babble of conversation rose through the Hall, until the herald raised his hand for silence.

"Hear this!" he said, his voice ringing out so that all could hear. "The eld called Dain stands accused by Prince Gavril of crimes and foul deeds against his person. His highness will lay those charges now."

His face alight with eagerness, Gavril stepped forward and pointed at Dain. "In the afternoon of this day," he began with great formality, "this pagan creature did walk into the common chamber of the fosters and interrupt my conversation with Mierre and Kaltienne. He did swear at me and give me great insult, then without provocation he drew his dagger and attacked me, with intent to commit grievous bodily harm . . . or my death."

Dain stiffened, incensed by so blatant a lie, but he'd been warned not to speak out of turn. It took all the willpower he had to stay silent, even as hostile murmurs rose through the Hall. Their emotions beat at him, stronger than ever: *guilty/guilty/guilty/guilty*.

Clenching his jaw, he drew his bard crystal from beneath his doublet and clutched the pendant in his fist. He thought of Thia, his beloved sister, whose pale, blonde-haired beauty had been like a song in the air. She would not want to see him here, judged for his life by this assembly of men and bound by their treachery and lies. He thought of her proud spirit, her courage that had never faltered, even in her final hours as she lay dying of a Bnen arrow.

If he did not prevail tonight, he would join her spirit in the third world. But he would not go like a baseborn coward, cringing and pleading for mercy.

Dain stared coldly at Gavril, whose lying tongue had finally fallen silent. Mierre and then Kaltienne were brought forward to speak their lies. Furious, Dain kept his shoulders erect and his chin high. Gavril had hated and persecuted him from the first day because he was an eld; there was no other reason. The prince's blind prejudice did him no credit, and someday perhaps these men and others who followed him would see the truth of his character and follow him no more.

When the accusations ended, silence hung over the Hall.

Dain faced the assembly, refusing to act guilty or let his fear show. He had no witnesses to contradict the lies Mierre and Kaltienne had spoken. Truthseeker lay at his feet. He wished with all his heart that the sword would spring into the air, guided by the hand of Olas, god of war and justice, to smite them.

But that was an unworthy wish, Dain told himself. His problems were his own, too small for the gods to concern themselves with. He had gotten himself into this by his own actions and choices. Foolishly, he had played into Gavril's evil hands.

The Hall seemed to grow warmer as someone else spoke at length. Dain stopped listening and let his mind drift. His arm was throbbing more than ever. He could smell the food not yet cleared off the tables. His stomach growled and rumbled, and it took all his willpower not to grab some of the table scraps at his back. Between his wound and his hunger, he felt faint. Yet he was determined to stand tall and look brave.

Something pale and indistinct near the ceiling caused the banners to flutter. Trying not to sway, Dain let his gaze wander upward. He frowned at the shape, which swirled like mist and was no creature of this world.

His mouth went dry and for an instant he knew fear. But he sensed nothing evil about it. His eyes closed a moment, fighting off a wave of weakness, and when he opened them again the mist was forming itself into the likeness of a man such as Dain had never seen before.

He blinked, unable to believe his eyes, and glanced swiftly around to see if anyone else noticed this vision. But Lord Odfrey was speaking, and all eyes were trained on the chevard.

Dain found his gaze drawn back to the vision. This stranger was an awesome sight, a handsome man in the prime of life, broad-shouldered and strong, with a chiseled face too angular to be Mandrian. There was a look of the eld to his features, although like Dain his frame was as large and muscular as any human's. His breastplate of gold embossed with symbols of hammer and lightning bolts gleamed as though with a life of its own. In his right hand this man held a magnificent sword with a blade that shone white and magical. His thick black hair fell to his shoulders, held back by a circlet of delicate gold that only enhanced his masculinity. His ice-blue eyes were eagle-keen.

They pierced Dain as though they would look deep, to Dain's very soul.

Unable to draw a complete breath, Dain felt his knees buckling. He tried to kneel before this king, but the apparition pointed his sword at him and his deep voice rang through Dain's mind, "Kneel not to me, Faldain of Nether."

Dain gasped. From the corner of his eye he saw Gavril glance at him sharply, but Dain's gaze remained rapt on the king. His heart was pounding with suppressed excitement. *Faldain of Nether.* The name ran through his thoughts. In his mind, Dain replied, "Great One, what would you have me do?"

Again the apparition pointed at Dain with his mighty sword, which glowed now to a blinding degree, like a tongue of white flame. "Beware!" rang the words in Dain's mind. "Danger lurks close. You must not fail."

Dain frowned, finding this warning hardly useful. He had little chance of prevailing at this trial, especially the way truth was being mocked tonight.

"How can I win?" he asked the king. "Have mercy, Great One, and show me the way."

"The way is already known to you. Lose not your courage against your foe."

"But—"

"The danger is not what you think. Beware, Faldain. Pay heed to my warning."

The apparition vanished, leaving Dain shaken and disoriented. He lifted his hand to rub the sweat from his brow, and wondered if his own weakness had made him imagine the vision.

Yet its words still echoed in his mind. Frowning, Dain slowly turned the warning over and over in his thoughts. Some spirit from the third world had reached through to warn him of danger other than what he faced right now.

The hair suddenly prickled on the back of his neck. Were Nonkind here, concealed in the hold, perhaps in the Hall itself? He sensed nothing, yet his sense of unease grew rapidly.

Lord Odfrey was saying, "I will remind you of how this boy first came to us, starved and wretched, how he did risk his own life to save that of the huntsman Nocine, who stands now at the rear of the Hall."

As he spoke, he pointed at the man. Many of the assembly twisted their heads to look. Others did not.

"Dain rode into battle unarmed at my back that day," the chevard continued, his voice hard and measured. "He risked his life to guide us to the dwarf raiders who had done wrong to Thirst. He risked his life to save mine."

The chevard pointed to his scarred face. "Thanks to this boy's quick actions, I survived my wound and lived. It was your wish, knights of Thirst, to make him a foster. I grant your petition and allowed him to stay as one of us, to be trained at arms. It has been our united intention that he one day be knighted and serve Thirst in its defense. You know his good qualities, which are many. But, yes, he has had his moments of mischief. What boy does not?"

A few of the knights chuckled, but others stayed silent, frowning while they listened.

"He disobeyed me a few days past and went forth in the smith's company to help him buy sword metal from a dwarf. Since Dain was raised by Jorb the swordmaker, it was not unreasonable of our smith to ask for his help in securing a good price."

Behind Lord Odfrey, Gavril was sighing impatiently and fidgeting. Dain stared hard at him, wondering where the Nonkind could be and how he could stop the proceedings to warn Lord Odfrey.

As though feeling Dain's stare, the prince glared back until Dain shifted his gaze away.

"In leaving the hold without permission, Dain did wrong," Lord Odfrey continued, his speech apparently endless. "But who among you cannot remember your own boyhood escapades?"

There were more chuckles, but Dain hardly noticed that the chevard's words were swaying the knights in his favor. He wondered if the chevard had yet answered the direct accusation Gavril had laid.

Lord Odfrey pointed at Dain. "Many of you have worked with Dain, and sought to assist him in his training. Others of you have supervised him in his chores. Have you known this boy to lie? To ever strike someone else in anger? To treat anyone cruelly or unjustly?"

The chevard paused, holding the assembly with his stern

gaze. "The answer to each of those questions is no. For the months he has lived among us, has he not had ample opportunity to do harm against myself, against any of you, against even the prince, had he wished? Why has he chosen to attack his highness now? Did he attack at all, or did our prince misunderstand boyish high spirits and—"

The stench of something rotted and foul reached Dain's nostrils. "Stop!" he shouted loudly.

His interruption silenced Lord Odfrey, who swung around to glare at him. Sir Bosquecel scowled. Others glared at Dain for daring to interrupt.

"You have not leave to speak, Dain," Sir Bosquecel said in annoyance. "Await your turn."

Dain paid them no heed. He looked in all directions, seeking the Nonkind that was among them. Released at last, as though the creature could no longer contain itself, a foul stench so overwhelmed Dain's senses that he wanted to retch. Swallowing, he looked but saw nothing wrong.

Everyone was staring at him, and Gavril said, "He is surely mad, or pretending to be so. It is a thin defense."

Even now, Gavril refused to accept any beliefs or abilities save those that he valued. Despising him for a fool, Dain said, "There is a Nonkind here."

Sir Bosquecel and Lord Odfrey swung around in alarm. Sir Polquin swore aloud and reached for his sword hilt.

"Where, Dain?" Lord Odfrey asked. "In Thod's name, what is it? Where is it?"

Dain could not tell him, for as yet his eyes could not penetrate the creature's spell of concealment. He shook his head in frustration. The stink intensified, worse than ever, causing the hair to stand up on the back of Dain's neck. It had to be close now, must be coming closer, yet he saw no movement save that of a knight, striding forward from the back of the Hall. Dain eyed him narrowly, unsure. He was unwilling to make the wrong accusation.

"Dain!" Lord Odfrey said sharply.

He drew a sharp breath and glanced at the chevard. "I cannot see it, but it's here in the Hall. It must be a shapeshifter."

"Gods!" Sir Bosquecel said, half-drawing his sword.

Sir Los stepped in front of Gavril with his hand on his own weapon.

Gavril laughed scornfully. "Will you believe more of his nonsense? Will you let his spells and lies cloud your minds?" He held up his gold Circle and aimed it at Dain. "This pagan has no—"

One of the wounded men jumped to his feet, knocking Sulein aside, and suddenly shimmered and changed shape, becoming a shadowy, snake-headed creature with black, leathery wings. It screamed, and the sound pierced Dain's ears.

Several knights cried out, clapping their hands to their ears and sinking to their knees. The shapeshifter flew through the air so swiftly it was only a blur, and came straight for the front of the Hall. It aimed itself at Gavril, who was standing dumbstruck with horror. The prince raised his Circle, but Sir Los pushed Gavril back and swung his sword at the shapeshifter's belly.

His sword glanced off the creature's hide without effect, and the shapeshifter sank its poisonous fangs into Sir Los's throat. Sir Los screamed, a high, keening sound of death, and his sword fell from his slack fingers as the creature pulled his body up into the air and drained the life from it.

With shouts, Sir Polquin and Sir Terent rushed at it, striking to no avail. Through the Hall, there was shouting and pandemonium. Lord Odfrey and Lord Renald bellowed orders that went unheeded in the confusion.

The priest held up his brass Circle, but retreated, wailing a prayer aloud. Someone rushed to grab one of the torches and whirled it about so that the flames popped and guttered. Gavril rushed foolishly at the shapeshifter, brandishing his Circle and his jeweled dagger, and Lord Odfrey flung himself at the prince to save him. One of the shapeshifter's leathery wings struck Lord Odfrey and knocked him sprawling to the floor. He lay still, unconscious or perhaps dead, his forehead bloody.

Sir Bosquecel grabbed Lord Odfrey's shoulders and dragged him out of the thing's reach just as it struck viciously. Its fangs snapped on thin air, and it screamed in rage.

"Back, demon of the second world!" Gavril shouted.

The shapeshifter turned on the prince, who flung his dagger at it. The pretty little weapon bounced harmlessly off the creature and clattered on the floor.

Gavril brandished his Circle. "By my faith, I order you back!"

The shapeshifter shimmered and suddenly took man-form again. It laughed, a horrible guttural sound that could never have been made by a mortal throat, then shifted back into its true form. It flapped its wings and snapped at Gavril, unfazed by his religious talisman.

Gavril's face had turned white. His hand trembled as it held the Circle even higher. "This is a holy object. It *must* drive you back!"

The shapeshifter lunged again, snapping its poisonous jaws right in Gavril's face.

He dropped his Circle and cringed back, flinging up his hands to ward off the creature. "No! No!" he screamed in terror.

Dain was the closest to the prince. Without thinking, he whirled around and grabbed a handful of salt from the seasoning bowl on the table, then stooped and picked up Truthseeker.

The embroidered cloth fell away from the carved blade as Dain swung it up and around.

The shapeshifter seized the prince in its talons and reared back its snakelike head to strike. Running to them, Dain flung his handful of salt at the monster and shouted, "By salt and holy steel do I banish you from this world!"

The salt stung the hide of the shapeshifter, which shrieked in agony and began to flail like something crazed. One of its wing tips nearly knocked Dain off his feet. Ducking, he regained his balance, but the shapeshifter's talons were tearing long gashes in Gavril's legs. The prince screamed. Gripping Truthseeker with both hands, Dain lifted the heavy sword. In that instant, he felt its power come to life, channeling up his wrists and arms all the way to his heart. He heard himself say words that he did not understand, yet they made the very air thunder. His bard crystal pendant sang a note so piercing and pure that Dain's ears rang. He swung the sword with all his might.

Bursting into flames as it whistled through the air, the god-steel blade sliced through the shapeshifter's thin neck and set it afire. In seconds, the creature's entire body was ablaze. It screamed and shrieked, writhing in its death throes, then exploded into ashes that rained down upon Dain.

In the sudden silence, the air reeked of smoke and Nonkind stench. Truthseeker's blade flashed fire a moment longer, its power shaking Dain's teeth. He could feel his whole body glowing and his hair standing on end. Then the flames went out, the light in the sword dimmed, its power faded away, and it became once more just a weapon of surpassing beauty.

Dain stood there, feeling weightless and light-headed. He could hear a roaring sound, muted and far away. He saw individual faces that he recognized in flickers of clarity. Thum, his freckles standing out boldly in his white face. Sir Bosquecel kneeling over Lord Odfrey, who was holding his head and trying to sit up. Sir Polquin, also on his knees, his lips moving but no sound coming forth. And Gavril, lying on the floor near Dain, torn and bloody. The prince was crying with pain and the aftermath of his fear, but he was alive.

Dain drew a deep breath, feeling neither relief nor regret, feeling nothing at all. He had saved the life of his enemy; that was all he knew.

Suddenly Truthseeker was too heavy to hold. He struggled with it, knowing he must not insult the blade by dropping it on the floor.

A hand gripped Dain's wrist, then gently took the hilt from his bloody grasp. He realized dimly that his wound must have opened. He could feel blood running down his arm inside his sleeve.

The hand belonged to Sir Terent. His ruddy face entered the diminishing circle of Dain's vision and knotted itself with concern. "Dain," he said. "Release the sword."

Dain thought he had, but when he looked down, his fingers were still gripped, knuckle-white, around the gold-wire hilt. Frowning, he forced his fingers to loosen.

Sir Terent reverently took the sword away and handed it to someone that Dain could not see. The absence of Truthseeker's weight was a relief. Now Dain had nothing left to anchor him. He felt himself floating farther and farther away.

"Dain," Sir Terent said. "Dain, lad!"

But the mists closed around Dain, and he was gone.

When he next opened his eyes, the sun was shining through a narrow window straight onto his face. Squinting, Dain tried to lift his head, but it weighed too much.

The pungent smell of herbs wafted beneath his nostrils, making him sneeze. Sulein bent over him, smiling through his dark, frizzy beard. "Ah, he is with us again. This is good."

Dain glanced around, but he did not recognize the small,

whitewashed room. Its shuttered windows were open to admit the fragrant summer air. He lay in a tall bed with heavy posts.

Sulein retreated, and Lord Odfrey appeared at Dain's bedside.

The chevard looked solemn and troubled. A bruise marred his brow, but otherwise he looked hale. He seated himself gently on the side of the bed and stared down at Dain.

"How are you, lad?" he asked. His voice was gruff, and he cleared it loudly.

Dain considered the question. "Hungry."

Amusement lit the chevard's dark eyes. His smiled warmed his face and took the sternness away. Turning his head, he asked Sulein to convey a message to the kitchen, then he swung his gaze back to Dain.

"What," he asked mildly, "shall I do with you?"

Memory was returning to Dain fast. He frowned, feeling his worries return. "The trial," he said. "Will it finish today?"

"The trial is over," Lord Odfrey said. "No fault was found in you."

Dain grinned with relief. "No fault?"

"None. You saved Prince Gavril's life in front of us all, or don't you remember?"

Dain frowned, the memories bobbing and turning in his mind. "Has his wound been salted and cleansed in the proper way?"

"Aye. And after all Gavril has done against you, I marvel that you care."

Dain's frown deepened to a scowl. Lord Odfrey mistook his concern. He cared nothing for the prince. But if darkness should possess Gavril through tainted wounds, everyone in the hold would be at risk.

"How the shapeshifter got in past our safeguards, the priest still has not explained to my satisfaction," Lord Odfrey said. "These are troubled times we face, now that Nether no longer stands against them with us. Had you not been there, Dain, many would have surely died, the prince among them."

Dain looked away, and could not feel entirely glad.

"Gavril is not wholly bad-hearted," Lord Odfrey said softly as though reading Dain's mind. "Just spoiled and ill-taught by ambitious men. He was mistaken in his belief that you meant him harm."

Dain sat bolt upright. "I never attacked him!" he said furiously. "There was no mistake about—"

"Dain," Lord Odfrey said, gripping his hand. "Hush. The matter is closed. You are cleared of all accusation."

"But he—he—"

"It is over," Lord Odfrey said in a tone that permitted no further discussion. "Be glad."

Dain sighed and nodded, knowing he must do as Lord Odfrey advised. Perhaps Gavril had learned a lesson from this experience. Perhaps now he would be more tolerant of beliefs that were not his own. Perhaps he might even see some good use in having an eld around.

"Was he much hurt?" Dain asked.

"His leg will pain him for a while, but he will mend," Lord Odfrey said. "By the king's birthday, he'll be well enough to do his part in his knighting ceremonies."

The king's tournament. Dain nodded, feeling fresh disappointment wash through him. He would see none of the festivities at Savroix, but at least he was alive and not to be punished. He could accept that as enough.

"Lord," he said, gazing up at Lord Odfrey, "there is something I would ask you."

"Yes?"

"It's about Thum."

"Yes?"

"You have no squire," Dain said, frowning as he sought the best way to phrase his request, "and Thum would be good in the job."

"Would he?" Lord Odfrey said. His voice was neutral. His dark eyes held no expression at all.

This was not promising. Dain frowned and tried to think of a way to persuade him. "Thum is smart, lord, and loyal. He never loses things. He works hard. He would make you a worthy squire."

"Thank you for your advice, even if it is unasked for," Lord Odfrey said. "I have already placed him in that post."

Dain's gaze flashed up, and he smiled, although to his surprise his spirits suddenly felt lower than before. So Thum would be the one foster permitted to go to Savroix later this summer. Well, he deserved the trip. He was a hard worker and a good friend. But somewhere beneath Dain's gladness lay an empty feeling that he could not drive away.

"Now enough about Thum," Lord Odfrey said. "The knights ended your trial, but there are other matters between you and me that are not settled."

Dain swallowed hard, expecting lecture and punishment. "Yes, lord?"

Lord Odfrey stared at him, and with a sudden frown stood up and began to pace back and forth. "Damne," he muttered. "I came here prepared to reprimand you for leaving the hold without permission, for not governing your damnable temper as you should, for causing me more worry than a man should have to endure. Never do that to me again."

Dain stared at him in surprise. "No, lord," he said after a moment. "I won't."

"You must learn discipline. An order is an order. If you like or dislike it, that does not matter. If your commander cannot count on you to obey him in all areas, then he cannot depend on you in battle either."

Dain hung his head. "Am I to be flogged?"

"Thod knows you deserve it," Lord Odfrey said grimly, then paused next to Dain and ruffled his hair with a gentle hand. "But, no. I think you've been through enough."

Relief filled Dain, and a great weight came off his shoulders. He glanced up and saw Lord Odfrey smiling at him. Dain smiled back, glad that they were friends again.

"Impossible brat," Lord Odfrey said with feeling. "How did you learn to swing a sword like that? How did you make it flash fire hot enough to destroy a Nonkind?"

"But it will always do so against them," Dain said in surprise. "Truthseeker is—"

"It is not made of magicked metal!" Lord Odfrey said too quickly, as though he perhaps feared that it really was. "I do not own a weapon that is forbidden by Writ."

"No, Truthseeker is not made of magicked metal," Dain said, wondering how Lord Odfrey could own such a holy weapon and not know what he had.

The chevard released his breath. "Thod be thanked. I thought you were going to tell me of some power I didn't—"

"It's made of god-steel."

Lord Odfrey stared at him, looking dumbfounded. "What?"

"Aye. God-steel. Have you heard of it? It's rare and very old. The metal is so hard that dwarves who have found pieces of it in places of ancient battles cannot hammer it. They cannot soften it with fire. They cannot work it at all, despite their skill. Some ancestor of yours must have fought in the great battles of long ago."

Lord Odfrey sank down on the edge of the bed again, as though his legs would not hold him. "Gods' mercy," he whispered at last. "I cannot believe it."

"The power was not mine," Dain said, surprised that Lord Odfrey had even thought so. "Everything lay inside the sword."

Lord Odfrey ran his hand across his face. "My father was afraid to touch it. I have never carried it in battle."

"That's where it belongs," Dain said. "That's what it sings for."

The chevard turned his gaze on Dain and frowned. "I have heard it said that the dwarves believe metal sings. You can hear it, can't you?"

Dain's smile faded. He met Lord Odfrey's eyes and knew he must tell the truth. "Aye. I felt it speak to me. It told me its name, and I believed it right to use it. Or, in doing so, have I broken another law?"

"No, lad," Lord Odfrey said kindly. "You used it for the greatest good possible, that of saving someone's life."

"It is an incredible weapon," Dain said, remembering the feel of it. "I would see you use it—"

"Nay!" Lord Odfrey said hastily, standing up again. "My father warned me as his father did warn him, that it is too strong for mere men to handle. And if you are right about its being made from god-steel, then my father spoke truth. Mortals have no business with such weapons. But you swung it as though it had been made for your hand."

"Desperation, lord, that is all."

"False modesty does not become you," Lord Odfrey said. "By the laws of our church, men cannot own god-steel."

Dain looked up in alarm. "You will not destroy it, lord! You will not fling it in the river."

"I should," Lord Odfrey said, but shook his head. "Nay, I will not. My father told me it was won as a prize in battle by our ancestor."

"It was a very great reward," Dain said. "Your ancestor must have fought bravely indeed."

Lord Odfrey nodded and blinked in amazement. "Godsteel," he said softly, looking secretly pleased. "Well, well. Let this be our secret, Dain, kept between you and me. Let the others think you have powers against the Nonkind if they wish."

"But I do not—"

"It does no harm. Otherwise, I must explain the sword, and I would rather not."

"Of course," Dain agreed quickly. "I would not wish to cause you trouble."

Lord Odfrey smiled. "Enough about Truthseeker. You saved the prince's life. And the king has already sent his gratitude."

He reached into his pocket and drew forth a rolled-up parchment, which he handed to Dain.

"How did it come so quickly?" Dain asked, puzzled. "When this all happened only last night, how did he know?"

Lord Odfrey chuckled. "Be at ease, lad. There's no magic here. You've been asleep five days since you swooned. I thought you might never awaken, but Sulein assured me you would recover."

"Five days!"

"Aye. No wonder you're hungry, eh?"

Dain nodded. He unrolled the parchment slowly, having trouble because his wounded arm was so heavily bandaged he could barely move it. Lord Odfrey held one side of the parchment while Dain unrolled the rest.

There were many seals and flourishing signatures, but it was all written in the same small characters that Sulein had showed him earlier, characters that Dain could not read.

He frowned in shame, realizing what it meant to be ignorant. "I cannot read this, lord," he admitted.

"No, your education has far too many gaps. That is why I wanted you to begin lessons with Sulein. If you are to live in Mandria, you must be able to read and write our language."

"Sir Terent cannot read," Dain argued, staring at the crown drawn above one signature. He guessed that it must say "Verence," and felt awed. "Sir Polquin cannot either."

"I would have you do better in life than a middle-rank knight," Lord Odfrey said firmly. "To be an educated man,

Dain, is to have as much treasure as a storehouse of gold pieces."

Dain sighed, thinking of endless days cooped up with Sulein in his dark tower room, studying letters when he would rather be riding and practicing swordplay. He nodded at the paper before him. "What does this say, lord?"

"It says, Dain, that I have permission to take you before King Verence and request that you be made my ward and heir."

Dain blinked, and at first he did not believe he had heard correctly. He met Lord Odfrey's dark eyes in wonder and disbelief, and felt amazed past words. "What?" he gasped.

Lord Odfrey's face held a mixture of hope and longing. "Does my petition please you?" he asked, and his voice was vulnerable.

"Please me?" Dain echoed. "Oh, yes!"

Lord Odfrey's whole face lit up, and he held out his hand. Dain gripped it firmly, his throat suddenly too choked to speak.

"Ah, Dain, it will be good to have a son again. Since you came to Thirst, you have lightened the sorrow in my heart. I have watched you, hoping to see you prosper and develop. Many times these past months my heart longed to speak to you about this."

"I didn't know," Dain said softly.

"No, it has been something for me to work out alone. That night of the trial, when you refused to flee the hold because I would have to stand accused in your place, I knew that you were as true as ash wood. And I believed then that you might perhaps hold some fondness for me as well, as a son has for a father."

Dain opened his mouth, but his emotions were too tangled for him to speak.

Lord Odfrey frowned and gazed into the distance. "You see, Dain, while you have lived here, you have acted at times like a wild spirit caged. I feared you would decide to leave us at any time. I dared not let myself become too fond of you, or start thinking of you as the son I needed to replace my poor Hilard. I didn't want to be hurt again. And then you did leave."

"Lord—"

"No, let me say this. I have nearly lost you twice now. Perhaps I have been too strict with you, as I was with Hilard. Had you been more sure of your place here, you would not have misunderstood me that day of the contest."

Dain was astonished to hear Lord Odfrey apologizing to him. "Lord, don't! It is I who must ask your pardon for—"

Lord Odfrey met his gaze, and Dain's sentence faltered to a halt. "Would it please you to stay at Thirst, to one day hold it after me as chevard?"

"I—"

"Think on it," Lord Odfrey said as though afraid that Dain would refuse. "I have told you too much too fast. You need not answer me now."

Dain struggled to swallow the lump in his throat, wanting to give his answer, but too overwhelmed to find the words he needed.

Lord Odfrey stood staring down at Dain. "If you agree, the king is willing to hear my petition. This paper almost guarantees that he will grant it."

Dain frowned. "Lord, you do me great honor. But will you not suffer by naming an eld into your family?"

Lord Odfrey shook his head. "I think not. Indeed, I care not. Mine is an old family, well established in honest service. Court politics have never interested me. Besides, the king does not hold the same views as his son, although I hope your bravery has changed Prince Gavril's opinions on many things. King Verence remembers the old days, and old alliances."

Dain thought of his vision the night of the trial, of the black-haired king who had appeared to warn him and who had called him "Faldain of the Nether." The missing prince of that troubled realm. He shivered, afraid to think Sulein's guess might be right. Dain thought back to the night he had dreamed himself drowning in water and a girl had summoned him forth to her bidding. Had she not also called him Faldain?

He frowned, wondering now if he should not tell Lord Odfrey of these things and ask his advice. But seeing the hope and hesitation tangled up in Lord Odfrey's face, Dain could not bring himself to speak of it. He had no proof, and in himself he was not sure. It seemed too great and wondrous an identity to wish for. And if he made such a claim for himself, he might lose Lord Odfrey's offer altogether. No—Jorb, who was always practical, had taught Dain to always take what was sure, never what might be.

Dain looked up at the man whom he so admired, whom he'd wished could really be his father, and who had now extended that tremendous honor to him.

He smiled shyly. "Lord, I would be honored past all I can say to—to be your ward."

Lord Odfrey let out his breath explosively and grinned. "Truly?"

"Aye."

They gripped hands again, and tears of happiness misted Lord Odfrey's eyes. Dain could hardly meet his gaze, for Lord Odfrey shone with such pride and affection that he felt dazzled.

"My son," Lord Odfrey said softly, and his voice shook with emotion.

Dain thought of the home and family he'd lost less than a year past. Now he'd gained both again—not the same ones, of course, but perhaps almost as good. Perhaps—except for Thia—better.

He drew a deep breath of happiness and looked up at Lord Odfrey. "My father."